The Bermondsey Bookshop

Mary Gibson

HEAD
of ZEUS

First published in the UK in 2020 by Head of Zeus Ltd
This paperback edition first published in the UK in 2020
by Head of Zeus Ltd

A catalogue record for this book is available from
the British Library.

ISBN (PB): 9781788542654
ISBN (E): 9781788542630

Typeset by Silicon Chips

Printed and bound in Great Britain by
CPI Group (UK) Ltd, Croydon CR0 4YY

Head of Zeus Ltd
First Floor East
5–8 Hardwick Street
London EC1R 4RG

WWW.HEADOFZEUS.COM

For Jo

I

Cuckoo in the Garret

1920

'Oi, Noss Goss! Where ya goin'?'

'Mind your own business and me name's Kate!'

Noss. She'd earned the nickname because her family thought she asked too many questions. Which was true. Not stopping, she sped past the young boy, her dark curls tumbling from their restraining clips. He was lounging against the ancient brick house, one of a long row that descended in ever-increasing dilapidation towards the Thames. Here they halted in a tumble of sagging roofs and broken windows.

The boy, her fourteen-year-old cousin Stan, stuck up two fingers. 'Only asking!' He pushed himself off the wall and ran to keep up with her.

'Ask no questions, you'll be told no lies. That's what your mum's always telling me. So, shut yer gob and piss off. I'm late for school!'

She soon outstripped him and he yelled, 'Janey says you're common as muck and your mother was a slut!'

Kate slammed to a halt. She'd risk the cane and book for being late rather than let him get away with that. She sprinted back towards him and, barely stopping, swung her fist into his cheek, speeding off again before he could retaliate. She smiled as she ran.

'I'm telling me mum! She'll chuck you out and good riddance!' he called after her, rubbing his face.

But Kate ignored the stupid boy. He was only copying his older sister, Janey, who'd made it her life's mission to ruin Kate's.

After school Kate hid herself in the garret, keeping out of Aunt Sylvie's way, until she heard a voice sharp enough to put her teeth on edge. 'Kate, get yourself down here!'

She hadn't got away with it after all. Stan had dropped her in it. Kate took a deep breath and ducked down the steep garret stairs, taking her time. This was the one place she would never hurry. Her mother had died after a fall from the garret stairs in the house next door, which had once been Kate's childhood home. Kate didn't intend to follow her. Aunt Sylvie would have to wait.

'You took your bleedin' time!' Her aunt had the *Bermondsey Recorder* open on the kitchen table.

'Sorry. I never heard you,' Kate lied. She'd found it best never to mention her mum to Aunt Sylvie. When she'd first gone to live with her aunt, Kate had been full of childish questions about her mother. Why did she have to die and leave her? What had she looked like – for her face had faded over time – but most of all, she'd wanted to know that her mother had loved her.

Aunt Sylvie was a tight-lipped, sharp-tongued woman and would answer, 'You and your questions! This…' she'd pinch Kate's small nose, 'will get you into trouble one day. Curiosity killed the cat.' And once, when Kate had asked 'which cat?', she'd got a slap for her cheek.

Now she stood, waiting for Aunt Sylvie to speak. Asking no questions.

'It says here,' her aunt prodded the column of situations vacant, 'Boutle's is looking for girls. Get yourself ready, we're going down there.'

'Now? Why?'

Aunt Sylvie rolled her eyes. 'Why d'you think? You're fourteen now and it's time you got yourself a job.'

'Why can't I wait till the end of the year, like everyone else?'

'You need to start paying your way.' Aunt Sylvie got up, closing the subject.

'But I ain't finished me education. Not even got me report or nothing!' Kate's naturally rosy cheeks flushed deep crimson.

'Finished your education? Don't make me laugh! You'll never be no more'n a skivvy or a factory girl,' her aunt sneered, then muttered, 'That's if you don't end up on the streets. Like mother, like daughter.'

Kate should have been used to the insults, but she clenched her fists. 'Don't you talk about my mum like that, you mean old cow!'

Aunt Sylvie had a powerful right-hander that came out of nowhere. A sharp slap squashed Kate's rising anger and she cursed her own quick temper. Why could she never keep her mouth shut?

'I'll say what I bloody well like in me own house. Now go and put your best frock on, and comb your rat's tails. We're going down Boutle's.'

With her cheek stinging and her blood pumping, Kate dashed out of the room straight into her cousin Janey, who put out a solid arm to bar her way. Janey was eighteen now and thickset. She pinched Kate's nose, making her gasp for breath.

'You got your answer there, didn't you, Noss Goss? Right across your earhole!' Janey smirked.

Kate slid under her cousin's imprisoning arm, giving her a parting kick in the shin. Janey answered with a clout, which Kate evaded, wrestling her to the floor. She grabbed handfuls of her cousin's straight sandy hair and tugged hard.

'Mum!' Janey screamed, and Kate leaped for the stairs. 'I'd kill you if I wasn't clocking on in five minutes, you gypsy brat!'

'You couldn't catch me if you had wings on your feet!' Kate laughed and, reaching the shelter of the garret, slammed the hatch closed.

The fight with Janey was nothing unusual. Her cousin had tormented Kate from that day, eight years ago, when she'd arrived at Aunt Sylvie's house, clutching her father's hand and full of questions. Why had her mum gone away? Why was her dad leaving her here? Janey hadn't taken long to coin Kate's nickname of Noss, but it had taken years before she'd stopped asking: 'why?'

The garret was scary. Unseen creatures scurried among the high rafters, approaching and retreating, never showing themselves. It was dark. The tiny dormer window, with three panes boarded up, let in scant light. The roof space loomed above, its timbers black. She pushed open the dormer and let weak sunlight spill in. Looking out over the saddle-backed roofs of the terrace tumbling towards East Lane river stairs, she let her eye rest on the sluggish Thames. It flowed just yards from the last house in the lane.

At least she had the garret all to herself. She'd shared Janey's bed until she was ten, and there hadn't been a night when she'd not been pinched, prodded and kicked out of bed, often waking up on the cold lino in the early hours. When Aunt Sylvie finally gave in to Janey's pleadings and removed Kate from the bed, there was only one place for her to go. The cousins all shared a bedroom, but she certainly couldn't go in with Stan. He was getting curious enough about her developing body as it was. No, Aunt Sylvie said, the garret was where she belonged. But on days like these it felt not so much a punishment as a blessing.

She remembered that other garret, in the house next door to Aunt Sylvie's. It had been her childhood home until she was six. Her parents had rented a room at the top of the house, with the garret as a bedroom for all of them. It was one of the few sharp memories of her life before coming to Aunt Sylvie's. No, Kate thought. This garret wasn't such a bad place. It certainly felt more like home than anywhere else in this bloody house.

She breathed musky river air deep into her lungs and noticed that the trembling in her body slowed. So, she would be a factory girl. Why was she surprised?

'You'll be all right, Kate, gel,' she whispered.

She spent a full five minutes trying to tame her black curls. 'Gypsy rat's tails', Aunt Sylvie called them, swearing Kate never used a comb. But however hard she tried to repress the springy ringlets, they managed to escape. In the end she yanked them into a tight knot at the nape of her neck. She took down the ugly brown frock from its hook on a rafter. Even the smell as she slipped it over her head made her gag. It had covered Janey's body for far too long before being handed down to Kate. It smelt of her cousin. She tugged at the hem.

'Ugh! You must look like Granny Erlock,' she said, grateful there was no full-length mirror in the room to confirm her judgement.

'Come on, I ain't got all day!' Aunt Sylvie's voice boomed from below. 'All the jobs'll be gone before we get there.'

Their walk to the factory in Wild's Rents was largely silent, except when Aunt Sylvie told her to slow down. Kate, quick in her ways, would always run rather than walk, and she continually found herself a few strides ahead of her aunt.

'We ain't runnin' a race!' Aunt Sylvie complained.

'I thought you said we needed to hurry cos all the jobs would be gone?'

'You've always got to have the last word,' Aunt Sylvie puffed. She was a short, sandy-haired, square-built woman of about forty, but she looked older. A perpetual frown of disapproval creased her forehead, at least when Kate was around. They traipsed up Long Lane and as they turned into Wild's Rents, Kate spotted the factory. She deliberately said nothing, enjoying her aunt's confusion as she searched for the building. It could hardly be missed. An insistent, deafening thud came from stamping machines cutting out tinplate; stinking black solder fumes snaked above a hotchpotch of buildings. Kate slowed down at the gates – they looked like the entrance to hell. She wanted to cry. But Aunt Sylvie turned back, giving her a searching look, and instead of crying, Kate grinned.

'You cheeky mare. You're dragging your feet on purpose! Get in 'ere and don't you dare show me up.' Aunt Sylvie grabbed her arm, pulling her into the factory yard.

Kate was expecting a grilling. But the energetic, bright-eyed factory manager surprised her with a pleasant smile and a brisk, kindly manner. Almost as if he knew how daunting the place must appear to her.

'We'll take you on for a trial. You'll be under Miss Dane in the soldering shop. Seven shillings a week – that all right, Mother?' Aunt Sylvie nodded eagerly and Kate guessed she'd never see a penny of those seven shillings.

'You can start tomorrow, then, Miss Goss. Eight o'clock, sharp!'

Tomorrow! She felt a mixture of excitement and nausea, which must have been obvious, for the manager smiled. 'Don't worry, I was your age when I started here – oh, about twenty years ago. You soon get used to the smell and the noise – first five years are the worst!'

She giggled and Aunt Sylvie jabbed an elbow into her side, not understanding his joke.

Once home, Aunt Sylvie surprised her by saying she could keep a shilling of her wages for herself. Of course, it would have to buy her clothes and soap, which took the shine off a little. But still, a whole shilling to spend on herself seemed like a fortune.

'Can I go and tell me mates I won't be going back to school?'

'All right, but don't stay out late. You get yourself to bed early. If you're late clocking on, you'll get a fine and it won't be me paying it! And no hanging round the gas lamp with them boys!' Aunt Sylvie lowered her voice as if Kate, who was waiting to make her escape, couldn't hear. 'Don't want history repeating itself.'

Kate's heart suffered a familiar wound. The soft memory of her mother, battered by small, daily hammer blows of innuendo, had long grown pitted and faded. Aunt Sylvie never missed a chance to make it clear that Bessie, Kate's mother, had tricked Archie Goss into marriage. The nature of the trickery was unclear to Kate, but her mum, she said, was a devious tinker slut, born in a caravan and brought up in Romany Row. A shell, like the toughened tinplate she'd soon be working with, had gradually wrapped itself around Kate's heart. She had learned it was best to preserve the memory of her mum in its sealed casing, locked away even from herself.

Aunt Sylvie wasn't her only relative in East Lane. In the first house, farthest from the river, lived her spinster aunt Sarah. And this evening, feeling suddenly ashamed at having to explain to her friends why she couldn't return to school, Kate decided to go there instead. Neither of her aunts had warm temperaments but at least Kate had something in common with Aunt Sarah – they both loathed Sylvie.

'She sent you round for your tea again?' Aunt Sarah asked. It was a running battle between the two women as to whose responsibility Kate was, Sylvie arguing that as Sarah had no kids, she should have been the one to take Kate in.

'No. She's making me start work early.'

Aunt Sarah rubbed finger and thumb together. '*Money*. That's all she cares about, apart from Archie, of course. Sun shines out of our brother's arse, according to *her*.'

'How does she know, when we never see his arse?' Kate asked, grinning. She sat at the kitchen table, eyeing some warm jam tarts.

'You're a cheeky little 'a'porth.' Aunt Sarah pushed the plate towards Kate. 'Here y'are. Don't tell *her,* though.'

'Why don't me dad never come to see me?' Kate asked, chomping on the hard pastry. Aunt Sarah was a terrible cook, but the jam made up for it.

'He's been busy making his fortune, according to *her.*'

'What, for eight years? It's taking him a long time.'

Aunt Sarah sighed. 'He never got over your mother. He don't want to come back here and be reminded.'

This was one of the variety of reasons she'd been given over the years for her father's continued absence. None of them made sense to her. 'D'you think he'll *ever* come for me?'

'Course he will. Don't forget he had five years in the army. You don't make no money in a war... well, not unless you're selling the guns, you don't.' Aunt Sarah sniffed. She had very strong opinions and would share them freely with whoever would listen. 'He'll make it up to you, Kate. I'll say this for him. He's a clever man. Our mum and dad scrimped and scraped helping him go to college. Give him everything. Us girls didn't get a look in. Anyway, he was always very good making money. I wouldn't be surprised if he's abroad, we ain't heard in a while...'

'What's he like?'

'Smart! Always dressed lovely. Handsome! Like I said, he got a scholarship. A cut above the other boys. That's your father. Too good for the girls round here, including your mother... well, that's according to *her.*'

'Why?' Sometimes, if Aunt Sarah was in a good mood, she would let slip pieces of information that Sylvie kept a tight lid on.

'How many times have you been told to keep your questions to yourself? Sylvie don't like us talking about it. Have another one.' She pointed to the jam tarts and leaned her elbows on the table. 'But I'm not answerable to *her* and you're old enough to know now.'

Kate felt her heartbeat quicken at the prospect of finding a new piece in the puzzle of her life.

'She tricked him into marrying her.'

Kate felt immediately deflated. 'I know that.'

Aunt Sarah cocked her head to one side. 'But you don't know how, do you?'

Kate shook her head.

'She got herself pregnant! So then course he had to marry her.'

'Why?'

'Jesus, no wonder you got yourself that nickname! Why? Because when a woman's got herself pregnant she's a slut – unless the man marries her, that's why.'

Kate had a vague idea of how a woman could get pregnant and she was pretty sure she couldn't do it alone.

'So, me mum, she got herself pregnant. Was it like the virgin birth and Dad felt sorry for her, like Joseph?'

'Joseph! You're sharp enough to cut yourself. That's what I get for answering your bloody questions. Go on. Get back to *her*.' Aunt Sarah stood to shoo her out.

'One more question – please. Tell me what she looked like, me mum – was she pretty?'

Aunt Sarah stopped for a minute and studied Kate. 'Bessie, pretty? Archie thought so. Hair black as yer hat, eyes blue as the sky. If you really want to know, go home and look in the mirror, gel. That's why Sylvie took against you. You're the face cut off of your mother.'

That night Kate slipped up to bed early, grateful she had an excuse to escape before Janey got back from an evening out with her workmates. The garret was reached through her cousins' bedroom via steep, ladder-like steps, at the top of which was a hatch, normally propped open so that Kate could hear Stan's snores or Janey's scolding. Kate squeezed between their empty beds. Stan's was curtained off, though it offered Janey little privacy, another reason Kate preferred the garret.

She climbed the stairs, pushed open the tiny dormer window for air, hung up her brown dress and lay down on the narrow bed. It wasn't so much a bed as a shelf: a few wooden planks, supported by roof struts. Its timber, black like the rest of the roof, was as old as the house, which had been there for at least two hundred years. Her mattress was of plain ticking, stuffed with straw from the nearby stables. She pulled the blanket up under her chin and, staring through the dormer at a thin sliver of moon, she began to conjure the dream of her dad returning for her.

It was a nightly ritual she looked forward to. She wove the tale into many strands and numerous variants. Now she smiled at the image of her dad turning up at Boutle's on her first day. Disgusted with Aunt Sylvie for sending his daughter to work at a tin basher's, he would call her out from the factory in front of everyone. All the other girls would look impressed as he drove Kate away in his own motor car. Dark green with silver chrome it would be. They would stop off at Aunt Sylvie's to get her clothes and Janey would be sick with jealousy. 'Oh, don't worry about those old rags, Sylvie,' Dad would say. 'I'll buy my daughter all new!' And then they would drive to a lovely house over the other side. Mayfair, maybe. But tonight, she had barely reached the new house before she was lulled to sleep by the soughing river, sucking and shushing along the foreshore.

She was soon asleep and must have slept deeply, for she didn't hear the hatch close, nor the wooden latch turn. But in the morning, after the dawn had turned the river red and she'd hurriedly slipped on her everyday blue frock, she discovered that the hatch was stuck fast and as she tugged at it, she heard Janey's laugh below.

'I told you I'd get you back!' Janey called up through the closed hatch. 'You made me late, now you can have a taste of your own medicine. You won't be clocking on today, you tinker brat! And don't try shouting for help, Mum and Stan's already gone out. Bye!'

Her Aunt Sylvie wouldn't be back before twelve. She did early-morning office cleaning before going straight to the wharf on Bermondsey Wall to sort beans. Kate slumped back down onto her bunk. She'd lose her job before she'd even started! And if she did, Aunt Sylvie would get out Uncle Tom's heavy docker's belt. Aunt Sylvie's husband had died in the war, and whenever she got a good hiding Kate wished he'd taken his belt with him. She flung herself off the bunk and knelt down at the hatch.

'Stan! Are you still there? I'll buy you fags with me first week's money if you let me out!'

She was met with silence.

She stuck her head out of the dormer window, considering making the two-storey drop to the street below. But she could barely fit her head through the opening, let alone her whole body. She stamped on the hatch, jumping up and down, risking falling through and breaking her neck rather than let Janey win. But the thick old boards were iron strong. She was a prisoner.

Kate had heard tales that all the garrets in the lane had once been a single open attic space. Smugglers of old had used the long passage to get themselves, and their rum, ashore and onto the highway as discreetly as possible. They would land their contraband at East Lane river stairs, offload it into the first house and pass along the secret passageway to a waiting cart at the end of the lane, far from the customs officers on the river front. It might just be true. What if she could make the journey in reverse? But first she'd have to find an opening through her own garret.

She rarely ventured further than the area around her bed, but now she lit the lamp and held it high. She skirted an old tin box and immediately tripped over a beam. The paraffin lamp flickered. She'd used her last match to light it. Shielding it with a hand, she steadied herself, waiting until the flame settled. She felt her way to the end wall, but found no connecting door or entrance, just rotting lathe and crumbling plaster. She was about to turn back when she saw some crude planks nailed to the old lathes. Putting down the lamp, she tugged at a plank and tumbled to the floor, pulling the plank with her. Careful of the rusted nails studding the rotten wood, she worked on the next plank and the next until an opening large enough to take a broad-shouldered man emerged. Braving cobwebs and ancient droppings, she put the lamp through into next-door's garret. But what if it was still being used as a bedroom, just as she and her parents had once done?

She peered in. It was empty. But it no longer resembled the cosy place her mother had made it when Kate was a child.

Instead, the large bedstead and washstand, with its pretty china bowl, had been replaced with a narrow cot, covered in sacks, and a table stacked with empty beer bottles. This must be where next-door's grandfather slept and drank his remaining years away. But, fortunately for Kate, he was out or downstairs. She crawled through and tiptoed across the cluttered floor, hearing echoes of her younger self reciting nursery rhymes back to her mother as they lay together in the big bed. She never remembered her father being with them. Though he must have slept there sometimes. It seemed strange to be in this place for the first time in eight years. Seeing it like this made her old life seem even further away.

She found what she was looking for. This time it was easier. A hinged door with a wooden catch allowed her easy access into the next garret. Filthier than her own, it looked like the last occupants had been the smugglers themselves. Clay pipes littered the floor, and bunks similar to hers lined the eaves. The dust of ages on the garret floor moved and she cried out as it rippled towards her. She leaped over the rat as it scurried past. Not caring now if she alerted the inhabitants below, she scooted for the end wall, but was astonished to find there was none. An unbroken roof space ran the length of several houses. All she had to do now was get through centuries of bird droppings, old nests and spiders' webs – and the quicker the better.

Shielding the lamp, she sprinted the length of the attic space until her way was blocked by another wall. This must lead into the last, most dilapidated house in the lane, where mad old Longbonnet lived in the few habitable rooms. Why they called her Longbonnet Kate wasn't sure; either it referred to her tall fedora with its black feather or, more likely Kate thought, her extremely long nose. She had a squint-eyed stare that had given all the kids in the lane nightmares at one time or another, simply because of the tales they wove around her. Longbonnet had once chased her all the way to Parker's Row because Kate had mimicked the old woman's cracked, quavery voice for her friends' entertainment. But when she caught her, Longbonnet had given Kate a penny – for giving her a bloody good laugh, she'd said. Still, Kate didn't fancy meeting Longbonnet today on the garret stairs.

Quietly, she examined the plaster wall till she found a similar square opening as in her own garret, but there were no planks covering this one. She eased herself through and felt her way till she came to a brick wall. This was definitely the end of the terrace, the last house of East Lane. The river – and freedom! – were just a few feet away. 'But how the bloody hell do you get out of here?' She looked up, asking the ancient cross-beams.

And the answer came from out of the shadows in a cracked, quavery voice that made Kate jump. 'This way.'

Kate whirled round to see Longbonnet herself, pointing to a wooden pulley, with a frayed fragment of rope running to a narrow door in the back wall.

'I... I...' Kate stuttered, backing towards the door. 'I'm escaping,' she finally managed.

And Longbonnet shook her greasy ringlets. 'You think you are... go on... out, quick!'

Kate darted to the door, flung it open and flew down wooden stairs leading to a cobbled yard below. Thank God for old Longbonnet – and the smugglers. She was free!

★

Like a greyhound let out of the gate, Kate ran all the way to Boutle's. 'Please, God, let me be on time and I'll start going back to Mass!' she pleaded.

But when she arrived at the factory and bounded upstairs to the manager's office, her heart sank. His cheery smile of yesterday had been replaced by a frown. Pulling out a watch from his waistcoat, he tapped it. 'What time do you call this, Miss Goss!'

'Sorry, sir!' She was aware of a trickle of sweat making its way towards the end of her nose. She cuffed it. 'I was detained on an unforeseen family emergency, sir.'

His frown deepened. 'Oh! I know you were detained all right, but what was the nature of this emergency, might I ask?'

She took in a deep breath and blurted out: 'False imprisonment!'

He seemed to consider this seriously before asking, 'Whose?'

'Er.' She fiddled with the belt on her dress and realized that the frock was now more black than blue and was ripped at the hem. God knows what she must look like. 'It was me stepsister... well, it was her that locked me in the garret. So, I reckoned if the smugglers could escape through the garrets, so could I, and I crawled through them all, though they was bloody scary, and I run here as fast as I could!' She finished on a breathless, high-pitched note and saw him cover his mouth.

'I see. Well, Miss Goss, you've shown great determination to get here for your first day of employment, and I like that in a young person.'

'Will I get a late fine?' she asked, thinking of Aunt Sylvie's warning.

He smiled. 'Not this time, but might I suggest a visit to

the ladies' for a quick wash and brush up? Those old garrets seem to have left their mark on you.'

He gave her directions and it wasn't until she looked in the mirror on the lavatory wall that she realized what he meant. Her face was as black as her hair, which looked like a nest vacated by some of the rats she'd surprised along the way. There wasn't much she could do with the hair, but she scrubbed her face with a piece of grey soap until it stung.

When she entered the soldering shop, Miss Dane, the forelady, gave her a broom and a cloth and explained her job – sweeping up and tidying around the benches. Some of the women raised their heads and then their eyebrows at the sight of her and she felt her face turn scarlet. Kate gave the young woman whose stare lasted longest a bold grin. 'Me complexion's naturally rosy.'

'And I suppose you'll be telling me your frock's naturally filthy, you cheeky little bugger,' the young woman said, with a half-smile. 'Here, come and clear round this bench, and watch your hands! These soldering irons are red hot.'

The day passed quickly enough, with plenty of fetching and carrying and cleaning to keep her busy. But she wasn't looking forward to answering Aunt Sylvie's questions about her ruined frock. She tried to slip in unnoticed, but Stan was lounging in the lane and wandered over, looking surprised as she approached.

'How did you get out? I opened the hatch when I got back from school and you was gone! I thought you'd run away. No such luck!'

'Sod off, Stan. You could have helped me.' He came in with her and as she tried to sneak upstairs, he called Aunt Sylvie's attention. 'Mum! Kate's ripped her dress!'

'Look at the state of you! Didn't they give you an overall?' Aunt Sylvie asked, inspecting the stains and lifting the torn hem.

'They didn't have one to fit me,' she lied. 'It's filthy there.'

'Well, you'll have to wear it till you can afford to get another one at the old clo' market. Get it washed and dry it over the range.'

This was the only conversation she had with her aunt about her first day at work. Not that she cared. What was there to say about sweeping up solder and washing off flux anyway? But as she was helping Aunt Sylvie make the tea, Janey walked in, and the look of astonishment on her cousin's face was reward enough for a good day's work done.

2

Blood on the Lino

1920–23

Kate soon learned that Miss Dane had eased her in gently to the soldering room on that first week. She had sent her on errands all over the factory, either taking order slips to the tinplate store or checking the solder and flux supplies. Another of her 'jobs' was running to the grocery shop on the corner of Wild's Rents to get Miss Dane her daily sandwich. Kate seemed to be everywhere *but* the soldering room. And when she picked up her first wage packet, she felt that perhaps factory work was going to be more fun than school.

It was during her second week that she realized she'd actually become a slave in hell. Eighty women worked ten hours a day soldering seams on all manner of tins, from large paint drums to fancy biscuit tins. Along each of the four workbenches were ranged twenty coke ovens. These kept the soldering irons white hot at all times. The whole room was a gigantic furnace. Ash blew out of the ovens in grey powdery clouds every time a soldering iron was inserted or removed, and it was Kate's job to wipe the soot from around the ovens and benches, keeping the surfaces as clean as possible for the women to work. Flux fumes, thick and tacky, stuck to her throat, while the smell of solder burned her nostrils. And because Kate was incapable of moving slowly, she was covered in a sheen of sweat from clocking on till clocking-off time.

Marge, the young woman who'd met her with the boldest stare on her first day, had proved to be one of the friendliest. She urged Kate to slow down. 'You've got to learn to pace yourself, Kate,' she'd warn, ''oss you'll waste away. You ain't chubby as it is!'

And it was true. After a while, the blue frock began to swamp her, and as she grew taller the hem rode ridiculously high. It would be months before she could afford a new dress out of her shilling allowance, but when she pleaded for a loan, Aunt Sylvie refused. She suffered agonies of embarrassment as the dress grew shabbier. And all her pre-sleep dreams became prayers that her dad would come back before it fell apart completely.

But Archie Goss didn't come back to save her, not during the first month at Boutle's, nor the first year. She became even more inventive in weaving her bedtime tales about him, constructing elaborate reasons for his failure to return to her.

Only when she was asleep would he appear in the sort of dreams she could not control, and sometimes they were not happy ones. They might end with Archie shouting at the shadowy figure of her mum, blaming her for some small offence. Or he would be walking away from Aunt Sylvie's, as on that first day, not even stopping to kiss Kate goodbye. Surely in reality he *had* stopped to kiss her? Or was that just another of her dreams – waking or sleeping – which were shared with no one? Her sorrow at her abandonment and her fading hopes of a rescue were hidden just as carefully as the memory of her mum. No one would know about them. She'd make sure.

By the time she was seventeen, Kate was as tough as the sheets of tinplate stacked in the yard and as sharp as the guillotines that cut them. She needed no one but herself.

'Conny, move yourself. Sweep up this solder, me feet's sticking to the floor!' Kate called to the girl whose job it now was to clean the soldering room.

She was sure she'd been twice as quick when it was her job to keep things tidy. Surely, she'd jumped to it before the ash from the coke ovens had even built up? She hadn't had to wait for Miss Dane to come and chase her. But Conny was impervious. The girl circled the broom around Kate's feet, languidly succeeding in moving debris from one spot to another, raising clouds of coke ash in the process.

'Giss that broom, Conny, you're making it worse!' Kate cleared the area around her bench in a few swift swipes. 'And see if you can wipe a cloth from one end of me bench to the other before you come and pour out the tea!'

Conny gave her a slow smile and a nod, failing to be cut by the sarcasm as she swirled the cloth around the bench in sleepy sweeps. Kate peeled off her overall and Marge, the young woman who'd first taken Kate under her wing, gave her a shoulder barge as they walked to the end of the bench for their tea break.

'Why don't you go a bit easier on that poor girl? She ain't on piecework, is she? And she's working clever! Like I always told you to do. You've got to pace yourself. Besides, you ought to remember what it's like doing the dirty work.'

'We're all doing the dirty work! There ain't *no* clean work in this place, not unless you're in the office.'

Kate picked up one of the tin cans they'd converted into teacups, soldering on the handles to save their fingertips from scalding. She spooned condensed milk in and eyed the oil drum that served as a tea urn. Each of the benches had a similar makeshift urn, with a tap soldered on and heated by a coke oven. Conny hadn't even got the water boiling and was still finishing her cleaning.

'Oh,' Kate said, exasperated, 'I can't wait for her, I'm gasping.' She began spooning tea into the large pot. 'I'll make it meself.'

'How's things at home?' Marge asked, pointing to a bruise on Kate's cheek.

She shrugged. 'You know me Aunt Sylvie – always quick with her hands. But she'll come unstuck one day.' Kate pressed the bruise, which was still tender.

'What did you do this time?' Marge asked, sipping the scalding tea as quickly as she could – their tea break only lasted ten minutes.

'I caught Stan spying on me through the hatch when I was getting changed for bed! So, course I give him a whack and pushed him down the stairs, dirty little sod. I'll have to keep the hatch closed, but it's stifling up there this weather.'

'He should know better than to upset you by now!'

'It's getting worse there, Marge. Not just Stan. Janey never stops going on at me. She thinks I'm her skivvy. I'm just hoping she'll meet someone and get married... Just think, Marge, there's some poor unsuspecting feller out there, having a lovely life, and he don't know what she's got in store for him.'

Marge chuckled. 'You're terrible.'

'It wouldn't be so bad if I could keep more of me wages, but sometimes I don't even have enough for a bar of soap.'

'Don't seem fair, love, having to buy your own soap out of the shilling she gives you back.'

Kate put down her tea tin. 'Fair? Life ain't, is it?'

When the dinner hooter screeched their release, Kate hung around, waiting for Conny. She saw the girl ambling up the factory floor, head down, in a world of her own, and had to call her twice before she looked up with a slow smile. Kate beckoned to her.

'Conny, I daresay you think I'm nagging you all the time. But if you don't start moving yourself, you'll still be sweeping up when you're sixty!' Kate knew that Miss Dane had spotted early on that she herself was a quick learner as well as a hard worker and so she'd progressed quickly to the factory floor. But Kate suspected Conny wasn't so much stupid as bone tired.

'What's keeping you awake at night?' she asked.

Conny looked up in surprise. 'How did you know that?'

'You got purple rings as big as saucers under your eyes. And I swear half the time you're leaning on that broom just to keep from falling over.' Kate paused. 'So, why ain't you getting no kip?'

Conny's eyes brimmed with tears, but she shook her head. 'I can't...'

'You got your own bed?'

She nodded. 'But I'm in the same room as me brothers – Wally, he's five, and our little Alfie, he's only three. Wouldn't be so bad if it was just them, but me two stepbrothers are in with us as well.'

Kate nodded her head slowly and said in a low voice, 'Is one of the boys pestering you of a night?'

Again, Conny's eyes filled, but this time she gave a short nod. 'Reg. I'm laying awake, waiting for him to start. I do me best to stop it, but he's getting strong now, Kate, and I don't know what to do!'

'Listen to me, Conny. I'll tell you exactly what to do. Come here.'

She led Conny to one of the coke ovens. A dozen soldering irons were waiting to go in. She picked one up. 'See this? Quick, put it in your bag. You keep it in bed with you and if Reg starts tonight, you give him a bloody good wallop round the head with it! He won't trouble you no more. In fact, I never go to bed without one meself!' She grinned and Conny gave her a grateful hug. 'Thanks, Kate.' She smiled shyly. 'You know I never mind you telling me to gee up – at least you notice me. No one else ever has – let alone that I've got dark rings!'

Conny left her with the beginnings of a spring in her step and the soldering iron tucked inside her bag.

Though Kate was happy she'd found a solution for Conny's problem, her own home life was still too full of them. She'd had her struggles with Stan, but although he'd still peek at her if he could, he'd not bothered her so much since she'd armed herself with the soldering iron. As the day wore on, the heat from the coke ovens intensified and the fumes thickened, but still she dreaded going home. For even the hell of Boutle's seemed preferable to Aunt Sylvie's.

*

It was Friday – bath and hair-washing night. Kate's job was to fill the copper in the scullery with water, then set a fire beneath to heat it up. First, she carried the tin bath into the kitchen from the yard and then filled it with bucket after bucket of hot water from the copper. The family took it in turns, each dirtying the water a little more. First Aunt Sylvie, then Janey and Stan. She had to make do with what was left after the others had finished.

Tonight, she waited for Stan to go up to bed before lowering herself into the bath with a groan. With only a small square of Sunlight soap to wash her body and hair, it wasn't a luxurious bath, but she was grateful to be rid of the stench of solder, however briefly. As she reached over for the jug, her hand found a bottle. It was Janey's Amami shampoo. Aunt Sylvie had forked out a small fortune for it and Kate knew the almond oil magic ingredient turned her cousin's thatch of sandy hair into shining spun gold. She normally used shavings of Sunlight soap, which turned her own dark curls to wire wool. 'You could scrub a pan out with yours, Kate, gel,' she muttered, regarding the half-empty bottle of shampoo. 'She'll never notice a little bit,' she told herself, unable to resist pouring some onto her palm. It smelt exotic and she inhaled deeply, rubbing it well in, enjoying the prospect of shiny hair tomorrow.

She rinsed it off and sat in front of the fire, drying her hair with her own towel. One of her first purchases with her allowance had been the whitest, fluffiest towel she could afford. For some reason Aunt Sylvie begrudged Kate using the family towels and she'd always dried herself on pieces of cut-up old sheets. But the white fluffy towel was more than a luxury, it was a link to another life. The feeling of being lifted from the tin bath by her mother, wrapped in a white towel, pre-warmed at the fire, was one of her sweetest memories of a time when she'd felt precious, and she took as much pleasure in the memory as in the towel itself.

Kate would have to empty the bath before she went to bed and hang it back out in the yard. But just for a few minutes, sitting alone, she returned to thoughts of her dad. Why couldn't he spare even a day from his business – whatever that was – to come and see her? Her aunts might *say* he was avoiding painful memories of her mother, but Kate felt it must be something else. Surely a bad memory wouldn't keep him from his only child. Perhaps he'd been ill and they hadn't wanted to tell her? Or his business had got into trouble and he was just waiting for things to pick up before he came. He wanted it to be perfect for her. That must be it.

It was on the following evening that Janey rushed into the kitchen, breathless and indignant, waving her shampoo.

'You sneaky tea leaf, Kate Goss. You've used all my shampoo! And don't look all innocent, I know it was you. I left it in the kitchen after our baths and you was the last one in here.'

Kate was sure she'd used only a tiny amount. Janey must have put a mark on the bottle, and considering it was left handily beside the bath, Kate suspected she'd walked into a deliberate trap. What a fool.

'I never touched your stinking shampoo. Why would I want to smell like you?'

Janey had made her accusation in front of everyone just as they were having tea. If there was one thing Aunt Sylvie hated it was disruption at mealtimes and, as a child, if she was late coming to the table Kate would always get her knuckles rapped with a spoon.

Now Janey launched herself at Kate, giving her a clout around the back of the head. She might have accepted that without retaliating, purely to keep Aunt Sylvie from weighing in, but she couldn't swallow the jibe that followed the blow.

'You're just like your filthy tinker of a mother. Born in a filthy caravan, bet she never had a wash, let alone a bath!'

The memory of the fluffy white towel and her mother's careful arms lifting her up stung Kate's eyes with angry tears. She stood up with a roar so fierce her cousin blanched. Kate kicked over her chair and, scattering dinner plates from the table, lunged for Janey's throat. As Aunt Sylvie tried to restrain her, Kate turned on her aunt with a snarl that brought fear to the woman's astonished face. Then, grabbing Aunt Sylvie by her shoulders, she tossed her aside.

Janey backed away, but Kate sprang, pinning her cousin to the kitchen door, before pounding her fists into the girl. 'You don't talk about my mum!' She emphasized each word with a blow. And as Janey slipped down, cowering on the floor, her hands covering her head, Kate's blows battered her. Still, Kate felt an unsatisfying lack of contact with Janey's skull. She felt hands grabbing her, pulling her from her wailing cousin, but her pure intention to inflict damage wasn't to be diverted by the combined weight of Stan and Aunt Sylvie. She kicked back like a mule and Stan retreated, but not before she'd twisted to knee him in the groin. For some reason Aunt Sylvie let go briefly, long enough for Kate to deliver a final, satisfyingly solid punch to Janey's nose. This time the girl screamed in agony as blood spurted, coating the back of Kate's fist. She breathed in the sweet relief of anger expressed more fully than in all the long years of her torment. Janey was at the receiving end, but it could have been any of them.

Suddenly she was aware of another stream of blood, flowing over her arm, and it wasn't Janey's. It was a steady red jet, gushing out of her own arm, and now she saw the cause. A kitchen knife was sticking out of her forearm and Aunt Sylvie's hand was gripping the handle.

It was only then that Kate felt pain shooting up her arm, grabbing her heart, knocking the breath from her. She pulled away but Aunt Sylvie's hold was strong and the effect was to drag the knife along Kate's arm, scoring it deeply. She cried out and Aunt Sylvie let go, rushing to help Janey.

'You've gone and broke her nose! Hold this over it, love.' Aunt Sylvie used her apron to staunch the blood pouring from Janey's nose. 'Stan, run round the doctor's. She can't breathe.'

There was a shift in Kate's vision, which she knew was not physical. She was seeing through the eyes of her childish self, all the horror-struck faces in the room were hazy, the one clear image that was sharp-edged and bright was that of her father. If he could see her now. He would be sorry. Sorry he'd left her to their mercy.

'Dad,' she heard herself whisper hoarsely as she reached for him, before falling, the knife still firmly embedded in her blood-drenched arm.

When Kate woke, she was aware of her arm only as an agony-filled balloon, twice its normal size. The knife had been removed and her arm expertly bandaged. What struck her immediately was not that she'd been stabbed, but that she was in the front room. The front room was out of bounds to her, unless it was to dust. She'd sat in there no more than a dozen times – once for every Christmas she'd spent here. The fact frightened her. She must be dying if her aunt had allowed her to be placed on her best furniture. Still being paid for on tick, it was now in danger of being ruined by Kate's blood, as it flowered red on the white bandage. She called out, but the house was all quiet. On the mantelpiece the heavy, wooden-cased clock ticked with ear-splitting precision. Through the sash window Kate saw a reddish full moon, lurid against an inky-black sky. Everyone must still be asleep. She tried to get up from the sofa, but was immediately pinned by pain, like a moth to a board. She grimaced, making no sound. Instinctively feeling that, more than ever, in this house she needed to stay invisible, unheard. Just until morning.

Stan was the first to venture in. She heard him breathing over her and woke to find his face inches from hers.

'I thought you was fuckin' dead,' he said and then grinned. 'You might wish you was once Mum's finished with you!'

'How's Janey?' she croaked, propping herself up with her good arm.

'Her face's wrapped up like a mummy and for once she can't open her gob, so you done us all a favour there. You've got a right-hander like Jack Dempsey's,' he said with grudging admiration. 'The doctor says you've broke her nose.' He shook his head. 'I heard Aunt Sarah say once that your dad had a vicious temper. Maybe you take after him more than your mum, though don't tell anyone I said that.' He hitched up the collar of his jacket and walked out, leaving the door ajar.

She had no memory of her dad's temper, but then half her memories had been supplied by Aunt Sylvie, who never criticized Archie Goss. She swung her feet onto the floor, cradling her arm. It *would* have to be her soldering hand, damn it. She grimaced. Perhaps she'd be joining Conny today, back on cleaning duties. Better that than be sent home with no pay. She guessed she'd have to keep Aunt Sylvie sweet for a year after this lot.

She heard movement in the kitchen and got up. She might as well get it over with and face the old witch. Besides, she needed to know if her injury was as serious as it felt. She pushed open the kitchen door and took in the blood-spattered wall, and then the reddish stain on the lino. Her aunt was on her knees scrubbing at it with soapy water. She looked as if she'd seen a ghost.

'What are you doing up? Go back in the front room. The doctor said you wouldn't have the strength to walk after all the blood you lost!' Her aunt's face was grey and there was something in her eyes Kate hadn't seen before. Was it guilt?

'Did you think you'd done me in?' Kate asked, but she saw no remorse in her aunt's eyes. Rather, Kate's presence seemed to cow her, which was a new experience. She stared at her aunt and saw it again. Fear. Not for Kate's safety, but for her own. Aunt Sylvie was frightened of her! Though she couldn't imagine why – after all, Kate hadn't been the one brandishing a kitchen knife. 'You thought I was coming in to finish what I started!' Kate looked down at her aunt and laughed. Which was a mistake.

'Don't you threaten me, you vicious little cow!' She threw the wooden scrubbing brush at Kate. It missed. 'I ain't having you in this house to murder us in our beds!'

Kate didn't move. Her aunt stood up and pointed to the old tin box from her garret.

'Get your clobber and sling yer hook out of it. It's all there.'

This was the last consequence Kate had imagined. She'd expected a thump from her aunt and the silent treatment from the others.

'But I ain't got nowhere to go! This is me home.'

Her aunt pulled a face of disgust. 'This ain't your home! And it never has been. If it hadn't been for my Archie begging me to look after you, I'd 'ave chucked you back to the tinkers you come from. But I've done me duty.' She folded her arms. 'You're old enough now. You can go and see what it's like fending for yourself.'

Kate tried desperately to stop her body from trembling. She wanted to draw on the anger of last night, but it had burned away to a spluttering ember. She blew on it. 'You'll be in trouble with my dad when he comes back!' she yelled. 'Wait till I tell him you've never give me a penny of what he sends!'

Aunt Sylvie gave her a pitying smile, but there was no compassion in it. 'My brother has got more important things to worry about than you, and in case you hadn't noticed he's not been near nor by you for ten years.'

Kate's lips trembled. 'Nor you,' she said carefully and watched as her aunt's face flushed.

'Because he's been abroad building his business! He writes to me.'

Now she had Kate's full attention. 'You never told me that! Did he say anything about me?'

Aunt Sylvie shook her head slowly. 'Not a word. I told you years ago, Kate. You died to him the day *she* did. And I lost me brother because of *her*.' Kate had never seen her aunt cry, not even when Uncle Tom was killed in the war. But now a single tear trickled down her pallid cheek. She turned away.

'You're not welcome in my house. Go on, out of it, and don't you dare show your face here again!'

'Don't worry. I wouldn't come back to this shithole, not if you paid me!'

Kate picked up the pathetically light tin box and charged out of the house into East Lane. When she heard the door click shut behind her, in spite of having no idea where she'd sleep that night, she felt a surge of irrational elation. There were many things Aunt Sylvie had said which she didn't believe, but her aunt was right about one thing – this had never been her home.

3

The Tin Box

1923

Kate picked up the tin box and lifted the lid. A quick glance confirmed it contained all her belongings. Her best brown frock, her coat, a change of underwear, her soap and the fluffy white towel. Along with it was her mother's rosary, holy medal, prayer book and a bottle of Atkinson's White Rose perfume whose contents had long ago evaporated. Kate let her feet take her to the only place that felt like home – Boutle's the tin bashers in Wild's Rents.

When she got there, Miss Dane immediately noticed the bandage.

'What's happened there? Did you cut it yesterday on the tinplate?'

Kate nodded. 'It's nothing much.' She walked to her bench but Miss Dane insisted on replacing the bloody bandage. Like all the supervisors, she carried dressings and plasters for on-the-job first aid. The forelady dipped into her deep overall pocket and brought out a roll of bandage, some gauze and a small pair of scissors. Miss Dane had been with the firm for over twenty years, in which time she'd treated everything from burned fingertips to severed hands. Now concern clouded her face as she peeled off Kate's bandage.

'This looks too deep for a tinplate cut.' The soldering room was the least hygienic of places, but Miss Dane went to work, deftly applying the fresh gauze dressing and bandage. Normally, she kept a strict distance between herself and 'her girls', but today she broke her own rule.

'Kate, I'm not stupid.' She kept her voice low. 'This is from a knife. Who did it? Do you want me to get the police in?'

Kate shook her head. 'No! It'll just make more trouble. It was my fault anyway. Got into a fight with me cousin and Aunt Sylvie stopped me with a kitchen knife…' Saying it out loud made her feel ashamed. But Miss Dane was the nearest thing to a confessor and so she added, 'I was sorry I broke Janey's nose, though… it was crooked enough as it was!'

Miss Dane's shoulders shook as she suppressed her laughter. 'Kate Goss. No one gets anything over on you, do they?'

Perhaps her remorse hadn't sounded sincere, but she hadn't meant to be funny.

'Well, sometimes they do. Aunt Sylvie's chucked me out and I've got nowhere to stay tonight. So, the last laugh's on her.'

'I'm sorry, love. Can you go to a friend?'

Kate nodded.

'That's good. But you can't work with your arm in this state.'

'Oh, it's all right, really. I can still use me hand!' Kate wiggled her fingers and kept her face rigid as pain shot up her arm.

Miss Dane looked doubtful.

'Why don't me and Conny swap?' Kate caught Conny's eye. 'I'll teach her how to solder and then I'll do her cleaning afterwards.'

'Conny? Solder?' Miss Dane shot a sceptical look at the young girl, who was vigorously swinging the broom over an already-clean patch of floor.

'Why not? She's been practising with the irons in her own time, ain't you, Conny?' Kate winked at the girl, who jumped to attention.

'Oh, yes, Miss Dane. Kate's already taught me ever such a lot!' she said, with a secret smile.

'I suppose it won't hurt to train her – just for when we get absences. But are you up to the cleaning as well, Kate?'

Kate gave a disbelieving, wide-eyed stare.

'Silly question, there's not much you can't tackle, is there? All right, get to work, the two of you.'

Conny was delighted with her sudden advancement but spared a thought for Kate, who was setting out the irons, solder and flux for her.

'You can come home with me tonight, if you got nowhere else to go.'

But Kate knew the offer was meant to be refused. Where would she sleep? And besides, she didn't fancy another fight tonight fending off Conny's stepbrother.

'Thanks, Conny, but I'll find somewhere. So, here's your soldering iron. Did you get any practice last night?'

'Too right I did. And I reckon me stepbrother come off worse than your Janey. But, honest, the offer's there if you want – it'd only be a blanket on the floor, but it's better than the streets.'

Perhaps it would be, but Kate wasn't that desperate yet. Besides, she thought there was one person who might take her side.

As it was Saturday, the factory closed at dinner time, and that afternoon, Kate hurried back to East Lane. She peered along the street and when she was sure neither Aunt Sylvie nor her cousins were about, she knocked on the first house in the row. Aunt Sarah opened the door.

'Oh. You're alive, then. I heard the screams all the way down the lane. You'd better come in.'

Her aunt lived in one ground-floor room, sharing a scullery with Polly, a girl who occupied the downstairs front room with her baby. Polly was unmarried, but not the only one in the lane to find herself in that predicament. She wasn't shunned as much as might have been the case in the more respectable streets. A family of ten shared the top two rooms and the garret. It was a noisy, smelly house and Kate didn't want to ask, but she had little choice.

'Aunt Sylvie's chucked me out. Can I sleep in the scullery till I find somewhere?'

'Pity you didn't pull out the knife and stick it in *her*! Done us all a favour. I'll make us some tea.'

She hadn't said yes, but she hadn't said no and Kate sat down, hopeful. Aunt Sarah would never be pushed into anything, which was probably why she clashed so severely with her bullying elder sister. Kate looked around the room, which was the equivalent of the kitchen in Aunt Sylvie's. There was a single bed against the wall, a chair by the fireplace and a small deal table under the window overlooking the backyard. In the scullery Kate heard her aunt moving slowly around, looking for a second cup and saucer. She didn't entertain much. She came back with the tea things on a tray and a plate of the perennial rock-like jam tarts.

'Thing is, Kate, if the landlord found out you was staying, he'd evict me for subletting. He done it to Mrs Freeman two doors down and she ended up in the workhouse. I can't afford to lose me room, Kate.'

'Course not. Don't trouble yourself, I can sort meself out,' Kate insisted, trying not to think of a night under one of the railway arches. 'I'll just finish me tea and be off.' She drained her cup.

'Now, don't take offence. Sit down, for gawd's sake. I wouldn't stoop to *her* level and see me brother's girl on the streets. You can stay till Monday, that won't hurt. Polly won't tell on me.'

'It'll just be for two nights, I promise,' Kate said, knowing the risk her aunt took was high, though she wouldn't want a hug or even thanks for it. 'At least now I'm not with Aunt Sylvie I'll be able to keep all me wages. Twenty-two bob a week, all to meself!'

'And how far do you think that'll go?'

'But I'll get an extra six bob when I'm eighteen,' Kate added hopefully.

Aunt Sarah shook her head. 'You'll need more than you think for a room and your keep. I can't manage it on just me Southwell's money. You'll have to take in home work like me, or do cleaning, else you'll starve, gel.'

But Kate wasn't daunted. She was strong, quick and, more importantly, her youthful confidence hadn't been knocked out of her as it had Aunt Sarah. 'I don't mind taking on extra work. I won't be skivvying for Aunt Sylvie – it'll feel like I'm on holiday! I'm just worried about finding a room. Do you know of anywhere I can try?'

'I'll look around for you. But if it comes to it, you might have to swallow your pride and ask *her* to take you back.' Aunt Sarah's face twisted in disgust. 'But if it was me, love, I'd rather sleep on a park bench.'

Kate spent a couple of uncomfortable nights on the stone scullery floor, wrapped in Aunt Sarah's large coat. On the first night, as she lay awake with her wounded arm throbbing, trepidation fought with elation at her unforeseen freedom and she wondered about Aunt Sarah's circumstances. For so long, Kate had dreamed of being rescued by her father – once his business had become successful. But what of her aunts? They had never seemed to expect anything from him, even though they all lived on the sharp edge of poverty. Archie Goss must be something very special, to have deserved such unquestioning loyalty and love from those two tough-hearted women. She gave herself a luxury which she'd learned to ration. She conjured a waking dream, screening it on the cream distempered ceiling – a flickering moving picture of her father's return.

Kate left Aunt Sarah's early Monday morning, carrying the tin box under her arm. She thought she would search for lodgings on the way to Boutle's. There was a room to let in Abbey Street, but fleas were jumping off the rugs and Kate made her excuses to the landlady, hurrying out of the place, scratching at her ankles. Long Lane looked more promising. Interspersed between the business premises were a number of houses with rooms for rent. She tried several, but they were all being let out as two or three rooms and far too expensive. She searched among the terraced houses in Wild's Rents during her dinner break, finding several single rooms, but with rents so high she'd struggle to find food and coal money. It looked as if Aunt Sarah was right – if she didn't want to starve she'd have to beg Aunt Sylvie or earn more, and she wouldn't beg.

She came back to the soldering room in a state of barely suppressed panic. Her arm was still throbbing, but when Miss Dane told her she could carry on with cleaning tomorrow, she insisted she'd be well enough to start soldering again. Piecework would save her. Tomorrow she would solder twice the tins she normally did and then she'd be all right.

At the end of the day, she walked with Conny into a grey evening of thin drizzle. She hadn't mentioned her plight again, but now Conny asked, 'Did you find anywhere to rent?'

'Oh, yeah. I got a room in Dockhead.' She hoped her smile didn't look too false, for she felt her lip tremble as she lied.

Conny looked pleased. 'Oh, I am relieved. I didn't like to say it but me stepmum wasn't too happy when I told her you might be coming to stay.'

'Conny! You shouldn't have said anything – the last thing you need is upsetting her, the old cow.' She squeezed Conny's hand and told herself to feel grateful that she had no evil stepmother or aunt to contend with now. Her only hardship would be a night on the streets, and it seemed preferable.

She'd had nothing to eat since breakfast and was so hungry she felt sick. She turned down Decima Street, heading for the dining rooms attached to the Methodist Central Hall. She could get a sixpenny supper there, which would leave her with only half a crown till payday. She hung about outside for a while, knowing she should save her money and just buy a bun. But the smells of sausages, tomatoes and onions sizzling away were too tempting and she went in. The dining rooms were bright and welcoming, and as she ate her sausage and mash, she compared it to teatime in Aunt Sylvie's, where the food would certainly be worse quality. She would have had to cook it, wash up and suffer Stan's jibes about her red face or Aunt Sylvie's moaning about her cooking skills. She was far better off here. The one thing she regretted losing was her old refuge in the garret.

She stayed for as long as seemed decent without buying anything else and left as night was falling. Her feet took her in the direction of East Lane. She stood outside Aunt Sarah's door and before she could stop herself, she'd knocked. But hearing her aunt's 'Hold on, I'm coming!', she changed her mind. Dodging into the yard of nearby Peabody Buildings, she peeped around to see Aunt Sarah on her doorstep, looking up and down the lane before shaking her head and shouting to the empty street, 'You kids! I know where you live!'

Kate simply couldn't risk getting her aunt thrown onto the streets. And, ashamed at her own weakness, she turned away, taking another route to the river. The drizzle had stopped but her coat was damp and the air chill. She faced the truth that there would be no warm bed for her tonight.

Kate comforted herself by remembering Aunt Sarah's judgement that a bench would be preferable to living at Aunt Sylvie's. 'You'll be all right,' she told herself. 'Things could be worse.'

She emerged at East Lane Stairs. The dark expanse of the slow Thames spread out before her. By now, gas lamps had been lit and on the far bank a few strands of golden beads reflected in the water. But here at the top of the stairs, all was in deep shadow. Looking quickly over her shoulder, she descended the slimy stone steps to where rows of lighters had been tied together. Their long, low hulls bobbed in jostling pairs, making it hard to judge their positions. She hesitated on the final step, then, holding her breath, she jumped. Panicking in mid-air, she thought she'd missed the lighter's edge, but her toe caught it and she stumbled forward, grabbing a rope, which just stopped her from tumbling into the water. Kate wriggled underneath the tarpaulin and, tunnelling her way like a blind mole into a mound of sacks, she made herself as snug as she could be in a bed that lurched alarmingly at every tug of the tide. She shut her eyes tight as the lighter bumped against its neighbour with thuds so loud she was sure the hull must burst open. She shivered. Pulling scratchy sacks up around her chin and easing muscles tensed rigid against the cold, she let the river's steady rhythm rock her into a fitful sleep.

She woke to the squawking of gulls. Uncurling her stiff limbs, she stuck her head above the tarpaulin and saw birds wheeling around a passing barge. The sun rose, brightening the barge's dull ochre sails to deep red. The smell, as it came nearer, revealed its fishy cargo. A crewman standing on deck spotted her, waved and shouted: 'Who was too drunk to get home last night?' He grinned and she waved back eagerly, glad to see a friendly face after her lonely night on the Thames. She needed to move quickly now, before the wharfside workers started arriving.

Groaning, her joints protesting, she straightened up and was about to jump onto the stairs when she spotted two dockers peering over the river wall.

'Oi, what you doing down there? You're trespassing!' one shouted as they began running towards the stairs.

Grabbing her tin box, she leaped up the stairs and collided with the nearest docker, a lanky chap with a long reach. She dodged him, skidding as he tried to grab her, then set off at full pelt.

'Let her go, Arthur!' the other laughed as the lanky docker pursued her. 'She's like a bloody greyhound, you'll never catch her! My money's on Blackie!'

Kate shot a look back at him, her dark curls flying as she ran. 'You backed the winner!' She grinned, before hurtling into Channel Row and the streets beyond.

Her lighter bed had been carrying a smelly load and, she suspected from the docker's comment, a dirty one too. Her aunt hadn't forbidden her to visit and so she made Aunt Sarah's her first port of call.

Polly answered the door, her baby propped on her hip.

'I've come to see me aunt. Sorry if I got you up.' Polly gave her a curious stare, but stood aside to let her into the passage.

'That's all right, I've been up ages. He's had me awake half the night!'

'He's bonny,' Kate said, pulling a face at the baby, who was so large she thought he must be eating poor Polly alive.

'I don't think your aunt's awake, though. It's a bit early, ain't it?'

But Aunt Sarah was up, still in her long nightdress and not expecting visitors. As Kate opened the door her aunt yelped, putting a hand to her heart. 'Kate! What you doin' here so early?'

'I slept at me mate's, didn't want to outstay me welcome, so I thought I'd come here for a wash.'

'Well, you bleedin' need one. The state of you! Have you seen yourself?'

She looked in the mirror above the mantelpiece. Her face was black, as were her hands and clothes.

'Where d'you sleep, in the coal cupboard?' Aunt Sarah asked. 'If your father could see you now, he'd be mortified. What a disgrace.'

Kate felt unjustly condemned for untidiness and snapped back, 'Well if he *was* here, I'd have been living with him and then I wouldn't be such a disgrace!'

'Take off your coat.' Aunt Sarah ignored her comment. 'I'll see if I can get the worst off. Get yourself in the scullery and boil a kettle!'

When Kate judged herself presentable enough to please even her father, she joined Aunt Sarah. Breakfast was tea, bread and jam. Her aunt was never short of jam, as she often smuggled out the odd pound of strawberry or blackcurrant from Southwell's jam factory.

'Wherever your mate put you last night, you can't turn up for work looking like a chimney sweep every day, Kate. You'll have to find somewhere else.'

No doubt Aunt Sarah was right. But the lighters were the best she could find during the following week. The different cargos made for different beds, but the sacks of peanuts were too noisy and the nets of coconuts too lumpy. When, after three nights, Kate couldn't face another on the Thames, she had an idea. Arriving at Boutle's, she went first to the cloakroom in the basement and tucked the tin box in her locker. The cloakroom was a new benefit, hard won by the workers' association, and had been converted from a storeroom. Before that the women had hung their coats by their benches, so that they were covered in soot by the end of each day. The cloakroom had a fresh coat of green paint and beneath the rows of lockers were long benches. It had struck Kate that a bench here would be a comfier bed than a lighter.

That night after the final shift had clocked off, she slipped back into the factory while Cecil the watchman snoozed in his box over a mug of rum-laced tea. She was so relieved to be somewhere safe and warm that she almost relished a night on the hard bench. Slipping through a basement window she'd wedged open earlier, she dropped into the corridor near the cloakroom. The place was different in the dark and she felt along the tiles till she found the door. The cloakroom seemed less welcoming now, and the sounds filtering in from the steam room made her jump with every hiss. She lay on the bench, her coat for a blanket, and sought sleep, but there was nothing here to lull her. No gently rocking Thames, no sighing tide. She felt lonelier than ever. She sat up and reached into her locker. Taking out the tin box, she felt a wave of sadness wash over her. This was her whole life. Feeling the contents rather than looking at them, she clasped the piece of soap, stroked the rolled towel, then she drew out her mother's rosary and, letting it run through her fingers, she let silent tears fall.

After each night in the black bowels of the factory with its creaks and hisses, Kate couldn't wait to get to Aunt Sarah's where, for a brief hour, she felt like a normal person who lived in a house and not out of a tin box.

One morning, without warning, Aunt Sarah announced, 'Anyway, I've found you a room.'

'Really!' Kate broke into a smile. No more freezing, filthy lighters or dark basements for her. But her aunt put up a hand. 'Don't thank me too soon, you ain't gonna like it…'

'If I can afford it, I'll like it.'

'It's ten shillings a week…'

'What! That's a bit steep. I won't have enough to live on!'

'Well you ain't found anything cheaper, have you?'

Kate shook her head. 'I'll just have to go cleaning,' she said, calculating how much extra she'd need to earn.

'Thing is, love, the reason you might not like it ain't so much the rent – it's the place next door to *her*!'

There was only one *her* that Kate knew of. She groaned. 'Well that's no good, is it?'

'No need to snap at me. You don't have to speak to her, do you?'

'Sorry, Aunt Sarah, but I don't want to be reminded every day—'

'You sound just like your father.'

If she hadn't known better, Kate might have taken that for a criticism of him.

'I'm not like him. Everyone says I take after Mum.'

'Don't matter now. But I tell you one thing, it'll drive *her* mad, if she's got to look at your face walking past her window every day!'

'All right, I'll go and see it.' The idea of irritating Aunt Sylvie appealed even more than the prospect of a warm bed.

It was only when she arrived at the house that she realized which side of Aunt Sylvie's the house was. It was actually her childhood home. She followed Mr Weston, the landlord's agent, up the garret stairs, which were now boxed in so that she wouldn't have to go through someone else's bedroom.

She pretended to be uninterested. 'I've only come to see it cos me aunt sent me – ten shillings seems a lot for a garret!'

She barely recognized the garret that she'd escaped through three years earlier. The beer bottles and sacks were gone, plaster repaired and new window panes fitted. There was a bed, a washstand and a chest of drawers. It looked far more like the childhood room she remembered and was certainly more habitable than her garret in Aunt Sylvie's. She looked around without speaking, feeling as if she'd come home. But the agent mistook her silence for hesitation.

'You'll have use of the downstairs scullery. But if you're not interested...' He turned away and she had a moment's panic, thinking of the cold and lonely nights she'd suffered.

'No! I'll take it. But I can't give you the rent in advance.'

He pretended to reconsider, but she knew not many people would put up with a garret at ten shillings.

'All right, but if you're late paying, you're out.'

The sense of relief was so overwhelming she skipped out of the house and didn't see Aunt Sylvie until they were face to face.

'Oh! I thought *you'd* be back!' Her aunt folded her arms, blocking Kate's way. 'Realized how lucky you was, have you? Come begging me to take you back? Well, the answer's no. You're not coming inside this house to attack me children again, so you can slink off back to *her* up the lane and perhaps she'd like to feed and clothe you for the next twelve years!'

Kate stared at the woman in whose care her father had placed her. 'You're a mean old witch and when my dad gets back, I'll tell him exactly how *lucky* I was, don't you worry!'

Aunt Sylvie flinched. It was liberating to have the illusion of independence, the freedom to tell her aunt exactly what she thought of her. But it was only an illusion. When rent day came around, she might well be back again, and then she really would be forced to beg.

Happiness had never been something she looked for. A quiet day, with no insults or wallops, that was the best she could imagine. But now she thought she remembered this feeling. She was happy. Here in her childhood garret. Here where the walls and rafters had witnessed her earliest happiness, the feeling began to return.

When she moved in, she first made sure to check the end walls. On Aunt Sylvie's side, the planks of wood she'd pushed through to make her escape three years earlier had been nailed back, and at the opposite end there was the same hinged opening, with its small wooden fastener. Once she'd checked no one could crawl through, she felt safe as well as happy.

It wasn't easy to keep up the rent payments, but if there was ever a choice between the rent and a loaf of bread, she would choose the rent. Her only worry was the stab wound, which wouldn't heal. She pushed herself to seam more tins than anyone else, but one morning in the soldering room, about a month after she'd been injured, she paid the price.

'Bloody hell!' Kate felt something rip. She turned her wrist to get a better angle with the soldering iron and almost dropped it.

'What's the matter?' Marge glanced up from her work.

'The cut's opened up.' She waved at Miss Dane. 'Toilet break!' She wasn't letting on. The forelady had warned Kate she wouldn't heal while she kept putting strain on her arm, but Kate couldn't afford to go back on cleaning duties.

When she returned from her toilet break Miss Dane called her over. Kate hoped she hadn't noticed the damp patch on her overall arm, where blood and pus had seeped through. But a number of women were already gathered around the forelady's bench and none of them looked happy.

Miss Dane looked awkwardly at Kate. 'I'm sorry, love, but I've just heard from the office – you're getting your cards.'

It was like a blow to the chest. 'But why? Miss Dane, you know I'm a good worker. I can't lose this job!'

'If it was up to me, I'd keep you on. But you're not getting the sack. Only being put off for a couple of months... till business picks up again. Couldn't you go hopping?'

Tin making was oddly seasonal. The work tailed off in September when the demand for paint tins dropped. The lay-off always dovetailed nicely with September's exodus to the hop fields, so, if they were lucky, women could swap tin bashing for picking hops. But it was too late for Kate, who'd never been affected by the yearly lay-off before.

'If I'd had a bit of warning it would've been nice! There won't be no places left on the hop farms now!' Kate paused. 'Is it cos I ain't as quick as I was?'

'No! You'll get your speed up. More likely it's that your wages are due to go up once you're eighteen and they don't want to pay you full whack for standing idle. You'll have till the end of the week to find something else,' Miss Dane said, turning away to give the bad news to the next girl.

Kate was only one of many. But for her, all the rediscovered happiness dissolved in a moment and she was left with an anxious void. Happiness was precarious. She remembered now why she had never looked for it.

4

He Who Runs May Read

That evening Kate went to see Mr Weston. The landlord's agent lived at one of the posher houses at the top of the lane and considered himself superior to all the other residents. He held the power of life and death in his hands, so perhaps he deserved to feel better than everyone else. If you missed the rent and he liked you, he'd give you some leeway, and if he didn't, you'd be out on the streets or in the workhouse. He was forever snooping and reporting back to the landlord if he caught anyone subletting.

'Hello, Kate. Yours is not due till tomorrow,' he said, seeing her into the front parlour that acted as the rent office. Kate eyed the open ledger on his desk, dreading totting up her own red entries for late payments. She fumbled in her bag for the rent book.

'Thing is, Mr Weston, I'm getting put off for a couple of months and I was wondering if I could pay you a bit less and make it up later. I'm going back full time in November.'

His smile faded and he shook his head. 'If we did it for one...'

'I know. But I've always been regular.'

He shook his head again. 'We're not a moneylender.' She supposed it was because he represented the landlord, but he always referred to himself in the plural, like the king or the Holy Trinity.

'What am I going to do?' The question was addressed to herself, but Mr Weston answered.

'*We* are not a moneylender, but we know one. They might help you out. Tide you over till you get back on your feet?'

Kate jumped at the lifeline. 'How much will they lend me?'

Mr Weston laughed. 'As much as you like. Just make sure you can pay 'em back!'

Kate took the address from him. The nearest thing to a moneylender she knew was old Mrs Page in George Row. She had a licence for a loan club. If you needed clothes or furniture you went to her, she bought the stuff and you paid her back with a bit of interest. But she never lent actual money. Kate had heard of others – the sharks – and they were the ones you fled from during the night.

But it occurred to her she might not need a loan – perhaps it was time to test her long-held dream. On the way home from the rent office she stopped at Aunt Sarah's.

'I need to write to me dad.'

'You don't know his address.'

'That's what I want to find out! Where is his business?'

Her aunt barked a laugh. 'Timbuktu, for all I know. Abroad somewhere.'

'Well, how do you know that? He must have written to you sometime in the past twelve years! Why won't none of you tell me? He's me dad!'

Aunt Sarah heaved herself up. She was a big woman who moved far too slowly for Kate's liking. She pulled out a case from under her bed and rifled around, finally pulling out an envelope.

'Here. This is the last address I've got.' She handed it to Kate. 'It won't tell you much, though – that was five years ago, just after the war. He wanted to let us know he was alive. Says there he's going to Canada. Something to do with the fur trade.'

'Five years ago! Why didn't you tell me?'

'Didn't seem worth upsetting you for. You always had this idea he'd turn up on your doorstep, and there he was, going the other side of the world. What good would it have done you?'

'So, you don't even know if he's still there?'

She shook her head. 'He always said he wouldn't set foot back in Bermondsey till he'd made his fortune. *Her* up the lane'll tell you different, but I don't think it could've been a big success in Canada. Not yet, anyway.'

'Does he mention me? In the letter?'

'Read it.'

She read it – twice. He mentioned her once. *I trust my daughter is well and Sylvie is looking after her.*

And she wanted to shout at the letter, *No, Dad! No, she wasn't looking after me.*

'He was never a very feeling sort of chap, my brother Archie. More of a thinker,' said Aunt Sarah, taking back the letter.

The moneylender was a woman, but nothing like old Mrs Page. She was in her forties, with dyed blonde hair and bright red lips. When Kate explained what she wanted, the woman flicked ash and put down her cigarette. 'I'll get my... Mr Smith. I don't deal with that side of things. I thought you'd come cos you was in trouble.'

'I'll be in trouble all right if I don't get the rent money on time.'

The woman sniggered. 'I meant the other kind of trouble, the nine months sort?'

'I'm not a slut!' she said, remembering the lifelong slurs on her mother.

'Don't take offence. I'll get him. He'll sort you out. But if you ever did need to get rid of anything – you know. You come to me.'

Mr Smith came in from a back room and she risked offending him by asking if he was licenced.

He answered by pointing to a certificate on the wall and then drew out a pad of preprinted forms interleaved with carbon paper.

'How much do you need?' He didn't look at her.

She'd decided on the bare minimum, just enough to pay the rent for two months and avoid starving.

As he took down her details, she felt as if she were in a bank manager's office. Mr Smith even looked like a bank manager, with his sober suit and his oiled hair, parted in the middle. He clenched a pipe between his teeth as he pressed down on the carbon paper. He smelt of a sweetish cologne which made Kate feel faintly sick. As she read over the agreement she baulked at the eyewatering interest rate and even as she signed, she feared Mr Smith wasn't the man to trust with her future. But her need and her instincts were in such conflict that she ignored the one to serve the other. She emerged from the house with her knees trembling and five pounds in her purse.

★

It was during the afternoon shift that Marge told her about an advert for a cleaner.

'It's a funny little place, probably won't pay much.'

'That don't matter, Marge, I need every penny I can get. Where is it?'

'Bermondsey Street, you can't miss it, it's painted bright bleedin' orange!'

'What do they sell?' she asked.

'I can't say for certain, love, didn't look in the window. Haberdashery, I think. I only noticed the advert on the door cos I was thinking of you.'

Kate didn't really care what they sold – if she could earn enough money cleaning, perhaps she'd just be able to pay Mr Smith back the five pounds. After her shift, eager to beat anyone else to the job, she set off at a trot in search of the bright orange shop, drawing a few stares, for only common girls ran in the street. The disapproval only made her run faster, and when she came to the orange shop she was out of breath. She smoothed her hair and, as she did so, noticed a blue-and-yellow sign swinging above the entrance. Fancy lettering proclaimed: *He Who Runs May Read*. She wasn't sure what that meant, but she pushed open the door to a satisfyingly loud ringing of the bell.

It was not what she'd expected. *Books!* There were shelves of them, all shapes, sizes and colours. *Books in Bermondsey?* Kate was struggling to understand. What useless businessman had decided it was a good idea to sell books in a place where most people struggled to afford the rent? And what on earth would they want with a cleaner? A chandler's or an ironmonger's, she could understand. But books were a clean trade. Marge was right, this one wouldn't pay much.

She had given herself a stitch and now wiped her sweaty face with the back of her sleeve, wishing she hadn't lost half her hairpins on the way. When no one responded to the ringing bell, she strolled to a large table at the back of the shop, which was littered with books. Picking one up, she took a deep breath, attempting to slow her pounding heart. The book, bound in red leather and stamped with a golden flower design, was *Grimm's Fairy Tales*. There had been no books at Aunt Sylvie's, but a memory surfaced, of illustrations glowing with colour, just like these, and her mother's lilting voice, reading to Kate, who always asked: 'Read it again.' Lost in the memory, she didn't hear someone coming down the stairs.

'Is there anything I can do for you?' The cultured voice seemed to accuse her of some wrongdoing.

Kate clutched the book defiantly. 'Well, I've run, so I think I may read!' she answered, pointing to the sign hanging outside the shop.

The young lady broke into bright laughter. 'You certainly *may* read! That *is* what we promise at the entrance.' Her long, pale dress swished as she approached the table and Kate noticed she wore a loose cotton housecoat to protect it. It was much prettier than the Boutle's overalls.

The woman offered her hand. 'How do you do. I'm Ethel Gutman. Proprietor of the Bermondsey Bookshop.' She looked too young to be the owner. She wasn't conventionally pretty, but she was striking, with dark, straight hair looped back in a bun. Her face and nose were long and thin. Beneath straight dark brows, eyes of intense warmth fixed Kate with a curious stare. Glancing at the red-and-gold book, she said, 'I adore the Brothers Grimm, so blood-curdling their version of "Cinderella", don't you agree?' And she gave an appreciative shudder.

Kate felt wrong-footed for an instant. It was as if she'd intruded into this woman's private parlour. It didn't look much like a shop. The long table, although full of books, was surrounded by wooden chairs, as if ready for dinner. Beside the table was a prettily tiled fireplace. Two hangings, brightly painted with elaborate vases and foliage, shaded the long windows, protecting the books from the late-afternoon sun.

She couldn't believe Ethel Gutman really wanted her opinion about the Cinderella story, so she said, 'Anyway, I ain't come to read, I've come to clean.'

'Well, my idea, of course, is that you can do both.' Miss Gutman smiled and paused, but when Kate didn't answer, she went on, 'But let's talk about the *cleaning* first!' The dark eyes were bright with interest. 'And have you had much *experience* of cleaning?' She mimed a vague circular action, polishing the air.

Kate stifled a laugh – it was obvious that Miss Ethel Gutman had none. 'I've certainly done me share, miss,' she said, thinking of the hours spent blackleading Aunt Sylvie's range. 'I'm quick, thorough and hardworking...'

'I'm sure you are. I have to warn you – the hours are rather odd. We cater for the working man, so we're closed during factory hours, then open from four thirty until ten thirty, sometimes eleven if there's a lecture. So, your cleaning duties would have to fit around those times.' Her tone was hesitant, almost apologetic.

'I can do that!' Kate answered quickly. 'I'm getting laid off from Boutle's for a couple of months. So, I can come during the day.'

'Perfect! Sorry – not perfect for you, of course. But I'm

afraid we can't offer full-time employment, we'd only require you for three days a week…'

Looking around, Kate couldn't see how the place would need even that much cleaning.

'That don't matter, I'm looking for an early-morning and an evening job as well.'

'Three jobs? Won't that be too much?'

'Oh, no. I'm used to hard work. Besides, there's no one else to support me now. So, I've got no choice.'

'I'm sorry. Have you been orphaned?'

It seemed an oddly personal question and Kate was about to take offence, but the woman's expression was so kind she decided to tell her the truth.

'Me mum's dead. I've been living with me aunt, but we didn't get on… she threw me out.'

'That's very unfortunate. And your father?'

'He's presently away on business, miss. But he'll be back soon,' she said, wanting no more questions.

'Well. Let me show you the rest of the place and explain your duties before you make up your mind.'

She spoke as if Kate had a choice, and Kate decided that in spite of her odd, over-familiar ways, she liked the woman. She led Kate upstairs to another room that looked even more like a parlour, with easy chairs, small tables, shaded lamps and a couple of bookcases. The walls were painted with a frieze of such bright yellow and blue that it seemed to leap out at her.

'This is the reading room. It's open to any working person and for sixpence a month you may become a member – after a few months your subscriptions will be offset against the cost of any books you purchase. A working girl such as yourself might soon build up a very fine library.'

No wonder she loved the Brothers Grimm – Miss Gutman

was clearly living in a fairy-tale world herself. Kate decided it was best to be gentle with her, as if she were a child.

'It's a question of *space*, miss. You see, I ain't got much *space* for books.'

'I do understand.' Miss Gutman put a hand on her arm. And Kate thought, *No, you don't.*

'But anyone is welcome to come along and read here after their working day – quite without charge!' She led Kate on a circuit of the room, stopping to adjust a vase of yellow chrysanthemums.

'This room is used for our Sunday lectures, which, again, are free for all to attend. On Mondays we have a French class here…' She paused, giving Kate the chance to express an interest. 'Yes, well, Tuesdays are elocution lessons, Wednesdays we have play and poetry readings. Our numbers are growing and quite frankly, they can be a messy bunch! So, as well as cleaning the shop, we would *like* you to clean this room.'

Kate's only experience of an interview had been for Boutle's, but she was certain this one must rank as unusual. She wasn't sure if she was being assessed as a cleaner or a possible member.

She didn't like to disappoint Miss Gutman by showing no interest in the book side, but she had to put her straight. 'I can't see me having time for the French classes. But I'll do your cleaning – what days do you want me?'

'Mondays, Wednesdays and Fridays. Our rate of pay is one shilling and sixpence per hour.'

Kate tried not to look impressed, but she couldn't help smiling. This was a better hourly rate than at Boutle's! She found herself wishing that bookselling were a dirtier trade – then they'd need even more of her services. They agreed she would start on Monday, and Miss Gutman told Kate that either herself or a volunteer would be at the shop to let her in.

As the young woman let her out, Kate pointed to the sign. 'What does that mean, Miss Gutman?'

'Ethel, please. We're all on first-name terms in the Bermondsey Bookshop. But thank you for noticing our sign – not many people do. It's Habakkuk – chapter two, verse two.' She struck a pose and, lifting both arms, holding her head high, declaimed in a loud voice, as though she were a prophet of old: '"Write the vision and make it plain upon tables, that he may run that readeth it."'

Kate nodded her head. 'Mmm, but I still don't understand what it means.'

Ethel Gutman dropped her pose and laughed. 'I believe that admitting our ignorance is the first step to wisdom! The meaning? I like to think of it as a promise – that somewhere there is a place where working men and women, always hurrying, may sometimes stop and read in peace.'

'A refuge,' Kate said, thinking of her garret.

'Exactly, my dear.'

Kate had to work out her week's notice at Boutle's, during which she intended to fit in the bookshop cleaning during her dinner break. She'd also managed to get a few hours' cleaning at the Hand and Marigold pub and had spent the early hours mopping up last night's spilled beer and cleaning the men's urinal. After the sapping heat of soldering all morning, she found herself wishing for an hour to herself and a chance to rest her slowly healing arm. But the bookshop was a lifeline, and she ran all the way to the bright orange shop.

'Are you always out of breath?' Ethel Gutman asked, letting her in.

'Didn't want to be late!' Kate gasped. 'I'll start upstairs. You said it'd be messy after a lecture?' She wanted to make sure she'd heard correctly.

'Excellent idea. We had Mr de la Mare speaking last night!' she said, waiting for Kate to be impressed. 'And, as you can imagine, there was a *huge* crowd, people even had to sit on the stairs! It really was an excellent evening, and he honoured us by reading some of his own poetry...'

Kate couldn't imagine. She had no idea who Mr de la Mare was. She began edging her way into the back room. Ethel Gutman called after her: 'The cleaning cupboard is—'

'I know! You showed me.'

Kate soon emerged from the back scullery with a broom, mop, bucket, duster and polish. She brushed past Ethel, giving her a friendly smile, but one which invited no more conversation. She wasn't here for chit-chat and she wasn't here to continue her education – Aunt Sylvie had put her right on that score the day she'd dragged her along to Boutle's.

'Yes. You go on up. Can you manage? Sorry about the mess!'

Kate had been wrong. Books were not a clean trade after all. The cosy, refined reading room she'd first seen was now looking a bit like the Hand and Marigold, but without the beery aroma. A long refreshment table was piled up with dirty teacups and plates of half-eaten buns. Overflowing ashtrays and discarded programmes littered the smaller tables, which had all been pushed back along the walls to make room for rows and rows of chairs. She let out a long breath. 'Phew, get wired in, gel,' she told herself, tucking her curls under a red bandana and slipping on her factory overall.

She cleared the room, stacking chairs and rearranging reading tables and lamps as she remembered them. Then she set about emptying ashtrays and clearing the debris. Adjoining the reading room was a small kitchen with a hot water geyser over the sink where she could wash up crockery. Books had been left lying about, and she tidied these into piles, not knowing where on the shelves they should go. Half an hour had passed before she'd even started cleaning. Filling a bucket from the geyser, she mopped, swept and polished until the room shone and then swept the stairs as she descended.

Ethel Gutman was at the large table at the rear of the bookshop, together with a pretty, small-boned young lady. They were surrounded by piles of typewritten pages. The girl was making rapid red marks all over one sheet while Ethel seemed to be doing some sort of craft work with blue paper and a jar of paste.

'Ah, Kate! This is Lucy, one of our gallant volunteers!' Lucy looked up, giving Kate a brief nod, before quickly bending her head to her work. 'We're just now going through the articles for the first number of our very own publication.' Ethel held up her craft work. It was a blue magazine cover with a yellow title label on the front. 'A mock-up for our quarterly. We're calling it *The Bermondsey Book*. What do you think?'

Kate glanced at it. 'Same colours as the walls?' She nodded towards the painted friezes. This woman liked bright colours. Ethel Gutman looked slightly deflated.

'It's very nice. Sorry, Miss Gutman, I haven't got time to do any more cleaning today. Do you want to inspect upstairs?'

'Ethel, please. And of course I don't need to check! I'm sure you've done an excellent job. It's not as bad as this every day – I warned you the lecture crowd is a messy bunch…'

'It's no different to the Marigold – when people are enjoying themselves, they don't want to be bothered tidying up, do they?'

'Quite so.' Ethel Gutman smiled, but Lucy remained buried in her manuscript and she gave an irritated shake of her head as she crossed out something in red ink. Kate wondered if she'd done anything wrong. But she preferred being ignored to being engaged in chat about a world that wasn't hers.

'I'll concentrate on the shop on Wednesday, then,' she said, massaging her injured arm and hoping the French and elocution classes enjoyed themselves a little less than the lecture crowd.

When she returned to the bookshop on Wednesday there was no answer to her knock, so she tried the door, which was unlocked. She found Lucy alone, and Kate gave her a friendly nod.

'I'm sorry, I didn't hear you knocking,' the young woman said, dabbing at puffy eyes and blowing her red nose.

'I'll be out of your way in a minute, miss,' Kate said, remembering the girl's previous irritation and knowing that sometimes it was worse if people asked you what was wrong. But when she came out with her bucket and mop, Lucy was slumped over the table and her tears were flowing fast enough to soak the latest article for *The Bermondsey Book*. As Kate edged past, she could see words on the manuscript already disappearing into a violet wash of ink. It wasn't her problem. It was best to stay out of it… but she thought of someone's hard work, just melting away because of this silly girl's tears.

'Miss,' she whispered, then, getting no response, louder, 'Miss! You're losing your words...'

The young girl looked up with a desolate expression. 'You are quite right. I *have* lost my words. I am rendered speechless... that he could be so cruel!' And she waved a letter at Kate.

Kate used one of her dusters to blot the running ink. 'I meant *these* words.'

'Oh no, Ethel's Introduction! Have you managed to save it?'

She plucked the tear-spattered paper from Kate's hand and read: '"In an age of lost fairylands, disenchantment broods darkly..."' She held the paper up to the light filtering through the painted window hangings. 'Darkly over what? Lord, her opening sentence has been washed away! Can you make it out?'

Kate took the paper. '"Disenchantment broods darkly over thoughts and things"?'

Lucy looked at her properly for the first time. 'Oh, yes. You're quite right. Well – thank you, er, Kate, is it?'

'I've got to start me cleaning.' And she handed the sheet back to the girl, who studied it closely.

'Please, just one second, your eyes are obviously better than mine. Half of the last sentence has gone too. She slaved over it! Here... "sensitiveness to beauty and desire for knowledge..." What's the rest?'

Kate shook her head – this time she could see only violet smudges – but then a theatrical voice rang out from the doorway: '"... sensitiveness to beauty and desire for knowledge are as keen in mean streets as in Mayfair"!'

'What have you done to my immortal words, Lucy?' Miss Gutman asked, not seeming at all upset.

'Nothing! I was just reading them to Kate... so inspiring!'

While Miss Gutman took off her coat, Kate began cleaning. She flicked the feather duster over books and polished bookcases. When she came to mop the floor, the three of them, now seated round the table, picked up their feet without being asked and continued their conversation as if she wasn't there.

'John, this is a *very* good piece. We'd be delighted to include it.'

'Really?' He sounded surprised. 'But are you sure your readers will be interested in a docker's typical working day?'

'Yes, yes, we've had many requests to include articles by local people. *The Bermondsey Book* is for new voices, not just the old guard. So long as it's well written, we'll take it. You should be very proud of this.'

The young docker didn't look at Kate as he left, but he stepped over her broom, careful to avoid the little pile of dust she'd already collected.

As the door closed behind him, Ethel said to Lucy, 'John Bacon is such a modest young man, don't you think? So clever, so promising, it's such a shame – if he'd been born in Mayfair, he'd be a household name by now...'

'It's just as you wrote, Ethel: "sensitiveness to beauty and desire for knowledge are as keen in mean streets as in Mayfair".'

Kate began to dust a porcelain figure on the mantelpiece. Aunt Sylvie would have called it a 'dust harbourer' but Kate had never seen anything as delicate and realistic.

'The way he's overcome such a sordid home life... that mother of his!' Lucy said with a shudder.

Kate began polishing the brass candlestick. She didn't know if John Bacon was clever, but she knew that in East Lane everyone called him Rasher – the boy who had had his pick of the girls when they all used to hang around the gas lamp after school. The sort of boy who wouldn't look twice at the likes of Kate Goss in her threadbare dresses and her cardboard-stuffed shoes. The boy she'd been in love with for as long as she could remember.

After she'd finished her cleaning and was washing cloths in the downstairs scullery, Lucy came in.

'I apologize for my silliness earlier. And thank you for your quick thinking with that duster!'

Kate wrung out the mop, running it under the tap till the grey water turned clear. 'That letter. You shouldn't put up with it, you know, not if someone's treating you bad. The more you try to please 'em, the worse they get. Bullies love a weakling.'

'You sound like an expert.' She eyed Kate's strong hands as they squeezed the mop dry. 'But you don't look like a weakling.'

'I've had years of being treated bad – from my so-called family. Best thing ever happened to me was when Aunt Sylvie chucked me out. It never seemed like it at the time, though.'

She took off her overall and stuffed it in her bag.

'The letter is from a young man. He says he loves me. But then I found out he's actually kissed my best friend! I was so hurt, I've cried for a week.'

Lucy was a beautiful young girl, with a halo of fine, fair hair and large blue eyes that were still slightly bloodshot.

'Words are cheap,' Kate said. 'It's what people do that

matters. If he's cruel to you, then no matter what he says, he don't love you.'

Lucy looked taken aback. 'No. I suppose he doesn't.'

'I'd give him the elbow if I was you.'

Kate might have had experience of being bullied, but she'd never experienced being ill treated by a chap – nor of being well treated by one either. Rasher had been the only boy she'd ever noticed with anything other than revulsion or disdain. Perhaps Stan's gropings had put her off men, and she'd long ago accepted that her love for Rasher was nothing but a childish fancy – until today, when the rush of excitement at the unexpected sight of him had caught her off guard. He seemed not to have noticed her, and she was glad, preferring to keep her feelings for him as just another secret fantasy, along with the dream of her father's return.

But it seemed she wasn't the only one with a secret. How could it be that Rasher, who'd left school at fourteen, was here, writing an article for Ethel Gutman's new publication? He'd been in the year above her at school but had no reputation as a swot. If Miss Gutman thought his home life was sordid, she'd never been down East Lane. His mum hadn't been a bad woman, just too drunk most of the time to look after her son properly. Kate had often helped her home in the evenings and Mrs Bacon had always resolved to stay sober the next day.

When Kate left the shop, about to set off at her usual trot, Rasher stepped out of a side alley.

'Hello, Kate,' he said, looking shamefaced.

'Oh, so you know me now! Why didn't you say hello in

there? Was you too embarrassed to let on you know the cleaner in front of your posh friends?' She hurried past, eager to put some distance between them.

'Don't be stupid!' he said, falling into step with her.

'And you're so clever, *John*?'

'I was a bit embarrassed, but not for you, for me. Don't tell anyone in the lane about seeing me in there.'

She shrugged. 'Why would you worry about that? No one's interested in you.'

'Thanks!'

In fact, the opposite was true – she knew a few girls who were very interested in Johnny 'Rasher' Bacon, and many boys who'd have liked to understand quite what he had that they hadn't.

She relented. 'I just meant you shouldn't worry what people think. But I am a bit surprised to see you here.'

'Why?'

She shrugged again. This was the longest conversation she'd had with him since she'd stopped playing with the kids in East Lane and started at Boutle's. She felt unusually tongue-tied. 'Because you're not that sort of bloke – you never wanted to be anything more than a docker – did you?' This sounded even more insulting and she just wished she could shake him off. But Boutle's was still some distance away.

'Don't remember you ever asking me what I wanted to be, you just took it for granted. Same as everyone round our way.'

'What made you go there?'

'To the bookshop? One of the union blokes – Ginger Bosher – he took me to a lecture on the trades union movement. And then I started using the reading room, they've got all of Marx and Engels. Anyway, I'd rather go there after work than back home!'

'I thought your mum's been better lately... but don't you feel awkward with them lot? Your accent's a bit different to theirs...'

He shook his head impatiently. 'They don't care about that, and nor will the readers. Besides, they can't hear my accent when they're reading my articles, can they?' He gave a short laugh, pleased with the idea.

They had reached Boutle's.

'You should give them a chance, Kate.'

Kate pulled a face. 'I don't trust 'em. They pretend we're all the same, but I don't need to be friends with them, I just need a few extra hours' work! If they could give me that, I'd love 'em!'

'Oh, you're a hard-hearted woman,' he laughed, and she liked that he'd called her a woman and not a girl.

His eyes held hers with a confident gaze that brought back that rush of excitement she'd been trying so desperately to suppress. She hoped her rosy complexion masked the undeniable blush rising under his lazy stare.

'Want to come for a drink one night?'

Kate was taken by surprise and blurted out, 'I can't, sorry. I've got to work...'

'Every night?'

'If I can. Boutle's are laying me off and Mr Weston's charging me ten shillings a week.'

'For a garret!' His anger flared quickly. 'The robbing bastard! You see, Kate, that's why we need to get ourselves a voice and be heard – *The Bermondsey Book* – it's international! Canada, Russia – just think, they'll all read what it's like to live on dockers' wages or to want something better for yourself than living six to a room in East Lane... Don't you see?'

This Rasher was totally different to the one she'd known on the streets. But she thought she did see. And she repeated Ethel Gutman's last line to him, mimicking her dramatic tones: '"... sensitiveness to beauty and desire for knowledge are as keen in mean streets as in Mayfair"!'

He laughed with delight. 'You sound just like Ethel!' Then he leaned closer, so that she could see the tiny gold flecks in his eyes, forming what looked like a star around the dark pupils. 'You really should come out for a drink with me, Kate Goss,' he said, with certainty.

5

A Fairy Godmother

Mr Smith's five pounds had only lasted two months. Kate had expected them to stretch for longer, and had hoped another couple of cleaning jobs would come along in the meantime. But so many women were laid off during autumn that most part-time jobs had already been snapped up.

It was cold in the garret. A sharp wind crept under the eaves and pierced holes left by broken roof tiles. The roof leaked and rain drummed an irritating tattoo into a zinc bucket. She would have to go back to Mr Smith for another loan. But she'd already fallen behind on the repayments on the first. She doubted he'd give her another. If she could only hold out till Boutle's called her back, she might be all right. She couldn't afford paraffin for the oil lamp and stove – in fact, she'd stopped buying everything except a weekly ounce of tea and loaf of bread. The jam came free from Aunt Sarah.

She jumped as someone rapped on the garret door. The boxed-in staircase could only be accessed from the first landing, so whoever it was must have been let in by the family downstairs.

'Who is it?'

'Stan.'

She opened the door a crack. 'What do you want?'

'I've got a message from Mr Smith.'

'What have you got to do with him?'

'I work for him,' he said, with a self-important smirk.

'Mr Smith can tell me himself.' She slammed the door and put her back to it, feeling it rattle as he tried the handle.

'Ain't you curious, Noss?'

'Piss off, Stan. I'm getting ready for work.'

'That's a porky. I know you've only got shitty cleaning jobs now... that's why you can't pay him. But Kate, you don't want to upset Mr Smith... I might be able to help. Open up.'

'All right. But keep your hands to yourself. I've got me soldering iron in here!'

He swaggered in, hands held high, like an innocent. 'You ain't got nothing to worry about. I got a girlfriend, and I ain't done bad for meself neither, for a ginger. She's a looker.'

He wore a cheap new suit that creased around his body.

'Don't offer me a cup of tea, I know you ain't got it.'

'I wouldn't give you the dirt off me shoes. What's the message?'

'Clever bitch. You'd better be careful, gel, you might want my help sometime. The message is "pay up". What did you think it was, an invitation to Sunday tea? Mr Smith ain't happy. Says he's been reasonable, but his patience is wearing thin... very thin.'

Stan sat himself on the edge of her bed and patted the blanket. 'Come and sit with your old cousin. See if we can't work out a repayment plan, eh?'

'Oh, for God's sake, Stan. You're not fourteen any more. You've delivered the message. Now you can go.'

As she went to open the door, he made a grab for her, pulling her down on the bed. She'd lied about the soldering iron. This was her haven, her refuge. There had seemed no need.

'I can afford sixpence a week, Kate. I'll make the repayments for you... if you're friendly.'

She battered his solid chest, but he grabbed both wrists, squeezing so hard she thought the blood might stop pumping along her veins. She twisted and turned like the eels on the fish stall down the Blue, evading his grasp, till he was red in the face with frustration. As she felt him relax she brought up her knee and heard a high-pitched squeal.

'Ah, that's the dear old cousin I remember!' she said, leaping off the bed and grabbing the enamel teapot.

'Here, don't go without your cuppa, Stan,' she said, swinging the pot so that it cracked against his skull. He rolled off the bed and stumbled for the door, covering his head as she aimed again. 'Leave off, you mad bleedin' gyppo! You've had your chance. I've delivered the message, but I tell you, gel, you ain't got it, you just ain't got it.'

She pushed him out and as he stumbled down the stairs, he called, 'I won't be so friendly next time!'

She ran all the way to Boutle's. It was lunchtime, but Miss Dane was sitting at her table in the deserted soldering room, eating her usual corned beef and mustard pickle sandwich, which Conny had collected from the corner shop.

'Have you got a minute, Miss Dane?'

'Kate!' She smiled and wiped yellow pickle from the

corners of her mouth. 'How you been, love? Sit down, you look a bit pale.'

'I'm all right, Miss Dane. Just come to see if they'll take me back yet.'

'They'll send you a letter. Should be end of November. Didn't you get yourself another job?'

Kate pushed her curls back, aware that she was breathing heavily, but not because of the run. 'I've got a couple of cleaning jobs, but... I'm in a bit of bother. I got a loan out...'

'Oh, you never did! Kate, you silly mare.'

'What else could I do? I really need to get back to work, though. I've gone and upset Mr Smith.'

'Who's he?'

'The moneylender.' Her lips were dry and she swallowed hard. Miss Dane was her last hope. 'He's just sent Stan, me cousin, to get the repayments. But I haven't got the money. It'll be the heavy mob next. I know it.'

'How much did you borrow?'

'Five quid.'

'How far are you behind?'

'Two weeks – it's a tanner a week.'

Miss Dane put up a finger. 'Wait a minute.' Her head disappeared under the bench and Kate heard her rooting about in her bag.

She came up with a half crown in her hand. 'Take this and get your payments up to date. He might lay off then.' Miss Dane gave her an uncertain smile. 'I'll have a word upstairs, Kate. See what I can do.'

But although she didn't look convinced, Kate felt near to tears at the woman's kindness. 'I'll pay you back,' she said.

Miss Dane shook her head. 'Sounds like you've got enough to pay back as it is.'

★

She went straight to Mr Smith's. Jean, the platinum-haired woman, whose relationship to Mr Smith wasn't quite clear, let her in, greeting her like a long-lost friend.

'Where've you been, darlin? We ain't seen you in a while.' The red lipstick was so thick it cracked when she smiled.

'It's only been two weeks!'

Jean raised her eyes in sympathy and adopted a confidential tone. 'I know how it is, the time runs away and before you know it...' She paused, her eyes hardening, 'you're in arrears!' She dropped her voice. 'Mr Smith gets unhappy when it comes to arrears. You don't want to make him unhappy, darlin'. You done the right thing listening to Stan. Go in.' She put a hand into the small of Kate's back and shoved. 'He's in the office.'

Mr Smith was going over a ledger, dressed in his bank manager's suit; it was hard to connect him to Stan's clumsy attempt to frighten her. He glanced up and gave her a curt nod. Picking up his pen, he immediately began writing in red in the ledger. 'Kate Goss. Two weeks' arrears.'

'Here's one and six, this week's as well.'

'You pay double for arrears. Two and six.'

'Double!' That was the half a crown gone already. She'd hoped to get a sixpenny supper tonight.

He looked up, unperturbed, as he opened a large cash box and shook it at her. 'I see you've got the exact money.'

She nodded and put the half crown into the box. Without warning, the lid of the box slammed onto her hand, trapping her fingers, and she cried out, 'What are you doing?'

He leaned his whole weight onto the lid of the cash box, and the more she tugged, the harder he pressed. 'Stop it! I'm paying you back!'

Mr Smith clenched the pipe tight in his mouth, keeping up the pressure. 'Miss Goss, be under no illusion. I am not a charity. And the next time I send you a friendly message I expect you to treat my employee with respect and pay what you owe there and then. Next time I won't send a relative...'

He let go and she cradled her throbbing hand.

'You can't do this to people. It's assault!'

'And you're free to report this little accident. But I wouldn't be happy... I wouldn't be happy at all.'

He leaned back, puffing impassively on the pipe till the acrid smoke made her cough. 'Good day to you, Miss Goss.' He turned away and Kate left, holding her hand to her chest, determined not to cry.

Jean let her out and with a pat on her shoulder said, 'If you need some quick money, I can get you work... easy work, know what I mean?'

Kate was about to thank her, then saw beneath the smiling exterior. Under the face powder, rouge and lipstick was the old hag in the fairy story Mum had once read her. And she remembered how, even as she listened to the terrible fate that awaited little Hansel and Gretel, her mouth had watered at the idea of a gingerbread house.

'N-no thanks!' she said. 'I won't be late again...'

Back in her garret, she plunged her hand into the bucket of rainwater and let the tears fall until the throbbing eased. Her arm had only just healed, and now her soldering hand was damaged. She had never felt more alone. She lay on her narrow bed and stared out of the dormer window at a steel-grey sky, letting herself drift into the old tale of her father's return. But this time it didn't work. Like 'Hansel and Gretel', it was just another fairy tale.

She heard the wind whispering her name, but it sounded as

if it were coming from outside her door. 'Kate, Kate?' a faint voice called.

She opened the door to see little Emmy Wilson from downstairs. She was cradling a saucepan. 'Mum says I've got to say sorry.'

'Why? What have you done?'

'I let that Stan in. He told me he'd come in the night and kill baby Stevie if I didn't... Sorry.'

Kate crouched down to Emmy's level. 'Tell your mum it's all right. Stan's a big bully and it's not your fault.'

'I'll tell her. Here, she sent you up this.' She handed Kate the saucepan. 'What's left of our rabbit stew, and she says we'll make sure he don't get in again.'

Kate took the pot and placed it carefully on the table before giving Emmy a hug. 'Sorry I haven't got a penny for you,' she said.

'Don't matter, Mum says we have to share and we don't want no payment.' The little girl drew herself up and Kate said, 'Your mum's a very kind lady. Tell her I said thank you and I'll give her back the pot tomorrow!'

Kate devoured the rabbit stew, trying to ignore her suspicions that she was eating Mrs Wilson's tea. When she'd scraped the bottom of the pot, she felt less hungry but, more importantly, less alone than she had an hour before.

Wednesday was an easy day at the bookshop. She couldn't see the point of the Tuesday elocution lessons. Who were they for? Certainly not the middle-class volunteers or the students who came from all over London to attend the Sunday lectures. So they must be for the locals. But she couldn't believe many Bermondsey people felt the desire or need to acquire a cultured accent. And the proof was that the elocution class was usually a small one. But whoever attended, they were a considerate lot and always stacked the chairs away before leaving. She was especially grateful today, as she'd have had trouble lifting chairs with her swollen hand. She gave the reading room a quick mop and polish and went down to the shop. Ethel Gutman had been joined by a woman Kate hadn't seen before. They were seated at the large table. Deep in conversation, they hadn't noticed her arrival. The woman wore an expensive-looking cream wool coat and a wide silk hat with a feather that fluttered as she spoke. In her late forties, she was older than the usual volunteer. Kate moved along the bookshelves and, careful to use her left hand, flicked the feather duster in time with the woman's hat. She was smiling to herself when the woman shot a look in her direction. Kate felt caught, and yet how could the woman have known that the feather on her head was being imitated? Kate made her movements a little less jaunty and turned away to clean the window display.

She pulled aside the lace curtain, which hung on a brass pole at the window, and reached over to flick the displayed books with her duster. She looked through the glass pane at sleeting rain and noticed a young man staring at her. He was wearing a tweed jacket and a pale peaked cap and held leather driving gloves in one hand. She expected him to look away but he stood back a little and continued to stare. Perhaps he wanted to see the books on display and she was blocking his view. 'Sorry!' she mouthed before giving one final flick of the duster and drawing the curtain again.

The shop bell clanged loudly and the young man walked in. 'Aunt Violet!'

He had a pleasant voice and he brought in the fresh smell of rain on tweed along with a sharp cologne. He took off his peaked cap and she darted out of his way as he went to greet Miss Gutman and the lady.

'Ah! My chauffeur's here! Miss Gutman, this is my nephew, Martin North.'

Kate slipped into the scullery. She filled the zinc bucket slowly so as not to drown out their voices.

'We've been talking about Miss Gutman's magnificent work here, making books available to working men and women – as well as her famous lectures. I'm going to be her latest patron!' The imposing woman had an almost girlish excitement about her. 'What do you think, Martin?'

'Marvellous idea! I've heard such good things about the Sunday lectures. I'm particularly interested in art history – do you have a programme, Miss Gutman?'

'We do!'

Kate peered round the door and saw Miss Gutman searching in completely the wrong place. 'Oh dear, I'm sure they were here. I do know we'll be having someone coming to speak on art – very soon. I can't quite remember...' She was getting herself in a state. Kate had picked up that Ethel was not the best of businesswomen. She left the financials to her husband, who was older than her and wealthy enough to subsidize the shop. 'I'll have to send you one.'

As they chatted Kate left her bucket and ran upstairs. When she came down with a programme the young man was already steering his aunt out of the shop. 'Come along, Auntie Vi, I know you love it dahn 'ere amongst the costermongers but we ain't got all day!' he said in a bad cockney accent.

Hot with a sudden anger, she shoved a programme into his hands and, unable to resist, addressed him in his own plummy accent. 'Mr E. Clephan Palmer of the *Daily News* will be giving a *thrilling* lecture on "The Failure of Art"!' Then dropping into his bad cockney, 'That's if you fancy comin' dahn 'ere again.'

His face paled. 'I beg your pardon. Thank you for the programme. Most kind,' he mumbled and hustled his aunt out.

She daren't look at Miss Gutman – no doubt she'd lose her job for offending the newest patron – but with her face still burning, Kate could finally see the point of the Tuesday elocution class.

Miss Gutman put a hand on her shoulder and Kate turned to face her. Ethel was laughing. 'You have a great gift for mimicry, Kate. I'm sure you'd be a welcome new voice in the Wednesday play readings. Come tonight!'

Play readings! Living on tea and air, she barely had the energy to do her cleaning, let alone prance about pretending to be a fine lady. This woman had no idea about real life in Bermondsey. She sighed. 'No thanks, miss. I haven't got the time.' She pushed back her curls under her bandana and Miss Gutman gave a gasp.

'What have you done to your hand?'

'Caught it in a door,' she said, making her escape to the scullery. 'I'll just finish polishing the floors then I'll be out of your way!'

When she came back with her duster, she was relieved to find Miss Gutman had gone upstairs. She knelt and dipped the duster into the tin of polish.

'Hello, Kate,' a voice said quietly, and at the sound of Rasher's voice, her heart beat a little faster. He stepped around her kneeling figure. *Damn!* He would have to come in right now, when she had her skirt hitched up and her hair stuffed into an old bandana.

She sat back on her haunches and pulled her skirt down. 'Miss Gutman's upstairs.'

'I've come to see you.'

'I told you before, Rasher. I can't go for a drink with you,' she replied wearily, but firmly. She guessed he was between girlfriends and at a loose end – there was no other reason for his persistence.

'It's not about that – though you will, one day,' he said with that cocky grin of his. 'Listen, I've heard the talk in the lane about you getting in trouble with that shark Smith. Let me help.'

'Did you get called on today?'

'No, I wasn't lucky.'

'Then how can you help me? You've got a mother to keep in Guinness,' she said, immediately regretting it.

'You're so sharp you'll cut yourself one day. I wasn't offering you money...'

'What were you offering then?'

'You'll find out.' She could see he was exasperated with her. But she couldn't help that. At the moment she had energy enough to keep herself alive, and that was all.

He was staring at her hand. 'Did Stan do that?'

She stuffed her hand under the overall. 'You can't keep no secrets in the lane, can you? It wasn't him, it was his boss.'

He squatted down beside her. 'Let me go and sort him out. Me and my mate big Ginger Bosher'll pay this Mr Smith a visit.'

'No! I can't have anyone else getting in trouble over my silly mistake.'

He shook his head. 'I don't understand your family. They've just chucked you to the wolves. What did you ever do to them, Kate?'

'I think I had the wrong mother.'

He nodded. 'I know what that feels like!' And they both laughed. 'The times you helped her home, Kate! You were a good kid.'

And in spite of all her resolutions, she couldn't help feeling pleasure that, back then, he had noticed her after all.

He pulled a rolled-up manuscript out of his jacket pocket. 'Better get the deathless prose checked over by milady upstairs!'

That evening, she went down to the end house in East Lane. Mad Longbonnet's backyard was unusual for having thick greenery sprouting from every corner. Cobbles had been dug up and patches of earth filled with all sorts of weeds. Once, Kate had fallen in the street and bumped her head on the kerb. Longbonnet had come out with a green, smelly compress of comfrey leaves and put it on the swelling egg. Her playmates had frightened her with tales of poisonous witches' brews. But, miraculously, the swelling hadn't lasted more than a day.

She slipped into the yard, making sure Longbonnet wasn't about, and began tugging up handfuls of comfrey.

'You remembered!'

Kate jumped. It was Longbonnet. The woman walked on silent feet and was always appearing out of nowhere. Kate eyed the back gate.

'Don't run away, Kate Goss. I got a better remedy for that hand. Come inside.'

Kate shook her head.

'I ain't gonna eat you.' And then she gave a brown-toothed smile. 'My gawd, it's like looking at Bessie when she was your age.'

The old woman shuffled off, and Kate followed her into the house. She allowed her hand to be slathered with a brown, foul-smelling ointment and bandaged.

'Comfrey and paprika. Keep it like that and you'll be good as new by the end of the week.'

Kate had lost all interest in her hand. 'Bessie? Did you know my mum?'

'Course I did. And your grandmother. When we all used to live in Romany Row. Your poor mother should've stayed there. Worst thing she ever did, coming into that family. The Gosses was a cold-hearted lot. And that Stan... he's always had his eye on you – now you've given him a way in. Silly mare.'

Longbonnet sounded suddenly not mad at all. She leaned close, her long nose almost touching Kate's. 'You should get away from that family, oss they'll be the death of you, just like your poor mother.'

A chill enveloped her. 'Whatever they are, it's nobody's fault she fell down the stairs. It broke me dad's heart!'

Longbonnet shook her oily hair, ringlets screening her face as she turned back to the ointment. 'Do as you please. You're as stubborn as she was. But one day you'll remember what I said. Then you come to me.'

Dismissed, Kate ran all the way to her own house. Longbonnet had never talked about her mother before. Why now? She wasn't going to let an old woman with a faulty memory upset her but, mad or not, Longbonnet was right about the ointment, for the following morning Kate was astonished to find her bruises gone and her fingers looking much less like sausages.

*

On Friday when she went to the bookshop, Miss Gutman appeared to be waiting for her.

'Before you begin, Kate, I'd like to put a proposal to you.' Kate hoped she wasn't going to renew her attempts to enrol her in the play readings. She was about to make an excuse when Miss Gutman took her damaged hand and examined it. 'It's looking much better, but a little bird told me what the cause was. And I would like to offer my help.'

Kate pulled her hand away. 'I'm sorry, Miss Gutman, but I'm getting along fine. And it's kind, but I can't accept charity. No!' She was intensely embarrassed. The woman took her hand again and held it gently. She was trapped.

'I understand. The little bird also explained that. But what if I were able to provide you with a few extra hours' work each week? Would that help?'

Kate would have fallen and kissed Miss Gutman's feet if the woman hadn't been holding on to her hand.

'Yes, yes it would! But what is there to do?'

Miss Gutman went on to explain that the numbers attending the lectures were now so high that they needed help setting out the room and serving refreshments afterwards. 'Also, I know you weren't attracted to the idea of joining the drama readings, but they are putting on some productions and would be very glad of some help backstage – though as yet we have no stage – costumes, props and so on...'

Kate almost laughed, but she veiled her delight as she asked, 'And the rate?'

'One shilling and sixpence, as for the cleaning.' Miss Gutman gave a businesslike nod as if to emphasize this was not charity.

Kate was nodding her head before Ethel Gutman had even finished. 'That would be acceptable, miss – Ethel. Thank you!'

Being paid for making tea and playing theatre felt like one of her mother's fairy tales, and she smiled when she asked herself who the fairy godmother might be. She had her suspicions, but Rasher Bacon just didn't seem the type.

Everyone was so smartly dressed. Kate was glad she was invisible. Most of the work had been done before the audience had arrived to fill the reading room to capacity. She'd moved the small tables, put out rows of chairs and put the kettles onto the range in the tiny kitchen. She'd laid out the tea things and plates of buns. She planned to stay on afterwards to clear it all up, saving herself a job the next day. From the half-open kitchen door, she surveyed the crowd, who were mostly young. She could spot the Bermondsey boys and girls immediately. They were smart, but the cut and quality of their clothes set them apart from their middle-class counterparts. Also, once the lecture had started, it was obvious to Kate they listened more intently, some leaning forward resting chins on hands, others taking notes. The students who'd found their way to this out-of-the-way part of south London seemed rude in comparison, interrupting the speaker, shouting out questions and witty comments, whilst others lounged in their chairs and some chatted to their neighbours. But the speaker seemed a jolly chap, taking it in good part and coming back with enough quips to make the audience laugh. She just longed for it to end. The question of whether 'Art' had failed seemed far less pressing than when she could eat next. Even with the extra work Miss Gutman had given her she was barely able to afford the staples and felt half-starved most of the time. She'd been unable to resist pocketing one of the buns she'd put out. She should save it for breakfast, but the temptation was too great. Sod it. She needed something to keep her going. And this bloke was enjoying himself far too much – he'd go on forever. She stuffed half the bun into her mouth just as someone poked his head around the kitchen door. It was Martin North.

'Oh! You're all a-tremble like a guilty thing surprised!' he laughed. 'Ethel says you'd better bring the tea out now, or else Mr Palmer might go on till midnight!'

She nodded, unable to speak due to the bun filling her mouth, and turned away to the teapots, aware that he was still there, staring at her. She swallowed and turned to him with a glare. 'I was hungry!'

'I'm sure you're allowed a bun…' He came into the kitchen. 'Anything I can do?' he went on, stuffing his hands in his pockets and staring some more.

Did he enjoy embarrassing her? 'No, just get out me way… please.' She reached past him for a tray. Why did men always think hanging around in the kitchen amounted to helping? 'If you really want to do something you can take out these teapots.'

She followed him with jugs of milk just as the question time was coming to an end.

'I believe I have won my point, have I not?' Mr E. Clephan Palmer cast a bright eye over his audience. 'For if art were not a failure wouldn't it have more to do with real life? Shouldn't we rather be governed by artists than politicians?'

'No!' Rasher Bacon stood up. 'The purpose of art is to take us beyond so-called real life!' She was surprised to hear a chorus of 'hear! hear!'s.

Martin put down the pots and, unable to resist diving in,

called out, 'But imagine the fun we could have as a nation if we had Mr Osbert Sitwell as foreign secretary!'

Rasher sat down and Kate noticed that the kohl-eyed blonde woman sitting next to him frowned at the interruption and put an encouraging hand on his arm, leaning in close to whisper in his ear. Perhaps Kate had been mistaken about Rasher being between girlfriends – the blonde looked totally smitten.

'Good idea!' Mr Palmer responded to Martin's suggestion. 'And what about Mr Bernard Shaw as prime minister!'

'No! It should be good old Alf for PM!' someone shouted, referring to Dr Alfred Salter, Bermondsey's revered MP.

'Give Conan Doyle the Home Office! He'd soon sort out the police!' suggested the young blonde woman, and Rasher gave her an appreciative smile.

'As a personal friend of Mr Conan Doyle, I am positive he'd turn it down – not important enough!'

The audience's laughter drowned out his next sentence and Ethel Gutman took the chance to bring questions to a close. Suddenly the audience realized how thirsty they were and began crowding around the tea table. Kate began pouring from a heavy teapot and was concentrating hard on not spilling a drop onto the white cloth when Rasher appeared. He picked up another pot and began filling cups.

'Do you know the chap that muscled in on my question just now?' he asked.

'Oh, Martin? He's just someone's nephew.'

'It looked like he knew you.'

'No! He's a bit odd – I think he just likes to slum it. But your blonde friend didn't look too happy with him interrupting you.'

'Oh, Pamela? She can be overprotective.' He smiled

thoughtfully. 'She might look like a dumb blonde, but she's a student at the LSE, absolutely brilliant – helps me so much with the writing.'

And Kate wished she hadn't mentioned her. 'Anyway, you'd better take her a cup of tea,' she said, turning away to serve someone.

'She had to leave. I'll make myself useful here if you don't mind.' He grinned.

When the crush had died down, she thanked him for his help and then added, 'Thanks for getting me these extra hours – I know it was you.'

He shrugged, not denying it. 'You wouldn't let me sort out Mr Smith, so...'

As she put down the milk jug she swayed and he caught her. 'You all right, Kate? You look a bit peaky.'

'I'm fine. Just need some air. How long do they usually hang about?'

'It could be gone eleven. Can I walk you home?'

'If you like,' she said. After all, it would be rude to refuse her fairy godmother.

6

Rasher

The Hand and Marigold was not the sort of pub frequented by the young – for the latest jazz songs and dancing you'd have to go to the Folly at Dockhead – but there was a warmth about it, with its glowing gas lamps, veiled in a fog of cigarette smoke, and its friendly crowd of regulars. The Marigold had its fair share of old ladies in black porkpie hats who sat for the whole evening with a pint of Guinness, singing the songs of old Ireland. And around the bar lounged working men – from Boutle's, Hartley's and Pink's jam factories or costermongers from Tower Bridge Road market. It wasn't the most glamorous place for their first drink together, but it was convenient, as the landlady had recently offered Kate barmaid work on a couple of nights a week and they'd arranged to meet during her break.

She knew the minute Rasher walked into the Marigold, even though she was concentrating on pulling a pint for Sean, the pianist. There was a little pause in the chatter and some heads turned. Rasher wore a wide, peaked cap and dark blue suit which hung well on his tall, slim figure. He was clean-shaven and his even features had a fineness about them that made him stand out in this crowd of weather-beaten traders. People stared at him as he made his way over to the bar. He looked like no other docker she'd ever seen and she suspected he knew it.

'Goin' on me break, Mrs Hardiman! All right?'

And the landlady nodded. Kate placed the pint of beer on the lid of the upright piano. 'Play something, Sean, it's a bit quiet in here!'

She and Rasher were probably the youngest in the pub, which made them even more an object of attention. She was glad when the old ladies started talking about this year's hopping trip. Their laughter became raucous as one of them launched into a tale.

'My Bill comes wandering back from the pub pissed as a puddin', can't find our hut so he gets in bed with the widow next door! She let him stay there all night an' all, filthy cow! Gawd knows what they got up to.' The old lady gave a disgusted sniff. 'I never asked, but she had a bleedin' smile on her face the next day and so did my old man! She was welcome...' The old lady paused to sip her Guinness.

Rasher looked at Kate and raised an eyebrow. 'Are these your regulars?'

She nodded. 'I like them. I only have to serve them the one pint all night.'

'Wasn't exactly what I had in mind when I asked you for a drink.'

'Well. I'm here.'

He smiled and raised his glass.

'But I'm not sure why you asked,' she added.

'And I thought you were cleverer than that.'

'You've never taken any notice of me, not since I started work at Boutle's. So, why now?'

She didn't really know why she was being so awkward. This was a moment she'd dreamed of when she was a young girl. But now it was here, she felt safer pretending not to care.

He leaned forward. 'To be honest, I think it was your impression of Ethel Gutman got me interested!' And he laughed at the memory. But then his expression turned serious. 'And I *did* notice you in the lane. I noticed every time you picked my mum up off the street, brought her home and put her to bed. And I noticed every time the others took the piss out of her and you didn't. I was just too embarrassed to say anything then.'

She was glad he hadn't insulted her by pretending he'd noticed her for her good looks.

'Why were you embarrassed?'

'Wouldn't you be if you had a mum like mine?'

She thought for a moment. 'I'd love to have a mum like your'n. I'd love to have any mum.'

'Sorry, Kate. I'm stupid.'

'Suppose you are – for a clever boy…' she teased. 'When did you start the writing?'

'Oh, that.' He blushed. 'When I was at school. But only in secret, just for myself. In between looking after Mum.'

'I had a book once,' she said wistfully. 'But if Aunt Sylvie found me reading, she'd give me such a walloping. She said I got enough of that at school. So, I'd read in the outside lav. *Grimm's Fairy Tales* it was called. But one day she dragged me out, tore up all the pages and stuck 'em on the spike for toilet paper. So I give up on books after that.'

'She's a witch.'

'Hmm, but I've escaped now…'

'Is your dad dead?'

'No! What makes you think that?'

He shrugged. 'Because no one ever talks about him.'

'Oh, my aunts talk about him, they just never tell *me* anything. They reckon he's coming back to Bermondsey when he's made his fortune.'

'What about you?'

She shifted uncomfortably in her seat. She didn't want to divulge her greatest dream. And suddenly that gave her an understanding of why he hadn't wanted anyone in the lane to know about his writing.

'I don't *talk* about him. But I think about him all the time. He'll come back for me.'

Rasher nodded. 'He'd be mad not to.' His eyes held hers and she looked away, conscious of how scruffy she must seem in the dress she'd mended so many times it couldn't take another darn. Was he playing with her? He obviously had ambitions and she knew he wouldn't stay a docker forever. He'd probably take up with that clever blonde, Pamela, and move away as soon as he could. She stood up abruptly.

'Well – back to work!'

'Oh! Already? I wanted to ask you something, and don't get offended. Are you all right for money now? I mean, can you keep up your payments to Mr Smith?'

'Some weeks. If I get enough work in the bar…'

'And what do you do if you're short? Not eat?'

She hugged herself, hoping somehow to disguise the skinny waist and bony ribcage.

'Let me help, Kate.'

'No, no. I'm all right. And once I'm back at Boutle's…'

But she'd begun to despair of ever going back there. The lay-off had made her realize just how vulnerable she was. She never thought she'd miss the hard, filthy work of tin bashing, but at least she'd earned enough to keep the wolf from the door. These past months, the wolves had been howling and she feared she'd be their next meal.

He watched her go back to the bar, taking his time drinking his beer. When she next looked in his direction, he was gone. *He won't do this again in a hurry*, she thought, convinced that she'd put him off for good.

A few days later, she was hanging out washing in the backyard on the one line each family took turns using. Because she always had so little laundry, she did hers mid-week, leaving the copper, wringer and washing line free for the Wilsons to use on Mondays. It also meant that she never had to hang out washing on the same day as Aunt Sylvie next door. But Stan had got wind of her weekly routine and now poked his head over the fence.

'Your feller made a big mistake going after my boss like that,' he smirked. 'Mr Smith'll have his balls cut off and fed to the fishes.'

She said nothing, but he continued to grin at her. Finding himself ignored, he stepped over a broken bit of fence. The sheet billowed on the line, obscuring him. Suddenly she felt herself seized from behind, his hands making clumsy grabs for her breasts. She twisted out of his grasp, picked up a piece of broken fencing and swung it in a low arc.

'Blimey, Kate!' he yelled, rubbing his shin.

'Stan, you're an ugly bastard and your breath stinks, what makes you think I'd want your filthy hands all over me? If you carry on, one of these days I'll end up smashing your brains out!' She squared up to him with the plank.

'You're a nutter! I was only giving a friendly bit of advice.'

'Well thanks, but I don't know who you're talking about. I haven't got a feller.'

'I ain't silly,' he said with an oily smile. 'That Rasher'd like to get his hands all over you too.' He curled his lip and turned to go. 'But Rasher won't last long if he carries on. My offer's still there if you want your debt paid off.' He turned to go, but as he left he ripped every bit of her washing from the line and trampled it into the dirty cobbles.

She gathered up her clothes and the bed sheet. Finally, she pulled the now-filthy white towel to her breast, briefly putting it to her cheek. But she had only the smallest piece of Sunlight soap left. She put the towel back into the washtub and began scrubbing. Everything would have to stay dirty for another week. But not this.

She stood on the top step and knocked loudly on the door, which rattled in its frame. The place was barely a house. It was more a narrow yard between two buildings that had been covered with a roof and furnished with a door at some time in the distant past. There were no front windows, but Kate knew that there was a top-floor back window and a glazed door on the ground leading to a narrow passage which ran down to the Thames.

The woman who answered her knock might once have been pretty, but her features had bloated, so that her nose and cheeks were differentiated by the merest indentation, as if someone had started to model a face in clay and had given up on the fine details. The eyes had receded into pockets of flesh, and her voice was deep with gin and Woodbines.

'Hello, Kate!' she rasped. 'I ain't seen you in ever such a long time. Come in, darlin', I'll put the kettle on.' She stumbled back into the gloomy interior and fell into the main room, which contained a bed, a table and a range.

Kate helped the woman to her bed, saying, 'Thanks, but I can't stop for tea.' She knew there would be none in the house anyway. 'I was wondering if your Johnny was in?'

'I don't see much of him, love. I don't think he's here... let me go and look.' She attempted to get up and fell back onto the bed. The room was so full of gin fumes that Kate's eyes watered. Mrs Bacon, finding herself flat on the bed, curled up, closed her eyes and began snoring almost immediately. Kate looked around, remembering how immaculate Rasher had looked on their drinks night. She wondered how he even kept himself clean in this place. 'He must go to Bermondsey Baths,' she muttered to herself.

'Yes, I do. Sixpence a week for a bath and tuppence to do the laundry. Welcome to the family estate.' Rasher stood in the doorway of what looked like a cupboard. He was wearing an old, baggy pair of corduroys, held up by braces over a collarless shirt, but still he managed to look good. 'What can I do for you?'

'It's what you can't, Rasher. You went to Mr Smith! What's the matter with you? You've got responsibilities...' She looked at Mrs Bacon and Rasher did too.

He sighed. 'I'd better cover her up. She's there for the night.'

'Stan paid me another visit.'

'Did he touch you?'

'Oh, only the usual groping. I'm used to it. If I'd had my

soldering iron instead of a plank of wood he'd be walking around on crutches. He says Mr Smith is coming after you. What have you done?'

'It took some hard negotiation, but he's agreed not to charge you interest. At least you won't be paying him back for the next five years.'

Mrs Bacon stirred and Rasher beckoned Kate to follow him. Through the cupboard door was a set of narrow stairs, leading to his room. It was like walking into another world. This room was spotless, with a yellow coverlet on the bed and a rug of modern design. An armchair was placed beside the tiny fireplace and a bookcase held volumes she recognized from dusting them in the bookshop.

'Did you buy all these out of your sixpenny subs?' She ran her fingers along the spines, reading their titles aloud.

He joined her. 'It's a good way to build up a library.'

'Well, let's hope you live long enough to enjoy it.'

'Oh, he won't risk doing anything to me. I just told him to lay off you or the police would come and ask to see his licence.'

'But he's got a licence!'

Rasher shook his head slowly. 'If you'd looked at that certificate behind his desk properly, you'd have seen it's fake. I think it's a swimming certificate.' He laughed and she felt stupid.

'I was just desperate for the money.'

'That's what the likes of him bank on.' He went to the bookcase. 'But let's not talk about Mr Smith any more. Here. It's a present.' He handed her a book, bound in red leather with gold blocking on the front.

'*Grimm's Fairy Tales*!' As she flicked through the pages a bittersweet wave of remembrance washed over her. Each tale held her mother's voice, each illustration was heavy with the memory of something loved and lost. For a moment she couldn't speak. 'You remembered,' she said eventually. 'You could have bought another Marx.'

'I could have. But I already know everything he's got to say. I don't know everything about you.'

Looking up from the pages, she studied his face. She looked past the perfect features, the full lips, the beautifully shaped head. She looked into his eyes and saw someone who'd been hiding for all the years she'd known him. 'Thank you, Johnny. This is the nicest thing anyone's ever done for me.'

He came to her side and, taking the book from her, laid it on the chair. Brushing away a tear with his thumb, he said, 'Don't cry! It was meant to cheer you up.'

'It has done!' she sobbed as he put his arms around her. She hadn't meant it to happen, she'd come here angry, but now, as she looked up into his eyes, just for a moment dropping every defence, she kissed those lips which had always seemed too beautiful for the likes of Kate Goss.

That night, after her work in the Hand and Marigold was finished, she took the *Grimm's Fairy Tales* to bed with her, and by the light of the oil lamp she reread the stories that had thrilled her as a child: 'Rapunzel', 'Snow White', 'Cinderella' and all the others. And she realized that Ethel Gutman had been right about them – some of the scenes were truly blood-curdling. Why hadn't she been frightened as a child? Perhaps her mother's comforting presence had overridden any sense of peril. But now, she knew they were true. Life *was* harsh and cruel and if the princess ever found her prince, it usually involved a fair amount of gore and some savagely inventive deaths. She was pleased to read some new stories, including the tale of 'Faithful John', which brought a dreamy smile to her face. *Faithful John*. She didn't think that, after today, she could ever think of him as Rasher again.

She was woken early next morning by shouting and banging, coming from the street below. She flung open the dormer and looked down.

'Oh, yes, that's right, you hide yourself up there, you vicious tart!' It was Aunt Sylvie and she was kicking the front door.

'I'm not hiding! Keep your bloody voice down, Aunt Sylvie, or you'll wake up the whole house.' As if on cue, Mrs Wilson's baby began to wail and Kate heard Mr Wilson open the window and call down, 'What's all the row about? I've been at work all night and I've just got to sleep!'

'Sorry, Mr Wilson!' Kate shouted, leaning far out of the dormer. 'I'm coming down.'

She'd woken so suddenly that now she felt herself trembling as she slipped on her frock and coat. Whatever she'd done wrong, she wasn't going to have a slanging match with her aunt on the doorstep.

But she didn't get a choice. Aunt Sylvie grabbed a handful of her hair and dragged her out of the house and down the lane towards the river. Kate struggled all the way, but her aunt merely yanked harder and twisted Kate's curls more tightly.

'Ow! Let me go! What have I done?'

'What have you done? You ungrateful little cow. I've brought you up like one of me own and now you've put my Stan in hospital! That Rasher boy might have pulled the trigger but you loaded the bleedin' gun!'

What had Johnny done now? 'Has Stan been shot?'

Aunt Sylvie gave an almighty tug and Kate fell to her knees. 'You know what I mean, you cheeky mare. You always was a sly, sneaking child – you're behind it. You set your fancy man on my son and now I might lose him.'

Curtains twitched and heads poked out of windows as neighbours enjoyed the spectacle of Aunt Sylvie dragging her the short distance to Johnny's house. Some who were ready for work came out a bit early to see the fight. When they arrived at the narrow house with no windows, her aunt, without letting go, began kicking on Johnny's door. He was already dressed, ready for work himself.

Aunt Sylvie aimed a left hook at his jaw. He dodged the punch and brought up a hand to catch her fist in a grip which forced a cry from her.

'Mrs Lynch,' Johnny said politely. 'Why don't you let Kate go? Then I can let you go.'

Aunt Sylvie released her grip. Kate was free. But her aunt was not, and she began kicking out. Johnny's long arm held her easily at a distance.

'Sylvie! Come indoors, have a cup of tea. Don't stand out there in the cold.'

Johnny raised his eyes as his mother appeared.

'And you! You drunken slut. It's no wonder he's turned out a killer, the way he's had to drag himself up.'

Mrs Bacon's lip trembled and she shot Johnny a bewildered look. 'My boy, a killer?'

Aunt Sylvie was heavily built and strong, but Johnny easily hoisted her off her feet and into the house. Kate followed, shutting the door behind her, feeling as if there were far too many bodies in the tiny room.

'Now you listen to me, you evil bitch.' Johnny's tone had hardened now they were out of public view. 'Stan's not dead, and he's not going to die. He's had a bloody good hiding, which you should have given him years ago, instead of using a motherless little girl as your punchbag.'

Aunt Sylvie opened her mouth to speak.

'Shut up and listen to me. Stan won't be giving Kate any more trouble... and if you want him to stay healthy, neither will you. Understand?'

His eyes that yesterday had been so clear, revealing so much to her, were now intense and impenetrable. 'Understand?' he repeated.

Aunt Sylvie nodded.

Kate prided herself on being able to read people – certainly she could read them better than any book – but this contained anger of Johnny's was somehow more frightening to her than an uncontrolled outburst. His fury, focused into a menacing power, made him unreadable to her and far too unpredictable for her liking. For an instant she regretted letting her guard down last night, wondering what else Johnny Bacon had kept hidden about himself for all these years.

Aunt Sylvie stared at Mrs Bacon as she meekly held out a cup of tea for her. Except it wasn't tea. It was hot water, with some condensed milk stirred into it.

'Aunt Sylvie hasn't got time for tea, Mum,' Johnny said, suddenly gentle. 'She's going to see Stan in hospital.'

Mrs Bacon's puffy face creased in concern. 'Oh, I am sorry to hear that, Sylvie. Wish him better for me, won't you?'

Aunt Sylvie gave Mrs Bacon a look of disgust and muttered, 'Blind drunk!'

Which proved too much for Johnny. 'You're not welcome in my mother's home,' he said, manhandling her out of the door and closing it softly behind him.

Kate didn't look at him. Instead she went to Mrs Bacon.

'Did I do something to upset Sylvie?' the woman asked, a bewildered look on her face.

'No! Of course not, Mrs Bacon. You know what she's like… short fuse! Why don't you let me take that,' she said, easing the teacup from her hands. 'I'll top it up, shall I? You go and sit down.'

She reboiled the kettle and found a few leaves of tea in a paper bag.

'Have you been behaving yourself, Johnny? Are you in trouble with Sylvie Lynch?' Mrs Bacon asked Johnny, whose eyes, as he looked at his ruined mother, were once again clear as day. What they revealed touched Kate's heart. She wouldn't show him how angry she was with him. Not now.

'I'm late for work, are you OK?' He gave Kate an enquiring look.

'We'll talk about it tonight – at the bookshop. I'll look after your mum – don't worry.'

Her extra duties now included setting up, clearing away and serving refreshments for the Wednesday night play-reading group. She'd finished her usual cleaning when Lucy came to show her how the group liked their chairs set out.

'In a circle, with a chair here for the director – me!'

Kate arranged the chairs, placing a copy of the play on each of them.

'*Pygmalion* tonight! We found *Androcles and the Lion* so entertaining we thought we'd give Mr Shaw another go. Actually, Ethel is a friend of his and she's hoping he'll give us a lecture one Sunday. We're branching out from reading into productions, which will be such fun! And we'll need your help for those too, Kate!'

'I ain't doing no acting! I told Miss Gutman that.'

'No, I understand. But we really need help with costumes and props, that sort of thing.'

Kate wasn't going to turn down work. 'All right, Miss Mannheim.'

'Lucy, please, Ethel insists it's always first names at the bookshop. Besides, I feel you know me *so* well. If it hadn't been for your good advice, I believe I'd still be pining for Henry Baynes. But what about you, Kate? Do you have a young man you pine for?' A secret smile played on Lucy's pretty lips.

Kate didn't mind giving advice, but she wasn't so good at taking it and she always felt uncomfortable when Lucy or Miss Gutman wanted to treat her as a friend. But Lucy's expression was eager, open and innocent of anything but girlish curiosity.

'I'm not pining for no one.' She went to the kitchen and Lucy followed. The young woman made a show of helping with the cups. 'But there *is* someone?' She gave Kate a sidelong glance. 'And I think I know who it is. I can understand – he's very handsome – and I'm sure he's taken with you too.'

Kate hadn't credited her with so much sharpness. How could she know about Johnny's interest in her when Kate had so recently found out herself?

'You're wrong.' Kate shook her head, wanting to maintain the secret. All day long she'd been wondering if it wouldn't be wise to pull back from the brink of this particular dream.

'All right then, I'll say who I think it is... it's Martin North!'

Relieved, Kate heard her own laugh ringing round the kitchen. 'You must be joking!'

Lucy looked puzzled. 'No! Actually, I'm not.' There was a pause and Kate could see her thinking. 'Oh, I'm sorry!' Lucy put a hand to her mouth. 'Has he sworn you to secrecy? His mother's a dreadful snob.'

Laughter bubbled up again and Kate couldn't restrain her giggles. 'I've hardly spoken to Mr North!'

Lucy flapped a hand impatiently. 'Oh, what does *talking* matter? I've seen him looking at you. Poor thing, he's like a stricken animal.'

'Well, he can look all he likes, but he won't be touching!'

Now Lucy laughed. 'All right, if you say so.' And she left her to greet her class. Kate peeked out from the open kitchen door, watching excited little groups arriving, full of chatter and laughter. There was obviously a hierarchy, with the star parts sitting nearest to Lucy. She overheard one of the female leads giggle and mention the 'scandalous line'! Kate made a point to listen out for it from her hideaway. Although they took up at Act Three, she quickly got the gist of the story. A flower girl and a middle-class man? Lucy's stupid idea about Martin North was obviously the result of reading too much Mr Shaw. But some of the readers were good enough to have her believing in them, and when the tea break arrived, she was surprised at how swiftly the time had passed. This felt nothing like work and she hated the idea of proving Miss Gutman right, but she would have loved to try her hand at Eliza. The actress playing her was making a mess of it and Kate had only spotted the 'scandalous line' because the girl had made such a fuss and blushed before she said it.

After the reading was over and the last of the group had left, Kate filled the silence of the deserted room with the clatter of crockery. But as she cleared away, she heard echoes of the actors' voices.

'Not bloody likely!' She whispered the 'scandalous' swear word Eliza had used and smiled to herself. Whoever thought that was scandalous needed to spend a day or two in East Lane! Turning from the table to face the room, she spoke the line again, louder this time. 'Not bloody likely!'

She was startled by three loud claps, which came from the stairwell. Johnny stuck his head around the door. 'You've already learned your lines! You'll be on at the Star Music Hall next!' He stood laughing at her and she was about to smile back, but then she remembered.

'I've got a bone to pick with you.'

'I'm sorry I had to leave you with Mum,' he said, mistaking her.

'That was no trouble at all. Your mum's lovely. And Aunt Sylvie was wrong, she wasn't really drunk, just a bit confused.'

'Drink doesn't make her nasty, but I think it's addled her brain. You just have to remind her what day it is sometimes,' he said matter-of-factly. 'Why are you upset with me then?'

'You're good at looking after her, you've been doing it so long. But, Johnny, I don't need you looking after *me*! I know you meant well, but I didn't ask you to sort out Mr Smith or beat up Stan. You might have brought yourself up – but so have I. I don't need no one's help.'

She said it as firmly as she could without seeming ungrateful. This morning's anger had virtually gone, but its cause was still there. He'd assumed a right that wasn't his. It hadn't been his place to step in and save her. And she'd had the uncomfortable feeling that if she let herself rely on Johnny it would be disloyal to her dad. For in her dreams it had always been her father who'd be coming to rescue her. He was meant to be her protector – one day.

He nodded slowly. 'I overstepped the mark. I'm sorry. I get a bit hotheaded sometimes.'

It had made her uneasy that their first kiss should be followed so closely by their first argument, but if there had been any remaining anger, he'd just defused the last of it with his apology.

'But you do know your Aunt Sylvie was blowing it all up. Stan's got a broken cheekbone and two shiners.'

'Oh! Well, I can live with that. Just don't do it again.'

'I won't need to,' he said with a cocky grin, looking more like the Rasher she'd known as a child. But however confident he was, she couldn't believe that there wouldn't be consequences.

7

Nora

Kate was dreading it. Even though Johnny had persuaded Mr Smith to drop the interest, she still had to repay the loan. She made her way reluctantly to the moneylender's house. The blonde woman threw open the door and, with a stony face, stood aside to let her in. As she entered, Kate felt herself trembling, imagining the woman attacking her from behind. But no blow came as, without a word, she showed Kate to the office.

Mr Smith smiled at her as if she were his long-lost daughter. 'Ah! It's young Kate Goss. Come in, sweetheart. Have a seat.'

She'd never been invited to sit before. The sixpence was sweating in her hand and she just wanted to drop it and run. His smile never faltered as he waited for her to speak.

She coughed, choking a little as the words tumbled out. 'Mr Bacon says you're waiving the interest on my loan so I've come to pay me tanner.' She held out the money.

He gave a hearty laugh. 'Quite right! The interest's a trifle. There was some misunderstanding over my status, so – purely as a gesture of goodwill, you understand – I'm letting you off – you'll just be repaying the principal.'

She thought she preferred him vicious. But then he opened up the cash box and, remembering the pain of crushed fingers, she hastily dropped the coin into the box before snatching back her hand. He kept the fixed smile on his face and turned to her with eyes like stone.

'And if I can ever do anything else to help Mr Bacon or yourself – you can be sure I will.'

He turned away and she rushed out of the house. In the street she put the hand that had held the sixpence to her face. It had the oily smell of dirty silver. Johnny might think he'd tamed Mr Smith, but the man's offer of help was more chilling than any threat and she knew, if he ever got the opportunity, he would do them harm.

She hurried home to get ready for her afternoon's cleaning at the bookshop and was surprised to find Janey standing outside Aunt Sylvie's house. Janey stared at her and as she passed grabbed her arm. 'You nearly got my brother killed, you ungrateful gypsy brat.'

Kate yanked her arm away. 'If it had been me, I'd have made a better job of it,' she said nonchalantly, pushing past her.

Up in her garret she threw open the dormer window and leaned out – just in time to see the motor taxi turn up. It was like watching a wounded hero returning from the war. Aunt Sylvie helped Stan from the taxi, which was such a rare sight in East Lane that a circle of curious neighbours quickly surrounded it. *Dear God in heaven, he's only bloody waving!*

Kate thought as Stan raised a weary hand in greeting to his well-wishers. Janey rushed to her brother as if she really did love him and Aunt Sylvie nodded regally to the crowd, making a show of helping Stan walk, though there was nothing wrong with his legs. As he made his way to the door, he looked up to her high perch and before she could duck back in, he pointed two fingers at her, aiming an imaginary gun. She replied with two fingers of her own.

What a big kid. His threats didn't scare her half as much as Mr Smith's niceties. She turned back to the envelope she'd picked up from the doormat on her way in. The letter was from Boutle's. Before she read it, she gazed deep into the blackened roof space. Sometimes she thought she could see lights up there, pinpricks, twinkling like daytime stars. Perhaps they were just tiny holes in the roof, but she liked to think of them as her own private slice of heaven. *Please, please, let them take me back!* Praying, but not to God. In this sparse room, where she'd slept as a child, she'd recently found herself talking to her mother. Asking for advice, for help, for comfort. If anyone ever found out, she'd be sent to Cane Hill asylum for certain.

We are inviting all women who were laid off in September to return to work. Wherever possible, previous positions and salaries will be offered.

'Thank you!' she offered up to the little daytime stars, which seemed to shine the brighter. She wondered if Johnny would understand.

She sorted through the orange crate which served as her larder: the remnants of this week's groceries were a pinch of tea and half a loaf, along with a dish of dripping and one of jam from Aunt Sarah. Just enough for breakfasts until she started work. But if she could keep on her extra jobs at the bookshop and the Marigold, life would take a turn for the better, she was sure. She'd be able to pay her rent and her loan and still have two pounds to spend on food and clothes. Riches! She clutched the letter to her heart like a holy relic and thanked her mother for watching over her.

The memories had begun to return soon after she had moved in here. The landlord had changed the room so much that the mere look of the place couldn't have prompted them. It must have been the feelings. She felt safe and in danger all at the same time. She wished she had a better memory of her father during those childhood days. But his prolonged absences meant that in her mind's eye he was always coming or going, and she remembered, now, that her mother would change at each arrival and departure. There was one time when she'd been snuggled up in bed with her mother and had drifted off to sleep blanketed in love and security. But she'd been woken by the noise of her father's return and found the bed empty. Creeping to the hatch, she'd looked down into the room below to see her parents kissing. She'd felt rage, jealousy, and she'd begun to scream. It was one of the few times her mother had spoken harshly to her. Calling up to her not to be so silly, that this was her daddy and she should be happy to see him. Kate only knew that when her father was back she lost her mother. Perhaps all kids felt like that sometimes, she didn't know. But she remembered he usually brought her presents from his travels. He would smile, ruffle her curls and always send her to bed early. It was on one of his visits home that she was first banished to a bed of her own. But it was in his absences that she got to know him best. For then her mother would talk about Archie Goss to Kate in such glowing terms that her childish imagination made him the sort of prince who appeared in *Grimm's Fairy Tales*.

Her mother said he would come back and take them to a beautiful place, which Kate imagined as a castle, in a country full of trees, flowers and streams. There would be plenty to eat and new clothes every day and her mother would have someone else to do the laundry. And so, Kate found herself both longing for and dreading her father's return. But now she was grown up and the years had robbed her of so much, she was left only with the longing.

The relief at getting her job back was quickly tempered by the realization that, with morning and evening jobs as well, she'd usually be working a fourteen-hour day.

'Where are you rushing off to?' Marge asked her on her first Monday back.

'The bookshop!'

'I've got you a nice bit of meat pudding we can heat up in the coke oven. You need feeding up, gel!'

'Thanks, Marge, but I can't stop. This is the only time I've got to do their cleaning – the hours are so awkward. Still, I'm not complaining – if you hadn't found it for me I would've starved while I was laid off.'

Her friend looked her up and down. 'Seems to me like you starved anyway. I'll save you a bit for your tea.'

Kate waved her thanks and scooted out of the factory. During the lay-off she'd got used to hanging about in the shop, chatting to whoever was volunteering. Sometimes she'd even stayed till opening time at four thirty, when workers coming home from nearby factories or shops would start to pop in. Often Johnny would come to meet her. Then they'd sit in the reading room together and he would talk about the stories he planned to write. Always he'd offer to take her to eat at the Central Hall Dining Rooms before her bar stint at the Marigold, knowing as he did that at home the orange crate was bare. Sometimes she would accept, and gradually her unease over his flashes of rage diminished as he revealed more of his kind and generous nature. There were, too, the walks home after the Marigold closed, when she let go of doubt and, giving in to the sweetness of his goodnight kisses, she seemed to know all she needed to know about Johnny Bacon.

Johnny wasn't the only person she'd started to trust. Slowly, she'd begun to feel exactly the way Ethel Gutman had wanted her to feel. As if she were one of the club, even one of a family. And Kate wouldn't let her down now that she was back at the factory. She'd carry on doing all the work Ethel had given her – just in double quick time. Today, however, she was surprised to find the shop locked up. She'd expected Miss Gutman would be going through the submissions for next quarter's *Bermondsey Book*. Johnny had been talking about it for weeks. The December number was now proudly displayed in its bright blue-and-yellow cover on every free shelf and Johnny had been asked to submit another article for the March edition.

Kate knew where the spare key was hidden. She reached into the crack below the step and eased it out. The reading room wouldn't take long – she'd done as much as she could last night after the lecture – and now she quickly mopped and polished. Afterwards she hurried down to do the shop, but at the bottom of the stairs, she paused. Someone had let themselves in.

Kate had never experienced being stopped in her tracks by someone's appearance, but now she was faced with the most beautiful woman she'd ever seen, and all she wanted to do was stare. The woman, who looked in her mid-twenties, was wearing a white fox-fur jacket over a grey day dress. The hem was cut in the latest handkerchief fashion, which revealed far more than was usual, and Kate couldn't help noticing her long, slender legs in their silk stockings. Everything about her was graceful. Her neck rose swanlike above the white fur collar. One hand rested on her hip and with the other she drummed a distracted tattoo on the table. Kate studied her perfectly sculpted profile. Visible beneath the wide-brimmed grey hat were fine, arched brows and long, dark lashes. Her nose was straight and delicate, her cupid's-bow lips half parted, almost as if she were about to speak. Kate had never seen feminine perfection until now. The women she'd grown up with had been forced to build an inner strength and a hard shell. Her mum had seemed the exception – but she knew her memory was filtered through loss. Ethel wasn't conventionally pretty, Lucy was. But neither had the impact of this woman. She seemed as perfect and vulnerable as one of the porcelain figures on the bookshop mantelpiece. Kate thought the woman might easily be shattered by a look. The only strong feature about her was her chin, which jutted slightly beyond her lower lip. But this was the very thing that made her beautiful, for without it, she would have been merely attractive. Instead, she was stunning.

The woman turned, without appearing to see her. Kate didn't know what to do. Should she ask her who she was? Or would that seem rude? She decided to go about her business. She didn't own the shop, she was just the cleaner. But as Kate moved towards the scullery the woman became aware of her and asked, 'Excuse me, do you happen to know where Miss Ethel Gutman is?'

When she spoke it was like music that you wanted to stop

and listen to. She had a faint foreign accent, which added to the sing-song quality of her voice. Kate was aware of her own silence.

'Umm. No, madam,' she said finally, ducking into the scullery. She felt flustered as she gathered her cloths and a tin of beeswax; she couldn't help notice her own chapped hands, her fingers that, even now, still bore traces of bruising. She held them up. The hands of the lady waiting out there in the shop were protected by fine kid gloves. 'Oh well, at least you work!' Kate said to her hands.

'They look as if they work very hard,' the musical voice declared, and Kate turned to find the woman standing at the scullery door.

'Oh, madam, don't come in here, you'll get your clothes dirty!'

The woman stood on the threshold and eyed the bucket and mop which blocked her path. 'Do you think Ethel will be long? She said I should meet her here this afternoon. I know I'm a little early, but…'

'You could wait in the reading room… upstairs?' Kate waved her duster at the woman, hoping the threat of dirt might make her move. 'It's quite comfortable.' She needed her out of the way now – she'd have to fly round with the beeswax as it was or she'd find herself with a late fine.

The woman agreed and followed Kate upstairs. 'Help yourself to books. Here.' Kate grabbed a copy of *The Bermondsey Book*'. 'This one is good. My friend Johnny Bacon wrote it. She opened it at Johnny's article and left the woman to her reading.

As she polished the downstairs table she noticed an earring. A pearl drop. She suspected it was real. She ran upstairs with it. 'Is this yours, madam?'

The young woman put a hand to her ear. 'Oh, dear, yes. My husband would have been very upset if I'd lost this. He gave them to me as an anniversary present.' She tried to put the earring on but fumbled and dropped it. Kate dived under the reading table.

'Got it!'

'Would you mind helping me? My husband loves to see me in them, but they're so fiddly it takes me ages to get the things on.'

Kate stood beside her, feeling oddly shy to be touching the delicate ear. Deftly she found the piercing and hooked the earring through the lobe. Then she spotted something on the slender neck. 'Oh, madam. You've got a bruise there.' She lifted the loop of shining hair and touched the purple-and-green mark. It was an oldish bruise, like those on her own fingers, and she guessed it had once been black.

The woman's creamy cheeks paled even further. 'Yes, as I said, I'm very clumsy.'

'You must be, if you picked up someone's hand and put it round your neck!' Kate was immediately horrified that she'd actually spoken her thoughts aloud.

'What a ridiculous idea!' The woman gave a nervous laugh. 'No! That bruise is from a choker – it matches these earrings. But it really is too tight... My husband is having it altered, actually.'

But Kate wasn't convinced. She'd earned enough of them from Aunt Sylvie over the years to recognize the type of bruise fingers made.

'Sorry, madam. My mistake.'

'Yes. It was,' the woman said, with a small flash of steel. Which Kate thought was all the better for her. Perhaps she wasn't porcelain all the way through.

*

Kate had been docked half an hour's pay for being late back at lunchtime and Miss Dane hadn't been happy with her. She found herself wondering about the perfect woman who'd cost her sixpence. She didn't look the normal type of young volunteer, but then again, nor did Mrs Violet Cliffe, who, Johnny said, had already proved her worth, using her contacts to line up all sorts of well-known speakers who otherwise wouldn't have ventured to Bermondsey. But Kate thought the woman in the white fox fur didn't have that necessary idealistic gleam in her eye. So when she arrived to make the tea for the Monday-night French class, she was surprised to see the mystery lady seated at the front and leading the class. The new French teacher glanced at her for a brief second then looked quickly away, and Kate noticed that tonight she'd wrapped a white scarf round her slender neck.

French class never usually finished late, but tonight the students gathered around their new teacher and it was dark before Kate finished clearing up. When she arrived at Dockhead, she saw what looked like a Sister of Mercy from the convent standing in the shadows. It crossed her mind that this was an unusually tall and well-built nun, but as she hurried by, she felt a hand grab her wrist.

What she'd taken for a wimple was in fact Stan's head bandage, secured under his chin. She laughed at him. 'You look a right idiot in that!'

'Oh yeah?' he said, through an immobile mouth.

'Got a gobstopper in your mouth, Stan? I can't understand a word!' She grinned and he twisted his grip tighter, till her wrist burned.

'Wanna know something that'll make you look like the

idiot – *Noss* Goss? For someone's always asking questions, you don't know sod all about nothing.' He attempted to laugh, but winced.

His two black eyes, staring from beneath the bandage, gave his face a skull-like look and she might have been frightened if he hadn't looked so ridiculous.

'Heard from your rich dad lately? When's he coming to take you away from all this?' he mocked her in a falsetto voice with a fluttering of his sandy eyelashes. 'Oh, I forgot... he's overseas, ain't he? So rich he can't afford a fuckin' stamp to send you a letter from Canada?'

She wouldn't give him the satisfaction of taking his bait. He'd love an excuse to wallop her. She wrenched her hand away.

'But he don't *need* a stamp, cos he's back in this country!'

She froze.

'Now who's the idiot?'

His small eyes glittered with enjoyment as he watched her dry-mouthed shock.

'You're a liar.'

'He's even been to our house. That's how much he cares about you, couldn't be bothered to pop next door and say hello!'

He was so pleased with himself he forgot his pain and shouted after her as she ran from him.

'He ain't interested in you!'

At that she wheeled round and, at a run, took a swing at his laughing face. 'Take it out of this!' she shouted, smashing her fist into his broken cheek.

'Ow! You soddin' crazy mare! Don't you know it's broke!' He held his face, grimacing in pain.

'Good! Well, now it's twice as broke!'

She ran to East Lane, but instead of going straight to her own house, she stopped at Aunt Sarah's.

Her aunt's long grey hair was in plaits and she was hugging a hot water bottle. 'I'm just going to bed, Kate. Can't it wait till tomorrow?'

Kate shook her head. 'No! I just found out me dad's back in the country! Why didn't I know?' She heard her voice crack and controlled herself. Aunt Sarah was never moved by tears. 'I *should've* been told!' she said, more firmly.

'So should I!' her aunt said, her shock genuine.

Kate sat in Aunt Sarah's kitchen and watched as she relit the gas lamp. Her hand shook as she fiddled with the mantle till the warm glow filled the little room.

'Who's told you Archie's home?'

'Stan! He says Dad's even been to their house!'

'No, love! He's having you on. Just getting his own back for that hiding Rasher Bacon give him.'

'I'm not so sure. He looked so smug.'

'I know. When his piggy eyes close up. Mean little git. But I would've known. Archie would've let me know.'

'Would he?' Kate said. 'Or would he have told Aunt Sylvie and expected her to let you know?'

Aunt Sarah, always looking for something to blame on her sister, didn't take much convincing. 'That's *her* doing. It's just like her to keep it from me. *Jealous!* I bet she's told him a pack of lies about me... and you, probably.'

'Why lie about me? And why wouldn't he have come to see me, when I'm only living next door?'

Aunt Sarah shook her head. 'He's a mystery. He never does things the way normal people do. You could offend him and not know it. Not till he turned his back on you in the street. But then he could just as easily come up and give you a kiss and a fiver, you never knew where you was with our Archie. But *she's* interfered. I'm sure of it, Kate.'

'How can I find out? Aunt Sylvie wouldn't tell me.'

'No, she won't tell you. But I'll make bloody sure she tells me – don't you worry about that!'

Kate waited while Aunt Sarah changed out of her nightdress, putting on her stays and thick stockings. She pinned up her plait and shoved a shapeless hat on her head.

'Come on. Let's go and sort her out.'

For once Aunt Sarah seemed to be moving swiftly, and Kate followed as she marched to Aunt Sylvie's. Her knocking was loud enough to wake the whole street, but there was no answer.

'Get yourself out here, you spiteful, jealous cow!' Aunt Sarah yelled and knocked again.

Aunt Sylvie flung open the door. 'What are you shouting your mouth off for now?'

'I want to know why you've not told me Archie's home.'

Aunt Sylvie looked at Kate. 'Why've you brought her?'

'She's his daughter when all's said and done and you've got no right to keep him from her – nor me!'

Aunt Sylvie gave a smirk. 'Archie goes his own way. If he wants to see either of you he can. I'm not stopping him. Anyway, whoever told you he's back is a bleedin' liar. I ain't seen me brother in years.'

And she slammed the door in their faces.

Kate despaired. 'Perhaps Stan did make it up after all, just to upset me.'

'Maybe he did, love. But you shouldn't be upset by your father, not after all these years. Don't pin your hopes on him and you won't be disappointed, will you? Still – I wouldn't put anything past *her*. And I tell you what, there won't be no one coming and going at Sylvie's house from now on that I don't know about!'

Kate and Johnny sat drinking in the bar of the Hand and Marigold during her break.

'Have you seen the bookshop's new French teacher?' Kate asked.

Johnny nodded. 'I think she's a friend of Mrs Cliffe. Why? Are you thinking of learning French? I'd come with you!'

He looked so eager she didn't like to laugh, but she did. 'Me? French? I can't even speak English properly, can I?'

'Why do you say that?'

'Being around people at the bookshop – I know me accent's terrible.' She twisted the glass around in her hand.

'I like the way you speak – but if you're not happy with it, go to the Tuesday elocution classes.'

She made a face at him. 'Classes, classes! You're always so...'

'So what?'

'I don't know... you think anything's possible, but it isn't.'

'Ha! *Isn't! Isn't!* You said "isn't" instead of "ain't" – so anything *is* possible!'

She joined in his laughter. At least Johnny could always cheer her up. She'd never been ashamed of her cockney accent, but her doubts about her father's opinion of her were disconcerting.

'Stan told me my dad's home, that he's even been to Aunt Sylvie's and he's not interested in seeing me.'

'Stan? I told him to stay away...' He clenched a fist and was almost out of his seat.

'Settle down, Johnny.' She took hold of his hand. 'There's

no harm been done...' But she didn't dare tell him Stan had grabbed her.

'But there has been harm,' he said, suddenly calm, intertwining his fingers with hers. 'He might not have touched you but he's hurt you. Your dad wouldn't come home and not see you. Forget it, Stan's lying.'

'Perhaps... Aunt Sylvie did deny it. But Aunt Sarah thinks Sylvie's been putting in the poison about me, telling me dad I don't want to see him.'

'That's possible.' He considered it for a while and then shook his head. 'Sylvie never does anything unless she'll get something out of it, and I can't see where the profit is. Can you?'

She couldn't and her unease began to subside as they chatted about other things, until he came back to her original question.

'So, have *you* met the French teacher?' he asked.

'Oh, yes.'

She remembered the slender neck, the white fur collar, the purple-and-green bruise, and was unsure why she was so interested. But then she remembered Conny – how she'd put up with that stepbrother – and she thought of her own trials with Stan. She decided not to say anything to Johnny. After all, she could be totally wrong. But if she was right, she was prepared, one day, to offer the perfect lady a soldering iron.

It wasn't until the following Monday that she saw the French teacher again. Kate was in the reading-room kitchen, cutting slices of fruit cake for the tea break. Ethel liked to run the place as if it were her own home and she insisted on offering refreshments at every event. Which was fortunate for Kate, as when her own food ran out she was quite happy to survive on leftover buns or cake. She always left the door half open while she was cutting the cake. Kate hadn't earned her nickname for nothing, and she had the ability to home in on any conversation across a room. Now she heard the musical voice. Nora, the French teacher, was talking to one of the students, a young boy of about sixteen, who was mumbling his appreciation of the lesson so far.

'You really bring the language alive, especially with all those examples of life in France. Are you French?'

Kate was grateful that the boy was as curious as she was. She laid down the knife.

'I was born in this country – my mother was English. But Father was French and they moved back to France when I was a baby. I was brought up in France – until the war…'

Her voice took on a sad note at the mention of the war. Perhaps she'd lost her parents then?

'Well, you've got a better accent than our last teacher,' the young boy said in a confidential tone. 'He came from Birmingham. I'm glad we've got you.'

Kate peered through the open door. The young boy was gazing at the woman adoringly, which, Kate thought, she must get a lot of. The new teacher turned away and began walking towards the kitchen. Kate snatched up a cake plate and went into the reading room – she didn't want to be cornered by the woman. She was feeling far too embarrassed by her outburst to this stranger.

Without looking up she swerved around Nora and dumped cakes and teapot onto the table. For the next half hour she was busy pouring teas and cutting more cake. But when the class began to disperse, Nora's sleek head appeared at the kitchen door.

'Thank you, the cake was delicious!'

'I didn't make it.' Kate tried not to stare at the white scarf.

'Well – the tea was very good too.'

Kate thought it wasn't hard to make a decent cup of tea, but she smiled at the compliment.

'I just wanted to let you know, my husband was most grateful to you for finding my earring. He wanted me to give you this.' She handed Kate half a crown.

'Oh, no! I can't take that!' Kate said, thinking: *I don't want nothing from your grateful husband who's probably given you more bruises than you'd find on the 'specks' chucked under a fruit stall.*

'He insists,' Nora said, putting the half-crown on the kitchen cabinet and giving her a worried look. Perhaps the husband would check that she'd done as she was told. For the woman's sake, Kate picked up the coin.

'All right then. Please tell him thank you.'

The teacher smiled, appearing relieved.

'Did you get the choker back?' Kate asked as Nora turned to go.

'The choker?'

'The one that was too tight.'

Nora nodded. 'Oh, *that* choker – yes. It's much better now.'

For a moment their eyes locked and Kate knew what lay behind the wary look clouding those lustrous eyes. She knew what it was like to fear that even your most secret action or word might earn a blow. And she knew she hadn't been mistaken after all.

'Goodnight, madam,' Kate said.

'Nora. Call me Nora.'

8

Martin

1924

The man was always staring. Martin North was getting on her nerves. Whenever he came to the bookshop he seemed to be in the way. If he brought his aunt Violet, he'd leave Mrs Cliffe with Ethel and wander over to wherever Kate was cleaning. He'd watch her as she worked, barely saying a word, not even offering to put out chairs if she was setting up the reading room. If he came to a lecture she'd catch his eyes on her when she was serving tea. If she stared back he never looked away. She was used to being ignored. Even in such an unconventional place as the Bermondsey Bookshop, she was still only the cleaner, and whatever she'd learned about the owner, the volunteers or the members was what she'd picked up because, as Janey had always said, she was a 'born nosser'.

And he always seemed to catch her at the most unflattering of times. Like now, cleaning the outside lavatory, which was little more than a shed in the shop's yard. She was backing out, swirling the mop over the brick floor, when a noise from behind made her start.

Martin North lounged against the scullery wall, a cigarette dangling from his mouth, and, as usual, he was staring at her.

She tutted, obviously louder than she'd meant to, because he stood up. 'You must think I'm very rude,' he said in that even, pleasant voice of his.

She shook her head and, tipping the pail of dirty water into the drain, spattered his cream-and-brown brogues with grey spots. This she was quite pleased about, but he didn't seem perturbed. 'It's just that I think you're a remarkably striking young woman.'

She was disappointed to find that Lucy had been right. 'I've seen you looking at me, but you might as well know I ain't having none of it. So just sod off and leave me to get on with me job.'

She picked up the zinc bucket, her cheeks burning with anger, tinged with fear. If he wanted to, he could complain to Ethel about her. The bookshop work gave her as much as half her weekly Boutle's wage. It would be a lot to lose.

He sauntered after her into the scullery. 'I think you've mistaken me, Kate. You don't mind if I call you Kate? Ethel likes—'

'Yeah, I know – first-name terms, but just 'cause you're a friend of the boss, that don't mean you can take liberties with me!'

He ran a hand through his thick brown hair and gave an embarrassed laugh. 'I never meant to offend you. Please, let me explain.' He pulled a small book from his jacket pocket and put it on the draining board. 'Open it.'

The scullery was tiny and she had almost to touch him to reach the book. He pushed it towards her and took a quick step back into the doorway, making her feel a bit like a dangerous animal. The book was bound in black leather and its pages were thick, smooth and creamy. They were full of pencil sketches. All of her.

Some were just heads, her dark curls escaping from the bandana she wore while cleaning; some were of her swollen-knuckled, solder-burned hands that she hated so much; others were back views. There she was stretching to reach that damned top shelf with a feather duster. She went hot with shame at some of them, showing her squatting or kneeling, the folds of her overall stretched over her breasts or behind. Ugh! She hated them all – all except one. This one, where he'd caught her not cleaning, but reading.

She remembered exactly when it had been. Martin had come up to the reading room with the excuse of delivering a message from Ethel. She'd barely noticed him. For once, he hadn't seemed to linger. She'd been tidying books strewn about the reading room, and a copy of *The Bermondsey Book* had caught her eye. She hadn't ever read Johnny's first article. She suspected she was frightened to, in case she found out that he was far too clever for her, beyond her in everything but upbringing. But she'd quickly become engrossed, astonished to find passages that were very funny, others that were very sad, but that all were revealing. She felt a secret pleasure when she realized she could find out so much more about Johnny here than he could ever tell her. Martin had caught that very moment, when she'd realized and smiled. She liked the drawing, but she hoped Johnny never saw it. It revealed much too much about the depth of her feelings, certainly more than she'd ever confessed to him.

'I don't blame you for not being impressed. They're very rough.' Martin tilted his head to look at the reading sketch.

'But of course, the finished article will look much better – that's if you agree to let me paint you.'

She was bewildered. What she'd seen in most of those sketches was a drudge. 'Why would you want to paint me?'

'Why? For having to ask the question, I suppose. Just because you really don't know.'

'Know what?'

'That you're beautiful.'

'Oh, now you're taking the mickey.' She pushed aside the sketchbook and he caught it as it tumbled to the floor.

'You may not have Lucy's fine clothes, nor Ethel's perfect diction – but you... you're like a light in a dark, dark room. You glow.'

She certainly was glowing now. Her cheeks burned with embarrassment.

'Don't mistake me, I will pay you. To be an artist's model is not for the faint-hearted, Kate. You need stamina. And after seeing how you scrub those floors... well, I know you've got plenty of that!'

He smiled and she wondered if she could put up with him. But the rates he offered, though less than cleaning, were more than at Boutle's and it would be worth it to get Mr Smith out of her life.

'I won't take me clothes off.'

'No need. I've yet to see a woman who can make an overall look quite so... interesting.'

'Interesting?' Marge said, pulling a face. When Kate got back to Boutle's that day, she hadn't been able to resist telling her about the surprising offer Martin had made. 'If he's interested in your arse, then I wouldn't go to no studio with him, love.'

They stood at one of the coke ovens and Kate was glad that the heat masked her blush.

'He's interested to *paint* it, Marge. And it's good money,' she protested.

'These posh blokes are the worst, and he's an *artist* as well!' Marge said. Although she was only a few years older than Kate, she acted as if she were worldly-wise.

'When did you ever meet a posh bloke – or an artist?'

Marge didn't answer. She drew a soldering iron from the oven and inspected its white-hot tip. She was wracked by a bout of coughing. 'Bloody fumes. I didn't get a wink of sleep last night with this cough.'

And now Conny took the opportunity to weigh in. 'She's only saying, watch where his hands go! And if he asks you to stay late one night – don't!'

It seemed that everyone had judged the 'posh bloke' before he'd even lifted a paintbrush. It made Kate want to defend him, however much he irritated her.

Not long after she'd taken Martin up on his offer, she was working a bar shift in the Hand and Marigold when Johnny walked in. She never got tired of seeing him come through the doors, knowing that he was there especially to see her. Since they'd begun courting, he made sure he saw her most days. Perhaps it was just his familiarity that made her feel so good, but tonight she was reminded that his familiarity was still tinged with an unpredictability that could surprise her.

He'd bought her a drink and he pushed it towards her when she joined him at the table.

'The Marigolds are in good voice tonight,' he said, nodding

towards the regular old ladies, who were singing 'Galway Bay': *If you ever go across the sea to Ireland…*

'Hmm. They've got lovely voices, just a shame they don't all start in the same key!' He chuckled and handed her his latest article for *The Bermondsey Book*.

'I know you're not interested in reading my stuff, but you might like this one. Apparently, the subscribers want more "local colour"! I've treated them to a day in Dockhead – you'll recognize some of the neighbours in East Lane, but I've changed the names.'

She took the manuscript. 'If I get time,' she said, knowing that she'd read it as soon as she got home.

'Funny how you can make time to "study" Martin North's paintings, though! Don't bother.' He snatched the manuscript from her.

There it was again – the surprise. That flash of anger. She didn't like it, but she liked his jealousy. Even if it was ridiculous.

'Don't be stupid, Johnny. It's just a modelling job. I'm not interested in his *paintings*.'

'But you are interested in him!'

She grimaced and shook her head. 'No! And he's only latched on to me 'cause I'm different from the sort of woman he's used to. I'm just a novelty.' She took back the manuscript. 'I know what, I can read it while I'm modelling! He wants to do two paintings now. One cleaning. One reading.'

He seemed mollified. 'All right, then. When are you going?'

'Saturday afternoon and Sunday. He's coming to the Sunday lecture, so he'll be driving me back in time for that.'

Johnny shifted awkwardly in his seat and pulled at his collar. 'I've got to say something, Kate. I know you've not had much experience with other fellers…'

'No? What's Stan, then?'

'Stan's an animal. I mean smooth-talking blokes like North.'

She smiled at him. 'Or like you?'

'What? Leave off.'

She waved the sheets of paper. 'Actually, I *have* read your first article...'

'And?'

'It was OK.'

He smiled into his beer.

Johnny stayed in the Marigold till closing time and then walked her home. But instead of stopping at her house, they carried on till they reached East Lane river stairs. With the coal store looming to one side and the council's refuse wharf to the other, it was a grim and smelly spot, but still, it had once been their playground, and they stopped at the wall where they had so often larked about as children. She remembered the games they'd played on the foreshore, looking for treasure.

'Do you remember our mudlarking?' she asked.

'And the barge hopping.'

Kate remarked that he'd been the most fearless of the gang, leaping from barge to barge far out into the river.

'Oh, I just never learned to be afraid. Never had anyone to tell me off, did I?'

'I always felt like the odd one out,' Kate said.

'Why?'

'Don't you remember?'

He shook his head.

'Because everyone used to take the mick – about the rags Aunt Sylvie made me wear and my dirty hair. They used to call me gyppo. You really don't remember?'

'No. I was too busy feeling the odd one out myself!'

'You?' she laughed. 'All the girls were after you and all the boys wanted to be you.'

'Didn't seem that way to me. I just thought everyone was laughing behind me back 'cause Mum made such a show of herself coming home drunk every night.'

He looked at her in the darkness and slipped his arm around her. 'Two misfits. We should do all right together.'

She leaned against him. Allowing the secret dream of her youth to play out. Testing to see if she really did love him, now that she was grown up. And when he turned her into his arms and kissed her – she found that she did.

However unconcerned she pretended to be, she was worried about going to Martin's studio. She didn't think he'd try anything on, but he was a complete unknown. Just like the place he lived. Fitzroy Square. It might as well have been the back side of the moon. He was cool and in control and she thought he'd probably mock her to his friends. She wished she could just see this as another job. She could solder a tin, mop a floor, serve a pint, but the idea of sitting still while a stranger stared at her for hours felt more dangerous than a stamping machine without a guard. Life had taught her the precious lesson of how to hide and disappear and stay out of people's way. Being on show would be the hardest job she'd ever done.

His car looked just right. It was dark green, with shiny chrome headlights and leather seats. But the man driving it was all wrong. It should have been Archie Goss, not Martin North, whisking her away from Boutle's gates, for that had always been the dream. She squashed the feeling, trying to enjoy her small celebrity. To be picked up in any car would make her an instant object of envy among the soldering shop girls, but to be picked up in a Rolls-Royce had set the factory buzzing and now she could see the van drivers and young apprentices craning their necks to get a better view, not of her but of the vehicle that she was now seated in. One young boy called out cheekily, 'Drive on, my good man, take me down the Blue to get me muvver's shoppin'!'

Conny and Marge, with huge smiles on their faces, were waving their arms as if she were leaving on a ship for America. Martin grinned. 'Wave back at your friends!'

'This is a bit of a show up,' she said, pretending to be annoyed. 'You should've met me round the corner. And you never said it was a Rolls!'

'Does it make a difference?'

She gave the girls a wave as the engine started up. 'A few hundred quid's worth, I should think.'

He laughed. 'It's not mine! It's my mother's. She lets me have it because when I'm not painting I'm expected to be everyone's chauffeur!'

'I told you I could get the bus! You didn't have to drive me.'

'I meant my family – not you, Kate. I was dropping Aunt Violet at the bookshop and besides, this is entirely a pleasure trip.'

He wove through the Saturday afternoon traffic, obviously an experienced driver. She was sure he was breaking a great many rules of the road as he cut across tramlines and shaved the sides of carts, drawing curses from cartmen. Once over Tower Bridge they cruised along beside the river, and she began to enjoy the experience. In the Strand, buses, cars and carts were so tightly packed they were forced to a standstill and Martin turned his attention from the road to her. Now that she knew he was looking at her as an artist, she supposed she should feel less self-conscious about his cool gaze. She didn't, but she'd have to get used to it, just as she had to the flux fumes and intense heat of Boutle's coke ovens.

'Do you like working at the tin factory?' he asked, as if reading her thoughts.

'It don't really matter whether I *like* it or not. It's a bit like hell – but it's saved me from starving and it's saved me from living with me aunt, so you *could* say I love it.'

'You don't like your aunt? I adore mine. Aunt Violet's a sweetheart. Hard to credit she's Mother's sister.' He tapped a finger on the steering wheel and for the first time Kate saw him rattled. She didn't think it was the traffic that was bothering him.

'Don't you like your mother?'

He barked a short laugh. 'Doesn't really matter whether I *like* her. You *could* say I love her.'

She began to warm to Martin North. He'd just told her he thought as much of his mother as she did of Boutle's the tin basher's. And he hadn't been guarded or cool at all in letting her know it.

When they turned into Fitzroy Square and he helped her out, she wished she'd been able to afford a new coat. Two ladies walked past arm in arm, immaculately dressed, with fur collars turned up and hats so wide they touched. Kate had borrowed Marge's best coat, which swam on her and smelt of mothballs. Although the pedestrians were smart enough, the buildings in the square were soot-streaked and the railings around the central circular garden were peeling.

He followed her gaze. 'The garden is beautiful, isn't it?' She inhaled the smell of rain-washed grass and heard the sound of dripping trees. It softened the straight, sooty lines of the once-grand houses.

'Yes, it is.'

Inside Martin's house, a stone staircase curved up four flights. 'My flat's on the second floor.'

Every inch of wall in the stairwell was covered in paintings. Some were huge, others tiny. Many were nudes: the male ones made her look away and the female made her glad she'd insisted to Martin that she wouldn't be one of them.

'Are these all yours?' she managed to ask.

He nodded, unlocking the door to his flat. 'Yes. The other residents let me use the staircase as a gallery. Very useful for prospective buyers.'

She followed him into a room whose walls were covered in painted friezes and panels. The colours reminded her of a fruit stall in Tower Bridge Road. Oranges and plums fought with apple greens and lemons, all against a background of tin blue. None of the furniture was new. The velvet cushions were faded and worn and a sagging sofa had been disguised with what looked like an old tablecloth.

'Oh! I didn't think it'd look like this!' she exclaimed.

'Like what?' he asked, flinging his cap onto a hook in the corner.

'Like the bookshop!'

'Ah! You have a good eye! Of course, the bookshop walls are largely my work.' He glanced pleased that she'd noticed. 'This is where I live and sleep.' He glanced towards a wooden screen, painted with flowers, and she saw the end of a bed. 'But this is where the work happens.' He flung open two tall connecting doors and she walked into a bright, spacious room. In spite of the grey day, the floor-to-ceiling windows let light into every corner. He walked to a paint-spattered easel and took down a smock.

'Here's my working attire, did you bring yours?' He rubbed his hands together, looking as excited as a child eyeing a jar of sweets.

She nodded and wrapped the brown overall around her. 'Are you sure you don't want me in a frock?' She'd bought a cheap second-hand dress at the old clo' market. It was ridiculous, she knew, to be spending money she didn't have, but she just couldn't face coming here in her old dress.

'No! Just as you are, and now, put on the bandana.'

The red bandana covered most of her hair.

'No. Too much hidden. Like this – may I?' he asked. 'More curls.' He teased dark ringlets from beneath her scarf, placing them artfully, as if they'd fallen over her forehead while she was working.

'Such beautiful hair,' he said to himself. 'Black with a flash of blue – a magpie's wing.'

The bare boards of his studio floor were dotted with a few rugs and now he kicked one aside, replacing it with a zinc bucket and scrubbing brush. 'I borrowed these from Aunt Violet's maid!' He looked pleased with himself. 'I want you like this.'

He knelt, picked up the scrubbing brush in one hand and leaned on the bucket with his other, as if so tired he needed to prop himself up. He looked over his shoulder, a startled expression on his face, as if he'd been caught in some guilty act. As soon as she took up the pose she knew it was one she adopted when she was sure she was alone and she was so bone tired she needed a rest. And if someone had come up on her silently, she might well have looked guilty. She wasn't being paid to rest.

'I've decided to do a triptych. *Cleaning. Reading. Resting.* I want to start with cleaning.'

He gave her a small cushion for her knees, which she hid beneath the folds of her overall.

'Once I start I never like to give up till I've got the outline done. Just tell me if you get uncomfortable,' he said reassuringly.

Then it was as if he disappeared altogether. Kneeling wasn't hard and she could rest on the bucket, but it was difficult to be under such intense scrutiny and yet feel entirely alone. He worked with such fierce, sharp brush strokes that she heard and sometimes felt the slate-blue paint splashing onto the canvas. She'd expected him to look at all those sketches and then make a more perfect copy now that he had her here. But he seemed to be painting the outline straight onto the canvas.

She lasted an hour before her thighs turned to burning stone and her back muscles to taut agony. The edge of the zinc bucket felt as if it might slice through her palm. She was used to hard work, she was good at shrugging off pain. But this was excruciating.

'Martin, can I move now?'

He hadn't heard her, but he'd said to let him know, so she said more loudly, 'Martin, I'm a bit uncomfortable, can I stretch yet?'

He seemed suddenly to realize she was there. 'What? No!'

He carried on for what felt like another hour, until she collapsed onto the bucket, then rolled into a ball, hoping if she stayed there the agonizing tightening of her muscles would stop. Then she pulled her legs under her, but an unbearable cramp seized her so that all she could do was yell, 'I don't want your money! I'm going home.'

He put the paintbrush down and without any warning

flipped her onto her back and pulled out her leg, shoving her foot up towards her head until she heard a crack.

'You keep your bleedin' hands to yourself! I told you, I'm not that sort of girl!' she screamed, kicking him in the stomach so that he staggered back against his paint table, scattering paint tubes, brushes and a full palette onto the floor.

'Ow! I promise I was only trying to help with the cramp.'

Now she felt stupid for mistaking his intentions. 'Well, you're a bloody torturer. I'm on me feet all night at the Marigold and I don't get cramp as bad as this!' Her calf muscles were rock hard. She got to her feet and grabbed her coat and bag. She was almost at the door when he caught her.

'I'm terribly sorry, Kate. I was thoughtless. I'm used to professional models... I just forgot you'd never done this before. Please, stay. We'll have a rest in the sitting room... Here, sit in this chair, it'll support your back.'

She felt as if he were talking to his Aunt Violet. 'I'm not an invalid – I just wanted to stretch a bit – but you wouldn't let me!'

'Sorry.' He scrubbed at his thick hair with paint-covered fingers.

She pointed. 'Now you've got a flash of blue as well!'

He teased out a long, blue-stained strand of hair over his forehead, going cross-eyed as he tried to see it, making her laugh in spite of herself.

'I'll get us some tea.'

'You're useless in a kitchen. Where's the kettle?'

'No! I insist, you stay there. We've got at least another hour's work. I shall wait upon you, mademoiselle!'

While he was brewing up on a gas ring in his studio, she rubbed her aching muscles and took a closer look around the room. Family photographs in silver frames lined the mantelpiece. She recognized his aunt in one, and there was a photo of a younger Martin in his army uniform. He looked so youthful she was surprised he'd been old enough to serve in the war. Perhaps he'd lied about his age. Next was a middle-aged couple she guessed were his parents. The man looked like an older Martin and the woman was a shorter, more forbidding version of Mrs Cliffe. She picked up the photo just as he came back in.

'Yes. She is *just* as terrifying as she looks. Pray God you never have the dubious pleasure of meeting her,' he said drily.

It was an awful cup of tea, though presented beautifully, with bone china and sugar lumps and tongs. She added as much sugar as would fit into the tiny cup. At least he'd made an effort. 'It's a shame you don't get on with your mother,' she said. 'I lost mine when I was little.'

'Yes, Ethel told me you were an orphan.'

'Did she?' She was surprised to have been the subject of their conversation. 'Why would she tell you that?'

'Ethel is a remarkable woman. She is exactly what she seems. She's kind, generous and she has a vision. She really does see her bookshop as a model for how things should be between the classes. To her we are all family.'

'But I'm not even a member.'

'I've heard that you're invaluable – and I'm not talking about sweeping floors.' His voice had taken on a gossipy tone and he offered her another tea. 'Apparently, Lucy tells me, you give very good advice about matters of the heart...' He winked at her.

'What's she been saying?' And soon, with the tea and the chat, her tired muscles relaxed and she found herself agreeing to undergo another hour of torture.

*

The following day there were more breaks and Martin worked slowly. She saw that his palette was dotted with mounds of oil paint, so she assumed he'd successfully captured her outline in blue, as he'd wanted to. He seemed more relaxed now, and during one of the breaks he showed her some of his paintings that had been covered by cloths and propped against the studio walls.

'These are commissions, waiting for clients to collect them.' Most were large portraits of fashionable ladies, generally seated. But one was so stunning it caught her attention. It was almost monochrome, with the woman's beautiful features chiselled by light, the dark hair framing an expressionless face, the white gown folded by shadows. It sent a chill through her. It was so cold.

She crouched to look at it more closely, just to make sure. 'I thought so – it's the French teacher! Do you know her?'

'Oh, yes, she's a friend of my aunt. Her husband wanted a portrait... but these lot just pay the rent,' he said dismissively. '*Here* are the ones I do for love.'

He led her to another stack of paintings. They were in a different style altogether, with broader, more textured brush strokes. The subjects were mostly working women, mothers and children, people going about their everyday business on buses, in shops or their workplaces. His expression softened as he looked at them. But then she saw one larger than the rest that had been covered. Curious, she lifted the cloth. It was of a woman standing by a window, head lowered, looking at what appeared to be a photograph.

'Oh, here's another one of Nora!'

'Yes, her husband rejected it. So, I painted that one.' He

nodded back to the cold-looking portrait. 'Apparently, it was more to his taste.' He was about to cover the picture again when she stopped him.

'But I've seen her with that exact same look!' It was astonishing to Kate that although the likeness didn't really show off Nora's exquisite beauty, he'd managed to capture her expression perfectly.

'What "look" would that be?' he asked in a cooler tone, making her wonder if she'd overstepped some invisible boundary of manners or class.

'Sad.'

'Really?' He gave her a searching look and drew the cover back over Nora.

She didn't comment further, but let him flick through more canvases until it was time to go back to work. She could understand why any husband wouldn't like that painting. It was as revealing as that sketch Martin had done of Kate herself reading Johnny's article. But however Martin North had come to know Nora, the painting was so tender Kate couldn't help suspecting she was more than just 'a friend of his aunt'.

Towards the end of the day he told her he wanted to work on the *Resting* painting.

'As I've never actually seen you resting, I need to make some sketches. I'm assuming you *can* rest?' She didn't know if he was being serious.

'I've got four jobs, and most days I work fourteen hours, so I usually rest when I'm asleep.'

He frowned. 'Well, surely there must be a *minute* during the day?'

He had no idea. But she sighed and thought for a moment. 'Yes. There *is* a minute.'

'Good! But you'll have to remove that overall.' He took it from her. 'Better. Now let's have a look at you. No. The frock will have to go too.'

She grabbed the overall back. 'I told you I'm not undressing for you nor no one! If you want a prostitute go up the 'dilly!'

'Oh, for God's sake, Kate. Why are you so suspicious!'

'Because you're a posh bloke!' she said, remembering Marge's warning, and, remembering the glimpse she'd had of a bed behind the screen, added, '*And* you're an artist!'

'Don't tar us all with the same *brush*!' he laughed. 'I only meant that, lovely as your frock is, it's... the wrong colour.'

'And that proves you're a bloody liar. The frock's a disgrace, but it's all I could afford.' She plucked at the dull green dress, feeling miserable.

'If you want me to be honest, I agree – the frock is hideous, but I have a box full of costumes. Come and help me choose.' He beckoned her as if they were children playing a dressing-up game, and his studied manner disappeared altogether as he opened an old leather trunk to reveal dresses, shawls, capes and robes of every hue and size, all neatly folded in piles according to colour. It was like a rainbow in a box and Kate was immediately entranced.

'Oh, I feel like I'm in Aladdin's cave!' She pulled out dresses of yellow and gold, shawls in soft shades of green and blue, there was a scarlet silk robe embroidered with dragons and clouds. 'What about this one!' She swirled it around her body, till she was sheathed in a dragon of gold and green.

He took it from her. 'Totally inappropriate. Something more suited to your age... ahhh, this.'

He held up a rose-pink fine lawn dress, with a low waist

and a scooped neckline. Delicate gold flowers and tendrils decorated the hem and waistband. She cradled it in her arms and smiled. She'd never worn any fabric as soft or pretty. 'It's lovely.'

'It's settled, then. So, tell me, about that minute when you can rest – what do you do?'

'I just look out of the garret window – at the sky and the river.' She wasn't going to tell him this was the time in the day when she often let herself dream of her father's return.

'Oh, Kate! You live in a *garret*? And you have a *dormer*?' He seemed excited. She nodded, and he made her describe the window and the view over the rooftops of East Lane. He sketched as she spoke. 'Perfect. Go and change now.' She picked up the dress. 'No, not that. The dragon robe.'

As she undressed behind the screen she dreaded what Johnny would have to say about it. She doubted she should be taking her clothes off in a single man's flat. But now she'd seen his painting of Nora, she guessed she would have nothing to fear from Martin North.

They arrived back at the bookshop only ten minutes before the Sunday lecture.

'Quick, you'll have to help me!' she ordered Martin. 'You put the chairs out and the lectern and a glass of water on a side table for the speaker. I'll do the tea things.'

She found Martin a decent enough helper when he was given specific instructions. 'Teacups and saucers – end of that table.' He saluted and dashed off with both hands full. Meanwhile, in the kitchen, she sliced cake and put out biscuits. When Johnny walked in they were still setting out tea plates.

He strolled over and planted a kiss on her cheek. 'You look lovely,' he said softly.

'Doesn't she just?' Martin swept past with a plate of fruitcake. Johnny ignored him. 'Is that a new dress?'

Kate smoothed out the rose-pink frock, which Martin had insisted she keep. 'Yes. It's from Martin,' she said.

'Martin?' His face registered disappointment, quickly followed by anger. 'Kate! You shouldn't accept gifts from a man like that. I warned you!'

'Shhh. He'll hear you.'

'I don't bloody care. I'm not having him ruin you. Tell me how much he pays you and I'll match it if you promise to stay away from him!'

She felt a surge of anger and was hardly able to speak. 'I'll choose who I stay away from – and if you're going to be like this, it'll be you!'

The audience beginning to arrive saved her from his answer, but she couldn't help noticing Martin's worried gaze following her as she rushed into the kitchen. She prayed he would stay out of her way this evening. Perhaps it wasn't fair, but instead of blaming Johnny for their argument, she decided to blame Martin.

As the speaker was introduced, she hid herself in the kitchen. She was so bone tired she propped herself on the kitchen stool, preparing to doze. Last week's lecture had been so dull she'd considered escaping through the kitchen window after an hour of the Reverend Ethelbert Goodchild's 'Glands and Their Effect on Personality'. But tonight, the speaker was a funny raconteur. Martin introduced him as 'my friend Mr Stacy Aumonier'. His subject was 'Stories and Storytelling' and within minutes he had the audience roaring with laughter. It was like watching a comedian at the Star Music Hall. He read one of his own short stories called 'The Octave of Jealousy' and she hoped it wouldn't be about jealous lovers, for she peeked through the door and saw Johnny looking dejected and unhappy. But Mr Aumonier's tale gripped her. It took an example from every class in England, from tramp to lord, and showed how each envied the other, the lord finally seeing true freedom in the tramp's life.

She felt she herself had crossed too many lines today. Surely it was simpler to stay in your place. If she'd never accepted the dress, she wouldn't have argued with Johnny. If Martin hadn't been wealthy, perhaps Johnny would have been less jealous. And look at the trouble those little class distinctions had caused in her own family. Her mother, never good enough; her father, heading for the middle classes, but dragged back down by marriage to a woman born in a caravan. Mr Aumonier's story was short, funny, bitter, wise. Just like the fairy tales in the beautiful book Johnny had given her.

She thought of his gift and realized that if anyone were hiding their true self it was her, not Johnny. She'd kept up her seeming indifference to him, a self-protection practised during all those years she'd felt unnoticed or even despised by him. And even though now she knew better, she couldn't seem to drop the act. She sighed and leaned her head into her hands. Hearing a sound behind her, she pushed herself off the stool. Johnny put a finger to his lips. He softly shut the door, took her in his arms and kissed her. 'I'm sorry,' he whispered. Do you forgive me?' What if someone walked in on them? But she could hear the laughter of Mr Aumonier's captive audience. She slipped her arms around him and, with her back against the door, pulled him close. 'There's no need for you to be jealous,' she whispered, their lips still touching.

'I can't help it, Kate. I love you.'

She knew this was the time to tell him she felt the same, yet the words wouldn't come, and for answer her lips met his with such passion that her feelings could never again be masked as indifference.

9

Rich Man, Poor Man

Martin seemed like a different person in the studio. More open, warmer, even eager to talk about his work or his difficult family. She began to understand that his cool, ironic manner was a mask. No one was what they seemed – she knew that much. Johnny had hidden his writing dreams, and she had tried to hide her feelings for him. With Martin, the mask made him behave as if he were set apart from others, always observing. But gradually he'd dropped his guard with her and she saw the man behind the mask. Though six years his junior, she sometimes felt much older. Especially when he talked about his mother.

'The old bat simply doesn't like me. Don't look so shocked. We expect that parents will love their children, but it isn't always the case. I suppose we've just never got on... though how I might have offended her as an infant I can't imagine!' He tried to make light of his mother's treatment of him, but Kate saw that he minded, or else why talk about it to her?

'Me and Aunt Sylvie didn't get on, but I bet your mother never stuck a knife in you!' She displayed the long white scar on her arm.

'Dear God, she did that? A bit lower and she'd have cut an artery. You could have bled to death! My mother's attacks are a little more subtle. She cut my allowance to a pittance after I insisted on becoming an artist instead of a banker.' He shrugged. 'If I want her money I'll have to toe the line. Needless to say...' He added more paint to his palette. '...I'm doing nothing of the kind.'

'I can understand her wanting you to have a bank job. It's more secure than painting, I should think,' she said, as if she'd ever known a bank clerk. She looked around the sparsely furnished room. 'The wages must be a lot better.'

He laughed, pausing mid-stroke. 'Slightly. Our family owns the bank!'

'And you're complaining!' She laughed and lost her pose.

'Sit still! Perhaps it seems ridiculous to turn down that sort of wealth. But I'm only doing the same as you. You're mistress of your own fate. You chose to leave your vile aunt, you keep body and soul together by your own hard work *and* you live in a garret!'

'Hmm. I do. But it ain't that comfy. It's draughty when the wind comes up under the eaves and things live in the rafters.' She gave a shudder.

'But the view...'

'Is lovely... for a minute a day.'

He was painting the *Resting* study now. But he'd decided instead to call it *Dreaming*, though she'd never confessed to him the subject of her thoughts during those few idle moments of her day.

A soft knocking on the flat door interrupted their conversation, and while Martin went to answer it, she took the opportunity to stand and stretch. She'd been bent forward, hands beneath her chin, gazing at the imaginary river for so long it hurt to straighten up. She twisted to ease the pain and glanced into the sitting room as Martin showed in his guest. It was Nora.

They stood at the far end of the sitting room, speaking softly so that she couldn't hear the words, but Nora was obviously upset. Martin took both of her hands and seemed to be reassuring her. Nora shook her head, that same sad expression on her lovely face, then she looked towards the studio. Her eyes met Kate's, who quickly turned back to the window and out of Nora's view. Someone shut the studio door and soon Kate heard raised voices. Nora's high, plaintive, and Martin's urgent, pleading, then impatient.

Kate knew she shouldn't be eavesdropping, but her curiosity, as it so often did, got the better of her. She moved closer to the door and heard Martin burst out violently, 'I've told you what to do, Nora. You must leave him. Right now, while you've got the chance!' She'd heard him ironic or gossipy, but never angry, and his outburst was more shocking because of it.

Now she was convinced. Martin and Nora must be lovers. She had thought the throttle marks around Nora's neck had come from a jealous husband, but they could equally have come from a jealous lover. Who knew? It was none of her business, she told herself. She just wished he'd come back in so they could get on with it. Martin always worked too long on Sundays and then drove at top speed all the way to Bermondsey so she wouldn't be late for the lecture.

There was silence and, after a few minutes, muffled crying and then footsteps approaching. She jumped back to her seat.

Nora's normally pale face was red with tears, though she affected a bright tone. 'Hello, Kate. Martin tells me the triptych is almost finished. He must have been working you very hard!'

'Oh, don't worry about Kate, she gives me hell if I do!' Martin quipped.

Didn't they think she had a pair of working ears? But they played the part of acquaintances very well.

Nora went to the easel. 'How lovely. Martin's captured that faraway look in your eyes beautifully – what are you seeing in your mind's eye, I wonder?' she mused softly. 'The garret reminds me of one I used as my bedroom the year I met my husband...'

'Not quite the same,' Martin said. 'Yours *was* in a French chateau, wasn't it? Kate was just explaining how draughty and infested hers is...'

'Chateaux are draughty and infested too.' She ignored him and smiled at Kate.

Martin lifted Nora's monochrome portrait and took it to her. But Kate could see no hint of that coldness in the woman who now stood examining her own image.

'Chibby likes this one better?' Nora asked Martin.

'Your husband was... entranced.' A secret look passed between them that Kate felt uncomfortable witnessing.

'When he returns from his business trip, I'm sure he'll send someone to collect it.' Nora's voice was as monotone as the painting, and she turned away with a look that verged on despair.

'I mustn't interrupt your work any longer, Martin. Don't

keep Kate too late... remember it's lecture night and the poor girl will want to arrive in one piece.'

Nora had obviously been chauffeured by Martin too.

The following morning Kate woke in the garret shivering and sweating. Every muscle in her body felt as if hot pokers were boring through it and she lay perfectly still, hoping this wasn't what she thought it was. But each breath from her crackling lungs told her it was 'Monday morning fever', the illness all the soldering girls succumbed to eventually. It was the metal fumes that gave it to you, but oddly the symptoms only came on after a Sunday away from the factory. Once it had stolen up on you, it would lay you low for a couple of days and Miss Dane always told them to stay at home in case it turned to pneumonia. But even if Kate gave the factory a miss, cleaners were two a penny and she couldn't afford to let down either the bookshop or the Marigold.

She rolled out of bed and was seized with a violent spasm of dry coughing that wrenched her already-aching back muscles. She threw on a coat to stop the shivering while she boiled water on the paraffin stove. Hugging herself, she scraped ice from the dormer window and peered over the snow-rimed roof. Martin's painting made her garret look romantic, but today what wouldn't she give to curl up on the chaise longue by the cosy fire in his sitting room?

She gulped hot tea and dressed hurriedly in her warmest clothes, descending as quietly as she could so as not to wake the Wilsons' sleeping children. Out in the street the sky was just turning pink and snow blew in sleety gusts, making the cobbles slippery underfoot. She was concentrating so much on keeping her footing that she didn't notice the slumped figure outside East Lane school until she was almost upon it. Someone had obviously tried to shelter in the lee of the school wall. As Kate bent over her, she saw it was a woman, her coat crusted by snow. She was curled up so that Kate couldn't see her face. But as Kate shook her shoulder, the woman's head lolled to one side. It was Mrs Bacon, and by the smell of her, she'd collapsed on the way home from the pub, which meant she'd been here half the night.

When Kate couldn't rouse her, she looked around for help, but the street was deserted. She sprinted to Johnny's house, knocking frantically at the door. He was there in an instant, already dressed for work.

'It's... your...' Kate paused, racked by a barking cough. 'Your mum... by the school. I can't wake her up,' she said, her teeth chattering as she was seized with a bout of shivering. 'I'll show you...'

'No, you're shaking, you get inside!' Johnny ordered. 'I'll find her.'

Within minutes he was carrying his mother through the front door. Kate had stoked up the fire and pulled a blanket from Johnny's bed, as there didn't appear to be one on Mrs Bacon's. Between them they stripped off her wet coat, frock and shoes and Kate wrapped her in the blanket. Through it all Mrs Bacon hadn't woken. Johnny pulled the bed nearer to the fire and laid her down gently while Kate began rubbing her hands and feet.

'They're freezing! Johnny, you'd better try to wake her up.'

He slapped her cheeks gently. 'Mum, you've got to come to now. Wake up!'

'Have you got any brandy in the house?' It seemed a silly question.

'No. But *she* might have.' He disappeared into the scullery and came back with a bottle. 'Tucked under the copper! After all these years there's not a hiding place I don't know about.'

He forced a dribble of brandy into his mother's mouth and then another. Mrs Bacon's eyes fluttered open. 'Oh, hello, Johnny. What time is it? Shouldn't you be at work...' Then she saw Kate. 'Hello, me darlin'. You been looking after me again?' She put up a hand and eventually found Kate's cheek to pat, but her fingers were colder than ice.

'Have you got any more blankets?'

He shook his head sadly. 'She pawned the bedding last week. I'll get it back today.'

'Coats, then?' He nodded and ran upstairs, coming back with a couple of his old jackets.

'I'm sorry, Johnny, I'm late for the Marigold. Will you stay with her?'

He nodded. 'But you shouldn't be going to work either. You look terrible.'

'It's just Monday morning fever. I'll be all right.'

He took hold of her. 'Thanks, Kate. She could have frozen to death out there. I knew she hadn't come home, but I was just so tired last night... I'll never forgive myself if anything happens to her.'

She looked at Mrs Bacon. She'd seen her in worse condition. But the cold had seeped deeply into her bones. 'She'll be fine once she's warmed up a bit.' But Kate feared she'd need far more heat than the Bacons' paltry fire could supply.

'Don't go,' he said suddenly, and pulled her into the warmth of his arms. She held on to him tightly, wanting nothing more than to stay.

'I've got to, Johnny. I'm sorry.' She felt mean denying him, but he knew the consequences of losing any one of her jobs.

The Marigold cleaning alone would buy her coal for the week, and if this morning was anything to go by, she'd need it. 'I'll come tonight, after the French class is over. I promise.'

With thumping head and shivering limbs, she somehow managed to sweep, mop and polish the bars of the Marigold, and she was never gladder to see the Boutle's coke ovens. She knew that with a day or two of breathing in the metal fumes again she'd be fine. It was just like Mrs Bacon's hair of the dog: the poison was also sometimes the remedy. But Miss Dane caught her draping herself around the oven. 'Go home, Kate!' she ordered. 'If you're shivering you can't seam straight anyway.'

'No! It's not a bad bout,' she stuttered. Trying desperately to control her trembling limbs, she walked, under the suspicious eye of the supervisor, to her bench.

After cleaning the bookshop during her dinner hour, she didn't know how she would get through the afternoon, let alone keep going till the French class. But Marge and Conny covered for her. Marge gave her aspirin and Conny helped her out when her arms and hands shook too violently to hold the soldering iron. Somehow, she survived the day and after work dragged herself to the bookshop to set up the class.

She was surprised to find Ethel waiting for her. Bookselling duties on Monday evenings were usually given over to a volunteer.

'Kate, I'm afraid you won't be needed tonight, the French class is cancelled – Nora is unwell.'

'Oh, what's the matter?' Kate said, hoping her delight at being let off wasn't too obvious.

'I believe she had an accident at home.'

'Is it serious?'

'I think not. Mrs Cliffe tells me she's had a fall – some bruising, nothing broken, thankfully.'

'Is there anything I can do?' she asked, hoping there wouldn't be.

'Well, as you mention it, I suppose it's possible the students may wish to stay and practise conversation. In which case, perhaps you could give them refreshments as usual?'

She nodded wearily and Ethel stopped. 'Are you quite well yourself? You're looking slightly flushed.'

Kate felt sweat drench her whole body. 'No. I'm fine.'

'If you're sure...'

Forcing a smile, she nodded and went upstairs to set up the room. She had just stood on a chair to get the cake tin from a high cupboard when she heard footsteps on the stairs.

'Class is cancelled. The French teacher's not coming!' she shouted, hoping no one fancied conversing in French tonight.

'*Au contraire, le professeur de Français est ici!*' the musical voice rang out, and Kate swayed, light-headed now with fever. She tumbled down from the chair, sending the cake tin clattering to the floor. Nora rushed into the scullery carrying an armful of exercise books, which she dropped in order to help Kate to her feet.

'The French teacher is here! Are you hurt?'

'No. But I think the cake's had it.'

As Nora bent to retrieve the scattered cake, Kate noticed her smooth cheek bore the shadow of a bruise, hidden by a thick layer of pale make-up. A dark purple ring beneath her eye was more difficult to disguise.

'Should you be here, Nora? Ethel said you couldn't come because you'd had a fall!'

Nora was usually graceful in all she did, but as she gathered up the notebooks, she winced.

'There was no fall and I'm fine. I stupidly walked into a door, I'm terribly short-sighted!'

She struggled to take off her white fur collar. 'Anyway, I'd much rather be here than languishing at home!'

It was painful to see how brightly she hid her injuries, which seemed as if they extended well beyond her beautiful face.

Kate spent a grateful hour resting in the scullery. Lulled by the sound of Nora's lilting French, she dozed off, only to be woken by the cacophony of the class singing some French folk song.

After the students had demolished scones and tea, Kate was clearing up when Nora came to say goodbye.

'Here, let me help you,' Kate said as Nora struggled to put on her fur collar. Then, seeing that the poor woman could hardly raise her arms to put on her hat, she asked, 'Shall I?'

Nora nodded and Kate placed it on top of her sleek, dark hair. The woman must have had a cracked rib and you didn't get one of those from walking into doors. It wasn't her place to say anything, but what if this had been Conny or Marge? Would she just let it go?

'That was a bloody big door you walked into, wasn't it, Nora? You know what I do when I walk into them sort of doors? I get a soldering iron from Boutle's and I bash the living daylights out of them!'

The French teacher looked at her in astonishment and for an instant Kate thought she would get the same chilly response as before, but this time Nora smiled and then put a hand to her ribs. 'Don't make me laugh, Kate, it hurts. But really, you've got entirely the wrong end of the stick... or soldering iron!'

Kate didn't know what to believe now. But if the woman didn't want to confide in her, she couldn't force her to. She knew how lonely it could feel when you were the one being bashed and no one else seemed to think it worth noticing or stopping.

'All right. But if you need any help... at home, let me know. I'll come over, do your cleaning, make a cup of tea. Though I expect you've already got a cleaner...' She stopped short, feeling suddenly shy and stupid.

Nora put a hand on her arm and said, 'I may not need a cleaner, but I do need a friend.'

As they walked out into Bermondsey Street, now dusted with a fresh fall of snow, Nora's fur collar fluttered around her neck and Kate hugged herself, feeling as if she might faint.

'Chibby's sent the car.' Nora walked to a black Daimler idling outside the bookshop. 'Do you live nearby, Kate? Or can we drive you home?'

As she asked, Kate suddenly collapsed across the bonnet of the car. She was aware of never wanting to move from the deliciously warm spot and only reluctantly let go, slipping to the wet pavement.

She came round to find herself being lifted into the plush leather interior of the car by Nora's driver. Now it was her turn to have brandy forced down her throat. It burned like liquid fire and she choked.

'Sorry, miss!' She was horrified to have embarrassed herself in front of this perfect woman.

'You're not well. Why didn't you say? Tell me where you live. You can't possibly walk home.'

Kate couldn't think of anything worse than Nora seeing the place she lived, but though she protested, Nora refused to let her out of the car till she gave the chauffeur instructions. As the Daimler turned into the long, dark lane, she noticed the chauffeur's head darting from side to side. It no doubt seemed a place not to linger at night, ending as it did at the river stairs. It didn't help that the pub was turning out, and he probably feared for his boss's car.

'I'll be all right from here,' she said, reaching for the door.

'No! We'll help you up – it's a garret, isn't it?' Nora said, scanning the rooftops.

'He'd better stay here,' she said under her breath. 'He looks a bit nervous and you don't want anything to happen to your husband's car.'

Nora seemed to consider that. 'I'll come, then.' And she helped Kate into the house and up the stairs to the garret room, lit only by the moon bouncing off snow on the rooftops. It was better if the place stayed in darkness, thought Kate – then the beautifully turned-out Nora would not see her two frocks hanging on a hook, or the threadbare blanket, or the crate she used as a food cupboard. But Nora found the lamp and lit it, flooding Kate's shame with light.

Thankfully she stayed only long enough to help Kate to bed and to add a coat to the blanket. Kate was dimly aware of her saying goodnight before she fell into a feverish sleep. It was only when she woke up the following morning to a banging on the front door that she remembered her promise to Johnny.

She crawled out of bed and called down to the Wilsons'

rooms, in a voice that scraped her throat like gravel, 'Could you let him in!'

But it wasn't Johnny. It was a delivery, which the youngest Wilson boy carried up to her, and when she opened the box, he gasped. 'Look at all that grub!'

It was a food hamper. Tins of Scotch broth and salmon and ham, boxes of biscuits and porridge and packets of tea. Enough food to feed her for months.

'Who brought it?'

'Some bloke in a grey uniform. He come in this posh black car. Give me this for you too.'

The note, written on thick cream paper, read: *To speed your recovery. Nora.*

She gave the Wilson boy some of the tea and biscuits and a tin of salmon, with instructions to give them to his mother. 'No eating the biscuits on the stairs!' she said, and he gave her a grateful grin before clattering downstairs shouting, 'Mum! Guess what Kate give us!'

Wishing she had the energy to make some breakfast from Nora's gift, Kate instead went back to bed. Pulling up the blanket, she felt the softness of fur against her skin. Nora must have covered Kate with her coat, the white fur collar still attached. Perhaps, she wondered, across the gulf of wealth and class that separated them, it really was possible to find friendship.

When next she woke, soft, golden light from a low sun slid through the dormer. Had she slept all day? Johnny! She'd promised to go back last night. What must he think of her? She got out of bed too quickly and steadied herself, testing her limbs. She could stand, but she felt a cold wave of nausea wash over her. Metal fume fever could bring on sickness, but by now it ought to be abating. Perhaps she should eat. She opened some of Nora's biscuits and felt better. Then, dressing warmly, she emptied the box of food and put Nora's coat inside it. Hoping he'd be home, she went to Johnny's.

Dressed in his old corduroys and jumper, his hair uncombed, he looked drawn and pale.

'I'm sorry – I've not been well,' she said in explanation.

He pulled her inside and held her tightly for a long time.

'Thank God you're here. I didn't know what had happened to you – but I couldn't leave her last night.'

She felt his heart thumping in his chest. Then he held her at arm's length. 'What happened?'

'I'm all right now. I fainted at the bookshop, but I had a guardian angel. The French teacher drove me home! All I could do was fall into bed and I've slept all day. Johnny, I'm so sorry I couldn't come and help you with your mum.'

He led her to his mother. 'Her chest sounds bad, but then it always does, with all the fags and drink... She just can't seem to get warm.'

He pulled up several blankets she'd thrown off. He must have been to the pawn shop to redeem them.

Kate put a hand to his cheek. 'You're a good son, Johnny. Go to bed for a bit and get some sleep. I'll watch her.'

She sat with Mrs Bacon while Johnny slept, and after an hour she went upstairs. She didn't like to wake him, but she had to work tonight. He'd looked so exhausted he'd probably sleep for hours, and when she crept into the room, it was obvious he'd just dropped onto the bed and fallen asleep on his back, his arms flung wide. He hadn't had time to shave and his hair was tousled. He looked so young and so vulnerable that her heart went out to him and she leaned over to brush back his hair. He woke with a start. 'Is she all right?'

'Yes, yes, she's still asleep,' she said, sitting on the bed. 'But I'll have to go soon, I'm due at the bookshop.'

He pulled her down beside him. 'Well, I'm not letting Ethel have you.'

She nestled into his arms and felt his cheek against hers, not minding the rough stubble of a day's growth. He'd left the gas lamp burning and now, in its cosy glow, it was the most natural thing in the world to feel the length of his body against hers and his breath on her cheek and his lips on her mouth.

Eventually she pulled away and said, 'We need to get up. I'll make us our tea.'

'I don't know how you're going to do that when there's not a scrap of food in the house.'

She explained about the hamper and he said, 'Nora looks a bit on the cold side, but she's got a good heart.'

'She's not really cold at all.'

'Her husband must be pretty well off to have a Daimler.'

'I don't know. I think it's her money, not his. Martin told me she used to live in a chateau in France!'

'But that's no guarantee of anything. The aristocracy's not what it was, not since the war – and it must be even worse in France.'

She knew he wouldn't want to be impressed by her knowledge, mostly because it had come from Martin.

'Well, whoever's money it is, I don't think they're happy.'

'And how do you know that? Don't tell me, Noss Goss has been asking questions again!' he teased.

'Don't you call me that!' She thumped his arm. 'It's been bad enough putting up with it all these years from Janey.'

He mollified her with a kiss. 'You're right, I suppose I

don't like being called Rasher much. But I think Noss is just a compliment to your enquiring mind!'

She gave him a sidelong look. 'Well, this enquiring mind is going to the bookshop. It's the elocution class tonight. Come on, get up!'

After they'd eaten and she was putting on her coat, he said, 'You shouldn't be out in the cold. Surely they can put out the chairs and make their own tea?'

'Ethel pays *me* to do it. I'll come back later to see how your mum is.'

'No. Go straight home to bed. I think she seems a bit better now, don't you?' he said with a hopeful glance towards the bed. Mrs Bacon did seem to be sleeping more calmly, so reluctantly she agreed and picked up the box.

He showed her to the door. 'What've you got in there?' he asked, tapping the box.

'Nora's coat – she lent it to me. But Mrs Cliffe's teaching the elocution class, so I thought she could take it to Nora.' She opened the box. 'Beautiful, ain't it?'

He looked up into her eyes. 'It would be more beautiful on you. Try it on for me.'

'No!'

'Go on.'

It was good to see him looking more cheerful, and so she draped the coat with its fur collar over her shoulders.

He gasped. 'I was right!' He took her in his arms and kissed her. 'It makes me wish I was a rich man, so I could buy you a wardrobe full of clothes like this...'

She gave him a gentle shove. 'Well, I prefer you poor.'

★

Whatever she'd told Johnny about feeling fine was untrue. She was still in the grip of fume fever, but with the help of another night's sleep and more of the contents of Nora's hamper, she was able to force herself in to work the next day. Wednesday night at the bookshop had become one of her favourite times. The little kitchen was like a private box at the theatre and she'd begun to appreciate the play readings and the rehearsals. It was a surprise to find that Shakespeare wasn't as difficult to understand as she'd thought. They'd read some at school, but it had seemed as dry as dust to her then. Only now that she heard them performed did the plays come to life. She quickly realized that if the actors were good, the meaning shone through the old-fashioned language. The group was rehearsing for a performance of *The Winter's Tale*. And Kate was surprised to find that Ethel and Nora were among the cast. She knew that Ethel had been an actress before the Bermondsey Bookshop venture had claimed her – it explained her sometimes theatrical way of declaiming her instructions about what Kate should clean next: she was full of prithees and haplys, which Kate largely let go over her head – but Nora didn't seem the theatrical type at all. Perhaps she'd just rather be here than at home.

Before long Kate found herself riveted by the story of mad King Leontes, who cruelly abandons his daughter, Perdita, in that 'desert place'. And though Archie Goss wasn't a king or anything like, it made her wonder if something more than grief had been behind her own exile in East Lane. She'd certainly come off worse than Perdita – with an Aunt Sylvie instead of a kindly old shepherd to care for her. And yet it wasn't so much this part of the story that moved her as that of the king's falsely accused and harshly treated wife, Hermione

– who was being played by Nora. Kate felt an almost electric chill at the lines which Nora spoke with such calm dignity:

I am not prone to weeping, as our sex
Commonly are; the want of which vain dew
Perchance shall dry your pities: but I have
That honourable grief lodged here which burns
Worse than tears drown...

She knew the truth behind the lines, she'd known women like that in her own family: tears rarely shed and love seldom expressed. But whereas Sylvie was hard, her Aunt Sarah was simply stoical. She knew Nora was only acting a part, but Kate was certain that the woman's coolness was simply a protective shell that might fall away at the merest hint of warmth from another human being. She wanted to seek out that husband of hers and give him a crack with the soldering iron herself.

After the rehearsal, Nora came to the kitchen. 'Thank you for the return of the coat, Kate. But I meant you to keep it,' she said, holding it out to her.

'Keep it?' For a moment Kate couldn't understand why, and then she realized how poor her garret must have looked, and how Nora must have noticed that she had just the one coat. The kindness only made her want to cry with shame.

'It's really kind but I couldn't accept it.'

'But why not?' Nora's direct gaze showed no hint of offence. 'A gift from a friend, that's all,' she insisted, pressing the coat into Kate's arms.

Kate herself had felt the weight and warmth of the coat as a sign of friendship, so why did she find it so humiliating to accept it? Because Nora had probably a dozen or more coats at home, and that made a difference. However much Ethel wanted the bookshop to be common ground for the mean streets and the Mayfairs, there was still a gulf much wider than the Thames to be spanned.

When she visited the Bacons later that evening, she was struck by how much Johnny's hopeful demeanour had diminished in a day. His eyes looked bruised with tiredness and worry. At her enquiry after his mother, he shook his head. 'She's bad, Kate. Ginger Bosher came to see why I've not been at work. He fetched the doctor for me. Pneumonia's in her lungs and the drink hasn't done her liver any good either. He didn't seem to think…' Johnny covered his face. For all her failings, mother and son loved each other. And Kate couldn't help comparing Johnny to Martin, whose mother had given him all that material wealth could supply but not one ounce of love. She knew which of the two men was the richer.

10

The Bermondsey Triptych

The wind blew up East Lane from the river in great icy bursts, seizing every house in its iron-hard grip and shaking them till they rattled and cracked. The houses were so ancient they seemed to taint every life within them – however young – with their agues and their shivers. Kate's return to work and the renewed daily dose of solder fumes hadn't cured her as she'd hoped it would. The Monday morning fever had persisted for several weeks, breaking out every weekend. She'd made light of the illness, but secretly she feared this tightness in her lungs and crackling cough might become pneumonia – then she'd really be in trouble, for she could never afford the doctor's bills. Noxious fumes alone weren't to blame for her ailments, it wasn't just the place she worked in making her ill – it was the place she slept in and the place she dreamed in too. And that was something Martin could never convey in his painting of her garret. He was coming to the end of his triptych, putting in the finishing touches. But new bouts of coughing interrupted the Sunday modelling session and Martin told her not to come the following weekend.

'I can finish it without you, and besides, I want you fit for the private view!'

A small gallery near his flat was mounting an exhibition of his work, and *The Bermondsey Triptych,* as he called it, was to be the centrepiece.

'I don't think I'll come, Martin.'

'Of course you'll come! I want to show off my Bermondsey muse,' he said, with a proprietorial finality which only made her more stubborn.

'Well, I'm busy helping Johnny with his mum, so I'll be needed elsewhere.'

He considered her excuse for a few moments, then his face brightened. 'John must come as well. I'll send a nurse to look after his mother. He'll probably need a break and he's let me steal you every Sunday, so it's only right he should share in the glory. And you will be a glorious triumph, Kate.' He studied the painting and then looked at her with an affectionate and proud gaze. She wondered if he thought of her as a prize pet. 'But right now, I'm driving you home.'

She'd tried to hide her continuing illness from Johnny, for his mother's condition had worsened as she lay in the narrow house which caught the full venom of the river winds. Johnny had come less to the bookshop and the lectures so that he could devote himself to caring for her. But it was when he turned down Ethel's request for another article for *The Bermondsey Book* that Kate began to seriously worry about him. He would never abandon his dream of writing, not unless he expected the worst.

At least having a Sunday off from the studio meant she could spend the day with him. She'd saved the last tin of stew from Nora's hamper, and if she piled up the potatoes at least he'd have one good dinner this week. He let her in along with a snow flurry and then hurried to stoke up the fire. The coal bucket was nearly empty. He must have gone through a sack in a week. She didn't know how he was finding the money for it, as he'd not worked since Mrs Bacon had fallen ill.

'How is she?'

Kate followed him to the bed, where he stooped to feel his mother's forehead.

'She's burning up, but then she'll get the shivers so bad her teeth chatter. She can't seem to stay warm.'

'Is she eating at all?'

Johnny shook his head. 'Nor drinking.' Sadness and fear clouded his eyes and then he saw her unpacking her bag. 'Oh, Kate, I can't eat—'

'Yes, you can! If you get ill you can't look after her, can you?'

Johnny nodded. He'd handed the practical aspects of his life to Kate – washing, ironing and cleaning – while he bent his will to making his mother better. But Kate could see he was wasting away himself in the process.

'Johnny, love, come over here a minute,' she called.

Reluctantly, he left Mrs Bacon's side. She held his hands and kissed them. 'You're not going to help your mum by giving up your life. And she wouldn't want you to. Why don't you go to the lecture tonight – you wanted to hear this one. I'll stay here with your mum. Nora's volunteered to make the refreshments and Martin said he'll do the setting up.'

'Martin?' Johnny frowned. 'Have you been talking to him about me?'

She disliked his suspicious tone. 'No more than to anyone else. Everyone at the bookshop's been asking after your mum – including Martin. Anyway, you've got nothing to worry about with him. I think he might be carrying on with Nora.' She hadn't meant to voice her speculations, but she'd been so eager to reassure him.

'Nora? She's married!'

'And he's an artist.' Kate shrugged.

'If that's all it takes, I'm even more suspicious of him when it comes to you, not less!'

'Well, you needn't be. All I meant was that he likes to think he's a bit of a rebel. But don't you repeat what I said about Nora, not to a soul! It's just one of those feelings.'

He put his arms around her. 'There's only one feeling I'm interested in, and that's this.' He kissed her and instinctively she pulled away.

'What?' He looked hurt.

'Johnny, I can't! Not with your mum lying there...' She glanced at the sleeping figure by the fire. But he was too raw to see beyond his own jealousy.

'Is it really that? Or is it because you're more interested in your posh artist friend? What's he called his *Bermondsey Triptych? Cleaning, Kissing* and *Cheating?*'

She resisted slapping him but, tight-lipped with anger, she said, 'You might be out of your wits with worry, but you don't talk to me like that, Johnny Bacon. I hope you've got a tin opener 'cause that's the only way you'll be getting any dinner tonight!' Fury and fume fever were not a good combination. Her chest constricted and her breath came in painful rasps. She might have said more, but a fit of coughing silenced her. Flinging on her coat, she left him standing shocked and speechless. Once outside, she was immediately overcome with compassion for his sad, stubborn, stupid self. *Oh, Johnny, you silly 'a'porth*, she thought, but she wouldn't go back.

Unable to face her garret room, she decided she might as well go to the bookshop. It would be warm and she needed something to take her mind off the argument with Johnny. No doubt other girls would have swallowed his insult – after all, he was considered a catch in East Lane – and if she hadn't loved him so much, perhaps she would have too. But she did love him. And that made his suspicions even more hurtful. Perhaps, underneath it all, he believed her aunt's version of her mother – a slut who'd tricked Archie Goss into marriage – and deep down he felt the apple never fell far from the tree. Cold air flayed her lungs and misery scoured her heart as she walked quickly to Bermondsey Street, where light from the old church spilled onto a crystalline pavement. When she arrived at the bookshop, Martin was already arranging chairs.

'Kate? Why are you here? Is John's mother all right?'

'Mrs Bacon's not at all well. But Johnny didn't need me after all.'

'But still, you shouldn't have come. The idea was to give you a night off…' He tried to help her with her coat, but she shrugged him away.

'I can do that myself, and besides, I don't want a night off!' she snapped.

He took a step back. 'Ah, now, I've studied you for many an hour, Kate Goss, and I know what that face means. He's upset you, hasn't he?'

Martin sat her down on a chair, almost as if he were posing her for another painting. 'Tell me all about it.'

She felt she was back in the studio, where their hours of voicing whatever came into their heads had formed a sort of confessional trust between them. 'He's jealous.'

'Of what?'

'It doesn't matter.' She looked away.

'Not of me?' he guessed, giving a disbelieving laugh. 'Absurd!'

'That's what I told him!'

'Told who what?' Nora came out of the kitchen with a cloth in her hand. She looked chic even in the long black housecoat.

'Kate's John just accused me of having unworthy intentions towards her.'

A look passed between them and, almost as if they'd talked about it already, Nora repeated, 'Absurd!'

'Well, you've answered your own question – that's the gist of what I told Johnny!'

Nora wiped her hands, thinking. 'Perhaps Kate should stop sitting for you, Martin. It's not fair if it's making her life... difficult.'

But Martin waved a hand in dismissal.

'Kate does what she wants. She's a free spirit, like me.'

'Is she?' Nora asked drily, and then beckoned to Kate. 'Come on, let's leave our free-spirited friend here to finish his task. I know you don't trust me to make tea properly – even though I am half English!'

When they were alone in the kitchen, Kate set about cutting the cake into much smaller slices than Nora's and adding extra tea to the pots. They worked silently for a while until Nora said, 'Kate, you should know something about Martin.'

Here it comes. Kate tensed. *She's going to confess!*

'I've noticed he has a tendency to fall head over heels – very quickly – usually with the young women his mother would approve of least...'

Kate swallowed hard and blushed. Was she trying to tell her that Johnny was right about Martin? Or was she just jealous of Kate herself?

'You really shouldn't let Martin come between you and John,' Nora continued. 'He'll end up hurting you...'

Kate put down the knife and turned to Nora. 'Thanks for the warning, but I could say the same to you...'

'Whatever do you mean?' Nora's dark-lashed eyes widened.

'I'll be straight with you, Nora. I think *you're* the only woman Martin North's interested in. And I reckon you'd be better off if he wasn't...'

Nora put a hand to her ivory throat. 'No, Kate, you're wrong. When I came to England it was so hard – my mother's family wanted nothing to do with me. But Mrs Cliffe – and Martin – were my only friends here. Martin and I did become close, you have to understand we were both very young – it was natural. But I couldn't have survived without either of them.' Her pale face flushed, whether from anger or guilt Kate couldn't tell. She thought Nora would have said more, but just then Martin put his head around the door, begging a piece of cake before the proceedings started. Nora handed him a plate and turned away as he flashed Kate a broad smile.

Tonight it wasn't so much a lecture as a debate. The subject was 'Art Versus Industrialism', and Kate was interested, if only because one of the speakers was Ethel's husband, Sidney Gutman. She was curious about the man who paid her wages, for successful businessman Sidney subsidized the bookshop heavily. She usually preferred to listen from the kitchen, but tonight she slipped into the audience after the introductions had been made.

Sidney Gutman was older than Ethel; sober-suited and serious-looking, he at first seemed an unusual choice for the theatrical Ethel. But Kate quickly warmed to his no-nonsense style. His fellow debater argued that industrialism killed any artistic aspirations in its workforce and had just mentioned Boutle's to prove his point! She sat up, her interest piqued.

'Not far from here is one of these tin bashers of the soul!' the man said dramatically. 'How could anyone sensitive to culture or literature expect to survive with their sensibilities intact once in its satanic grasp?'

Sidney responded with the dry observation that even the most sensitive soul came with a body attached and those bodies generally needed to be fed and watered. Boutle's did the job admirably! Kate joined in the appreciative applause, for there were many in the audience employed in the leather trade or the food factories who had built up substantial libraries using the bookshop's 'tick' cards and Sidney was popular. With an affectionate look towards his wife, he gave her the rightful glory.

'And now we come to the very reason for the existence of this place – the Bermondsey Bookshop – a very bulwark against what my friend here so eloquently refers to as "the tin bashers of the soul". When, in 1921, my wife Ethel Gutman had the faith to open the portals of 89 Bermondsey Street to bring the love of books and the allied arts into the lives of the working men and women of Bermondsey, the naysayers were vocal. We were assured the adventure was doomed – the very idea – *books* in Bermondsey! Beer and boxing, yes, but *books*! Even the letting agent shook his head and prophesied the shutters would go up again in a matter of six weeks!'

He spread his arms to include the audience. 'And yet three years on – here we are! Proof incontestable that whatever industries the working classes may labour at – be it tin bashing or tea packing – the desire for knowledge and a love of literature are not quashed and indeed, given the opportunity, will manifest themselves in a surprising degree. We only hope that other such shops may soon be opened in all the poorer quarters!'

Needless to say, Mr Sidney Gutman's argument won the day, and now Kate could well understand what Ethel saw in him. But her pleasure in listening to his arguments was all wrapped up with Johnny and his hopes for himself and she experienced a sharp longing that he could have been here.

She decided to make up with him tomorrow before work. But late that night, shortly after she'd gone to bed, she was woken by a loud knocking. Instantly she was alert and, not stopping to look out of the window to see who it was, she ran down the garret stairs before Mr Wilson had even stirred from his bed. She fumbled with the stiff bolt and yanked open the front door.

'Can you help me, Kate?' Johnny's stricken face confirmed what she already knew. Her heartbeat seemed to slow and she felt a calm settle over her, even as she realized what she would have to face.

The silence of the house struck her first; Mrs Bacon's laboured breathing was now absent and the crackling fire reduced to grey ash. And yet the silence seemed to have a presence. She stood at the bedside and kissed Mrs Bacon's forehead. It had already cooled.

'When?'

Johnny blinked back tears before answering. 'Not long after you left.'

Kate pictured what she had been doing at the time – complaining to Martin, cutting cake, applauding Sidney Gutman. She should have been here, with him.

'I didn't notice she'd gone – not for ages. How couldn't I have known?' He paced the tiny room, hugging himself. She made him sit down. 'I knew something was different, and then I couldn't hear her breathing any more. She'd gone and—' His sentence was cut short by a shuddering cry. She enfolded him in her arms.

'Oh, Kate, what a bloody pitiful life she had – pointless, and now it's over. That's it – gone. I tried to make it better for her... I did.' He swept the tears from his cheeks and she waited till he could hear her.

'But you *did* make it better, Johnny. Just by being you. She loved you and you loved her and that was the point of her life... you.'

'No, no, if it was, why did she drink herself to... this...'

Tears caught at her throat, but her voice stayed steady: 'She loved you, but she didn't love herself – and that was never your fault.'

Kate woke with a start and a deep intake of breath. It was a while before she realized she was breathing without pain, and she said a silent prayer of thanks that the metal fume fever had lessened its grip. For today she would need all of her strength to help Johnny. The congregation numbered just four: Johnny, Kate, an old workmate and a cousin who'd known Mrs Bacon as a girl. Some of the neighbours in the lane stood respectfully at their doors as the coffin was placed in the hearse; they were the ones who knew too well what she'd suffered at the hands of a drunken husband who'd beaten her daily until he left her with a baby to bring up alone. It had driven her to drink and they didn't condemn. Others, like Aunt Sylvie, kept their doors firmly shut.

Johnny's normally assured expression was dimmed by loss. He was like a dark, thin blade, his grief so sharp she feared she'd cut herself if she reached out to him. But she did – linking her arm through his and never leaving his side through the whole sorry day. Johnny believed his mother's life had been a pointless waste, and in the days after the funeral he seemed intent on making his own life one too. None of the things that had once lit his eyes with enthusiasm could move him. He worked every shift he could, he stopped buying books or going to the reading room, the lectures, and he even gave up writing. One day, as she was dusting around the table where Ethel was proofreading the latest *Bermondsey Book*, she looked up suddenly and said, 'We haven't seen John Bacon here since his mother died... how is he?'

'There was only ever the two of them – Johnny and his mum. He's blaming himself because he wasn't enough.'

'Enough for what?'

'Enough to save her.'

She nodded as if she understood. 'I wouldn't presume to visit him at his home, but perhaps you could persuade him to take solace in his writing? Would you let him know that we've had interest from a publisher in his "Life of a Docker"? They feel it could be expanded into book form. Surely that will lift his spirits?' Ethel's concern was touching and she promised she would, hopeful that this might be the very news to dispel his sadness.

That evening after work, she rushed home and waited for his knock with excitement. They spent more time in her garret room now, as he hated spending time in the house where his mother had died. Her room had even fewer of the comforts of home than his house, but at least he could settle there.

She waited until she'd made him tea on the little paraffin stove and he was seated on the rag rug she'd made. His face was half obscured by the glare of the lamp, and at first it seemed he hadn't heard her, so she repeated herself. 'Didn't you hear me? A publisher, Johnny! It's your dream!'

But he shook his head. 'It's rubbish, all rubbish. A few printed pages squashed between two boards – what difference will that make to anything or anyone?'

'It will! You always said no one can hear your accent when you write. They'll take you seriously, they'll hear how hard it is to live—'

'Of course it's bloody hard to live!' He flared up at her quickly these days. 'It's hard to be *alive* – doesn't matter whether you're poor or rich!'

She moved the paraffin lamp so that she could see his face properly – every line of his handsome features seemed skewed with hopelessness.

'Well, don't do it to save the world, then. Do it to save yourself.'

He looked at her in silence for a while and then reached out his arms to her. She led him to her narrow bed and she tried as best she could to soften all the hard edges of his despair with her kisses.

Johnny had come for her sake. Kate hoped she hadn't made a mistake in persuading him to be here, but she was desperate for any way to rekindle his enthusiasm. His friends at the bookshop were coming, and perhaps Ethel might have the chance to reignite his interest in writing, or Ginger Bosher, from the Bermondsey contingent, might persuade him to read the latest trade union bulletin – anything to draw Johnny back into his own life.

Martin had insisted she pass on to Johnny his invitation to the private view of his latest paintings. At first he'd flatly refused, but Kate had appealed to his protective instincts, implying she'd be lost without his support. What did she know about the art world or posh London galleries? She'd be like a fish out of water. 'You'll know exactly what to do, Johnny. Imagine me on my own, standing around drinking wine, trying to make conversation with that arty crowd!' She'd laid it on thick, even though she felt no such trepidation. If any of these people could be induced to buy not one but three paintings of her, then they had more money than sense, and Kate could think of far better things to do with a few hundred quid. When she'd expressed that same opinion to Martin he'd laughed and called her a beautiful barbarian, which she'd taken as a compliment.

The exhibition was to be held at a gallery in a terrace of white stucco houses not far from Martin's studio in Fitzroy Square. The narrow frontage was deceiving. She and Johnny passed through the heavy wooden doors into the chequered-tiled hall and then into a single long gallery, which took up the entire depth of the house. She looked up at a roof that reminded her of an upturned glass-bottomed boat, flooding the lofty space with light. But it was an alien place. A high-pitched chatter like a twittering of birds in an aviary filled the room. Flamboyant dandies and sleek-haired women curved their bodies into self-conscious poses and lifted their voices to unnatural levels of brightness. They seemed determined to attract more attention than the paintings on the walls. But it was the walls which steadied Kate among all this strangeness.

They reminded her of Martin's staircase. Floor to ceiling, full of his paintings, and there she was – or rather three of her – taking centre stage at the far end of the gallery.

Now she was here, she found herself glad that Johnny was beside her, not for his sake so much as her own. The gallery owner hushed the chattering crowd and, in his flowery introduction to Martin's work, made special mention of *The Bermondsey Triptych* as the finest example of his new work. She gripped Johnny's arm as heads turned in her direction. She overheard a couple whispering, 'Where on earth did he find her? In a tin factory? How extraordinary!' And then another young man declared loudly, 'Seems more Botticelli than Bermondsey...' followed by tinkling laughter from his companions. She felt as uncomfortable as on her first day at Boutle's, when all the experienced girls had stared at her ragged frock and dirty appearance. Her face burned, but Johnny at that moment put an arm around her and whispered in her ear, 'North hasn't done you justice – my Kate's much lovelier than those three up there.'

But at the unveiling in Martin's studio, she'd been surprised to find she'd actually liked the triptych, which Nora had insisted so captured her likeness. *Cleaning* caught her looking exhausted and anxious – every job she did was hard work and her income always precarious – so why wouldn't she be? She was glad that in *Reading* her secret love for Johnny was plain for all to see, if they'd only known *what* she was reading. But *Dreaming* was her favourite. It was the one that really did capture her true self.

She'd spotted Ethel as they'd entered, and when the speech was over she saw her making a beeline for them. At that moment Nora appeared beside her. 'John, would you mind?' She put a hand beneath Kate's elbow. 'I need a word with

Kate?' Nora steered her in the direction of the drinks table. It was nicely timed, for Johnny, now standing alone, had no choice but to face Ethel's warm smile.

'Did you and Ethel plan that?' Kate asked as Nora picked up two glasses of champagne.

'Was it obvious?'

Kate nodded, taking an exploratory sip of the champagne. She wrinkled her nose. The bubbles made her want to sneeze and the sharpness stripped the sides of her tongue.

'Don't you like champagne?'

'There's not much call for it at the Hand and Marigold – and now I can see why,' she said, putting down the glass.

'I was so sorry to hear about John's mother. Ethel says they were devoted to each other. I envy him that... my own mother died when I was young.'

'So did mine.'

'Did your father bring you up alone – or remarry like mine?' She offered Kate a plate of tiny sandwiches and took one herself. 'I hated my stepmother,' she said, in a confidential tone.

Kate took a bite of the sandwich, disappointed to find it contained only cucumber. 'Oh, mine left me with an aunt – I reckon she was worse than a stepmother. At least you had your father to stick up for you.'

Nora pulled a face. 'It wasn't quite like that. He was besotted. He always sided with her against me.'

'Did she wallop you?'

Nora laughed. 'Oh no. She got a maid to do that. But she did lock me in a cupboard and leave me there all day when she said I was being "naughty".'

'And really you was good as gold, trying to please her all the time...'

'Yes!' Nora said. 'You too?'

'Until one day I realized nothing I did would ever be good enough – because she just didn't like me! Was it because of your stepmother that you came to England – to be with your mother's family?'

'No. It was Chibby, my husband's, wish. When we met, he was in the British Army, and his company were garrisoned in our town. He'd worked his way up the ranks to colour sergeant and when the Germans were making their final push, he was suddenly put in charge of a platoon and sent back to the front. He insisted I come to England – she hesitated – for my own safety.'

'Of course.' Kate was surprised – she'd imagined Nora's husband as a passionate, jealous Frenchman, but now her image of him changed. He turned into a sober British Army officer, undemonstrative but adoring and perhaps overly protective.

'I didn't want to come here. I was nineteen, all alone in a country I barely remembered. I often wished I'd stayed to brave the Hun – I'm sure they would have been less fearsome than my mother's family!' She laughed, but her expression was bitter. 'I was very unhappy.'

'But what about your father? Couldn't he help you?' Kate's imagination had seized upon the similarities between Nora's family history and her own, and she was hoping that Nora's story ended with a father who gave the wicked stepmother the elbow in order to reclaim his child from her evil aunts.

Nora shook her head. 'No, he'd died years before this, just as the war started.'

'Oh, that must have been so hard. And what happened with your stepmother – did she chuck you out?'

Here, Nora gave a mischievous smile and repeated in her

lilting accent, 'Oh no, I chucked her out! Father had seen through her by that time. He provided her with a small allowance in his will. Everything else was left to me.'

Kate nodded. 'So he did help you.'

'He left me well provided for, but how could that make up for the years of his love I'd lost?'

'I feel like that sometimes, but then I tell myself, when he does come back, I'll be so happy I won't remember all the years he wasn't there.'

Nora gave a rare smile. 'I think you are very wise for your years, Kate.'

Kate dipped her head at the compliment and then Nora asked, 'But what about you? Did your aunt "chuck you out"?'

'Yes, she did. Me and my tin box!'

She was explaining to Nora the nature of the tin box when Ethel joined them.

'I'm afraid I couldn't make any headway with John.' Ethel glanced towards the front of the gallery, where Johnny now stood, closely examining the triptych. He had a half-smile on his face as Kate saw him move on from *Cleaning* to *Reading* and take a step closer. His face was inches from the canvas and then she saw his smile fade and turn to a frown. She excused herself and went to his side. He turned to her with doubt-filled eyes.

'What's going on, Kate?'

'What do you mean?'

'With you and North.' He pointed to *Reading*. 'That's the way you look at me,' he said accusingly. 'Why are you looking like that, when you're with him?'

'Johnny! Stop it, I was just reading—'

'No!' He raised his voice. 'That expression… I'm not stupid, though the likes of North might think I am!' He bristled with a sudden anger.

'If you'll just listen a minute, I'll explain—'

But just then Martin came up to her with a breezy smile and took her elbow. 'I think I may have a buyer for the triptych!' He turned to Johnny. 'Can I steal her—'

Whether Martin had noticed Johnny's angry voice and had come to rescue Kate she couldn't tell, but she certainly knew he hadn't noticed Johnny's fist until it struck his jaw with an audible crack. Martin was sent toppling across the gallery, sending gilded tables and drink trays flying. He collided with a woman swathed in long bright scarves, one of which caught on the toe of his black patent shoe. He tripped and slewed across the floor, landing in a pile at the feet of the astonished gallery owner. Martin was quickly up again and came at Johnny with surprising speed, both fists raised in boxing fashion.

Her heart pounded. Johnny would make mincemeat out of him. She shouted, 'Stop it, Martin!', too late to stop his swift right hook from flooring Johnny, who shook his head, momentarily dazed. The gallery audience had formed a loose ring around the two men and Kate looked around, desperate for someone who might stop them. She spotted Ginger Bosher and ran to him as Martin waited, like a gentleman, for Johnny to get up.

'Ginger, can you get Johnny out of here – quick!'

But Johnny was already charging. His head connected with Martin's stomach, winding him. Before Johnny could follow up with another punch, Ginger Bosher's massive arms encircled him, lifting him off his feet. People turned aside, forming a clear path for Ginger to hustle Johnny from the gallery.

Martin straightened his shirt front and pulled down his cuffs as he came to her side. 'Are you quite all right, Kate?'

She nodded, her face burning with shame. He put an arm around her shoulder and took her off to a drinks table, offering her water. She kept her eyes lowered, not wanting to see the sidelong glances in their direction as people returned to their groups, pretending to talk about the paintings and drawing their own conclusions.

'I'm so sorry, Martin.' She was glad he shielded her from the rest of the room, even though all eyes were avoiding her now.

'I'll drive you home.'

She was trembling and felt cold suddenly. 'No. You stay, this is your day. I'll make me own way home.'

'You will not.' He looked around then beckoned to Nora, who had been hovering nearby. 'Will you sit with Kate for a moment? I just need to see a few more people, then I'm taking her home.'

Nora put a hand to his shoulder. 'Go. I'll look after her.' Her eyes followed him as he crossed the gallery and Kate thought she saw a flicker of doubt, but then she turned to Kate.

'Your Johnny's a fiery one. Jealousy is a torment when it takes you over.'

'It's not so nice being on the receiving end either – is it?'

Shortly afterwards, the crowded gallery emptied and Martin came to find her. He drove her back to Bermondsey in his mother's Rolls. She was silent as they wove their way through the early-evening traffic in Tottenham Court Road. He seemed unperturbed by the day's events, even humming softly to himself as they negotiated the crush around Trafalgar Square and crossed Waterloo Bridge. She gazed beyond the bridge to the darkening Thames, trying to fathom him. Sometimes his unruffled exterior annoyed her. She could see nothing worth humming about. Johnny had made a farce of what should have been Martin's moment of glory.

Once south of the river, she finally spoke. 'You don't have to pretend with me, Martin. I know you must be upset. Johnny's ruined it for you.'

Martin turned a smiling face to her. 'You're quite wrong, Kate. John Bacon has done me an enormous favour. *The Bermondsey Triptych* is apparently worth twice as much with a dramatic story attached to it – jealous lover, fisticuffs with the artist at its first showing, and who is this mysterious muse from Bermondsey who caused all the fuss? There was a bidding war for it – and I think I can finally chuck Mother's Rolls and buy myself a Baby Austin with the proceeds!' He laughed and then flinched, rubbing his face where the bruising was now evident. He turned into East Lane. 'Besides, he's just lost his mother, poor chap.'

She'd found that Martin wasn't easily rattled, but even so, she was impressed with this good-natured forgiveness. As they came to a halt outside her house, he added, 'The last thing he wants is to lose you as well.'

'But he's not going to!'

Martin turned in his seat and unexpectedly took her hand. 'Well, he might. If it has anything to do with me.' He leaned forward and put his lips to hers. It was the briefest of kisses, but when he pulled away he said, 'Cinderella is returned safely from the ball and I'm so glad I know exactly where to find her again...'

She was so shocked she could barely speak. She wanted

to say, *And what about Nora?* But he put a finger to her lips. 'Don't speak, don't break the spell, Kate. I want you to be more than just my model. I want to offer you a new life. Just think about it, think about me. Think about what John saw in my paintings of you that made him so jealous.'

He hopped out of the car and came around to open her door. A couple were strolling past and stopped to stare at the posh car, wondering to each other what on earth such a handsome, well-off couple were doing in East Lane, Bermondsey.

She didn't go to see Johnny straight away. She was too angry and too heartsick to face him. They had grown so close during the days of his mum's illness that he'd called her his anchor. And she'd let her guard down, pouring out all her love without reservation. But now she felt set adrift – his jealousy and his rage had cut the tie.

After a few days of soul-searching she went to his house. When he opened the door, he said morosely, 'I don't want to see you.'

Before he could shut the door, she slipped inside, following him into the room. He looked as if he hadn't changed his clothes since the fight at the gallery; still wearing his good shirt, he bore the bruises from Martin's fists. She'd expected him to be contrite.

'You're not still blaming me?' she asked, a hot surge of anger taking her by surprise.

'Why shouldn't I? You're the one who cheated.'

'You bloody idiot, Johnny Bacon, that's not true. I love you.'

He shook his head. 'I can't live like this, I can't compete with the likes of Martin North.'

He hadn't heard her at all. 'Well, perhaps I can't live like it either. Wondering when you'll get into a rage and start using your fists instead of listening to me... When you're angry like that, Johnny, I don't know you at all and...' She was left hanging, caught by the sudden realization of what frightened her most about his sudden rages – it was that he disappeared.

'I love you, Johnny.' She said it again. 'But I think it's best if we just go back to being friends. We'll both be happier,' she added miserably, hoping that he would raise his dear, familiar eyes to her and be himself again and say it would all be different. But instead, he turned away, saying nothing, and she could only take his silence as a goodbye. She let herself out and walked down to the river stairs, looking out over the Thames, her tears flowing as relentlessly as the tide.

It was shortly after Martin's startling proposal that Kate proved Nora wrong about her youthful wisdom. It turned out she had never been wise beyond her years when it came to her father. She had been blind and stupid and she found out just how much after a conversation with her Aunt Sarah. Kate often went to see her aunt on her evenings off, taking saveloy and pease pudding – Aunt Sarah's favourite. Kate had never received much attention from her when growing up, but now she felt sorry for the elderly spinster who for so long had been in thrall to the dream of her brother's return – the rich man who would save them all from East Lane. But one night she arrived at the house to find her aunt in tears. Kate had never before witnessed such a sight and for a moment she reacted as if hers were a normal family. She threw her arms around her aunt, asking what was wrong, only to be unceremoniously pushed away.

'Don't think this is 'cause I'm unhappy. I'm bloody angry, that's what I am – angry!' And her strangled sobs broke out again, halting and jerky as if she were swallowing a stone.

'I know that!' Kate lied. 'But what's stirred you up?'

'It's my brother – *your* father. I've found out Stan's been telling the truth all along. Archie's back in the country and never sent a word to me. I thought I was different to *her* up the lane.' She slapped her chest with her fat-fingered hand. 'That he'd never forget what I did for him... the sacrifices so he could go to St Olave's school, putting away out of me own wages for his uniform, more fool me. Shit's been me thanks.'

Kate let her aunt recover herself, not speaking until her tears had ceased. 'But, Aunt Sarah, how can you know for sure?'

'Because I took it into me own hands. Got in touch with cousin Bert in Bromley. Archie was always very friendly with him – he's got a few bob – and I says to meself, if Archie's been to see anyone, it's Bert. I got this letter today.' She flung it across the table to Kate. 'Bert says Archie's been back in the country all right and now he's sodded off abroad again. He don't care about his family, Kate. He never has!' She raised puffy eyes to Kate that were full of hurt. 'I've give up on him. You do yourself a favour and forget the ungrateful bastard,' she said, pointing a stubby finger at Kate.

Kate had only just begun to convince herself that Stan's 'revelation' about her dad had been a pack of lies, made out of spite, but now she felt as if a strong hand had reached inside to squeeze her heart till it hurt. She doubted that the particular moment Martin had captured in his painting *Dreaming* would ever happen again. Archie wouldn't be coming for her. She felt herself let go of the last faint hope and put a hand over Aunt Sarah's, asking dully, 'What did he ever give us anyway?'

After that, it was hard to live with what felt like a gaping hole in her heart. There were habits of mind that brought her continually up against this void, as if her thoughts had been used to circling a maze with Archie at its centre. A centre she now knew was empty. She wished with all her heart she could tell Johnny, but now she could never share her loss with him. For his had been so much greater. He had lost his mother, and since the fight over *The Bermondsey Triptych*, he had lost her too.

11

A Dangerous Situation

Kate never thought she'd be going to Lucy for advice. She had a sweet nature but, to Kate's thinking, hadn't an ounce of common sense. Now Kate found herself almost desperate to talk to the girl. As soon as Boutle's hooter screeched for the dinner break, Kate shot out and hurried to the bookshop. She knew Lucy was helping with stocktaking that afternoon and hoped to find a few minutes to ask her where she'd got the stupid idea that Martin was in love with her. She'd thought it was just Lucy's fantasy – a girl who seemed to fall in and out of love at the drop of a hat. But now Martin's declaration had proved Lucy right. So how had she known? When had he confided in her?

When she arrived, the shop was deserted, and she got on with giving the place a quick clean. She was upstairs mopping the reading-room floor when she heard the jangling of the door bell. Kate picked up her mop and bucket and descended, careful not to spill dirty water on her clean stairs. But it wasn't

Lucy who'd arrived. Instead, Mrs Cliffe stood in the shop, along with her chauffeur – Martin. Mrs Cliffe had a vague smile on her face and seemed at a loss. Giving her a quick nod of greeting, Kate was about to duck into the scullery when the woman asked, 'Would you happen to know, my dear, where the stock books are kept?'

Avoiding Martin's eyes, which were boring into her like hot soldering irons, she put down the bucket, wiping her hands. She hoped Martin was getting a good eyeful of her frayed overall and chapped hands. Her appearance alone, contrasting so starkly to the finely dressed Mrs Cliffe, should surely show him what an idiot he was being. She hadn't seen him since the private view, but she had received a letter in which he'd repeated his feelings for her, saying he hoped he'd made it clear he wasn't suggesting anything other than marriage. He'd ended by asking her if she would let him know when she came to a decision. She had replied, not because she wanted to but because she knew from bitter experience that silence and absence only stoked the fires of longing.

The foolish wish that she could run down to Johnny's house and ask him to check her spelling only confirmed her decision. After making several practice attempts on brown parcel paper from the bookshop, she then spent money she didn't have on some nice notepaper and painstakingly copied the best version.

Dear Martin,

I am writing because you asked me to. You said you wanted to show me another life. But, Martin, you already have done. I have seen the world you live in, and I know I would never be accepted into that world. Whatever Ethel might say about there being no class distinctions with people of like mind, I don't believe she's right. Especially when it comes to a marriage between the likes of you and me. I can't write about feelings, Martin, because they don't come into it. All I will say is that you have been very kind to me and I liked being painted by you and all our friendly talks. I will miss them.

> *Yours truly,*
> *Kate*

It wasn't eloquent; she'd only wanted to be clear. But at this moment, faced with him in the shop, her cheeks burned with embarrassment. He wouldn't take his eyes off her. And in front of Mrs Cliffe, whose mobile feather hat was now casting about the place like a lost bird.

'Here, Mrs Cliffe. In this cabinet.' Kate covered her confusion by bending down to retrieve the stock books. She put them on the long table. 'But wasn't Lucy meant to be stocktaking today?' she asked.

Mrs Cliffe approached, removing her gloves, ready to get her hands dirty in the cause. 'Something about a young gentleman – Lucy and her passing fancies. I can't keep up!' She glanced at Martin, who was standing by the door. 'You can go now, Martin dear. But be here at four o'clock sharp to collect me. It's bridge night at your mother's and you know how she hates to be kept waiting!' Martin examined his nails and Kate waited for him to obey, thinking how impossible it would be for a man like him to go against either his aunt or his mother.

'I'm afraid I have other business this afternoon, Aunt Violet. I'm taking Kate to a dance and she needs to shop for a new dress!'

Mrs Cliffe looked from Martin to Kate in disbelief and then gave a deep laugh. 'Who am I to stand in the way of a prince and his Cinders? I only wish I had a fairy wand with me.' She shook her head, still laughing. 'Off you go now, both of you. I need to get on with my stocktaking.'

Kate stood her ground. 'Mrs Cliffe, your nephew's a fool.'

She looked unperturbed. 'I'm sure his mother would agree with you, my dear.'

Kate headed into the scullery, where she tore off the apron and quickly cleared up, aware that he'd followed her. He leaned against the closed door. 'I'm no fool, Kate. I've never felt wiser. I'm following my heart – not my mother – and I *will* be taking you to the bookshop dance on Saturday.'

She turned to look at him while rolling down her sleeves. 'Didn't you get my letter?'

He nodded. 'But it's a dance, not a wedding. Ethel's invited everyone, staff, volunteers and members. I know John Bacon won't be escorting you...'

So, the word had got around that she'd broken it off with Johnny.

'What about Nora, who's escorting her?' she asked.

He seemed puzzled. 'She can't go. Her husband's due back from his business trip and, apparently, he likes her to be there to greet him.'

'Well I can't go either. I'm working on Saturday night at the Marigold.'

'I should have done another painting of you and called it *Frowning*.' His mouth turned down in a comic serious face. 'You need a bit of fun! You work so hard, surely you could take one night off? And if you're worried about me, you should know me by now – I'll be the perfect gentleman!'

But that was the thing. She didn't really know the most important thing about Martin – she didn't understand his relationship with Nora. And then, she knew nothing of his world. She didn't want to be just a novelty, nor a convenient little rebellion against his mother, without any consequences to himself. He might believe he was serious about her, but he could easily just be bored between paintings. She'd told him in her letter that feelings didn't come into it, but she'd grown to care for him, and she'd enjoyed their easy friendship. But any deeper feelings she might have for Martin North had been driven into the shadows by the fierce light of her love for Johnny.

'The perfect gentleman? No more talk about marriage!'

He laughed. 'Promise. And I meant what I said about buying you a new dress too. The success with the triptych is largely down to the model.' He waited for a response to his compliment, but she said nothing. 'Anyway – you deserve a share of the rewards.'

'You already paid me.'

He nodded. 'Yes, before I knew how much it was going to make me! Honestly, Kate. I would give you a share of the proceeds if I thought you'd accept them, so just let me do this small thing for you. A new dress, a delightful evening among friends. Nothing more. What do you say?'

He came to collect her from Boutle's at the end of the day. She'd made him promise to wait around the corner, as she couldn't bear listening to any more of Marge's warnings about posh blokes. She turned the corner of Wild's Rents and hurried to the Rolls, which was parked outside a pub. Slipping into the deep luxury of the car, she flashed him a bright smile. 'So, how often do you go shopping with girls?'

He started the engine. 'The shop owner is a friend of mine. He supplied that rose-coloured dress you looked so lovely in. He's staying open late, just for us!'

He drove through the early-evening streets, crossing the river by Waterloo Bridge, heading in the direction of his studio. She liked being driven by Martin – his hands on the steering wheel were deft and he drove with a sort of elegance, sometimes lifting a hand from the wheel to smoke a cigarette. But however fast he drove, she'd learned she needn't be anxious. He was always in control.

The shop, when they arrived in Great Portland Street, was a little unimpressive. Not much bigger than the Bermondsey Bookshop's, the frontage looked more like an ordinary house, except for the panelled front window, displaying just two dresses. Once inside, the owner kissed Martin warmly on both cheeks and Kate's hand as if she were a princess.

'Dear Martin! Come upstairs. We are well prepared for Miss Goss.'

They followed him into a long room, and Kate was astonished at the quantity of clothes crammed into it. There were rails and rails of garments, from wedding dresses and party frocks to tennis outfits. Martin's friend indicated a curtained-off dressing room, outside which were two armchairs upholstered in black-and-gold stripes. This was the very situation she'd tried to explain to Martin in her letter. She was so far from Bermondsey it might as well have been the moon. She knew that the owner, whom Martin introduced as Roberto, was just a shopkeeper, the same as Mrs Davies in the dairy in Wild's Rents, but here she felt uncomfortable whereas at the dairy she'd happily sit on a chair by the counter and chat. She tried to imagine Roberto's highly scented, perfectly suited figure running a second-hand stall down the old clo' market in Tower Bridge Road.

Martin gave her an encouraging smile and she wondered if now she was expected to go into the dressing room and try something on, but then from behind the curtain emerged a slim, long-legged woman wearing a tight ankle-length dress. She did a circuit of the room and then stood, hand on hip, in front of Kate.

Roberto looked in her direction, his chin resting on his hand. 'No. A little too old for Miss Goss, I think.' He clapped his hands and another girl appeared. Kate wondered how much they got paid for trying on dresses for other people. It was money for old rope. The black outfit was much shorter, with horizontal gold lace bands around the skirt. She didn't know if she'd be comfortable showing off so much leg and the second girl was dismissed. The two models alternated until they'd seen six dresses. While Roberto was behind the curtain organizing another one, Kate whispered to Martin, 'Can we go now? I can wear the pink dress you gave me.'

'Don't worry. Roberto's a genius. He's just warming up!'

The first model returned wearing a blue-and-violet dress. It was a shift style, but cut on the bias, so that it fell in elegant folds across the model's body, showing off her slim figure. A double hemline gave the appearance of a shorter skirt without exposing too much calf. The deep V-neck was squared off with a violet panel and the front decorated with a diagonal band of violet stitching. It was beautiful, and perhaps she had leaned forward in her chair, for Roberto swooped like an elegant swallow, leading the model to Kate so that she could get a better look. He appeared delighted.

'You picked the best! This is my absolute favourite. Would you like to try it on – just to be sure it's the right one? We may need to take it in a little here and there,' he said, eyeing her skinny shoulders.

Looking at herself in the dressing room, she appeared nothing like the Kate Goss she knew. The image blurred with tears as for a moment she saw herself walking into Boutle's wearing Janey's cast-off frock on that first day. Then her beautifully dressed self snapped back into sharp focus and the realization was heady – she could make this world hers with just one powerful word. One 'yes' to Martin would change everything. She turned to Roberto and said, 'This is the one.'

On Saturday night she emerged from her house, Nora's coat wrapped tightly around her, and pulled up the enormous white fur collar in the vain hope that she wouldn't be recognized by any passing neighbour. She was self-conscious enough without inviting any sarcastic comments. She kept her eyes firmly fixed on the pavement as she began walking to the end of the street. Martin had insisted he come to collect her, but she wasn't going to hang about for him – there was only one way into the lane, so she certainly wouldn't miss him. She looked up briefly and was surprised to spot a car approaching that wasn't the Rolls. Cars were such a rare sight here it struck her as odd that there should be two in the vicinity on the same night. But the small red car came to a halt beside her and the driver dropped down the window. 'I told you the triptych would buy me a Baby Austin! Hop in!' It was Martin. 'Isn't she beautiful?'

She examined the bright red body, with its shiny black wheel guards and gleaming headlamps. But the car had attracted the attention she'd wanted to avoid. Kids began to congregate and suddenly she heard Janey's grating voice calling her from Aunt Sylvie's front window. 'Oi, Noss Goss! I heard you was earning tart's money – what d'you have to do for a ride in that, eh?'

Martin's smile disappeared.

'Don't worry. That's just me cousin,' she explained.

'Oh, is *that* Janey?' He peered through the open window. 'I can see what you mean about the piggy eyes.' In their long hours together they'd swapped stories of their most loathed relatives. She'd heard plenty about his mother that could rival Aunt Sylvie's meanness. 'And is this the charming Stan?'

Stan was strolling towards them from Aunt Sylvie's. He wore a vest, his braces dangling around his waist, socks on his feet. He grinned. 'Oh, very nice. *Very* nice.' But he wasn't looking at the car; he was eyeing her up and down.

'Sod off, Stan,' she said, but as she attempted to duck into the car, his hand brushed her bottom and she paused to stamp on his shoeless foot.

'Ouch, you spiteful mare!' Stan hopped up and down.

'Let's just go, Martin, quick!'

As Martin started the car, Stan thumped the bonnet and shouted after them, 'So, I'll tell Mr Smith you've got enough to pay him back the lot!'

Martin sped away, and once they'd cleared East Lane he asked, 'Who's Mr Smith?'

'Oh, just someone I owe a bit of money to.'

'If you're in trouble I can always—'

'No, it's all right, Johnny got him to drop the interest. Anyway, you've done enough. Stan's right – for once! With the money I've earned modelling for you I can pay back everything I owe.'

He looked doubtful. 'So why is Stan involved?'

'He works for Mr Smith,' she said with finality, hoping he'd drop the subject.

'Well, your descriptions of the cousins didn't do them justice, Kate. They're far nastier.'

She leaned back into the seat, closing her eyes briefly, and he glanced at her. 'Have they upset you?'

'Oh, I couldn't care less what they think of me.'

But she wished with all her heart that Johnny hadn't come to his front door just as she was being driven away, for she did still care what *he* thought of her.

The St Olave's Institute was filled with faces she knew from the bookshop. The hall was decorated in the 'bookshop colours' of blue and yellow, bunting festooned the walls, blue cloths and vases of yellow flowers brightened the tables. The piano player was a bookshop member and she recognized the jazz singer as someone who'd given a lecture called 'German Lieder in Translation'. It was a memorable talk, because at first the man had threatened to send her to sleep, and then he had threatened to make her cry as he sang 'Night and Dreams' with piercing longing. The song was about someone who woke in the morning only to pray for the night to return so they could dream again. Tonight, his singing was much jollier, and suddenly she determined that she would be too.

She'd been amazed at how much a simple dance had meant to her. Before putting on her new clothes, she'd looked out of her garret window. All the greys and browns of the warehouses surrounding East Lane had turned golden – only a result of the low evening sun – but she took it for a sign that her new life was possible without her old dreams. Now she was here, she told herself she didn't need either her dad or Johnny in order to be happy.

As her coat and blue dress were gifts, the only things she'd had to buy herself were a pair of strapped shoes and a bottle of Amami shampoo. That afternoon, at the end of her Saturday shift, she'd gone to the Bermondsey public baths, taking the shampoo with her; she wasn't risking the frizz that their packets of pine needles usually produced. Now her hair was shining and her heart racing as Martin held out his hands.

'Dance?'

As the jazz singer got into his stride, couples were beginning to whirl around the smallish dance floor, gleefully bumping into each other. No one was trying to win any dance prizes tonight. She felt more confident. She put a hand on Martin's shoulder and he whizzed her elegantly into the crowd, dancing in roughly the same manner as he drove. After the singer paused for a drink, they joined Ginger Bosher, who was sitting out the dance with his wife, Fran. She was enviously eyeing the couples as they laughed and collided with each other.

'He can't dance,' she explained to Kate.

'Martin'll dance with you, Fran!' Kate suggested.

'May I dance with your wife?' Martin asked Ginger politely, and as soon as the piano started up, Fran was on her feet.

Watching them go, Ginger said, 'Thanks, Kate. It ain't much fun for Fran with me and my two left feet. He seems a nice chap.' Ginger nodded towards Martin. 'You seen anything of Rasher lately?'

'No.' She wished he hadn't reminded her of Johnny's figure at the door, watching her leave in Martin's car.

'It was a bloody show-up, what he done at the gallery, I'll give you that. But he's a good bloke, really.'

'You don't have to tell me that, Ginger. But I can't rely on him. I had enough of punch-ups at Aunt Sylvie's. I don't want to be with someone who starts using his fists every time he sees another chap paying me a bit of attention.'

Ginger nodded silently, his large feet tucked in so as not to trip the dancers. 'It's hard to understand it, if you're not the jealous type. I'm not. Look at her.' He nodded towards Fran and Martin. 'Having the time of her life and it ain't with me, but I'm not complaining.'

'Exactly! That's because you're thinking of Fran, not yourself. Johnny's had a lifetime believing he's some great catch that girls can't resist... he's too cocky by half.'

She didn't believe that and she didn't feel as harshly towards Johnny as she sounded. The truth was he didn't feel at all cocksure of himself where Martin was concerned; in fact it was the opposite, and she'd worked out that he'd rather be without her than live in fear of losing her. And all this was far too complicated to relay to Ginger Bosher right now.

Ginger took in a long breath. 'Trouble is, love, you caught him, hook, line and sinker, and if you'd seen the state of him the other night, you wouldn't say he was cocky, not at all.'

'Why?' she asked, surprised to find that Ginger knew his friend almost as well as she did. She dropped her indignation. 'What was he like?'

'He's ashamed of himself and so he bloody should be. But if you still care about him, I'd pay him a visit soon, love. The drink runs in his family and you don't want it to take hold.'

Martin delivered Fran back to her husband and invited Kate for another dance. But Ginger's news about Johnny had dampened her spirits and Martin noticed. 'Or maybe a drink?' He took her elbow, guiding her around the sides of the room to the refreshments.

A young volunteer served their drinks from behind the blue and yellow table. It was a night when Ethel had insisted all divisions of class or work should be banished, and the young woman serving was a medical student who travelled in from Kensington for the lectures.

'I should think it's a pleasant change to be on this side of the table!' he said, handing Kate her drink.

'A change? You could say that – I think it's more like a bloody good holiday!'

He laughed loudly, so that a couple of girls helping themselves to food looked up and smiled.

They took their plates of sandwiches to some chairs a little away from the singer. She hadn't eaten all day and the dainty ham triangles were good. She ate three before he'd even started his.

'Kate...'

She knew what was coming. 'No, Martin. You promised not to talk about it. Eat your sandwiches.'

Obediently, he chewed in silence, then brushed crumbs from his trousers, stood up and offered her his hand. 'Come on then, let's make the most of your holiday.'

After that evening Martin came for her once a week, usually on Saturday evening but sometimes on Sunday afternoons, when, as the first signs of spring appeared, they would motor out to Kent in the Baby Austin. The apple blossoms came early that year and she began to feel free, and sometimes even happy, as they skimmed along narrow lanes with clouds of white and pink frothing over every hedge. He never spoke again of loving her or marrying her. She knew that if he'd pushed the subject on the night of the dance, that would have been the end of it for her. But because he turned out to be just like Ginger Bosher, putting his own feelings aside, happy that she was happy, she carried on going about with him, trying out the new world that he offered, letting the unusual feeling of unfettered affection and fun be her guide.

But happiness, like the apple blossom, was double coloured. A stain of doubt over his history with Nora still cautioned her, but more than that, deep veins of sadness tinged her heart when she thought of Johnny. Ginger's warning about his drinking had been playing on her mind. Part of her thought she should just let it go, but she had told Johnny they could still be friends, and a friend wouldn't leave him to go the way of his mother. She made up her mind to pay him a visit, prepared for him to be as uncommunicative as when she'd last seen him. When he answered the door, his expression was muted, his eyes were red-rimmed and bruised with tiredness and he sported a two-day growth of beard. He looked as if he'd been sleeping in his clothes. He let her in without a word. She looked around the tiny room.

'Your mum's bed's still here.'

He looked at it, almost surprised. 'Oh, yeah. I didn't know what to do with it.'

'Perhaps you should give it to the Sally Ann – you'd have a lot more room.' She felt guilt twist her gut. She should have been here all along helping him.

There was a bottle of brandy on the table. She walked over to it and shook it – there wasn't much left. 'Have you been clearing out your mum's hiding places?'

'It's the last of it.' His gaze slid away to the scullery and she knew he had more there.

'Do you really want to end up like her?'

He clenched his fists and she prepared herself for an outburst. Instead he ran his fingers through his untidy hair. 'Sit down, Kate, for chrissake. Or ain't you stopping?'

She sat down. 'You can make me a cup of tea, if you've got any.'

Once she would have leaped up to make it, but now she waited while he filled the kettle and spooned tea into the pot. She looked for trembling, but his hands seemed steady, if a little grimy.

He put the tea in front of her and sipped his own.

'You need to sort yourself out, Johnny. Get down Bermondsey Baths, have a haircut and start taking a pride in yourself again. Your mum wouldn't be happy to see you like this.'

He sighed. 'My mum wouldn't have noticed if I'd gone out in the street stark naked, she certainly didn't care if me hair was washed.'

'When she was sober she did. What about when you was a kid and come home up to your neck in Thames mud? She tanned your hide – all the way up the lane and back again!'

The memory brought a smile to his face. 'She did, didn't she?' He rubbed tears from his eyes and they sat in silence for a minute until he had recovered. He got up and took the brandy bottle into the scullery. She heard him pouring the contents into the stone sink, then went to join him. He retrieved beer and spirits bottles from behind the kitchen cupboard and underneath the copper. She watched as he poured them away. When it was done, he said, 'Kate, I should've come and apologized. I should never have done that – at the gallery. You must have been so embarrassed, and I don't blame you for not wanting to have anything to do with me now.'

'It wasn't the embarrassment that hurt, Johnny. It was that you never trusted me about Martin. And it's not that I don't want nothing to do with you – I do still care about you.'

He looked her properly in the eyes for the first time. 'But I *was* right. You two are courting now.'

She hadn't come for a row. She took a couple of breaths before answering. 'No – you were *wrong*! But we go out to different places together. I'm trying to get on with me life but, Johnny, it's not what you think.'

His eyes suddenly filled with hope. 'If I get myself sorted out, would you give me another chance?'

She thought carefully before answering. 'Come and ask me that again when the old Johnny's back.'

But after that, days had passed and then weeks and Johnny hadn't come to her, and she'd not wanted to seek him out, for fear of what she might find.

Kate found herself looking forward to Monday nights. After the French class had finished Nora would help her clear up, and then, with the cosy reading room to themselves, they would talk. Kate found it hard to explain why it was so easy to be with Nora. It shouldn't have been. Perhaps it was Ethel's vision for the equalizing force of the bookshop; perhaps it was because the two women, for all their vastly different material wealth, had a similar family history; perhaps it was that Nora had always seemed friendless, lonely. Kate knew by now that her reserved manner could easily be penetrated and she was always glad when she could make Nora laugh – usually with her tales of the old 'Marigolds' or the Boutle's girls.

Tonight Nora seemed more subdued than usual. As they sipped hot cocoa and ate cake left over from class, Kate asked, 'Did I ever tell you about mad old Longbonnet?'

Nora shook her head and Kate got up, bent her body like

an old woman and imitated Longbonnet's direful warnings. Nora laughed at the imitation, but then stared into her cocoa, running a fingertip around the cup. Perhaps she wasn't in the mood for a chat tonight. Kate started gathering up plates. 'Well, I'd better let you get home.'

Nora's head shot up. 'Oh, no. There's nothing to go home for,' she said, sadness clouding her face.

'Your husband's away again?'

'He'll be back tomorrow. He's been setting up a new venture. It's a lot of work.'

'Do you miss him when he's gone?' Kate asked, aware she was on dangerous ground. Nora never seemed to like talking about her marriage.

'Well, of course, but to be honest, after he's home I often wish him gone again!'

'I can understand that. Men can get in the way, can't they?'

Nora smiled. 'Chibby doesn't just get in the way, he fills every available space in my life. When he's home he wants me all to himself – sometimes it's hard even to get to the bookshop. Though I'm determined not to give it up. I've so enjoyed it.'

'Has he asked you to give it up?'

'No, he wouldn't do that. It was Mrs Cliffe's idea for me to volunteer and Chibby is very keen to keep Violet happy.'

'Why?'

'Because she's largely funding his new project.'

'Oh? But why does he need her money when he's got yours?'

Nora flushed and Kate realized she had asked one of those questions that Aunt Sylvie used to answer with a wallop.

'I'm sorry! Sometimes I just blurt out these things, Nora! Just ignore me.'

But the damage had been done and she could see she'd

rattled Nora's usual composure. She lifted eyes, not angry but sad, and said, 'Kate, you always ask exactly the *right* question. The one other people won't. That's why I liked you immediately. The answer is that much of my inheritance is gone. Chibby made some bad business decisions, but he's convinced this latest venture will get us everything back. I'm sure it's largely why Violet agreed to help. She's doing it for me.'

'Good old Vi,' Kate said with a grin.

Again, Kate was rewarded with a chuckle from Nora. 'Speaking of good old Vi, she tells me that Martin's turned into quite a rebel and it's all your fault! You're seeing quite a lot of each other, I hear.'

'A bit. Whatever he says, I know it'll never come to anything.'

'And what is it he says?' Nora was alert now, her dreamy sadness seeming to have evaporated.

Kate shrugged. 'He's young in his head. He says he's in love with me. But you told me to be careful of him...'

There was a stillness in the air between them. Nora let out a long sigh. 'I can't really speak for Martin, but I do believe the situation is dangerous for you. Unequal matches are... full of challenges, my dear young Kate.'

Kate wondered if Nora was talking about her own marriage, but she daren't voice any more questions. She'd got away with one too many tonight.

'I'll be careful, Nora. I don't expect nothing of no one these days,' she said wistfully.

And Nora patted her hand. 'Perhaps that is the best way to be, after all.'

★

Her talk with Nora left Kate wanting to ask other questions. She knew more about Nora, but less about Martin. She had got used to his easy-going charm, and she wouldn't pretend she wasn't flattered by the attentions of such a handsome, wealthy young man. But she'd also found herself liking him so much more than she'd ever expected to. It wasn't that she had forgotten Johnny; it was that love had been transformed into regret. And so she'd locked him away in a secret part of her heart and hidden the key, even from herself. Nora was right – it was a dangerous situation.

Nora had left her saying she'd be back the following afternoon. Ethel was unwell, so Nora had volunteered at short notice to run the bookshop for the evening. Kate wondered how her husband would view her disappearance on the very day of his return. At lunchtime Kate tried the door, hoping Nora might already be there, but it was locked. She searched out the spare key from its hiding place and was opening the door when she saw Nora emerging from her car, a little further down Bermondsey Street. Kate decided to wait for her. But then someone else got out of the car. He came around to the passenger side and took Nora's hands in his. Kate's curiosity was piqued and, half hidden in the doorway, she studied him. He was a tall man, at least ten or twelve years older than Nora, elegantly dressed in a well-cut grey suit and black homburg hat. He had a pale complexion and a longish face with a neatly clipped red-gold beard. He leaned closer to kiss Nora on the lips. Now Kate stood, transfixed. Trying to think how he could possibly be here, kissing her friend. The only explanation was that this was Nora's husband. But that was impossible, for Kate knew the man. How she knew him, where or when she'd met him, she had no idea, but of one thing she was certain – she needed to find out before she could face Nora again.

12

Chibby

Kate ducked back into the shop, banged the door behind her and locked it. Her heart was racing and her blood pumping so hard she heard its dull thudding in her temples. Time seemed to stand still as she trawled her memory. How many striking, prosperous, powerful-looking men had she met in her lifetime? None. Her view of him had been fleeting but she concentrated on his features now: the pale, thin face, the hooded eyes – startling blue even at a distance. She replayed how he'd leaned forward to kiss Nora on the lips... It was perhaps the kiss that unlocked her memory – for although he was twelve years older than the last time Kate had seen him, the man who had just kissed Nora goodbye was not her husband Chibby, he was Archie Goss, Kate's father.

She could barely breathe. This was impossible! Unless she'd been mistaken. Had she for so long imagined her father's return that she put his likeness onto anyone who looked vaguely like him? She'd only been six when he'd left,

MARY GIBSON

but surely she could not forget her own father? She closed her
eyes, feeling a wave of nausea wash over her. It was true, she
knew in her heart that it was. But it would take time for her
brain to catch up with her heart and she didn't have time, for
Nora was knocking on the door to be let in.

'Kate, Kate! Are you in there? I can't find the spare key!'

Kate moved swiftly away from the door. First, she rushed
to the scullery, then changed her mind and turned, hurrying
for the stairs. From the reading-room window she'd be able
to check if Nora was alone. She twitched the painted hanging
and peered into the street below. Nora was still searching
for the key in its hiding place under the step. Abruptly she
stood and looked up. Nora had seen her. She smiled, then
mimicked a key turning in a lock. In a daze of uncertainty,
Kate moved to the centre of the room, tripping over a low
table as she went, seeming to view herself from a long way
off. This was so far removed from all her imagined reunions
with Archie Goss, if it really was him, that she had no plan
to follow. All her rehearsed speeches about missing him and
believing in him for all these years, all her practised scenes of
forgiveness, had evaporated at her first sight of him kissing
Nora.

On unsteady legs, she slowly descended the stairs. Feeling
sick, she took in a deep breath to still her trembling as she
fumbled to unlock the door.

'I've been knocking and knocking! Couldn't you hear me
from up there?' Nora took a step into the bookshop and then
stopped. 'Kate, you look like you've seen a ghost! Are you
feeling unwell?'

Kate shook her head and turned away, hiding her face. 'I'm
all right, thanks. I'll just finish off upstairs.'

Nora took off her gloves and hat, following her. 'No,

you're not all right,' she insisted, puzzlement in her voice. Kate's limbs were heavy, each stair a monumental effort. She kept her back to Nora, scared the woman might see into her heart. At the top step, she stumbled, and Nora, who was close behind, caught her before she could fall.

'Now I know you're not well, let me help you!'

Nora supported Kate to an easy chair and fetched water from the kitchen.

'Kate, this is ridiculous, you're working yourself to death. Do you really need three jobs?'

'Yes, I bloody well do! I never had a rich father to leave me a fortune like you, I've had to fend for meself!'

Nora's eyes widened in shock. 'I'm sorry. I know you've had a very hard life. I just thought that now you're doing more modelling for Martin, you might give up the bar work.' Her luminous eyes reflected hurt and concern, but not, Kate was ashamed to see, any anger.

'If I've said something to upset you, Kate, I'm sorry. I thought we were friends – that we could talk about anything. If it was what I said about Martin being dangerous before, well, I was only thinking of you.'

'It's not about Martin.' Kate's voice was harsh, and suddenly she felt cruel. It wasn't Nora's fault; she was obviously completely in the dark. 'It's not even about you,' she said, more gently. 'It's about the man who was in your car.'

Now Nora looked even more puzzled. 'Just now? You mean Chibby?'

So, it was true – Archie was her husband. 'That's what *you* call him.'

'It's a pet name. I've always detested Archibald. Actually, he came back from abroad only this morning, and I was a little worried about telling him I had to go out, but he had some business near London Bridge and said we might as well drive over together. I don't understand why the sight of him has so upset you. I must have made him seem quite a bully, but—'

'No, that's not it.' She took in a deep breath and fixed her eyes on Nora. Kate needed to be sure Nora had no idea who he was. 'You call him Chibby.'

'Yes, as I said.'

'My mum used to call him Archie. I used to call him Dad.'

Nora gripped the edge of the table, steadying herself. 'What? No, no, you're mistaken, Kate. Chibby can't be your father.' She was shaking her head, certain.

Kate nodded slowly. 'I know who he is. I've pictured him every night for twelve years, hoping he'd come for me, until I found out he's been back in the country for over a year and never told me.'

Nora shook her head. 'No, that can't be right... What's your surname, Kate? I don't even know it with Ethel's first names policy...'

'Goss, I'm Kate Goss.'

Nora looked relieved. 'Well then, that settles it, Chibby's name is Archibald Grainger. He's not your father, Kate.' She shook her head in disbelief.

'People can change their names – and I remember what me own dad looks like, Nora!'

Nora stood, like a pale statue. She plucked her lower lip, trying to make sense of Kate's revelation. 'I told you, I met Chibby when he was serving in France in 1915. Chibby told me he was a widower. Estranged from his family – they'd disapproved of his marriage. He said he'd raised himself up out of squalor, that the family was only interested in sponging off him... You have to understand, I was only sixteen when I met him. My father had recently died. I had no one. Chibby was much older than me, of course. He is a wonderfully capable man, accomplished, clever... I never questioned...' As Nora replayed her history, Kate thought she saw her certainty begin to evaporate. But now, she straightened her shoulders and thrust out her chin. 'I *know* he'll have an explanation for this.'

'Well, it'll have to be a bloody good one.'

The bookshop did not get cleaned at all. They talked until Kate's dinner hour was up, examining every possible reason for Archie Goss's or Chibby Grainger's behaviour. Before Kate returned to Boutle's, they agreed to tell no one else until they'd given him a chance to explain.

'I'll wait till tomorrow before I speak to him about it,' Nora said. 'It'll be eleven before I can leave tonight, and Chibby will be in bed before then – he's had such a long, tiring journey.'

'All the way from Canada?'

Nora nodded, looking surprised. 'But how did you know?'

Kate gave a bitter laugh. 'Whenever I asked Aunt Sylvie why my dad never came to see me, the excuse was either the war or his business in Canada. I got to hate the very name of the place.'

'It seems there are a good many coincidences...'

Soon Nora would be as sure as she was that Chibby was Archie, but let her go home and ask him for herself.

'We'll talk again about this tomorrow – after the play reading. I promise we'll sort all this out then, Kate.' Nora put a cool hand to Kate's cheek. 'You must take this evening off and try not to worry. I trust Chibby to do the right thing.'

For someone who'd just learned that her husband was not the person she thought he was, Nora was remarkably confident and self-controlled. Kate admired her. She was so much tougher than she looked.

Kate decided to follow Nora's advice. She'd skip her stint at the elocution lesson tonight, but she had to return to Boutle's this afternoon. She was grateful for the comforting familiarity and monotony. Heating irons in coke ovens, soldering seams, stacking completed tins, chasing the cleaner who'd taken over from Conny – all felt safe and secure. Only once she was home in her garret in East Lane did the real torment begin.

Though she thought she'd abandoned all her expectations of Archie Goss, that night, she realized he still had absolute power over her. The fairy tales she'd conjured about him still held sway and she wished she had no imagination. She wished she could be like Marge, who took everything at face value and romanticized no one, not even her husband, though she loved him. Don't be fooled by any man, Marge had warned her more than once. Don't be taken in by good looks, they're all selfish bastards underneath it, and it's the women make the sacrifices to keep things going. Why couldn't Kate be as practically minded? She knew it had something to do with her mother, and those fairy tales about scullery maids marrying handsome princes. Her mother. Whose voice was as sweet as Nora's, whose eyes as sad, whose touch as gentle. And then it struck her. The similarities: the dark colouring, the delicate features. Archie Goss had a type, and the original was Kate's mother.

She tossed and turned and lay for a while staring through the dormer window at the stars and crescent moon, slicing an indigo sky. She gave up and, lighting the lamp, pulled out her tin box and began looking for Archie. There wasn't much to go on. The photograph of him in uniform had always been a comfort: the face clean-shaven, not particularly youthful even then, when he must have been in his late twenties; the hooded eyes, sleepy, confident; the smile, lopsided, self-assured. But now she studied the background more carefully. The French town was in ruins, the blurry figures never of interest till now: an old lady carrying a basket; a shoeless boy, hands in pockets. But that young girl, leaning against a tree? Could it be Nora? And was that chateau in the distance hers? Archie's history, which Kate had largely written herself, now belonged to Nora. Even this photo, which Kate had treasured, imagining it had been taken specially for her, now seemed more like a memento for Archie's sweetheart. Even the cocky pose proclaimed him the conquering hero – a man his beloved could trust with her future.

She finally fell asleep in the chair with the tin box on her lap and was woken in the early hours when it clattered to the floor. When she thought of the day ahead and Nora's promised report of her talk with Chibby, she felt weary beyond her years. She wasn't even sure she had the energy or desire to face the truth.

They met in the Hand and Marigold before the play-reading session that evening. The snug had nothing to recommend it other than being little frequented and quiet. Kate heard the piano strike up in the saloon bar, another mournful Irish song – the only thing the Marigolds loved better than a sad song was a rude one.

This wasn't the best place to bring Nora, but she couldn't think of anywhere else. Though Kate's eyes had been glued to the snug door for ten minutes, Nora's appearance was still a surprise. She wore a dark green coat and hat, with a peacock-blue scarf wound around her slender neck. The perfect planes of her face were gilded by gas lamps dotted around the walls. She looked nervous.

Kate half rose, attracting Nora's attention, which was hardly necessary as there was no one else in the snug. She quickly sat down again, feeling so anxious she could barely breathe. Nora sat at the table and Kate, suddenly wanting to put off the conversation, asked, 'What do you want to drink?'

Nora reached for the small handbag she'd placed on the table. 'Please, let me pay.'

'There's no need. I work here. It'll be on the house.' Which wasn't true, it would be docked from her wages.

She came back with brandies, suspecting they would both be in need of them. Nora took a sip of hers and Kate a gulp. It burned her throat.

Nora got straight to the point. 'It's as I thought, dear Kate. Chibby has explained it all. It is a very sad tale indeed. And I believe every word of it.'

'Tell me the story, then.'

'I already knew that Chibby's estranged family was from Bermondsey. I think it was one of the reasons I agreed to volunteer at the bookshop when Violet Cliffe asked me – and perhaps for the same reason, Chibby was totally against it. He has no good memories of the place, nor of his family, a bad bunch, he says, whom he wanted to distance himself from. So he'd changed his surname, before he met me, from Goss to Grainger. When I told him about you and asked why he'd never mentioned having a daughter, he broke down completely. Chibby is devastated, Kate. Utterly heartbroken to think that you have been patiently waiting for him to come back all these years. I'm afraid you have both been wronged by a very wicked woman.'

Kate had forgotten to breathe and so her voice, when it came, was a strangulated whisper. 'Aunt Sylvie?'

She nodded. 'He entrusted you to her and she betrayed him. When he left for the war he sent his child allowance and most of his army pay to Sylvie and, of course, asked after your health, and always the answer came back that you were thriving and well cared for, but that you were not settling into life with the family.'

'Of course I wasn't, they treated me like a slave! And I don't know how much he sent home, but not a brass farthing was spent on me!'

'But Chibby didn't know that. Your aunt insisted you'd never settle if he kept coming and going in your life – and then later, as the war dragged on, she told him the most wicked lie of all. That you had turned against him, blamed him for leaving you, and refused point-blank to see him! Of course, now he's racked with guilt for not coming to see for himself. He trusted her.'

Kate sat back in her chair and took another gulp of the brandy; this time, it didn't burn enough. 'Why would she lie like that about me?'

'Spite and greed. When the war ended Chibby's army pay and allowance stopped. He went back into business, and of course sent money for you, but she wanted more and more. His business took off and he was bombarded with begging letters from the family. Chibby can be ruthless, I admit, and he squashed any idea Sylvie might have had that he was an endless money pot. So, she took her revenge. She deprived him of his greatest treasure.'

'Aunt Sylvie told me it was grief – the reason he never come back to Bermondsey to see me. Grief over me mum, because it brought all the memories back.'

'I know he loved your mother very much. And for a time, I think that grief might have been the reason, but then the war came, when every day could mean death. How would it be if he came back into your life one week, only to be removed the next?'

'He should have come himself, or at least he could have written to me!'

'He didn't think he would be welcome.'

'Sod welcome! He was me dad, he should have been looking after me!' A sob broke like a wave from the depth of her stomach and she swallowed it. What was the point of railing at Nora? She was only the messenger. Up until now, Nora had been intent on pleading Chibby's cause, but now Kate saw a slight nod of her head. An acknowledgement that he was not blameless. She paused and her gaze seemed to turn inward for a second. 'Chibby is not easy around children. He's a man of business, of action, he loves striking deals, he loves many things, fine food, music, books... but he does not love domesticity. It's why he's away so much. I'm sure half the time someone else could be overseeing those business transactions, but he must always go himself...'

'But he never even told you about me.'

Nora shifted uncomfortably in her seat. 'No. He wouldn't have done. The subject of children is a difficult one for us personally – we have our differences, Kate.'

She didn't want to press the woman about her marriage. It was enough that Nora had been faced with the secret of Kate's existence. She could imagine the conversation between the two hadn't been as comfortable as Nora might make out.

They sat in silence for a moment and then Nora said, 'When you meet him, you mustn't be disappointed if he seems...' She searched for the word '...cool.' Odd that it was the word Johnny had once used to describe Nora herself. 'He hides his feelings very deeply, but they are there.'

'So, he does want to meet me?'

'Of course he does! He needs to explain all this himself, but he thought it would be better for me to prepare the ground. In case you didn't want to see him.'

'I do! I've wanted to see him every day since I was six,' Kate said, remembering the last sight she'd had of him from Aunt Sylvie's doorstep. The lopsided smile, the slow wave of his large, freckled hand and how after he'd turned the corner, Aunt Sylvie had dragged her back inside. Now she wanted to kill her.

The drama group were reading *Lady Huntworth's Experiment*. She gathered from snippets overheard from the kitchen that the heroine was an aristocrat divorcee whose ex-husband had gambled and drunk away her fortune, so that she'd been forced to disguise herself as a cook to make some money. It was meant to be humorous and Kate smiled at some of the lines. She admired how the heroine bravely took on a world that was not her own. The girl playing the divorcee was far too young, but she had good timing and her posh accent was convincing. One line of the heroine's to her ex-husband struck her as oddly coincidental: *When [Father] died, I inherited a fortune – and my freedom – without much notion what to do with either. That was a bad year for me. I lost my father and I found you.*

At least during the play reading and afterwards, serving

tea, her murderous thoughts towards Aunt Sylvie had time
to subside. She walked home past Aunt Sarah's house and
found it hard not to stop and tell her aunt about Archie. But,
according to Nora, he regarded 'the family' as spongers, a
judgement she assumed must include her Aunt Sarah, who
had never struck Kate as being motivated so much by money
as by love. She might have pretended to wash her hands of
her brother Archie, but Kate doubted she really had. But it
was harder still to walk past Aunt Sylvie's, who she didn't
doubt was motivated entirely by money and not the least
by love. She halted for a moment, staring at the darkened
windows, realizing how much she'd changed. The old Kate
would certainly have kicked the door in and pulled the old
witch from her bed.

Her meeting with Archie would not be as she'd always
imagined it. Nora said he wouldn't come to Bermondsey and
was unsure if Kate would want to come to their home. He
would send the car to collect her – not from East Lane, but
from the bookshop – and they would meet at his business
premises, which he thought would be private enough, but
neutral. She wished Archie had come to collect her himself.
But perhaps a first meeting in a car would have been awkward.
She would have felt awkward going to his house too, so
maybe he'd got the meeting place just right.

She sat in the back as they drove across Tower Bridge and
passed the looming dark presence of the Tower. It was a warm,
bright day, but the massive, soot-stained old fortress seemed
to absorb all the light bouncing off the river. They circuited
the Tower and she was surprised when they turned into Lower
Thames Street and began slowing down. She knew that Nora
lived in Belgravia and she'd assumed that Archie's business
premises would be in the same posh area of London. Ancient

wharfside offices and the colonnaded Custom House took up much of the busy street. But as they approached Billingsgate fish market they slowed almost to a halt.

'Not far now, Miss Goss. That's if we can get through this lot!' the driver explained, tooting his horn at a young boy pushing a hand barrow piled high with fish crates. The whole street was jammed with barrows, horses, carts and lorries going to the market. As she peered through the window, some porters walked past, baskets of fish piled high on their flat, black hats. One turned his head to wink at her and still managed to keep his load balanced.

Eventually they turned down an alleyway, barely wide enough for the car, stopping outside a tall, narrow house with a bow window jutting over the river like a captain's cabin on a sailing ship.

The driver helped her out and showed her to the front door. He pushed it open and they stepped into a dim passageway. It was panelled with dark, old wood and the stairs in front of her were steep, furthering the impression that she'd entered a ship.

'I believe Mr Grainger is in the downstairs office.' He indicated a long bench for her to sit on while she waited to be announced. She felt sick with anticipation, half wishing that she'd never found her father, dreading the possibility that he would be different to her memory of him. Cool, as Nora had warned. But there was no more time to anticipate – the driver was beckoning her through. He stepped aside as she entered a spacious, shadowy room, wood-panelled like the passage and with a solid wooden desk in front of the bow window. Its dusty panes let in enough light to reveal, sitting in an armchair next to the fireplace, the figure of Archie Goss, her father.

At sight of her he stood up. Her brief glimpse of him in Bermondsey Street had been deceiving. Now, at closer quarters, he looked older than his thirty-seven years. The pale, freckled face was thin and full of fine wrinkles, and his wavy, sandy hair had begun to recede into a widow's peak. But the hooded blue eyes were bright and vital as they first narrowed, then widened to take her in.

'Hello, Dad.' She hesitated in the doorway.

'Katy? My little Katy?'

She was struck by a powerful longing as she remembered he'd been the only person ever to call her Katy. He opened wide his arms and she ran into them. Powerful arms that wrapped around her, clasping her tight against his muscular chest. He didn't speak as he held her, but she heard his heart pounding. Perhaps a sign that he'd been as nervous as herself. Eventually, he held her at arm's length.

'You've grown into such a beautiful young woman, Katy. The image of your poor mother.'

His voice sounded so different to her memory of it. Deeper, more cultured and assured, but to her his Bermondsey origins were still evident in certain words, and she was glad he didn't sound like a complete stranger. Now, after all the years of anticipation, she was struck dumb, overawed by his presence. He led her to the armchair opposite his own.

She was facing the bow window and could just see the muddy Thames flowing fast and high beyond. It suddenly struck her that opposite this office, downriver a little, on the south bank, was East Lane. What if one day she'd been looking out of the dormer at the lights on the north side and one of them had been his? She felt sad at the thought, and angry too.

'To think that all these years you've been just across the water.' She turned her eyes from the window, back to his. 'Almost touching distance.'

'Katy, I'm sorry. Sorry I never came for you. Sorry I believed Sylvie when she said you hated me. I know now what a fool I was, but I thought it was for the best not to upset you...'

She dropped her head, studying her tightly folded hands, noticing the knuckles had turned white. 'I never hated you,' she whispered, then went on as he leaned forward to catch her words. 'I always loved you, Dad, and I always knew one day... one day... you'd come back.'

'It makes me feel so much better to know that. Nora's told me a little of what you went through and I can't help blaming myself. I knew Sylvie was a money grubber, but I never expected she'd treat you so cruelly. I hear you've been nothing more than a servant in that house.' His large fist curled and he thumped the arm of his chair. She hadn't found him cool, as Nora had warned he might be. He'd greeted her warmly and now the blue eyes flashed and seemed to burn. 'Treating you like a skivvy! My daughter!'

She was wearing a green shift frock, with short sleeves and a white-trimmed collar. He seemed to be scrutinizing the frock and she felt an instant's awkwardness at its cheapness. Without warning, he stood and in one quick stride was beside her. Lifting her arm, he asked, 'Is that an old injury?'

The long white scar hadn't seemed to fade over time. It stood out a stark reminder of that violent encounter with her aunt.

'Oh, that. It's not old. Last year I give Janey a broken nose for saying bad things about Mum. So Aunt Sylvie give me this.' She twisted her forearm so he could better see the scar.

'Stuck a kitchen knife in me. But that's in the past. It did me a favour!' she said, affecting a false, bright tone. 'She chucked me out and I've been a lot happier living on me own, fending for meself.'

His eyes narrowed, so that the hooded lids almost obscured their brightness. Smoothing the scar with his powerful, pale hands, he said in a low voice, 'Sylvie will regret she ever laid a hand on my child.'

If only he knew how many times she'd felt that hand. But she wouldn't tell him, not now, nor ever.

'And did they always disparage your mother?'

'I never believed them, Dad.' She'd called him Dad, but the word seemed to mock her dreams of this day, for he didn't seem at all like her dad.

'They were against her from the start. Always complaining I'd married beneath me.'

'But you didn't think that, did you?' she asked.

He shot her a questioning look. 'How could I? I loved your mother!'

He let her arm drop and went back to the armchair. 'But now I want to hear everything. Everything you remember from your childhood to this day, everything that happened at Sylvie's. *All* the unkindnesses, all the slights, all the pains.' He'd obviously seen through her pretended unconcern. 'What's your earliest memory?'

He rested his elbows on his knees and leaned in closer. The large hands massaged each other and his intense blue eyes seemed ready to record every incident of her life. She felt her heart swell. She drank in the attention. This was what she had wanted, what she'd imagined it would be like to have him back. He was interested in her. Finally, she was happy.

'I remember the day you left...' She paused, and he interrupted.

'No, before that. Surely you must remember when you were very small and we lived in the garret?'

She smiled. 'I remember little things. Mum reading me fairy tales – she had such a beautiful soft voice – and even the scary bits didn't bother me, because she was there...'

She had noticed, while sitting with him, that his energy was channelled into a constant motion. He was either kneading his hands together or jiggling a foot or rubbing his face. But now his whole body was stilled. 'Yes, your mother was a great reader. Unusual for someone of her upbringing and heritage. The tragedy robbed you of so much – I wish you'd known her for longer. Remember anything about me from those days?' he asked, raising a thick, sandy eyebrow.

He seemed eager and she didn't want to disappoint him by saying 'you were always away', so she said, 'I remember when you came home you always made a fuss of me, and I remember how Mum used to give you all her attention and then I had to sleep in my own bed. I used to get a bit jealous!'

He laughed, the first time she'd heard that laugh in twelve years. It was more like a small explosion.

'You were always her little darling. There was nothing to be jealous of. From the day you were born, you were first in her affections.

'And the tragedy, do you remember that? I wasn't a good father to you then... I didn't explain, I was so wrapped up in my own grief. I'm sorry.'

She noticed he had twice referred to her mother's dying as 'the tragedy', as if it was easier for him to deal with a tragedy than a death.

'I don't, remember much about that night. Just the next morning when Aunt Sarah told me Mum had gone to heaven. It felt so lonely without her, and I remember I wouldn't let go of your hand. After you left me, being lonely just become a way of life.'

He reached across the small distance between them, taking her hands in his, and with fierce urgency said, 'You'll never have to be lonely again.'

13

Mudlark

She wanted to tell everyone. But most of all she wanted to tell Aunt Sarah, the one person about whom her father had expressed interest. At his office, when Kate had mentioned his eldest sister, his face had clouded with sadness.

'I would have liked to stay friends with Sarah,' he'd admitted. 'She did a lot for me when I was a boy. I was only twelve when your grandmother died and Sarah brought me up. But it turned out her and Sylvie are cut from the same cloth when it comes to money. As soon as I started making a success of myself it was all about what they could get out of me.'

'But they're not really the same, Aunt Sarah hates Aunt Sylvie!'

'That's just jealousy – Sarah thought I was giving Sylvie more. My family!' He'd shaken his head sadly.

She'd wanted to stick up for her Aunt Sarah, to say that the woman had idolized him, but how could she know anything for certain about either of her aunts when Sylvie had lied to her for years, deliberately scuppering all her childhood hopes and dreams?

'Perhaps Aunt Sarah's changed. She's getting old and she's all on her own. I think she'd just like a visit from you...'

He hadn't answered; instead, before she left, he'd asked her not to mention their reunion to either aunt. 'Leave all that to me,' he'd said. 'They'll find out soon enough.' But he hadn't forbidden her to tell anyone else.

The bookshop closed for three months in the summer. Ethel and her husband went on holiday to France, and the volunteers, many of whom were students, went back to their family homes. The orange shutters went up and the lectures and meetings ceased. Kate was surprised to find she missed Ethel and the women volunteers, for in spite of all her misgivings, she'd come to regard them as friends. But the more pressing loss was that of a good portion of her income, which was why she'd welcomed Martin's proposal of a new painting.

He'd finished his preliminary sketches and on a Saturday afternoon shortly after her meeting with Archie Goss, she went to Martin's studio. Now he was arranging her into just the right pose in front of the tall windows – which were a torment on this hot afternoon. Even though Martin had opened the windows, not a breath of air penetrated the room. She was hot and impatient.

'Why does it take so bloody long to set me up? You've got the sketches, can't you just do it from those?'

'What I'd really like to do is take you down to the Thames, tie you to a post and leave you there till the tide comes in!'

he replied testily, bending her body forward a little and tilting her head. She was meant to be looking for treasure in the Thames', mud and he wanted her to hold something between her fingers, then look up at him, as if she'd just found it.

'Perfect! Stay like that, it's exactly the way you looked when you found that clay pipe!'

It hadn't been much of a find. 'I wish I'd never taken you down the foreshore,' she grumbled, which was true. Not just because she'd set herself up for some uncomfortable hours holding excruciating poses, but because it felt disloyal to Johnny. Mudlarking had always been their childhood game, even though it probably had more significance in her memory than his. Most of the time when they'd played along the foreshore, he'd barely noticed her, which had only spurred her on to find some special treasure, one that would stand out from the endless fragments of green glass and tarnished metal. One time she'd found a silver coin, with an indistinct face on it. She'd given it to Johnny. And when they'd started courting, he'd told her he still had it. She hadn't believed him, until he'd brought out a little black bag of his own finds and there amongst them was her silver coin. She'd taken it as a sign that they'd always been bound – the coin sitting there for all those years had silently spoken of a love she'd never uttered. Now she didn't like to think of it. Perhaps she'd taken Martin to the Thames to punish Johnny. In any event, she now regretted it.

Today in the studio she had on the same small-brimmed straw hat she'd been wearing on their day of mudlarking, when Martin had made sure to take off his smart two-tone shoes, tying the laces together and slinging them around his neck. His white trousers, rolled up to his calves, had soon been mud spattered, but he'd just laughed, saying it was a small price to pay for buried treasure. He'd soon tired of searching out the flotsam and jetsam, though, and had leaned against a piling, sketching her against the backdrop of Tower Bridge. They'd soon attracted the inevitable attention of kids combing the mud and he'd seemed to enjoy that too, including them in his sketches. The thing about Martin, she had to admit, was that he was at heart a happy person, and when she was with him, she found it easy to be happy too. Besides, she couldn't be grumpy for long. The secret happiness about her father which she carried would break out at the oddest times. She'd passed Stan in the street and found herself smiling at him. He'd almost smiled back until he remembered that he hated her and told her to sod off. Now, in spite of her aching back as she held the pose, she smiled again.

'That's a very nice smile, but it's changed... you had the expression just right before.' Martin was working swiftly at his blue outline.

But she couldn't repress the smile.

'All right, what is it? Let me in on the joke.'

'It's no joke, Martin. It's the best thing that has ever happened to me!'

His face fell. 'You're back with John Bacon,' he said, laying down his brush and coming to her.

She shook her head, standing up straight. 'No, I'm not.' She paused, savouring the moment. 'I'm back with me dad!'

'Your father's home! Kate, that's wonderful news! But how?'

'It was an accident. I just spotted him in the street one day.'

Martin's smile was full of genuine warmth and delight. 'And he recognized you?'

'He didn't see me, but I got in touch and we've met and... Oh, Martin, I'm so happy!'

'I'm delighted for you, Kate! I know how much this means... And did he explain why he lost touch?'

She appreciated that 'lost touch'. It seemed so blameless, she and her father, like flotsam and jetsam on the Thames, no choice, no harm, just drifting apart. She was glad she could now give Martin the plausible, real reason, and it wouldn't reflect badly on her father.

'It turns out my aunt told him I hated him and didn't want to see him!'

'This can wait for later.' He wiped his hands and covered the painting. 'Come and tell me all about it.'

They went into the sitting room and he poured them some wine. 'To celebrate! I wish I had champagne.' He smiled as he chinked his glass against hers. 'So, you bumped into him in East Lane? Had he come back to see the aunts?'

'No, he doesn't want to see them, says they're money grubbers... Actually, I saw him a little while back outside the bookshop, with Nora.'

'Nora?' A flush rose from his neck to his cheeks. 'What on earth would your father have to do with Nora?'

'I can hardly believe it meself – I couldn't take it in, but it turns out my dad is Nora's husband!'

'Chibby?' Martin rubbed his temples, smearing them with blue paint like pagan tattoos. 'I'm sorry, I don't mean to doubt you, it's just confusing. Let me get this straight, your surname's Goss?'

She nodded.

'But his is Grainger?'

'He said he despised the Gosses, so he took his mother's maiden name.'

His eyes narrowed, and she saw a flicker of distrust. 'But how can *Nora's husband* possibly be your father?'

It was clear he wasn't happy for her now. 'You mean how can someone of Nora's class be married to someone from mine?' she snapped. 'Well, I'm telling you, Chibby *is* Archie, my dad, and if you don't believe me, ask Nora.'

She snatched off the straw hat, which unaccountably was still on her head. 'I knew all this stuff about being equal was a load of old codswallop. I'm going.'

He stood and caught her hand. 'Kate! Don't go. I didn't mean that at all. It's just such a shock. Sit down again, please. You forget, I've met Chibby and there's no hint of a Bermondsey accent and he certainly never refers to it.'

'Well, he wouldn't, he hasn't got a good word to say about the place.'

'And you're convinced he's telling the truth – about his long absence being your aunt's fault?'

'Of course he's telling the truth! He did admit he wasn't the best father, said he should have come for me whatever Aunt Sylvie said.'

'Well, that's something, I suppose.'

'You don't like him, do you?'

Martin looked away and then got up to pour another drink, which she refused. He strolled to the window and looked out over the small back courtyard.

'I think I should let you make up your own mind about Chibby – or Archie. What are you calling him, by the way?'

'Dad.'

Martin laughed and sat down again. 'Look, I haven't had a lot to do with him personally, it's only what I hear from Nora. But I don't think he makes her happy.'

'Maybe not, but that doesn't make him a bad man... I mean, he's not a wife beater or anything, is he?'

She watched as his face reddened. 'You would have to ask Nora.'

'I did notice something. The first time I saw her...' Kate pointed to her own throat. 'Fingermarks, here, and another time, a cut eye. You see it a lot where I come from, and believe me there's not enough doors in Dockhead for all those women to have walked into! I was sure it must be her husband did it, but now I know that's not true.'

Martin's mouth tightened into a straight line and, leaning his chin on his hand, he stared at her. 'Who do you think it was, then, if not him?'

'Jealous lover?' She tried to sound casual, but had wandered into a quagmire of her own imaginings and was finding it difficult to extricate herself.

'Say what you mean, Kate.' He'd put his wine down, his expression unusually hard.

'You said Archie doesn't make Nora happy, but I reckon you did... once, and when she went back to him you didn't like it.'

'Let's get this straight,' he said sternly. 'Nora and I are just friends.'

'Oh, Martin. I saw the painting of her – in that pile you "did for love"! I'm not an idiot.'

'And I'm not a bully. Do you really think I'm capable of hurting a woman?'

'No. But sometimes things can get out of hand. I broke Janey's nose once in temper. I just need to know, was it you, or was it me dad?'

Without warning he stood. 'I think I'd better drive you

home. Your question's a double-edged sword, Kate. Worthy
of a good barrister. What if I said it was your father that hurt
Nora? You'd think I was lying – or, if you believed me, you'd
hate me for spoiling your new-found happiness. And if I said
it was me? You'd throw me over in an instant!'

She wished she'd said nothing now – he was naturally
offended and hurt. But when Chibby had just been Nora's
anonymous husband, the relationship between those three
had had nothing to do with her; now Chibby was her father, it
did. She laid a hand on Martin's arm as he helped her on with
her coat. Turning to him she said softly, 'I'm sorry, Martin. I
know you wouldn't hurt a woman. I just can't believe my dad
would either.'

Archie Goss, though her father, was still a mystery to her,
known only through her aunts' stories or her own vague
memories. She would just have to let him prove himself to
her over time. And the following week he would get the
opportunity. For Nora sent a note inviting Kate to their home.

*Chibby was so excited after your meeting! I haven't
seen him as happy in a long time. We would love you to
lunch with us here on Sunday. Chibby is wary of going
to Bermondsey – he doesn't want to be anywhere near
the sisters – he's furious with them! We'll send the motor.*

As planned, her father's car came for her on a quiet
Sunday morning. There were enough people about for the
motor to attract the usual attention, though Kate thought
the neighbours must be getting used to the sight of her being
driven here and there. The driver opened the door and she

slid into the leather seats, pretending not to notice the curious stares. She began to understand how easy it was to get used to the trappings of wealth. But if Archie Goss had turned out to be running his business from a coster barrow in Petticoat Lane, would she have been as happy at their reunion? She knew the answer would be 'yes'.

They arrived at a pretty terrace near Belgrave Square and stopped outside a white house. There were steps up to the front door and steps down to a semi-basement below. A spiked iron railing ran along the front, and through the car window she saw the ground floor had two tall windows. At one of them, she thought she saw a curtain twitch. On the second floor were two delicate wrought-iron balconies and in the deep, tiled roof, she saw several dormer windows. They reminded her of home. Fear gave way to eagerness and she emerged from the car, mounting three steps to the wide, black door. But before the driver could even knock, it was opened by Nora.

She kissed Kate on the cheek and took her hand. 'He's waiting for you in the garden room.'

'Are you coming in too?' She gripped Nora's hand more tightly.

'I'll see you at lunch.'

She led Kate down the tiled hall to a pale green door, turned the brass handle and ushered Kate inside, whispering, 'He's so looking forward to seeing you again!'

A large bay window, letting in sun and a glimpse of green, dominated the room. She was aware of tasteful, light-coloured armchairs and a sofa arranged around the fireplace. On a small round table was a vase of creamy roses. She instantly recognized the delicacy of Nora's taste in the room but there, in the middle of it all, stood her father. A powerful, muscular presence, he was studying Martin's cool painting of Nora. He had his back to her, so she couldn't tell if he liked it, but she remembered the one he definitely didn't like. She took a step forward and he turned to her. She saw an instant look of shock, almost as if he wasn't expecting to see her.

'Dear God, Katy!' He approached with both hands outstretched. 'I thought it was your mother walking into the room.' His eyes glistened and now she could believe how, after all these years, the memory of her mother still haunted him. He took her hands, leading her into the room. 'I'm sorry, I can't stop looking at you!' He laughed and drew her to two chairs placed by the large window. She looked out on a small garden, full of roses in shades of white and cream, no doubt the source of the flowers on the table. Again, she saw only Nora's influence. Archie's frame seemed too big for the chair, his elbows sticking out over the arms and his muscular thighs filling the small seat. He'd seemed much more at home in his office.

'Pretty garden,' he said, following her gaze. 'All Nora.'

'It's beautiful. A bit different to the backyard in East Lane.'

He flinched. 'I'm sorry.'

'Dad, I won't be able to talk about my life if you keep saying sorry every time I mention the place. It wasn't your fault you was lied to.'

His face relaxed. 'All right, I'll stop, I promise. Just tell me more about your life.'

And so she did. From her earliest memories to her first days at school, the loss of her precious *Grimm's Fairy Tales*, her fights with Aunt Sylvie and her cousins, and starting at Boutle's. He listened intently; sometimes a pained expression crossed his face. And though she tried to, there was no disguising the harshness of that life. She wanted desperately to find some crumbs of comfort for him, some signs that her childhood had not been completely unhappy, and so she told him the story of her girlish love for Johnny, their games on the foreshore, how she'd loved playing along the street and making the other kids laugh with her mimicry. He seemed to be enjoying the tales, smiling and nodding as he recognized some of the cast of neighbours. But when she told of the day Longbonnet chased her to Parker's Row, giving Kate a sixpence instead of a telling-off, his expression darkened again.

'That old witch! I'm sorry to hear you had anything to do with her. She never liked me, would have stopped me marrying your mother if she could have done – same as all Bessie's family. We had opposition from every side – my sisters didn't like the marriage either.' He turned to look out of the window, but seemed to be staring past the roses to East Lane and his youth. 'They couldn't stop us. We were a love match, your mother and I.'

There was silence between them, broken only by the ticking of a glass carriage clock on the mantelpiece. He rubbed the plush arms of his chair and eventually slapped his palms down. 'Too much brooding on the past.' He looked up with a smile. 'We have all the future before us, Katy. And I intend to make up for everything you've suffered.' He smiled, stood and offered her his arm. 'But first, lunch.'

The dining room was every bit as elegant as the rest of the house; its wood-panelled walls were painted pale green, and the delicately turned chairs and oval table had a foreign look about them. Gold-and-green silk curtains, held back by tasselled braids, framed the long windows. Perhaps Nora was trying to recreate her chateau home. Or maybe all wealthy people lived in houses like this; Kate had no way of knowing. But if, as Nora had said, most of her own money was gone and Archie was looking for Mrs Cliffe's backing for his business, where was the money coming from to run this place? Whoever was paying for it, the house seemed to flow around Nora as if it emanated from her. Chibby was more like the ginger tom that had strolled into the pretty garden and made his home there, and Kate wondered if, even with all his accomplishments, he wouldn't be more at home in East Lane.

A young maid, in a black frock, white apron and cap, served the lunch. The girl had a miserable, sallow face. She served Nora and Archie first, kept Kate waiting and then plonked the plate on the table in front of her. She stomped out and Nora pulled a face at Kate. 'Sorry! Lizzie's new.'

Kate would have been miserable too. She'd been nothing but a maid for Aunt Sylvie's lot and many a time she'd have loved to tip the stew in their laps. It had certainly put her off going into service. Or perhaps the girl was just a snob, seeing Kate as an interloper whose proper place was downstairs scrubbing pans. But that was exactly how Kate felt too. It would take a long time to get used to her unearned shift in status.

She got through the lunch by pretending this was all one of her daydreams. Her dreaming self was up in the garret in East Lane, planning what would come next. What actually came next was a loud knocking on the front door; soon after which the maid returned, informing Archie that there was someone to see him.

'I'm not expecting anyone. Who is it?' he asked sharply.

'Wouldn't say, sir.'

'Well, tell them I'm not at home.'

The maid looked to Nora, who shot an uncertain look in

the direction of the hall. 'Don't you think, Chibby, you ought to just see—'

'No! Absolutely not, Nora.' The maid gave an impatient shrug and Kate noticed that she fixed Archie with a stare of loathing as she left. Kate was certain she mouthed 'arse'ole' before closing the door. Archie took up the conversation as if nothing had happened. He was obviously a man who valued his privacy.

'Nora, why don't you tell Katy about our little surprise?'

'Yes!' Nora said, looking pleased with herself, and was about to get up when the maid returned.

'Sorry, sir, they won't go away, says it's urgent.'

'Oh, for God's sake, all right! Nora, you take Katy upstairs and show her.'

He strode out and Nora gazed after him. 'His business drains him. He hates being disturbed at home.'

She followed Nora out of the dining room and peered along the hall to the front door. Archie's broad back blocked her view so that she couldn't see the person on the doorstep, but she could just about hear him. The voice was low, indistinct, and Kate thought the accent sounded more Bermondsey than Belgravia. Then she heard the visitor clearly say, 'You fuckin' better get a move on, hadn't you, Uncle Archie? He wants his money.'

As Nora led her upstairs, Kate looked back to see her father grab the man by his coat, put his face close and growl, 'Get yourself back to the organ grinder, you loathsome little monkey. And tell him an investment always carries risk.' Archie lifted Stan off his feet and shoved him down the front steps.

Kate knew exactly what had just gone on. She'd had

similar conversations with Stan and was unsettled to find that her father had his own dealings with Mr Smith – who'd obviously run out of patience. Perhaps it wasn't his sisters that he wanted to avoid by staying away from Bermondsey so much as Mr Smith.

Nora reached the top landing and, showing no sign that she'd noticed the encounter on the doorstep, beckoned her into a bedroom. It overlooked the garden and Kate heard a blackbird in the small rowan tree that filled her view. Late-afternoon light fell over a single bed with a pale violet eiderdown. There was a wardrobe and matching dressing table, with a silver-backed hairbrush and mirror. Nora sat on the bed, patting the eiderdown for Kate to join her. 'Do you like the room?'

Kate looked around appreciatively. 'It's beautiful. But, Nora, did you hear what was going on downstairs? Is my dad in trouble with a loan shark? Only I've had a bit of experience meself and I think he should just pay up and get himself out of it!'

Nora sat up straight. 'Kate, don't ever let him hear you talking like that.' She glanced towards the door. 'Chibby is a businessman and sometimes he has to make hard decisions. He absolutely wouldn't like you to question his judgement.'

'What, not even me?'

'Especially not you.'

Kate thought for a while. 'You're right. It's not like he's seen what I was like growing up – asking all my silly questions... I used to drive Aunt Sylvie mad!' She stroked the violet eiderdown. 'That's why they called me Noss. Dad's had no time to get used to me. But he will.' She grinned and was glad to see Nora's tense expression relax.

When Archie came in and found them sitting on the bed

chatting, he showed no signs of his previous anger and, like Nora, acted as if nothing had happened. Though Kate was longing to ask him about Stan, she realized she'd have to curtail her natural curiosity in order to keep her dad happy.

'Ah, my two girls, getting to know each other. What a lovely sight.' He rubbed his hands together. 'Have you told her?' he asked Nora.

'I wanted to wait for you.'

Archie looked pleased. 'Katy, we want you to visit us often and we thought it would be nice for you to have your own bedroom in our house.' He looked to Nora and nodded. She got off the bed and opened the wardrobe.

Kate looked from one to the other. 'This is for me?'

'Yes, this is your bedroom now, Kate, and here—' she swung the wardrobe door wide – are a few things I thought you might like.'

'But it's all too nice!' And to her own surprise, she began to cry.

Archie stuck his hands deep into his trouser pockets. 'Nora?'

She went to sit beside Kate and put an arm around her. 'None of that. Too nice, indeed! Come and look at these dresses and wipe those tears.'

'Thank you. You're both so kind.' She got up and embraced her father. 'I knew you'd be kind,' she said and, embarrassed, he patted her cheek.

'Well, I'll leave you to try on dresses. I'm afraid I have to go to my office. I'm sorry to leave you, but Nora will explain the rest of our little plan.'

He left, and while Nora took down several dresses, a jacket and a summer coat, laying them on the bed, she explained what Archie had meant. She repeated that they wanted Kate to visit often and get to know her father again. 'And then if you agree, we'd like you to come and live with us. What do you think of that idea?' Nora asked.

Kate was overwhelmed. She would move in tomorrow. She pretended to think it over and then said, 'It's a good idea to get to know each other first. He might end up not liking me. Probably I'll just be too annoying!'

Nora smiled. 'I don't think so. The danger is you won't be able to put up with him!'

She selected a yellow-and-white shift and took it off the hanger. 'Come and try this on,' she said, and began unbuttoning the back of Kate's dress.

'Your father has so many good points, Kate, and I would never be disloyal to him, but what we just witnessed, it's not uncommon. His temper flares up. I'm not making excuses, but I blame the war. He went through hell – well, they all did, how couldn't they come back changed? But Chibby, sometimes he's like two different men – a Jekyll and Hyde, almost. Usually he'll go out after an episode – to cool off – and when he comes home, he's the considerate, captivating man I married once again.' She helped Kate step into the dress and looked her in the eye for the first time in their conversation. 'It was my idea to have a trial period for you. I felt you should know everything about him first.' Kate wasn't sure if she'd heard a note of discouragement in Nora's voice, but then the woman added brightly, 'If it was up to Chibby, he'd have you moving in here tomorrow!'

She asked the driver to drop her off before they got to East Lane – she didn't feel like attracting any more attention today. He handed her the bag containing some of her new clothes;

the majority she'd left at her father's house. They were too fine for her life in East Lane; better they stayed in the pretty bedroom, ready for her possible future. But her garret was stifling, and after spending all day in her father's fine home, she recognized it for what it was. A hovel. It had always seemed a refuge, a symbol of freedom, a place to dream, and she found it strange that now the dream was a reality, she saw only the bare boards, the orange-crate cupboard, the rags she called dresses hanging from the rafters.

She went out, down to the Thames. The day had been so warm there were still some kids out on the foreshore paddling, others diving from lighters and swimming with ungainly strokes, fighting the swift tide. She leaned against the low wall by East Lane Stairs and watched them, envying their easy joy. They had all their dreams before them and she was beginning to understand that a dream realized is also a dream lost. She rested her chin in her hands, enjoying the breeze and the musty river smell.

She became aware of a presence. Someone else was leaning on the wall, a few feet from her. She looked to see who it was. Clean-shaven, immaculately dressed in a crisp, open-necked blue shirt and light trousers, Johnny tipped his cap. He was smoking a cigarette.

'Want one?' When she smiled at him, he strolled over and took out a packet.

They stood smoking silently for a while and she said, 'You look better, Johnny. I'm so pleased.'

'I came to see you earlier – you were out.'

She remembered their last conversation. When the old Johnny's back, she'd said, come and ask me again... But 'the old Johnny' wasn't the only one who'd come back, and now everything was changed.

'I was in Belgravia.'

He shot her a look of surprise and then she told him about how she'd found her father again.

'I'm happy for you,' he said simply. 'You've waited so long for him, you deserve a better life.' He flicked away the cigarette and looked into her eyes for the first time. 'You'll move away.'

And you'll move on, she thought, instantly knowing that the question he'd come to ask her would go unasked. Johnny would never hold her back and she would never give him false hope by pretending that she wouldn't leave. So she stayed silent, until he pointed to where a group of kids were grubbing in the mud.

'Remember the silver coin?' he asked, and she felt a sudden rush of love for him, wishing she were that young mudlark again, whose dreams were so uncomplicated and so unattainable.

14

Bermondsey to Belgravia

Aunt Sylvie stood like a solid block in her path.

'I want a word with you, Kate Goss!'

Kate wasn't surprised. Her father had told her he would be sending Aunt Sylvie a letter, expressing his anger at her lies and her appalling treatment of his daughter. If Aunt Sylvie hadn't been aware before that Archie had no love left for her, she was now.

'You've turned my brother against me! I'll have you, you evil little mare!'

Kate knew Aunt Sylvie's fighting style by now and easily dodged the hand reaching to grab a fistful of her dark curls.

'Me, evil?' She was retreating and Aunt Sylvie advancing – soon they would be at East Lane river stairs and Kate didn't fancy being tipped into the Thames. She ducked around her aunt. 'You're the wicked liar, telling him I hated him, when you knew full well all I wanted was for him to come and get me!'

But her aunt wasn't listening. She took another run at Kate, who stuck out a foot and sent her sprawling. Kate dropped down and put her knee into her aunt's well-padded stomach. Pinning her down and only inches from her aunt's face, she said, 'I've kept quiet because Dad told me he'd deal with it, but I swear,' and here her voice cracked, 'if it was up to me I'd creep into your house one night and stick a knife in your black heart, you old witch. You stole my dad from me!'

She knew she was making a spectacle of herself – what would Ethel and her new friends at the bookshop think of her? But she also knew that she'd felt robbed of her own anger when Archie had asked her to say nothing to Aunt Sylvie. Now it felt good to spill her venom – if not her aunt's blood – all over East Lane, no matter who was looking on.

She eased her hold and Aunt Sylvie scrambled to her feet, beating a quick retreat, fully aware that Kate was quite capable of matching her strength. Kate didn't think she'd have any more trouble from Aunt Sylvie, but she was worried about what her father had written to Aunt Sarah. She hoped he hadn't been too harsh.

The following day, after work, she went to the cook shop for a bowl of faggots, gravy and pease pudding and paid her aunt a visit.

Aunt Sarah looked grim and offered no greeting. Her hair, entirely grey now, was drawn back in a severe bun that made her podgy face look even larger. She turned and led Kate silently down the passage to her bleak room and scullery. The contrast to her father's fashionable house was stark. She'd placed an antimacassar on the armchair, stuck some photos from a countryside calendar on a wall, tacked a brass crucifix above her bed and propped a few photos of Archie and

Kate's grandparents on the mantelpiece. These few attempts at decoration only made Kate feel sad.

Aunt Sarah spread newspaper on the table and started dividing the faggots onto two plates. Before she sat down to eat, her aunt took something from the mantelpiece, put it in front of Kate and tapped it with an arthritic forefinger.

'There it is in black and white. He don't want nothing to do with me. Says I've only ever been after his money.' Aunt Sarah chewed thoughtfully for a while and then gave a bitter laugh. 'Well, it's been the other way around for most of his life, so what if I did think he'd want to give me a treat now he's flush? It's only what I'm due! But no, according to him, *she's* put the kibosh on all that. He says she's been lying to him for years, saying you hated him! Wicked mare. Did you know about this?'

'He told me. It's not your fault.'

'No, love, it ain't, but I'm tarred with the same brush.' She heaved herself up to clear away the plates.

'Let me do that.' Kate went to the scullery and made some tea. There were pathetically few groceries in the kitchen cabinet and Kate determined that when she'd got to know her father a bit better she would persuade him to help Aunt Sarah. She put the tea in front of her aunt, who in a rare show of affection patted her hand.

'You're the only one I got now, Kate. Seems strange, Bessie's daughter being me only comfort. Oh, I was such a cow to her. I regret it now.'

'He told me you and Aunt Sylvie were both against the marriage, and so was Mum's family. Are there any left?'

'Of your mum's family? Not that I know of... Well, only her down the end, if you can call her family.'

Kate was confused. 'Who down the end?'

'Old Longbonnet.' Aunt Sarah looked as if Kate should know this.

Kate gave a disbelieving smile. 'I didn't know she was related. She told me they all used to live in Romany Row, but she's never said anything about being related.'

Aunt Sarah sniffed and tapped out her clay pipe on the range. She made several slow attempts to light it. 'Well, she's your great-aunt, your grandmother's sister, I think.'

Kate sat back in shock. 'Why didn't no one tell me?'

'Didn't seem any point – the old gel's not right, is she? Never has been, and she got worse when your mum died. To be honest, some of the things she was saying back then nearly got her locked up in Cane Hill asylum!'

'What things?'

But Aunt Sarah waved a weary hand. 'Oh, she was raving. I can't remember. It's all a long time ago now.' Her aunt got up, with difficulty, went to the mantelpiece and took down the photo of Archie. She studied it for a few seconds and then placed it face down.

'One thing old Longbonnet did say all them years ago, she said to me, "Sarah, Archie Goss breaks everything and you'll be no exception, he'll break your heart one day." And no truer a word's been spoken. Perhaps she wasn't as mad as we thought she was.'

As the hot summer burned itself out into autumn, Kate found herself spending so many Sundays at her father's house that Martin began to complain he'd never get the mudlark painting finished. The truth was she'd been glad of an excuse not to see

Martin, even though she needed the modelling money. It had become awkward between them after Kate's confession she'd suspected him of hurting Nora – she couldn't really blame him. She'd probably spoilt whatever chance of a friendship they'd had. But during Archie's next trip abroad, she did agree to go to his studio, just so that the finishing touches could be added to *The Mudlark*.

He was placing her limbs in the awkward pose and she felt he was being unusually brusque and rapid.

'This is the last painting you'll do of me.' It was better to make a clean break.

'Why?' He pulled her elbow further forward, but his expression was unmistakably crestfallen. 'You can't stop now! You're my muse.'

He'd obviously forgiven her, or at least he still needed her.

'Well, if I do, then you'll have to pick a pose that's not going to turn me into a bent old lady before me time.' She groaned and, in an ancient voice, quavered, 'Oh, me poor old bones.'

He laughed. 'I've missed you,' he said, beginning to paint. 'Your father's monopolizing you! He's certainly making up for lost time. In fact, I bumped into John Bacon at the bookshop and we agreed, you've eyes for only one man these days.' She held her breath. 'And that man is neither of us!'

'You and Johnny agreed about something? You're telling me pork pies!' She covered her confusion with a laugh.

'We've buried the hatchet, didn't he tell you?'

She shook her head. She hadn't talked to Johnny since their last meeting at the river stairs.

'Well, in fact, he came and apologized for his behaviour at the gallery. I told him, all water under the bridge. He really is a decent fellow.' He held his brush mid-air for a moment. 'We both want what's best for you. That's another thing we agreed on.'

'Oh? You were having quite a little chinwag.' She nodded, wondering what else they'd been saying. 'Were you talking about my dad?'

'It would be strange if we hadn't. Whatever's happened between you two, John's obviously still concerned about your happiness, whether that involves me or your father.' He saw her frown and added quickly, 'He's not going to interfere, Kate. I explained that you and I are friends, but I admitted to wanting to be more... and that I would always put your happiness first.' He paused, peering closely at the canvas. 'And we shook hands on it.'

It felt almost as if Johnny had given Martin his blessing, as if he were tying up every loose end to do with Kate before moving on. She felt a painful tearing in her heart, as if its two halves were moving inexorably apart. And yet she wouldn't hold him back; she wanted Johnny to be happy too.

'Yes...' He raised his brush with a flourish. 'A very decent chap. It's finished.'

She groaned with relief at being able to move again and keeled over, curling herself into a ball before stretching her back like a cat. Offering his hand, he pulled her up, with a strong grip that propelled her into his arms. She saw a spark of desire in his eyes, and the way he was holding her told her it wouldn't take much to replace the veneer of friendship with something more serious. She pulled away.

'Can I see it?'

Not waiting for his answer, she went to look at *The Mudlark*. The paint still glistened, which was even more evocative of the oily, olive-green Thames. A smudgy yellow haze of sky made her feel hot with the memory of that warm day. She liked the way he'd painted her expression, a mixture of delight and pride in her treasure and of eagerness that he should share it. But then she spotted someone Martin had included in the background. Along with the group of kids combing the foreshore, a figure was outlined, almost a caricature. A ragged old woman, half-hidden behind a moored lighter. She was clearly looking in Kate's direction, and Martin had captured the long nose in profile so perfectly that Kate knew instantly who it must be.

'What's she doing there?' She pointed to the woman as Martin came up behind her.

'I don't know, she's just a scavenger. I thought she looked so odd I had to put her in... Why, do you know her?'

'Yeah, I do,' she said. 'That's old Longbonnet.'

She waited by East Lane Stairs. A warm autumn day had declined to a damp, foggy evening. The pewter veil hovering over the Thames crept up the lane, seeping into doorways, slithering along rooftops, and clutching at her neck with cold, slimy fingers. It was about this time every night when Longbonnet would make her way home from one of the 'rounds' that kept her body and soul together. This morning she had set out with two large wicker baskets on her arm and had spent most of Saturday, as she always did, selling bundles of watercress from door to door. Tonight she would go out on another round to the pubs, this time selling 'supper delicacies' of calves' feet and pigs' trotters. Kate was hoping to catch her between rounds.

She turned away from the river to see Longbonnet emerging from the fog. She was almost at her house before Kate could run from the stairs and catch her by the arm. The old woman whirled round, dropping one of her empty baskets onto the slick cobbles.

'Kate Goss! You scared me to death!'

Kate picked up the basket, thinking it was a strange turn of events that Longbonnet should be frightened of her. 'Sorry... I just wanted to ask you something.'

'Come in, come in! You can help me load up me pads with trotters,' she said, holding up her empty baskets.

The old woman's kitchen was steamy and thick with greasy cooking smells of trotters and calves' feet that had been bubbling away in cauldrons for most of the day. Longbonnet took off her coat and scarf and went to remove the pots from the range. 'Give us an 'and, gel,' she said, and Kate hurried to help carry the cast-iron pans to the table. She groaned with the effort. 'How do you lift these on your own!'

Longbonnet cackled. 'I'm stronger than I look. I'll get the pots and you can help me fill 'em.'

Kate clearly had no choice in the matter. Longbonnet lit the gas mantles and disappeared into the scullery. She came out with a tray of earthenware pots and lids and placed them on the table. She muttered to herself as she searched for an extra spoon in the cutlery drawer. Handing it to Kate, she explained what to do. 'Fill it up, but leave enough room on the top for the jelly. Like this.' She demonstrated once and they began dipping into the greasy stewpot and filling up pots with 'supper delicacies'. Kate wouldn't have touched them, but it was surprising what a man would eat after a heavy night's drinking.

They worked in silence for a while. 'So, Archie Goss is back,' Longbonnet said matter-of-factly. 'I suppose you'll want to go and live with him in his posh house over the other side.'

'How did you know?' Kate said, shocked that her secret was well and truly out.

Longbonnet's shoulders shook in a silent chuckle. 'I watch. I hear. I might have a wall eye, but I can see clear enough when it comes to this place. I see you coming and going, I see your face. You look happy, Kate. And it's what you always wanted.' She tugged on one of her pendulous earrings. 'And I might be old but I ain't deaf. I hear Sid Smith's popped out of his hole for a bite of a juicy worm.'

The picture made Kate's stomach turn as she spooned pigs' trotters.

'Don't look so surprised. There's nothing happens in East Lane I don't know about.'

'Mr Smith sent Stan to my dad's. He's got a posh house and a business, so why would he need Mr Smith?'

'Oh, them two. They used to be in some sort of business together. Thick as thieves. But I heard Archie left owing him money.'

'Why didn't you ever tell me you was my mum's aunt?'

'It wouldn't have done you 'a'porth o' good, gel. If you'd ever come running to me, Sylvie would've made you pay for it.'

'I wish I'd known.'

Longbonnet shook her head. 'Archie wouldn't have liked it either. If it was a choice between me and your dad, I know who you'd rather have. No. It's best as it is.'

'Dad's cut off both my aunts because of the way I've been treated.'

Longbonnet made a dismissive noise. 'He should have been here a bit sooner himself, then, shouldn't he?'

They continued to pot up the trotters and calves' feet till the pots were all full, then placed them into the long, flat baskets Longbonnet called pads. She covered them with white cloths and they left together, making their way down East Lane till they got to Kate's house. Here Longbonnet stopped, giving Kate a long, squint-eyed stare. 'I know you'll end up with your father. But if you ever need any help, you know where to find your Great-Aunt Rosina.' She tapped her long nose. 'That's me name,' she said, nodding her head, as if she'd conferred on Kate a great gift.

As Christmas approached, the Hand and Marigold got busier and Kate took on extra shifts. It was one early evening in December that she was shocked to see Johnny come walking through the door. Since the bookshop had reopened after the summer break, she'd seen him more and more in the company of Pamela, the clever blonde who'd helped him with his writing. She couldn't pretend she wasn't jealous, but no one would know it, certainly not Johnny. It wouldn't be fair. He sauntered over to the bar. He was freshly shaved and smelt of pine needles. He'd obviously been to Bermondsey Baths.

'Pint of bitter, please, miss,' he said with a grin. 'And have a drink yourself.'

'Thanks. I wasn't expecting to see you here. Are you all right?' Kate couldn't help looking out for signs that Johnny had simply papered over the cracks of his grief and would break out in some rash act of self-destruction at any minute.

A shadow passed across his face and he gave a brief sigh. 'I'm fine, Kate. It's just I thought I'd catch you here – you're always in Belgravia these days.'

It wasn't an accusation, just a fact, but she had to stop herself from apologizing.

'I've come here to ask if you want to spend Christmas with me.' His open, assured smile struck her with guilt. She hadn't even thought. 'Christmas Day in your garret's not going to be much fun for you – my house won't be a riot, but at least we'll have company.'

She could feel herself beginning to flush and she saw his smile fade. 'Oh, I'm stupid. Of course, you'll be going to your dad's.'

She nodded. Archie had invited her when he got back from his trip to Germany, where he'd spent a few weeks trying to expand his fur business. 'I'm sorry, Johnny. Dad and Nora asked me a while ago. He wants me to stay for a week...'

'Oh, well, just a thought.' He ventured a smile, but his disappointment was clear.

'What about your friend – Pamela? Won't you want to spend Christmas with her?'

He shifted awkwardly. 'Oh, no. Pamela's gone home to her parents for Christmas. I think she's a bit scared to tell them about me...'

'What if I ask Dad to invite you for Christmas Day too?'

'No!'

'Why not?'

'It wouldn't be right. He doesn't even know me.'

'He does. He remembers you – from when you were little. He told me he knew your mum.'

Johnny pulled a surprised face. 'I always forget he comes from East Lane.'

'Let me just serve this gentleman,' she said, turning to a customer, 'and then I'll take my break.'

At their usual table, she shared a sandwich with Johnny.

Kate said, 'I have trouble remembering Dad's a Bermondsey boy too. There's a lot of his history that's muddier than the foreshore. I found out he's had dealings with Mr Smith! Some sort of business deal years ago – and Mr Smith thought he'd been diddled. You'll never guess who he sent to Dad's house to squeeze some money out of him – Stan!'

Johnny whistled. 'What, to Belgravia! I bet that's one business partnership your dad regrets.'

Kate shrugged. 'He's always so confident. He talks as if he's the world's best businessman, but I think all his money's tied up in the business.'

'That's usually the way with businesses,' Johnny said knowledgeably.

'Doesn't stop Nora spending it like water! Every time I go there, she's bought me a new frock or pair of shoes.'

'She was brought up as some sort of princess, what can you expect!' He laughed, and it felt good to be talking easily with him.

'She showed me a photo of the chateau – I thought it'd be like Buckingham Palace but it's really just a great big house, with a few turrets stuck on the top.'

'Well, I've warmed to her. It seems she's treating you well... So's your dad, by the sound of it.' He hesitated, then asked, 'When will you go?' In spite of having drunk a pint of bitter, he seemed dry-mouthed, and she sensed he was holding his breath.

'He wants me to... soon.'

He let out the breath, drawing a pattern in a little pool of beer. 'You'd have to give up work at Boutle's – and here, and the bookshop.'

'No. I'd still come to the bookshop!' she said quickly.

'But not as the cleaner.'

She shook her head. 'I suppose not.'

She'd been happy in this limbo, going back and forth from Bermondsey to Belgravia, enjoying the luxury of having her father back without the pressure of choosing between his world and her own.

'But we'll still see each other, Johnny. I'll be a volunteer, like Nora, and I can visit you.' But even as she said it, she knew that choosing Belgravia meant leaving East Lane, and everyone in it, behind.

Snow was falling outside her garret and a little pile had been swept into one corner of the dormer window, blown there by the sharp river wind. Most of her new clothes were at her father's, but she'd brought back one outfit to wear for her journey to Belgravia this Christmas Eve. It was a dark-red, low-waisted dress, with buttons down the front and soft pleats around the skirt. She and Nora had chosen it together on a trip to Harvey Nichols, a palace of treasures she could not even have imagined a few months earlier. She tied a black ribbon at the collar and adjusted a low-slung black belt, then buttoned the long sleeves. The garret was freezing and she was glad of the warm dress, and even more grateful for her new black coat, with its fur stole – another present from Nora. She put on a close-fitting cloche hat, picked up her bag and looked around the garret. The violet bedroom in Belgravia would be warm, bright with electric lights, and heavy curtains would block out this freezing, snow-heavy wind. Increasingly the garret looked like the room of a stranger.

There was one thing she needed to do before she left. Although Ethel had always encouraged her to become a member of the bookshop, she'd never taken her up on it, until now. She'd wanted to give Johnny something for Christmas, something that would be as precious to him as the silver coin from the foreshore he'd kept all those years. There was a book he'd mentioned wanting, but when she'd asked Ethel, she'd been shocked to find it would cost 12s 6d, the price of a brand-new Witney blanket, or half the cost of this woollen coat she was wearing now. Although she accepted her father's hospitality and Nora's gifts, she hadn't yet given up all her independence and she still had to live on her wages. The only way she could pay for Johnny's book was to join the reading room and get her ticket made up with sixpenny subscriptions until she could afford to buy the book. *On the Art of Writing*, it was called, though she'd have thought Johnny knew enough about that already. The author's odd-sounding name conjured up a picture of someone in Elizabethan dress lying on a couch, sucking a quill pen and dreaming up stories. She was sure it would be a lot more serious than that. Johnny loved nothing more than a serious tome. Now she took out the book, carefully cut the price off the dust jacket, and put it into her bag.

When he opened the door of his house a small burst of warmth and light emerged.

'Kate! Haven't you gone to your dad's? Come in!' He looked so pleased and surprised, she hated to disappoint him.

'I can't stop. Dad's car's waiting round the corner. I just wanted to give you this.' She pulled out the book. 'A Christmas present.' She gave an involuntary shiver as she did so and he stood aside.

'Just come out of the snow. Your coat's getting covered.'

She stepped into the kitchen, pleased to see it looking clean and tidy. He'd even stuck some holly along the mantelpiece and hung mistletoe from the corners of the mirror.

'What's this?' He smiled as he unwrapped the book. 'The Quiller-Couch! How did you know I wanted this?' He opened the book, flicking through as if he'd like to start reading it immediately. She was glad of all the sixpences she'd handed over now.

'Oh, this is the best present anyone's ever bought me!' And he put down the book and, taking down some mistletoe from the mirror, held it high above them. 'Am I allowed a thank-you kiss?' he whispered.

She looked up into his eyes, feeling the warmth of his breath on her cold cheeks. She lifted her face and he kissed her still-smiling mouth. His lips were gentle, appreciative, and his kiss too brief.

'I hope you know you only got away with that because of the mistletoe,' she said, and he grinned. 'I'm sorry I can't stay... the car...'

'Yes, you said.' He held up the book. 'And thank you...' He opened the door and she went out into the snow. It stung her face and clung to her cheeks.

'I'll think of you every time I read it. Happy Christmas!'

She waved at him, his figure obscured by the flare of the gas lamp outside his house and soon smudged by snow flurries. 'Goodbye, Johnny!' she called back as an icy snowflake lodged in her eye, causing a tear to trickle down her cheek. By the time she'd brushed it away, he had closed the door.

Kate's room was just as she'd imagined it, warm and inviting. A fire burned in the pretty fireplace, and a lamp had been turned on. It was Nora who'd greeted her. Archie was still at his office, but she told Kate he'd definitely be home early that evening. Tonight, they were entertaining. A small gathering of friends and a few of Chibby's business associates, she said, nothing grand.

But Nora had a different notion to Kate of what grand was. When she came downstairs, wearing the cocktail dress that Nora had chosen for her, Kate felt like slipping away, back to Bermondsey and the familiarity of her garret. Men in evening suits and women in cocktail dresses milled around in the larger reception room. Lights blazed and glinted on crystal glasses, pale yellow champagne bubbled, and jewelled cocktails shimmered in wide glasses. She was dazzled and looking for an escape when Martin appeared. She grabbed his elbow and with a fixed smile on her face whispered, 'Save me!'

'Happy to.' He smiled, steering her towards the drinks table. He picked up two cocktails and found chairs half-obscured by a silk screen.

'Thanks,' she said, gulping the cocktail. 'Don't leave me.' She peered round the screen to see her father entering. Nora went to him immediately, greeting him with a kiss and putting her arm through his. He walked to the centre of the room, handsome and confident; she could see why Nora would be attracted to him.

'Do you know all these people?' she asked Martin.

'Good grief, no. They're mostly Chibby's friends.' His eyes had followed hers. 'They're a very fine-looking couple, aren't they?'

She looked for a sign of jealousy in his expression, but saw none.

'I can't believe I come from the same family as him, he's so handsome.'

Martin turned to her with a laugh. 'I personally think it's a very good thing you took after your mother – you look stunning.'

'Nora chose it.' She smoothed down the thin, silvery

cocktail dress and instinctively crossed her arms. She'd much rather have stayed in the warm red dress, but Nora had said it wasn't suitable.

'I'm not talking about the dress.' His eyes lingered on her face for a moment longer. 'When are you moving in here?'

'That's funny, Johnny asked me the same thing before I left.'

'Oh? You've seen him?' She thought she saw a flash of jealousy now.

'Just to give him a present – a book he wanted.'

They were silent for a while. Then she asked, 'Has Nora mentioned anything to you? About me coming to live here?'

'Yes.'

'She was worried I might find it hard to live with him.'

'Hmm. He'll be different with you.'

'I can't judge him properly, Martin. I don't know if it's the right thing to do.' She was surprised that she was looking for his opinion. Usually she made up her mind about people quickly and trusted her own judgement when it came to her first impressions. Why was she asking Martin? If he'd really had an affair with Nora, wouldn't he be the last person to give an impartial opinion?

'That's because you've spent too long dreaming, Kate. I'd say the best thing to do is leave things as they are for the time being.' He spoke casually, not urging her, and she found herself agreeing.

'Sometimes you can be very sensible,' she said.

He laughed loudly. 'I'm not sure I want you to think of me as sensible!' His laughter had attracted the attention of Mrs Cliffe, who now bore down upon them. 'Oh, no,' he said, 'she's got Mother in tow...'

Kate recognized Mrs North from the photo in Martin's

studio. The two women, though sisters, were unlike each other, not so much in features as in expressions. Mrs Cliffe had a benevolent vagueness that put Kate at her ease. But as the two women approached, Mrs North looked at Kate with undisguised hostility.

Martin squirmed in his chair before giving in to the inevitable and standing up to greet his mother. He kissed her cheek and almost hopped back, as if he'd been burned.

'This is Miss Goss, Mother... Chibby's daughter.' He drew Kate forward, and she thought he'd probably like to use her as a shield between himself and his mother if he only could.

Mrs North inclined her head. 'I understand you've only recently surfaced,' she said, barely concealed suspicion in her voice. 'And where did Chibby find you?'

Kate matched her frosty stare. 'Where he left me.'

She felt Martin's shoulders shaking and saw Mrs Cliffe's lip curl into a small smile.

'Ah. How interesting.' Mrs North turned away, leaving Martin and his aunt chuckling.

'Well, I've rarely seen my sister lost for words. Well done, my dear, for standing up to her.'

'Why on earth did you bring *her*?' Martin hissed.

'I didn't! It was Chibby's doing. He wants to interest her in the business as well.'

'Water from a stone. Good luck to him,' Martin said.

'Oh, he's got a golden tongue, Nora's Chibby – your father, my dear – he is a most persuasive businessman. He will make us all rich as Croesus!'

She left them. Martin downed his cocktail and Kate followed suit. 'I thought your mother was already rich!'

He nodded. 'She is, but you know how the song goes:

"There's nothing surer..."' he sang, flapping his hands, '"the rich get rich and the poor get poorer".'

'Oh, yeah. I know that one. *Ain't we got fun?*' she added sourly, looking around the room at all these people so eager to get her father's attention. No wonder it had taken him twelve years to 'find' her.

15

In My Father's House

1924–1925

On Christmas Day there were just the three of them. She'd only bought one present – the book for Johnny. She'd puzzled over what on earth she could give to her father or Nora when she could never match any of their gifts for her. So, for weeks she'd stayed behind at Boutle's for extra half hours here and there when her shifts had ended and, with Miss Dane's help, she'd acquired enough spare tinplate to make them each a present. For Nora she'd made a paperweight in the shape of a cat holding a ball. The ball spun on a spindle and could be run across the desk as if it were continually chasing the unobtainable. It was a simplified figure, but still recognizable as a cat. Nora had once told Kate she would love a cat, but Chibby forbade it, saying the creatures made him itch. For her father she'd crafted a cigarette tin, with an Egyptian-style sunburst design copied from a newspaper advertisement. She'd smoothed and polished it to a high shine that could be mistaken for silver, fixing a flat spring inside to hold the cigarettes in place. On the back she'd engraved *To my father, from your loving daughter, Katy.*

After lunch, when Nora handed her a package, Kate was glad of all those hours she'd spent fashioning their presents. At least she had something to give them. The box Nora had given her was lined with black velvet, on which nestled a gold wristwatch. It was beautiful. She gasped.

'For me? But... I can't take this!'

Nora smiled and looked at her husband as if they'd predicted her reaction.

'Yes, you can. And you will,' her father said, coming to help her put it on.

Kate raised her hand, admiring the watch, twisting it this way and that, letting them see how it fitted perfectly. And yet something inside shifted at the sight of it on her slim wrist. The object immediately made her someone else. She wasn't sure who that person was, but she knew how she felt – she felt indulged. Like a loved child.

She kissed her father and Nora and hesitated before picking up the bag containing her own gifts. 'They're not much compared to this,' she said, looking at the watch. She handed over the packages. Nora was eager, quickly unwrapping hers, and she laughed with delight. 'Ha, I've got my cat! See, Chibby! Where on earth did you find it, Kate?' She had discovered that the ball spun.

'I made it.'

'How clever of you!'

Kate looked to see if her father was equally delighted with his present. He'd been slower and was now examining the raised sunburst design, running his fingers over it. 'And you made this too?' he asked, and her heart swelled as he nodded appreciatively. 'You're a talented whitesmith, Katy.'

'It's only tinplate.'

'Of course. But your skill deserves a less humble material – I'll buy you some and turn you into a silversmith!' He turned over the case and after reading the inscription, he pulled out a handkerchief and blew his nose. 'I'm so proud of my daughter.' He stood and took something else from his jacket pocket; she couldn't see what it was. 'Katy, I promised you that I'd make up for all the years you had to struggle alone. You're a strong, clever girl and I know you've coped better than most could have, but still, you ought to have had your father with you. And now all that is about to change.'

He came to her and placed in her hand a small brass object. It was a key.

Nora saw her puzzlement. 'It's to our front door.'

And her father said, 'This is your house now, Katy. I think it's time for you to come and live here with us. Would you like that?'

The ball-chasing cat and the cigarette case were the last things Kate made at Boutle's. She was saying goodbye to the tin basher's forever. And though she wasn't sorry to lose the solder fumes and the metal fever, she would be sorry to lose her workmates. After Christmas she'd sent a letter handing in her notice and now she was at the factory collecting her cards and final pay packet. Marge and Conny both burst into tears when she came down from the office into the soldering room and broke the news. It felt good to be able to finally tell people that she had a father who wanted her, and a real home at last, but it was more of a wrench than she'd ever imagined. For they'd both been good friends to Kate. Marge, from her first day, had been her advisor about everything from flux to men, and poor little Conny had repaid Kate's early protectiveness with a loyalty that was unswerving.

'You're not leaving here without a do!' Miss Dane insisted, and even though the forelady wasn't a drinker, she insisted on organizing an impromptu send-off at the Hand and Marigold later that evening. Kate walked back out into the yard, where a lorry delivering tinplate was blocking the exit. She skirted it and was caught in a billow of black smoke belching from the coke-oven chimneys. Once out of the double gates and into Wild's Rents, she allowed herself to look back at the ramshackle collection of storage sheds and ancient buildings added to over the years. The old stables had been pulled down to make room for a new tinplate store and press room. It was an ugly, soot-stained, smelly warren, and yet it had been one of those unlovely havens she had always found for herself. Her father had called her a smith; she could thank Boutle's the tin basher's for that.

From the factory, Kate walked to the Bermondsey Bookshop and told Ethel she would be losing her cleaner.

'I knew it was coming!' Ethel exclaimed, throwing her hands into the air. She got up from behind the long table where she and Lucy were parcelling up the latest *Bermondsey Book* ready for despatch to various parts of the globe. Ethel had been very proud that the publication had gone international and so had Johnny, telling Kate that he'd even received a fan letter from a miner in the Transvaal.

'I'm distraught, my dear Kate.' Ethel took both Kate's hands in her own.

'Sorry to leave you in the lurch,' Kate said, looking round at the shelves of books. 'I'll miss keeping this place spick and span, but I can put the word out at Boutle's, see if any of the girls need extra work?'

'I'm not mourning the loss of our cleaner, but our rock! What will we do without you?'

Kate made a dismissive gesture. She didn't see herself as rock-like, but Lucy came to join them. 'It's true! You've done so much more than clean. I'd be married to that horrible boy I was so in love with if it weren't for your advice, and our dramatic productions would have been in tatters and our classes so much less fun without you!'

'Exactly!' Ethel agreed enthusiastically. 'We must arrange a little goodbye party.'

'Well, you could come to the Hand and Marigold tonight, if you want to? The Boutle's girls are giving me a send-off.'

From the looks on their faces she thought she might have put a little too much strain on the bridge connecting north and south of the river which Ethel had been so proud of building, but then a mischievous light shone from the woman's dark, intelligent eyes.

'I have been looking for an opportunity to enter a Bermondsey public house since I opened the shop in 1921. I would be delighted!' And much to Kate's surprise, Lucy agreed to come too.

As the door of the Bermondsey Bookshop closed behind her, Kate stopped to study the sign that swung above it. The painted torch of learning had faded since she'd first seen it, but the legend *He Who Runs May Read* meant so much more to her now. Almost as if the place had given her permission to become someone else – the orange door a portal to another world.

She had yet to find courage to say the hardest goodbye, but before doing so, she stopped at the Marigold to give her notice and warn the landlady that tonight there would be quite a few extra customers. She ordered some sandwiches and paid for them out of the allowance her father insisted she must now receive; she wasn't going to let the Boutle's girls pay for them. By the time she turned into East Lane the afternoon light was fading. She walked first to the river stairs, watching as a dull orange sun set over Tower Bridge. For a moment the brassy disc was suspended between the bridge's two towers, north and south, caught between two worlds – just as she was.

As it dipped and sank beneath the Thames, she turned away to see that Longbonnet was watching from her doorway. The old woman nodded her grey ringlets and pulled her shawl closely around her before beckoning to Kate.

'You'll be leaving then, gel,' she stated.

'I'm going to live with my dad,' Kate said, unsurprised now that the old woman already knew.

'Come in.' Longbonnet disappeared into the house, expecting Kate to follow. 'I won't be a minute.' The old woman went upstairs and returned carrying a small box.

She opened it and held out to Kate a gold belcher chain. 'That's yours.'

'Mine? No, I can't take this, Longbon— Aunt Rosina. It's too valuable!'

'Course it's valuable. It was your mother's. So were these.' Longbonnet pulled out a sovereign ring, some more chains, a brooch to fasten a shawl made of a silver coin, and lastly, a single, heavy gold earring shaped like a teardrop and pierced with a filigree pattern. 'One of a pair, the other's lost,' Longbonnet explained, placing the earring in Kate's hand so she could feel its weight. 'Bessie wasn't the poor slut they'd have you believe, Kate. She had her own money. It might not be like *their* money. We wear ours. Truth be told, there wasn't a lot left betime she died. But I've been saving this for when you really needed it.'

Kate was bewildered. She'd 'really needed it' when Aunt Sylvie had chucked her out and she'd been forced to borrow from Mr Smith, so why had Longbonnet waited till now? 'I'm grateful, but I think you should keep it. I don't need it now, me dad's giving me an allowance, you see.'

'Don't argue with me, Kate. But you just keep this quiet. Your darlin' mother give these to me before she died. It was her wish you should have 'em. "Keep it all safe for me little girl, Aunt Rosina," she said to me. "You'll know when to give it to her." It's your inheritance, Kate. Don't matter about what Archie Goss gives you or don't give you, a woman needs her *own* money.'

Mad old Longbonnet had been the scary figure of Kate's childhood, but now, wanting to honour her mother's wishes, she took the jewellery, kissing the old lady without any trepidation. She was learning that appearances are no indication of character and, as she felt the weight of her mother's treasure in her hand, she understood, too, that wealth was not the same as worth. For her the value of this 'treasure' lay simply in the connection it offered to her mum. Bessie Goss had worn it and therefore it was priceless.

She wasn't looking forward to telling Aunt Sarah about her move, but was relieved to discover that her aunt held no grudge towards her. She sent Kate off with only good wishes, refraining from any more complaints about Archie, until Kate promised to visit her soon. Her aunt held up a warning hand. 'If you come, you come, but don't make promises you can't keep, Kate. It's what he always did.'

Kate decided it was best to leave it to the street gossips to inform her Aunt Sylvie that she'd left East Lane for good. Let her figure out for herself where Kate had gone.

Her final visit was the one she'd dreaded most and now, standing in front of Johnny's front door, she rehearsed all the reasons why this wasn't goodbye. She felt a brief, cowardly hope that he'd be out. But when there was no answer her heart sank and she realized it wasn't a goodbye she'd come for, but a blessing.

It was all very well her dad saying he'd not have his daughter working in a factory, but by the new year the shopping trips with Nora and the stream of luncheon and dinner parties they gave had already begun to wear thin.

'I'm not complaining,' she prefaced to Nora as they sat in the garden room, drinking tea, 'but I'm used to being busy. Going from three jobs to none in as many weeks... well. I wasn't brought up to be a lady, was I?'

'You're every bit as good as any lady I've ever met!' Nora said.

Kate smiled at her protectiveness. Nora had a surprisingly strong maternal side beneath her impassive exterior. And she was another who'd taught her that initial impressions could sometimes deceive.

'I just meant I'm not used to idleness... not that I'm saying you're idle, but you've got all your charity work.'

'And you've got the bookshop.'

'Hmm, but that's only once or twice a week, and I mostly go to see the friends I made.'

Nora poured more tea and handed her a cup. 'And Johnny, of course. How is he?'

'He seems well, concentrating on his writing. The

publisher's collecting all his articles together and making it into a book. The title's going to be *Called On: A Docker's Life in Bermondsey*.'

'Yes, Ethel told me, he's done terribly well. But I meant, how is he coping with not seeing so much of you?'

Kate sighed. 'Bit better than I expected. I thought he'd miss me more!' She pulled a face.

'Has he found someone else, do you think?'

Kate nodded. 'Pamela, the blonde...'

'Oh, I know, kohl eye make-up? Always made sure she sat next to him in lectures?'

'You noticed! I knew he'd have no trouble finding himself another girl. I think she's got a lot in common with him – writing, you know,' she said, trying to be generous.

But it hadn't been easy, this fracture in her life. It had been too sudden and, though well-intentioned on her dad's part, too violent in its extreme dislocation. She felt loved, but she also felt adrift.

'I think you should take your father up on his offer of fitting out a workshop for your silversmithing.'

'I would if it was tin we was talking about. But I can't let him buy me silver. It's too expensive! I understand everything about money being tied up in the business...'

She hadn't probed Nora further about their finances, but she'd been surprised at how extravagant her father's tastes were. Now Nora was silent as she poured more tea. Eventually she said, 'It's something he can do for you. You should let him do as he wants.'

Because that's what you always do? Kate thought but didn't say.

'It's only because he can't bear me being a tin basher – a tinker, his daughter!' Kate had also learned that her father, in spite of his humble Bermondsey beginnings, was a bit of a snob. She shrugged. 'Funnily enough that's what they always called me at home, long before I got a job at Boutle's. Aunt Sylvie used to say, "You're a sly tinker, just like your mother!"'

Nora looked thoughtful. 'But she wasn't a tinker. She was Romany.'

'How do you know that?' Kate asked, surprised.

'Chibby talked about Bessie, when we first knew each other. He told me she was Romany royalty!'

'I never knew that...' Kate said, thinking of her mother's bequest, which she'd hidden away and told no one about, just as Longbonnet had instructed. 'I'm finding out more about her than I have in all my life. Do you remember I told you about old Longbonnet?'

Nora nodded. 'I do! You did a very good impression of an old lady.'

'I found out she's my Great-Aunt Rosina!'

'Really? But I thought Bessie had no family left. Perhaps Chibby didn't know.'

'Perhaps,' Kate echoed, while privately thinking that he must have.

'Well, getting back to your smithing, there's nothing stopping you from working in other metals if you feel you can't accept silver – what about bronze, or pewter?'

Kate considered for a moment. Tin and copper and lead shouldn't bankrupt her father. 'Maybe I'll do some of each.' She smiled at the idea. 'And perhaps he'd let me sell a few things.'

Nora looked doubtful. 'Chibby has strange, old-fashioned ideas when it comes to the women in his life. He wouldn't allow us to work.'

Kate remembered the years she'd slaved in the soldering

room. She kept her peace. It was another life. And he'd been deceived about her.

It had been good to be talking like this to Nora again. She'd become less of a confidante since Kate had moved in. There were now no more talks about the state of her marriage, no hints at her loneliness. Perhaps it was just that Nora was happier since Kate had come. But now she had an intimate view of Nora's marriage, Kate looked in vain for signs of the bullying she'd once suspected. In fact, if anything, she saw excessive devotion.

But she now understood better Nora's complaint that Chibby took up all of her life when he was at home. He was the same with Kate. Except she found him a welcome intrusion, one she'd dreamed of for most of her life, and she couldn't get enough of his time or his attention.

That evening, when she and Nora came back from the Sunday bookshop lecture, her father was home. He'd been on another business trip, this time to France, in the region where he'd met Nora. He was sitting at the piano when they came in and beckoned to Nora – he seemed in a sentimental mood.

'Remember this?'

He began singing in a rich, tenor voice.

Roses are shining in Picardy, in the hush of the silver dew,
Roses are flowering in Picardy, but there's never a rose like you!

And the roses will die with the summertime, and our roads may be far apart...

Here Nora put a hand on his shoulder as he came to the phrase – *But there's one rose that dies not in Picardy! 'Tis the rose that I keep in my heart!*

Nothing else was needed to convince Kate that she'd been mistaken in offering Nora the use of her soldering iron that day almost a year ago.

Kate soon discovered that her father liked to show off his 'two beautiful girls' – as she and Nora had become. When he wasn't travelling, this meant accompanying him on outings where they could be paraded in public, or to dinners, which usually involved business investors like Mrs Cliffe. Archie Goss was the sort of energetic powerhouse who slept little and packed more into a day than most people did in a week. Even his meetings with Nora and Kate were scheduled. And so in the last couple of weeks she'd seen quite a lot of Martin, when he'd been press-ganged into escorting either his mother or his aunt to one of Archie's social functions.

It was on one of these occasions that Kate casually mentioned to Martin the scene she'd witnessed, when Archie had sung his sentimental love song to Nora.

'It was sweet, Martin, so natural and loving – it made me realize what a fool I'd been to suspect him of ever harming her.' She spoke as to a friend, someone who might be interested in her guilt – and her happiness at finding herself wrong. She'd almost forgotten the alternative she'd once presented Martin with.

'Sweet? Natural?' He stared at her in disbelief. '*Now* you're being a fool! Chibby never does anything without working it out a year in advance. It was for *you*, Kate – not for her!' She jumped at the vehemence of his tone. 'And so now they're a picture of love's young dream in your eyes, what does that make me?'

If they hadn't been in the crowded reception room, with Nora and her father circulating and Martin's aunt and mother within earshot, he would have been shouting at her by now.

Kate explained that she'd discounted *all* her stupid judgements, including the ones that involved Martin. But he was furious with her. 'No! I won't listen to another word. I've had about enough of being branded a – oh, I don't know what you'd even call it! – a mistress beater! I shouldn't have to explain, I shouldn't have to talk about a married woman's private life. But I'll say it once and then I want you to leave it alone. When Nora came back to England seven years ago, she was nineteen, unbearably sad, beautiful, disowned by her family and very alone. I was eighteen. Of *course* I bloody well fell in love with her! And I think she loved me too, but only because she was so miserable.'

'So, I was right, you did have an affair...'

He pulled himself up to his full height and straightened his jacket. 'We were close, but it was all very innocent. She wouldn't allow anything more and we certainly never committed adultery, if that's what you mean.' It was an oddly legal phrase for him to use about someone he'd obviously adored.

She snorted her contempt. 'But you did in your heart.' She repeated the phrase that the nuns at her old school had used to warn their girls. There was no escaping the heart, she thought, it would trick you every time. And now that she knew the truth of it, she thought her own heart might be betraying her into falling in love with Martin after all.

'You don't understand – there are things I could tell you, but it would be breaking Nora's confidence. When Chibby came home from the war everything changed between us, and by the time you met Nora, yes, I might have still been a bit in love, but for her it was nothing but a friendship between us.'

'Then why did you tell her to leave him for you?'

'When?' She didn't think his shock was feigned. 'I never said any such thing!'

'You did! I heard you telling her, at the studio one day. You was both in the other room but I heard all right, you said, "You should leave him right now while you can." And that's why I don't believe you about *anything*.' Now she was angry with him.

'Whatever I did or didn't say to Nora, you'll have to ask her for an explanation. But I swear I never laid a hand on her!' He uttered the last phrase in a low voice, with great emphasis and a deliberate pause between each word, almost as if he were hammering a nail into her head. 'Whoever made those marks on her throat, it wasn't me…'

'And it wasn't my father.'

'Perhaps not, but she would come to me for someone to talk to and I have to warn you, Kate, your precious father is not always kind. That's the only reason I'd be urging her to leave him.'

Her immediate reaction was to defend Archie. 'I know he leaves her alone too much and then expects her to drop everything when he's back, but that's because he really does love her.'

Martin's lips compressed in disapproval. She thought there was jealousy there, but also something else.

'What ain't you telling me?'

He seemed to make a decision. 'I don't trust him.'

'Why not?'

He stared at her for a moment and then pulled her out

of the reception room, hustling her into the garden room. 'Listen, Aunt Violet befriended Nora when she first came to England. My aunt knows Nora's family, thought they treated her disgracefully, and she stepped in to help Nora with... everything. She's been a good friend to her ever since. But she might as well have not existed as far as Chibby was concerned... not until Nora's money started to run out. Then suddenly it was, "Oh, Mrs Cliffe, you must visit us here" or "You must come to the races, to the theatre..." She was invited to everything! And now my *mother*?'

She wanted to hit him. 'So, you're saying he just married Nora for her money?' A minute ago she had thought she was in love with him, and now she hated him. 'I think you're just jealous. And besides, I've seen them together, in private, and he's so romantic with her. You should have seen them the other night, I tell you, they were like newly-weds...'

He made a gesture of frustration and fixed her with a cold stare. 'You're famous at the bookshop, you know, for being able to read people, understand their insides, pinpoint the very thing that will bring them unhappiness – or happiness.' His scathing tone told her there was a 'but' coming. 'But you'll never be able to read your father, and you'll never understand those two, not until you've asked Nora about Paul.'

Martin had left the party without speaking to her again. Perhaps he never would. Over the next week she tried many times to broach the subject of the mysterious Paul with Nora. Normally so good at asking questions, Kate found this was one that she couldn't articulate. Whenever it was on the tip of her tongue, she'd lose her nerve. It was the fear of an answer she wouldn't like, she knew that. And so she let the pattern of their days as a new family continue, gradually coming to understand how it was that her mother had been so taken up with Archie whenever he'd returned from trips away when Kate was a child. When he was home, he made himself the centre of everything, and when he wasn't, you were left almost wondering what your life was for. This was the part of reuniting with her father that felt the least comfortable to Kate.

When Nora told her that Chibby would be away in Liverpool for a few days, Kate took the opportunity to begin constructing her own place, somewhere she could exist in the spaces between his absences, somewhere she could still feel herself. Although he'd been delighted when she'd agreed to his idea of a workshop and had asked for a list of things she would need, nothing had transpired. She decided not to wait any longer.

While her father was away, she began spending as much time as she could in the modest back basement room which had been set aside for her. She used her allowance to buy a small gas stove for heating the soldering irons. It was smaller but much cleaner than the big old coke ovens at Boutle's. She loved the peace and order of the emerging workshop. The semi-basement room gave a partial view up into the garden through French windows, so there was enough light to work by and good ventilation. She had begun by working on some design sketches of bronze stands and shades for electric desk lamps and decided the time was right to order tinplate, a small amount of copper and some lead. She hoped to buy all her materials at trade, so she decided to visit her old friend Miss Dane at Boutle's the following day to ask for her help.

Kate had been unable to get to the bookshop lately, nor had she seen much of Johnny. She missed them both and she missed

Bermondsey. She told Nora that she'd take the opportunity of her trip to Boutle's to volunteer for the evening shift at the bookshop. But when she arrived she found that more than enough volunteers were already on duty. She was tempted to go to Johnny's, but he'd probably be with the clever Pamela. It was easy to see how Archie Goss had drifted away from his Bermondsey family over the years; a shift up the social scale was more than just a change of location. All the bonds East Lane shared – formed from the daily fight against poverty, dirt and disease – had been weakened and she hadn't worked out a way to be both a Bermondsey girl and a young lady from Belgravia. She doubted she ever would.

She decided to make her own way home. She walked swiftly across Tower Bridge. The early-evening air was damp with the threat of rain and she belted her mackintosh tightly, pulling up the collar. The river was black ink and above it a luminous violet twilight. Looking always to her right, she sought out where the river inserted itself like a dark blade into St Saviour's dock. Just beyond would be East Lane Stairs and the place she still thought of as home. She kept her eyes fixed on that spot until she had to cross over the road and skirt the Tower for Mark Lane underground station. As soon as she got out at Sloane Square, the threatened rain shower arrived, and she trotted the rest of the way to her father's house.

Letting herself in, she was surprised to find the house empty. Nora hadn't said she was going out tonight. She shook out her mackintosh, kicked off her wet shoes and went straight to her workshop. Sitting at her new bench, she pulled out her designs. They were rough, untechnical, imprecise, but they were enough to be her guide. She began sketching a new idea for a geometric fan-shaped jewellery box, but the storm had made the house feel oppressive and she opened one of the

French windows. She looked into the inky shadows between shrubbery and trees and breathed in sweet damp air, listening as the weakening rain spattered a tattoo onto flat, black laurel leaves.

She was about to return to her sketches when she heard sounds coming from the garden room above. She froze, listening more intently. It might be the young maid-of-all-work, but this was her night off and normally she spent it with her chap – an errand boy from Harrods she thought nobody knew about. The sound came again and now it was recognizably that of weeping. Kate put down her pencil, crept in her stockinged feet upstairs and found the garden-room door ajar.

It was Nora, sitting in shadow. The twilight had deepened and she was only visible in the darkened room because of her pale dress. Her face was obscured by a loop of dark hair, her head bent over something she was holding in her lap. Her sobbing was gentle, sighing almost, as her shoulders rose and fell. But she'd made no attempt to muffle the sound. She obviously thought she was alone in the house. Kate decided to leave her in peace. If she'd wanted to share whatever pain it was that had caused these tears, she would have done so.

But as Kate turned away, the floorboards creaked. Nora looked up sharply. 'Who's there? Chibby, is that you?'

Kate saw her slip whatever she was holding down the side of her chair.

'Hello?' Nora half rose and Kate stepped out of the shadows.

'It's only me.'

Nora brushed away her tears. Her face was spectral, her eyes hollow, her expression agonized; Kate felt as if she'd intruded on something painfully private, but didn't know how to retreat. She decided not to pretend. 'Why are you crying?'

Nora dipped her head again and, unable to speak, covered her face with her hands.

Kate sat on the arm of Nora's chair and put an arm around her. 'Ever since I met you, you've been sad. You don't have to answer me if you don't want to, but, Nora, who is Paul?'

Nora gasped and searched Kate's face for an instant before taking in another shuddering breath. She pulled out whatever she'd hidden in the armchair and smoothed it in her lap. It was a smallish, dog-eared photograph. She handed it to Kate.

'Paul,' she said. 'My son.'

16

Reviled Beloved

1925

Kate stared at the photo. She had a million questions clamouring to be answered. Had Nora been married before? Wouldn't she have been too young? She'd been barely nineteen when Chibby had sent her to England. But what if the child had been born out of wedlock or Chibby had just married Nora to save her honour?

The boy was small-featured and dark-haired like Nora. The photograph showed the toddler from the waist up. He was delicate and small-boned, and there was something awkward about his posture, as if he'd been forced into one of those excruciating poses Martin chose for Kate. She guessed he'd been positioned to lessen his obvious defects – a twisted torso, one shoulder higher than the other. Large, luminous dark eyes seemed almost to plead with the camera to be released.

'It was taken for his third birthday. Chibby said we shouldn't have him photographed full length. He isn't properly formed,' Nora said, stroking the photo.

'He's a beautiful boy,' Kate said, looking at the exquisite features.

And Nora raised brimming eyes to her. 'Do you really think so?' she asked, with an almost desperate desire.

'Of course I mean it! He's the face cut off of you – and you're beautiful.'

Kate's words brought on fresh tears. 'You're so kind. When I first met you, I thought you were like your father. He can be a hard man, Kate,' she said, almost apologetically. 'But now I know you're not like him at all.'

'Now I can understand why you've always seemed so sad. For a child to die before their mother…' Kate couldn't really know what it was like, but she'd been a child whose mother had died before her, whose father had left her – she understood enough about loss. 'How old was Paul when you lost him?' She gave the photo back to Nora.

'You're right, to lose a child is agony.' Nora dipped her head, and her voice was so low that Kate had to lean in very close to hear the rest. 'He's been gone three years. I lost him when he was four. But, Kate, he isn't dead.' Nora pressed the photo to her breast and lifted her lovely face. 'Can you understand how hard it's been for me, to see Chibby welcome you home, his beloved child, when my Paul he reviled and sent away?'

'Nora, Nora.' Kate held the woman tightly as her sobs, no longer gentle, racked her entire body. 'I'm sorry. How could I have known? Why did my dad send him away? Was it because he's someone else's child?'

'No, Kate, you've misunderstood. Paul is Chibby's son! Though he wishes he weren't.'

Kate sat down, stunned, struggling to comprehend that her

father had another child she knew nothing about. 'Paul's my brother?'

Nora nodded. 'Of course.'

'How could he do that to his own child?'

Nora said, 'I've asked myself that a million times. As Paul grew older and his difficulty walking became more obvious, Chibby couldn't even bear to look at him. He said that the strain of looking after him was ruining my health, that it would be better for me to send him away to be looked after properly... And I let him. God forgive me, I let him.'

Kate held her tightly until she had cried herself to a miserable silence. Then all at once Nora pulled herself up straight.

'I shouldn't have said anything. And neither must you. As far as Chibby is concerned, Paul might as well be dead. He told me he did it for my sake, but I knew. My husband couldn't tolerate the imperfection, you see. And yet he's so different with you. It seems you're perfect.'

What happens when he finds out I'm not? Kate thought, even as her heart reached out to her unknown brother. Abandoned. Probably hoping for his father to come for him, longing to be the loved child, just as she had. It wasn't fair.

'Did Paul know why he was sent away – I mean, could he understand?'

'Are you asking if his mind is as imperfect as his body?'

Kate nodded. 'I suppose so.'

'Sometimes I wish it were, that he was as simple as some of the other souls in that place. He's not, though. He's sharp.'

Kate took the photograph again. Yes. Those eyes, so dark and deep, looked out on the world with a knowing that was faintly unsettling.

'He looks clever,' Kate said. 'And he looks perfect to me. I think Dad ought to bring him home.'

Nora got up quickly. 'No. You mustn't interfere. He won't have it and I don't want you to be hurt for my sins.'

'Hurt? How?'

'You're beloved now, but Chibby won't be crossed. He's fixed, do you see?' And she put up a hand and sliced it straight through the air, like the blade of a very long sword. 'It's his nature.'

'People can change.'

'Not Chibby.' She shook her head and then shuddered involuntarily. 'It's my cross to bear, Kate. Not yours.'

'But if he's my brother—'

'One that you didn't know you had.' Nora wiped any remaining tears from her cheeks. She stood straight-backed in the dark room, pale and impassive as the first time Kate had seen her.

'How could you have let him go?' She couldn't keep the accusation from her voice.

Nora said simply, 'Because he would have been worse off here. And a mother has to protect her child.'

Kate had a memory of her own mother, hugging her close and tight till it hurt. 'I understand.'

'Who is Paul?' She had wanted to know and now she had to live with the answer. Another unintended consequence of one of those awkward questions she always seemed compelled to ask. It hadn't seemed right for Kate to talk about her shock and confusion, not when Nora was quashing her own suffering. But that night as Kate lay awake in the pretty violet bedroom Nora had made for her, she probed those feelings.

The new understanding of her father's inflexible, remorseless pursuit of the finest in everything – even to his son's body – sat like one of the heavy meals she was becoming accustomed to, undigested, unwanted, but impossible to ignore. She turned her mind instead to Paul. She had a brother. She smiled into the darkness. 'Hello, Paul, I'm your sister,' she whispered, practising for that meeting which she knew would happen one day. And the feeling she had then was light, bubbling, like the first glass of champagne she'd ever tasted with Martin. Martin. Why had he put the question about Paul into her mind?

Martin opened the flat door wearing his artist's smock and warpaint. His hands, stained blue and red, had somehow transferred the oils to his hair and his cheeks.

'Oh, it's you!' he said.

'Nice to see you too.' She brushed past him, not waiting to be invited in.

'I'm painting.'

'I ain't blind.'

'I meant I've got a model here.' He blocked her way to the double doors of the studio, but she peered over his shoulder. A naked young woman was reclining on the chaise longue.

'I hope you've put a cloth on that couch – I sit there!'

'Not for some time you haven't.'

'I didn't think you wanted to speak to me, after…'

'What can I do for you?' he said, wiping his hands on his smock.

She nodded towards the model. 'First of all, you can tell *her* to get some clothes on. She looks a bit cold.'

Martin went in and muttered something to the girl, who

came out shortly afterwards, fully dressed and smiling broadly. 'Thanks, love, I just got a day's pay for sitting on me arse for an hour!'

She patted her pocket as she left. Martin came back in with clean hands and face, his expression serious.

'Sit down, Kate. Drink?'

She sat on the small sofa, hating his cool manner.

'You're obviously here for a reason,' he said, pouring himself a whisky and sitting in the chair opposite.

'I asked Nora about Paul.'

His expression softened. 'Oh, I'm sorry.'

'Why? You're the one who said I should.'

'I'm sorry because now you know who your father really is.'

'Is that what you wanted? To hurt me?'

He leaned back in the chair, looking at the ceiling. He sighed. 'What I wanted was for your eyes to be opened; I wanted you to trust me.' He gave her a despairing look. 'If you can never trust me, you can never love me, can you?'

She looked away, choosing not to answer his question. 'Well, I should've trusted you,' she said eventually. 'I can't believe my dad would do something like that to his own child.'

'Why not? He left you to rot in East Lane for long enough.'

'But he was always coming back!'

'And yet you met him quite by chance...' His tone was mocking.

'Stop it! I'm not stupid, Martin. I'm getting the picture. Dad's not perfect, he's not a soft-hearted man, he's even cold at times – but that's no crime. Look at you!'

'Me? Cold?' He gave a short laugh. 'Ridiculous.'

'All right – cool. With most people.' And as she said it, his eyes lingered on her, and she had to admit, their expression was anything but cold. Before she could say more, he crossed the room and took her in his arms. He kissed her, his lips hard, his unshaved cheek rasping hers, yet she didn't mind. Perhaps it was this that she had been waiting for: Martin's passion – or perhaps her own – for she'd never felt that irresistible draw to be close to Martin that she had with Johnny. But now, when he finally pulled away to look at her, she didn't want him to stop.

'Cool enough for you?' he asked, his mouth returning to hers. Till eventually, she had to put a finger between his lips and her own.

'I think I'll have that drink now, Martin.'

She smoothed her hair and her dress while he went to the drinks cabinet. She felt her heart thumping and her skin tingling. She hardly recognized herself as she took the whisky from him. Was she being a fool? But as he sat beside her, she studied him with fresh eyes. She'd always thought of him as boyish, but not today. It might have been the shadows cast by the stubble, but his chin looked stronger, his cheeks leaner and his brow more deeply furrowed. Up close she saw all the fine creases around his eyes etched by years and experience. She found she hadn't been seeing him at all.

'So. Do you think you could ever love me?' He put an arm around her.

'I don't understand why you'd want me to, Martin. But yes, I think I could,' she said, surprised to find it was true.

She felt his chest expand as he took in a deep breath. He fixed her with loving eyes and she didn't look away as he explained why he wanted her love. 'You're an extraordinary woman, Kate, and yet you don't know it. You're strong and funny and clever – here she gave a snort of disbelief – yes, clever, you've had no advantages to speak of and yet I do believe you could run the country if you set your mind to it! And did I mention you are creative and captivating and—'

'Oh, enough!' she said. 'You've answered my question.'

Leaning into him, with his arm around her, she was happy to speak of other things, but she let his loving declarations sink deep into her heart so she could remember them later. They talked about his work and she explained her whitesmithing venture. He was delighted at the idea, asking to see her designs, suggesting he could find a gallery that might sell them. But when she told him her father wouldn't like that, his face darkened.

'Will you still take notice of what he wants? Hasn't what you've learned changed your opinion of him at all?'

'Of course I still have to take notice! I'm living with him. But what he's done to Paul is wrong and I'm going to make him change his mind. Nora says I should leave it.' She stroked his arm. 'Will you talk to her for me?'

He thought for a moment, rubbing his stubbly chin with an insistent rasping.

'Well?'

'All right, I'll talk to her, but she won't listen to me.' He tried to kiss her again, but this time she pushed him away with a laugh.

'Oh, no. Not until you've had a shave.'

His eyes widened in disbelief. 'What, right now?'

'Now.' And although he made a mock show of being put out, she knew he was pleased and that today she could have asked him to do anything and he would have happily agreed.

Martin had made good on his promise and spoken to Nora about Paul. Since then, she'd been avoiding Kate. But this morning she and Nora were due to spend the day helping to organize the Bermondsey Bookshop's fourth anniversary celebrations. They met in the garden room and immediately Nora said, 'Kate, you shouldn't have gone to Martin.' She dropped her voice. 'What I choose to do about my son has nothing to do with him.'

'But he's your friend, you listen to him about other things, I just thought he could help you to see straight...'

'No! What makes you think you could talk to Chibby about Paul when his own wife can't?'

'I'm sorry. I know it's really none of my business. I won't say anything to Dad. But couldn't I at least visit Paul?'

'Absolutely not!'

'He's my brother! I want to get to know him. It's not fair I can't see him.'

Nora, who had been pacing the length of the garden room, stopped and turned to face Kate, a rare flash of anger in her eyes. 'It's not fair I can't either.'

'You don't visit him? What sort of a mother are you?' She looked at Nora, her chest tight with fierce judgement, which she knew wasn't solely aimed at Nora. 'You're as bad as my dad.'

She pushed back her chair and almost ran from the room. But Nora stopped her, tugging her back inside.

'Shush, Kate. I'm sure the maid eavesdrops and repeats things.' She shut the door with a firm click. 'First promise me you won't repeat things as well.'

She nodded, knowing it was a promise to keep secrets from her father, which made her feel unaccountably nervous. But she had to know.

'When Chibby sent Paul away, he found the school. A nice place, where Paul could develop to his full potential. But he said the only way we could all live happy lives was for us to forget each other.'

'He stopped you going to see Paul?'

The instinct for secrecy was strong in Nora. She dropped her voice even lower and looked over her shoulder, going to close a window.

'Not specifically. He *advised* it was necessary – if we wanted our son to have a full life. And he had the backing of the school. Their experimental method actually calls for it.'

She paused, and when she spoke again her voice was breathless and her words tumbled out. 'I didn't go for a year. I accepted what Chibby said, I wanted the best for Paul...' Nora wanted her actions to be understood, but all Kate could think of was the boy, waiting and longing. She offered no encouraging words. 'But, Kate, I couldn't carry on, it was breaking my heart. So, I do go. And I see my darling boy whenever I can. And I keep it from my husband. He'd be absolutely furious with me if he found out I've been lying to him. But it *will* come out – if you start questioning him.'

Kate nodded, frightened even to utter a sound. And then, taking Nora's hand in hers, she whispered, 'Next time you visit him, can I come with you?'

A small smile lit Nora's sad face. She put her arms around Kate. 'Yes, I would like that very much. And so would your brother.'

Set at the top of a lawned double terrace, the place looked more like a country house than a school. It was a two-storey mock Tudor building, with white walls criss-crossed by black timbering and large bay windows protruding at each end. They ascended two flights of shallow steps to the main door and at the top Kate looked back, gasping at the far-reaching view. It was beautiful. She could see for miles across the wooded, undulating countryside. She'd wanted to hate the place. But her father hadn't condemned Paul to a prison or a dungeon – it was a pleasant country house, surrounded by spacious, well-kept grounds. She took in the sweeping view once more and had to admit, in a comparison of where they'd spent their childhoods, the reviled child had done much better than the beloved.

The door was answered by a fresh-faced young woman wearing plimsolls, a bandana and a green gym tunic. 'Oh, hello! Have you come for the open day? It's not until next week.'

Nora had explained to Kate that family visits were restricted to 'open days' which occurred twice a year. Only on occasions of ill health or other family crises was this rule relaxed. Taking Kate to see her brother risked flagging up Nora's visits to Chibby. The principal, she had explained, might well make a fuss about it. 'I'm sure he's well-meaning,' Nora said, 'but he has a visionary gleam in his eye, and sometimes I think that's dangerous – especially in an unmarried man with power over the lives of the young.'

'A bit like a priest, you mean?'

'I suppose so,' Nora had said.

The gym teacher was studying them now, swinging the wooden hoop she was holding, clearly not inviting them in.

'I've come to see Paul Grainger,' Nora explained. 'I have permission for a special visit. I've brought his sister with me.' She drew Kate forward.

The teacher flashed a bright smile, her eyes narrowing with suspicion. 'You can wait in the breakfast room,' she said. 'I'll send for Mr Woolf.'

She stood aside, and it was only then that Kate noticed, standing behind her, a small troop of children. Silent, docile, not like any group of school kids she'd ever seen. They each carried hoops, ribbons or dumb-bells and were all dressed identically in green gym dresses or shorts.

'Hilary, will you take a message to Mr Woolf for me?'

Hilary, who looked about twelve, slowly repeated back the message to the teacher and then set off, in a strange half-skipping walk, on legs that looked like brittle sticks.

'He won't keep you long.' The teacher showed them into a room, the entire front of which was a glazed bay. The top panes were stained glass and a bright morning sun splashed colour across the furniture. It felt like a chapel. As they sat in silence, waiting for Mr Woolf to appear, Kate thought she had never felt so unprepared in her life. Not even her first day at Boutle's could compare to this. It was no good looking to Nora for help. The woman's habitual calm had deserted her and she sat twisting her fingers around the handles of her beaded bag. Kate wondered which she was more nervous about – Kate meeting Paul, or Chibby finding out.

Mr Woolf was wearing a sports jacket and an open-necked Aertex shirt. Kate noticed that he also wore leather sandals with socks, rather than shoes. His face was ruddy, his long fair hair swept back from a domed forehead. His smile was as bright and suspicious as the gym teacher's.

'Good morning, Mrs Grainger!' He extended a hand to Nora and then Kate. 'No need to go to my office,' he continued, indicating seats at one of the refectory tables. 'We like informality here. I understand the purpose of your irregular visit is to introduce Paul to his sister?'

Here his smile widened as he turned to Kate. 'A momentous day for both of you. But I would like to explain a few things

first. So that you understand the potential consequences...'
He paused and asked casually, 'I presume your husband, Mr Grainger, has agreed to the meeting?'

Nora swallowed, but she now wore her unruffled calm like a familiar coat. The fiddling with her bag, the chewing of her cheek had ceased the minute Principal Woolf had entered the room.

'Indeed he has! And he's very happy it should happen. Unfortunately, he's detained on business and can't be with us.'

She was an accomplished liar, but still Mr Woolf pressed her. 'I believe he has *never* visited his son on one of our open days?'

Nora shook her head. 'Sadly not. He is away for a good part of each year. And he believes in your method of separation – wholeheartedly.'

This seemed to satisfy Mr Woolf. Kate had taken an instant dislike to the man. Anyone who smiled so much would be suspect in East Lane, so why not in East Sussex?

The photograph of Paul had shown him as a three-year-old. Four years later, his body hadn't grown as it should. His legs and arms were skeletal, his hands and feet twisted inwards. He sat in a throne-like wooden wheelchair with leather straps designed to support his wasted muscles. It was evident from the metal-and-leather collar visible at his neck that he was wearing a back brace, but the curve in his spine was still noticeable. Only the brightness of his large, intelligent eyes had not deteriorated since that photograph had been taken. They hadn't altered. The face in the photograph had looked haunted, and so now his smile at the sight of Nora was a shock to Kate. Like the bright sunbursts that sometimes bounced off the murky Thames, illuminating all the gloom, Paul's smile was dazzling. Kate felt instantly happy.

He tried to get up, fumbling with the leather straps that held him. But before he could unfasten them, Nora was at his side, her arms around his twisted torso, his thin arms clasping her. Kate's happiness was instantly dimmed with dismay – the brace and his weak arms prevented him from squeezing Nora as tightly as he obviously wanted to.

'Mummy? Why are you here?' He had Nora's musical voice, but thinner and higher-pitched. He looked uncertainly towards Kate, who smiled encouragingly.

He asked Nora, 'Is my daddy with you?'

Nora stroked her son's cheek. 'Not this time, darling.'

'Oh. Next time?'

'Perhaps next time.' Nora looked over her shoulder, beckoning Kate forward. 'But look, I've brought someone else with me.'

He winced as he twisted to look at Kate, shrugging at the confining steel of his brace. Then he gave her that dazzling smile. 'Hello,' he said, and he put out a twisted hand, which she took in both of hers.

'Hello, Paul.' She glanced at Nora, who nodded her permission. 'My name's Kate. I'm your sister.'

He laughed, his eyes crinkling, almost closing in amusement. 'Don't be silly! I'm an only child.' He looked for confirmation to Nora.

'It's true, Paul. Your father was married once before and he had a daughter, Kate. It's the most marvellous thing that your father found her again. And she so wanted to meet you.'

Paul's eyes widened. 'A sister! Where did my daddy find you? Where do you live?'

'I used to live in Bermondsey, where our dad comes from. But now I live with him and your mummy.'

Kate saw Nora's look of alarm. Paul's lower lip trembled. 'I wish I could live with my mummy and daddy.'

Kate took his hand. 'Perhaps one day you will!'

Nora squeezed her shoulder hard, and Kate swallowed the promise that she desperately wanted to give.

Their meeting place was a wood-panelled common room, with a large table and chairs, some books and board games. They drew up chairs to the table where Paul sat. Kate had worried that he wouldn't like her, would even be jealous that she'd taken his place at home. But he was quick to commandeer her.

'You sit beside me,' he ordered. 'We can play.' It didn't matter that she was twelve years older, and Kate found herself easily enchanted. They were soon engrossed in a game of draughts, while Nora sat silently looking on, a smile on her face. Paul was sometimes clumsy with the pieces, but quick to seize every advantage. He outwitted Kate at every turn, which she didn't mind at all.

'Are you letting me win?' the little boy asked suspiciously.

'Oh, no,' Kate laughed, 'you're beating me fair and square.' And he looked pleased.

He didn't need to try very hard and in between hopping over her pieces, he asked her questions. Incessant questions. Why hadn't their daddy come to fetch her when she was small? What were his cousins and aunts like and were they his family too? Was it fun working in a factory? Did she like living in East Lane? In the end she couldn't keep up. 'Why, why, why. You ask so many questions – you're just like I was! Only I used to get a wallop for it when I was your age.'

He stared at her mid-move. 'I'm sorry they weren't nice to you, Kate.' Then in a low voice he added solemnly, 'They're not nice here either.'

Nora stirred from her silence. 'Paul, that's not true. They only do what's best for you. I know the brace is uncomfortable, but at least your back is a little straighter now.'

He pulled at the metal contraption at his neck. 'Not just this. They lock us in...'

It was just then that Mr Woolf returned after their allotted hour. Paul's previous animated manner changed instantly. His smile disappeared. And still clutching her final two pieces in his twisted hand, he let it fall over hers. He fixed her with those pleading eyes and whispered, 'Ask my daddy if I can come home – like you did.'

Her eyes stung, a feeling of utter uselessness overtaking her. If she had to leave him here each time, it would be agony to go on visiting him. Nora's torment must be impossible. Kate squeezed Paul's hand, almost wishing that she hadn't pushed so hard to meet the brother she could not help.

Nora kissed her son goodbye and Paul began to cry.

'Now, now, silly,' she reassured him, 'I'll be back next week – for the open day!'

But he held tight to her hands as she tried to leave. 'Soon, my darling, I'll see you soon.'

As Nora hurried from the room, Kate hugged Paul, hearing Mr Woolf tutting at her back, impatient for her to be gone. When they joined Nora outside, she was leaning against the corridor wall, her face full of misery, her eyes full of tears.

Mr Woolf said, 'You see why we do not encourage these sorts of visits. It only upsets everyone concerned – not least your child, Mrs Grainger!' His tone pretended sympathy, but the visionary gleam hardened into an unpleasant disapproval that made Kate want to flee the place and his presence. She understood why Paul wanted the same.

When her father came back from his trip to the fur trade exhibition in Germany, he sought her out straight away, greeting her with a kiss. He'd grown more demonstrative over the weeks she'd been living there and she'd become less shy of him. She helped him off with his overcoat, liking the feeling that he was hers. *Her* father. Liking that he still had the smell of soot from the train on his overcoat and a tobacco smell to his hair. She slipped her arm through his. 'Come and see my workshop.'

'Let your father rest for a bit. He's been travelling all night!' She hadn't noticed Nora coming into the drawing room.

'No, no.' He gave a weary smile and kissed his wife. 'My Katy comes first.'

And the warm glow of being at the forefront of his affections after all these years dimmed like a twinkling star. If she came first, there was another who came last.

In the basement, she pushed open the studio door, flicked on the electric light and let him walk in first. He looked admiringly around the little room. 'You should have waited for me to help with this! But I see you've gone ahead and done it all on your own.' He picked up tools and metals, examining them carefully. 'I'd have been the same,' he said approvingly. 'If you want something done, do it yourself. That's always been the secret of my success.'

He leaned against her bench and looked at her with a half-smile on his face. 'Your mother was very good with her hands.'

'Was she?' Kate asked, intrigued. 'What sort of things did she make?'

'Wooden things. Well, I'm ashamed to say she made pegs to sell. Before we were married, of course! I soon put a stop to all that. But she made other things, beautiful flowers made of wood shavings. Intricate, delicate. And then there were the peg dolls for you. Don't you remember?'

She shook her head. 'I don't remember much about Mum.'

'Good.'

'But I wish I did!'

'If you don't remember her, you can't mourn. I'm glad for your sake, Kate.'

'But I did mourn, Dad. I still do.'

He pushed himself up from the bench. 'Yes, well. I'm sorry. Very sorry. But that's the past. You have to let it go. Never look back, that's my motto.'

Perhaps it had upset him, talking about her mother. He'd seemed suddenly to lose interest. 'I need a hot bath,' he said. 'Don't work too late on your trinkets.' He was making her feel as if she'd done something wrong.

'Out of sight, out of mind?' she burst out.

He halted in the doorway. 'What on earth do you mean?'

'Is that the way you cope with the guilt?'

'I've got nothing to feel guilty about – I've admitted my mistakes. I shouldn't have left you. But I've taken you in now – given you the best… I don't know what's got into you, Katy, but I don't like your tone!' His lips turned white and his face, which had been grey from tiredness, was flushed with anger.

There was a game they'd played as children – a gang of them would take turns hopping on and off the back of the 'ha'penny bumper', the oldest tram in Bermondsey. They'd jump and jump, setting up a rhythm that caused the wheels to leave the track, sending the tram grinding and screeching across the cobbles. She felt now as if she'd just hopped onto that ha'penny bumper and started a fatal rhythm that she had no idea how to stop.

She jumped again. 'I'm not just talking about *me*.' And again. 'You tell me to forget Mum. Don't think about her and it'll be like she was never here. Is that the way you could leave me and take up with a sixteen-year-old girl?' She didn't know where the anger was coming from. She'd believed she only felt grateful to have him back, dizzy with happiness. But now the ha'penny bumper was off the rails and heading who knew where.

'I left to fight a war, you ignorant girl! I couldn't think about Bessie and I couldn't think about you!'

'That's what I mean! Out of sight, out of mind – just like my brother!'

He couldn't have looked more stunned if she'd shot him between the eyes. But in an instant he was walking towards her, fists clenched, stopping with his face inches from hers. She could see small beads of sweat collecting in the furrows of his brow.

'What are you talking about? You've got no brother.'

She drew back, dropping her eyes for an instant. If she let the lie go, perhaps the jolting runaway tram could somehow be halted, lifted back onto the tracks. She looked into his eyes and something compelled her to jump one more time.

'My brother's name is Paul.'

He grabbed her shoulders, his thumbs digging in to the soft hollows beneath them. 'She had no right to tell you about the boy. You will *not* mention his name again.' His voice was low, hard and deliberate. 'The boy won't make old bones, and if I choose to protect my wife from that inevitable pain, it's my affair. You won't interfere.' His grip tightened, but she resisted squirming. Instead, she held his gaze.

'But he's not dead yet! He's alive and he's lonely and all he wants is for you to come. Just like I did! Why should I have a home here if he can't?'

He took hold of her elbow and hustled her out of the studio, up the stairs to the drawing room. He kicked open the door. Nora's stricken face filled Kate with guilt and fear. *What had she done?*

'How dare you involve Kate in my family affairs!' He slammed the door behind him with his foot.

Nora stood up, looking ready for flight. But then Kate saw her studied calm settling like a soft fall of snow and her fear melting away. She spoke softly, in musical tones, as if soothing a threatening animal.

'Chibby, this has nothing to do with Kate. Let her go.' She put out a beckoning hand. 'Come here, come to me, Kate.'

Her father's hand relaxed for an instant and Kate darted across the room to Nora, who drew her close so that she could feel the woman's trembling.

'Exactly, Nora. This is none of Kate's concern!' His voice had an implacable, deliberate quality that tolerated no contradiction.

'It was my fault! I found an old photo, I made her tell me about Paul,' Kate jumped in. 'I'm sorry, Dad. But when I saw his photo I was so upset, thinking I had a little brother that died before I could ever meet him – well, I cried so much...' She spoke in a rush and stopped to gulp in air. 'Nora felt sorry for me and told me he was at a special school.' She dug her fingers into Nora's side, willing her not to contradict the lie. Then, looking from one to the other, she pressed on. 'The last thing I wanted was to cause any trouble. I'm *really* sorry.'

Her father's rigid face relaxed a little. His breathing calmed and he sat, motioning for them to join him. He couldn't meet Kate's eye. When he spoke his tone was softer. 'I accept your apology, Katy. You're soft and silly, like your mother. I understand you were upset. But this mustn't be spoken of again. Paul was *my* child and I did what I thought was best for him. I don't expect to be contradicted in my own home and so long as you understand that, you're welcome to stay.' He got up and, turning his now-ashen face to Nora, he said, 'You shouldn't have kept the photograph.'

Once he'd left, they sat in silence, holding hands. 'Nora, I'm sorry. I don't know what devil made me ask him about Paul. I'm always the same. You warned me what would happen.'

'He believed you, Kate. He has no idea about my visits and that's all I care about. My boy will never come home. But so long as I can see him…'

Kate thought this was scant comfort, but she wouldn't ever put Nora in danger of losing it again.

17

A Pair of Gold Earrings

In the following days the atmosphere in the house was chilly. Her father was polite to her, asking questions about her whitesmithing at breakfast, but he would leave straight afterwards for his office and spend most evenings either working or having dinner with clients. Kate felt she'd endangered everything about her new life and now she was determined to keep a curb on her curiosity. Nora spoke no more about Paul, almost as if there really was a chance the maid would overhear and tell her husband. Instead she and Nora spent the time finalizing plans for the bookshop's anniversary dance at Rotherhithe Town Hall. It was to be a much bigger affair than the last, which had felt more like a local Saturday-night dance. For this occasion, all the literary lights who'd lectured or written for *The Bermondsey Book* had been invited, so Nora felt it was essential for Bermondsey to put on a good show.

She'd also insisted Kate have a new outfit. It was the most sophisticated thing she'd ever owned. A black silk evening dress, low cut at the front and back, with thin shoulder straps, a straight sequined bodice and transparent layers of voile over a skirt, which finished just below the knee. It was daring and mature, and she'd had her hair cut into a curly bob to complete the look.

On the night of the dance, she stood in front of Nora's mirror, shocked at her own transformation. She could see nothing of the Boutle's tin basher in the young, well-to-do woman reflected back at her.

'You look lovely!' Nora said. 'But it needs something gold to lift it.' She took a chain from her own neck and held it against Kate's throat. 'No. Spoils the neckline.' Then she dangled it against Kate's cheek. 'Yes, some gold earrings might do it. Let's see what I have.'

Nora retrieved a large jewellery box from her dressing table and placed it on her bed. Pulling out several drawers, she rifled through her collection, setting out pairs of earrings on the bedspread. 'Nothing's quite right.' She got up. 'There are more in the safe in Chibby's office. If I can remember the combination!'

She left Kate looking through the black-velvet-lined drawers of earrings. She pulled out the last drawer. As far as she could tell, there was nothing different here, just more gold hoops, studs and dangling earrings. If her father was that strapped for business cash, she thought he need look no further than his wife's jewellery box. She reached to the back of the drawer and her hand found a larger earring, which she pulled up and swung in the light from the bedside lamp. It was a heavy, solid-gold teardrop, pierced with a filigree pattern. She went cold. She felt around in the velvet-lined drawers, pulling out everything to find the matching earring. But she knew she would find nothing. For its twin was tucked safely away, with the rest of her inheritance, in a box at the back of her own wardrobe. This was her mother's earring.

When Nora returned with more treasures, Kate's hand closed firmly around the golden teardrop.

'My goodness, you've had a thorough search!' Nora said, eyeing the bedspread. 'I told you there was nothing.' She opened the mahogany box she was carrying. 'Look! Here are the real old beauties. These are my inheritance – or what's left of it!'

In the end Nora abandoned the idea of earrings altogether and instead teased the sides of Kate's hair into dark kiss curls. The deep black of the dress was relieved with a long string of pearls. As she looped them twice around Kate's throat, Nora said, 'These were my mother's.'

How she got through the evening Kate didn't know. Martin's compliments and sweet words as they arrived and danced barely touched her. Even seeing Johnny and being introduced to Pamela, who clung to his arm as if she owned him, couldn't reach her. She'd dropped the second earring into her black beaded bag and had brought it with her. It dragged on her arm and burdened her heart as though it were made of lead rather than gold. She spent the entire evening wishing only to get back home to check it against her own earring. Perhaps, after all, she'd been mistaken. When she and Martin sat for a drink, she found herself constantly feeling the bag for the teardrop nestled within the black silk.

When the evening was blessedly over and she was back

in her room, she locked the door and took out the box containing her own inheritance. She laid Nora's earring beside her mother's. They were identical. Why the discovery of this second earring should have so upset her she wasn't sure. Of course, it was natural her dad should still have some things belonging to her mum. She wasn't even jealous that he'd given the earring to Nora. But the sight of the two earrings, together once more, filled her again with cold shock. She went to her dressing-table mirror and put them on. They were heavy, tugging on her earlobes; long, falling just below her jaw. She turned her head this way and that. The earrings swung, lit by her bedside lamp, their filigree pattern changing with every new angle. It was as she placed her hands on the dark oak dressing table and tilted her head to one side that she remembered something. The combination of smooth wood beneath her fingertips and a dazzle of gold in dim light sparked a long-cold memory, which now burst into flame. Her image in the mirror faded, replaced by a vision of her six-year-old self, crouched on the garret floor, black timbers smooth with age beneath her small fingers as they curled around the open hatch.

How had she got there? She probed and saw herself waking in the night, all alone. She'd been sent to sleep in her own little bed because Daddy was coming home tonight. But it was too dark and cold up here on her own, she missed her mum. She opened her mouth to call for her, when she heard noises downstairs. Raised voices, angry, then a sharp cry, followed by a loud thud that made Kate jump out of her bed. She pattered on bare feet, making no sound, slipping to her knees by the garret hatch.

What had she seen? She didn't want to follow the memory any further. She looked up now, trying to quench the fire of remembrance, and, staring back from the mirror, she saw a face rigid with terror. The same terror she'd felt when she'd peered through that garret hatch into the dimly lit room below. She forced herself back into the body of her small self. There was her mother, lying on the rug, her head tilted at an impossible angle, her eyes wide, unseeing, staring up at Kate. In her ears were the long, golden earrings she always wore when she made herself pretty for Daddy coming home.

Kate sat heavily at her dressing table, her fingers stroking its dark wood, as if she were smoothing out the pages of an old picture book. All the crinkles and rips were gradually forming into a clear picture. She saw a pair of hands, large, pale, freckled. She could not see any other part of his body, nor his face. Just the white cuffs of his shirt and the arms of a dark suit. The hands tugged at her mother's ears, tearing the golden teardrop, so that a bead of blood seeped and then sat on her white earlobe, like a ruby. Kate let out a whimper. The hand hastily grabbed the other earring and then was gone.

What happened next? She remembered curling into the smallest ball she could, her legs and feet caught up inside her nightdress, her arms wrapped around her knees, and there she had stayed, shivering, till eventually she must have crept back to bed and fallen asleep. The next day her life had changed forever. Though her aunt explained to her later that her mother's death had been caused by a fall, she had never once remembered witnessing that death, nor that someone else had witnessed it too.

She wrapped the second earring in tissue paper so that she would know which had been with her father all those years and which had been safeguarded by Longbonnet. And the following day she set off for Bermondsey, telling Nora she was going to visit her Aunt Sarah. It wasn't a lie – she would go to her aunt's – but first she went to the house at the end of East Lane. Longbonnet was home, opening the door dressed in the sacking apron she used when preparing her 'supper delicacies'.

Kate followed her into the kitchen, where the old woman briefly stirred a pot of trotters before putting a kettle on to boil.

'What's happened?' Longbonnet asked as she poured them tea.

Kate hadn't slept well, and perhaps there were dark rings under her eyes, but she was surprised that Longbonnet had so easily guessed there was trouble. She took the earring out of her bag and laid it on the table between them.

'Hmm. The one your mother left you. Don't tell me Archie's got you to pawn it already? I told you to keep it a secret!'

Kate gave a weary smile and shook her head. 'It's still a secret, but I've got a question about it. You told me Mum gave it to you as part of my inheritance.'

Longbonnet nodded and slurped her tea.

'But how could she have done that when she died wearing it?'

'Gawd spare us,' Longbonnet muttered, setting down her cup and crossing herself several times. 'What are you talking about, gel?'

Why would the old woman have lied to her about the earring? This was what Kate had come to find out. She looked at the gnarled, large-knuckled hands now making the sign of the cross. They looked strong as a man's...

'I'm talking about the night my mum died. Yesterday'— was it only yesterday? It seemed a lifetime ago—'yesterday, something happened and I remembered that I was there. I saw Mum... I saw her dead.'

Longbonnet fixed her with dark, searching eyes. 'Yes?' she said, warily but not questioning the truth of it.

'I woke up in the garret and I remember I saw Mum on the floor downstairs. She looked so strange, not moving, her eyes were open – but I knew she couldn't see me. She was dead. And she was wearing these earrings. So how could she have given one to you?' Kate repeated.

The old woman's gaze didn't falter. Instead she reached for the earring. 'She didn't give it to me.'

'Why did you lie to me? Did you go there that night?'

'No, darlin'. I only wish I had. Your poor mother give me everything else, just as I said. But not this.' She stroked the golden teardrop. 'She kept back the earrings for something to pawn on the quick. I found this one in the lane, near Bessie's house, the morning after she died. And I never told a soul, not a living soul, that I found it, nor that it was covered in that lovely girl's blood. What happened to the other earring, I never asked. I just dropped this in a cup of gin, put it away for Bessie's girl, like she would've wanted. It's what I done and it seemed for the best, and you can blame me if you like, but I thought it was the safest thing to do.'

Kate sat back. It had the ring of truth. But why safest? 'I remember there was blood.'

'Oh, shhh, shhh. Kate, don't tell me. Don't. I tell you, gel, blood's called to blood, that's why it's come back to you!' Now Longbonnet let out a wail, and a choked keening followed, almost as if the old woman had long forgotten how to cry.

Kate grabbed the gnarled hands. 'I've got to tell you! There was someone else there. I remember seeing the hands pulling

THE BERMONDSEY BOOKSHOP

off the earrings, and Mum's ear must have ripped, because that's where the blood came from. Didn't anyone notice it? Didn't they ask any questions?'

Longbonnet shuddered and clutched Kate's hand tightly. 'I wasn't there, love. Your aunt Sylvie took over. Said she'd found Bessie at the bottom of the garret stairs. Said she must have fell. I don't think I ever believed it, but, gawd forgive me, what could I do? Did you see who it was, with your mother that night?'

'No.'

'But you know who it was?'

Kate took out the other earring. Carefully unwrapping the tissue paper, she showed Longbonnet. 'I found this. Me dad had it.'

Longbonnet sucked in a sharp breath and pulled her shawl tightly around her.

'Be careful, me darlin'. Nothing'll bring her back.'

When she returned home, Kate was glad that Nora wasn't there to question her. She rushed to her room and collapsed onto the bed. Retching, she put a hand to her mouth, finding with the other a handkerchief to stem the bile rising there. A cold sweat covered every inch of her skin and she slipped beneath the violet bedspread, pulling it up beneath her chin. Squeezing her eyes shut, she tried to banish the vision of those hands. The large, pale, freckled hands which only while talking to Longbonnet had she realized were those of her father. No wonder she'd never wanted to remember. But now she had, she found herself desperate to flee the person she'd longed for through all those empty years. For those hands had not been gentle.

She felt her eyes filling with tears of sadness and regret. Her darling mum had been lying there dead, and those thick-fingered hands had treated her with nothing more than a frantic desire. And for what? Two pieces of gold. Kate covered her mouth to silence an anguished cry. There was nothing she could do for her mother now, but equally, there was nothing her father could do to stop her finding out what had really happened that night.

As she let her tears flow freely, a soft knocking came at her door. 'Kate, I didn't expect you back so soon. Can I come in?'

She hastily wiped her eyes. 'Yes, Nora. Come in.'

'Oh, what's wrong? Have you been crying?' Nora sat on the bed. 'I thought you didn't seem yourself last night. Was it seeing Johnny with that little blonde thing on his arm? Are you still carrying a torch?'

Kate shook her head. 'No!'

'Hmm.' She put a hand to Kate's forehead. 'You're very hot and you've not even taken your clothes off! Let me help you.'

Kate let Nora help her to change into a nightdress and went along with the fiction of a sudden fever. 'Perhaps I've been soldering too much. It's the metal fever come back, I expect.'

'Oh, Kate. Chibby will be so upset. The last thing he'd want is for this whitesmithing of yours to make you ill!'

'Don't tell him!' Kate pleaded.

Nora patted her hand and pulled the covers up under her chin. 'You have kept my secrets, how can I not keep yours?'

'I'll be fine by tomorrow. It's just a little dose, nothing like I used to get at Boutle's!'

She desperately wanted Nora to go. She needed time to think. Longbonnet had warned her to be careful. But no warning could put the lid back on Kate's burning desire to know what had happened to her mother. And now she'd convinced Nora her fever was mild, the woman seemed in the mood to stay. She brought water for Kate and sat back on the bed. 'This Saturday is the school open day,' she whispered. 'If you're well enough, will you come?'

And thinking of those ungentle hands, she replied, 'Nothing would stop me.'

The grassy terraces had been newly mown and the gardens were draped in bunting. Kate was surprised that, on this cold day, the children had been ranged outside the house to greet the guests.

'They look perished!' she said to Nora as they joined a stream of visitors ascending the shallow steps to the house. She spotted Paul, strapped into his chair, scanning the crowd for them. His face was pinched. 'Why don't they let them wear coats?'

Nora looked pained. 'It's the policy. They believe in fresh air, the colder the better. It's good for their lungs and circulation... so they say.'

Kate privately thought it was the best way to give them all pneumonia, but Nora was obviously feeling bad enough, so she kept quiet. Beneath a pewter sky, they were kept waiting outside the entrance until Mr Woolf arrived to welcome them. The principal wore the same sandals and Aertex shirt as on their last visit, but had added a baggy old sweater.

'Nice to see he's made a bit of an effort,' she quipped under her breath and was glad to see Nora smile.

'The children have prepared a welcome!' Mr Woolf clapped his hands and every child lifted a musical instrument of some kind. Recorders, small cymbals, bells and shakers – one child had almost disappeared behind a large drum. When they were ready, a music teacher led them in a folk song that was difficult to identify, as the recorders each seemed to be playing a different tune and the percussion section ignored the baton entirely. Paul caught her eye and grimaced. She daren't laugh, in case she dented someone's confidence. But she thought the teacher could have matched her pupils' instruments with their abilities a bit more skilfully. It must have been torture for them. All they wanted was to see their parents. But even when the song was over, Mr Woolf kept a strict hold on proceedings, giving instructions about the duration of the visit before pairing children with their families and sending them off under the watchful eyes of teachers and nurses.

Finally, Paul's turn came. He was like a fizzing bottle of ginger ale ready to explode. Only when they were in a corner of the common room, surrounded by chattering groups, did he let the glass stopper off. His twisted arms grasped first his mother, then Kate, in an awkward embrace.

'I'm so glad Daddy let you come to see me again!' he said to Kate.

She smiled. 'What you been up to?'

He pulled a face. 'Recorder practice. I hate it. I'm no good at music, but they make us all do the same thing. It's silly. I'd be better off doing my maths. That's what I really like.'

Nora stroked his hand. 'Paul is very advanced in mathematics.' He gave a little smile and was obviously pleased with his mother's praise. 'Have you been out of the chair much since we last saw you?' Nora asked and Kate looked at his fragile legs, doubting they could hold even his feather weight.

'No,' he said sadly.

'And what about the pool, have you swum?'

He fidgeted. 'The pool's for the older boys, Mummy. I told you that.'

'No. Surely not. Your father told me all the facilities were available to you.'

Kate could see Paul squirming uncomfortably. 'Do you need to go?' He nodded.

She offered to push him to the bathroom but was quickly overtaken by the male nurse. 'I'll take him, miss.'

She waited outside the lavatories and just as the door was closing, saw the nurse place powerful hands around her brother's thin chest, hoisting him out of his chair like a sack of coals before dragging him into one of the cubicles. Ungentle hands. She clenched her teeth, wishing her father were here so that she could break his nose, the way she had once broken Janey's. And then she feared her own temperament. What if the Gosses were simply a violent-natured family – and she was just like all the rest of them? 'Dear God, let me be a Dye in my heart,' she prayed, using her mother's maiden name.

When they emerged, Paul wouldn't look at her. He was a seven-year-old boy; perhaps he found it embarrassing to need help going to the toilet. She insisted on pushing the chair. 'I can manage!' she said and stared at the male nurse till he retreated. On the way back to Nora she noticed Paul's brace was chafing his neck. As she bent to adjust it she saw that his shirt was ripped near the collar. He pushed her away.

'I'm sorry, Paul. I was just trying—'

'It's not you,' he whispered, blinking back tears. 'I hate him.' He shot a look at the retreating nurse. 'I'm sure he hurts me on purpose. They all do it, slinging me about as if I haven't got any legs, but I can walk, Kate! It's just I'm too slow and they get impatient. It's quicker to stuff me in a chair.'

'Try not to be upset, Paul. Stay brave for your mummy and I promise, I'll get you out of here one day.'

He stopped crying and looked at her with a sort of adoration. 'I thought it would be my daddy that rescued me, but now I think it'll be you!' he whispered, smiling heartbreakingly up at her.

She realized what a terrible thing she'd done. The thing Longbonnet had warned her against – making a promise you can't keep. And she determined then that she wouldn't be the one to let him down.

Kate wanted to keep out of her father's way as much as she could. Should he decide to come home early from his office or take a day off, she couldn't trust herself not to confront him about the people most on her mind – her mother and her brother – so she volunteered for extra shifts at the bookshop to keep herself out of harm's way. Not long after the open day at Paul's school, Kate was serving a customer in the bookshop when Nora paid an unexpected visit. She waited patiently by the fireplace while Kate marked off the cost of the book on the young man's subscription card. When he'd gone, Nora turned to face Kate. She had the look of a hunted animal.

'What's the matter, Nora? Shouldn't you be with Dad at Mrs Cliffe's benefit concert?'

There was no one else in the shop and she drew Nora to the table at the back, where, beneath the overhead light, she could see her face more clearly. Though Nora had done her best with a chiffon scarf, the marks on her throat were visible to Kate, who was transported back to their first meeting in this very place. Back then, the bruises had already begun to fade, but these were purple and fresh. Kate knew Nora well enough now not to pussyfoot around the woman's misplaced loyalty and pride. 'What did you do wrong?' she asked, gently plucking the scarf from Nora's elegant neck.

Nora clutched at it but too late. The fingermarks clearly ringed her throat.

'Chibby found out about my visits to Paul.' Nora put up her delicate fingers to hide the imprint of those other, coarser ones.

'So, he did this?'

Nora didn't attempt to deny it. 'His temper has always been his failing.'

'Don't make excuses for him, Nora! This is a bit more than just temper. I can't believe I waited for him all those years and he turns out a bloody wife beater!'

Nora flinched, almost as if Kate had aimed a blow herself. 'So, how did he find out about the visit?'

'From Mr Woolf. Apparently, the school fees haven't been paid for last year. Mr Woolf telephoned to chase the money and told Chibby he hadn't raised the subject at the open day as Mrs Grainger and Paul's sister seemed to be enjoying the occasion so much, and he wouldn't have wanted to spoil it...'

'Oh, no. Did you tell him it was just the one visit?'

'He didn't believe me. It was terrible, Kate – his rage, when it comes... it's like there's a devil in him and nothing I say makes any difference. I thought he might kill me.' She massaged her neck. 'He'll feel awful tomorrow.'

Nora was trembling so violently she was unable to keep her limbs still. Kate put a 'closed' sign on the door. The reading room wasn't being used for a class that night, so she helped Nora upstairs and arranged two armchairs together so that she could lie down. She made tea, forcing Nora to have hers extra sweet.

'Has he always been like this?' Kate asked quietly.

'No. Before our marriage he never laid a finger on me. In fact, he was quite the opposite, treating me like a fragile doll, sending me to England to keep me safe – I was very young, only eighteen when I fell pregnant. But the war ended soon after I had Paul. Chibby came home, we married and things began to change. I sometimes wonder if he felt trapped into marrying me – because of the baby.'

It was a too-familiar tale – the same one her aunt had repeated about Kate's own mother. She sat in silence for a moment, taking in the sequence of events. 'So, you and Dad weren't married when Paul was born?'

'No, we weren't married. Why do you think my mother's family wanted nothing to do with me?'

'Why don't you leave him?'

'Because I love him. He was my salvation, you see. I was a sixteen-year-old girl in the middle of a battlefield, orphaned, alone. You can't imagine what it was like, with the constant shelling and my whole world obliterated, the terror as the Germans got closer and closer.' She shuddered at the memory. 'Chibby was there when I needed him.'

'But you said yourself, he was a different man then.'

Nora shook her head. 'I think he's the same – underneath. He feels such remorse, shame... afterwards. He cries. It's pitiful.'

Kate thought it was pitiful, but not for the same reasons as Nora.

'Besides, where would I go? How would I live? I have no money of my own to speak of, just the jewellery, everything else is in the business – and what about Paul's schooling?'

'What about it? Dad hasn't been paying the fees anyway!'

Kate said. 'And you don't really want him to stay in that place, do you?'

'No,' she admitted in a quiet voice. 'But let me ask you something, Kate. If you are so disapproving of Chibby, why don't *you* leave him?'

Clever Nora, to deflect Kate's questions with one of her own. She thought for a moment, wanting to be honest. 'Because I love him – or at least I've loved the idea of him for too long to let it go.'

'You see! We're the same, you and I, Kate.'

'Maybe,' Kate said, knowing that in one crucial way it wasn't true at all. They were both women who loved Chibby, both with inheritances depleted by him, but Nora looked on what was left of hers – those black velvet drawers full of gold – as a mere trifle and Kate saw hers as holding everything she most needed: answers.

18

Pieces of Silver

Kate didn't look up when her father came in. She was soldering a pewter inkstand, a present for Ethel, to mark the fourth anniversary of the Bermondsey Bookshop. It was the most ambitious thing she'd attempted. The inkwell was sunk in a solid pewter octagon with a hinged lid and she was attaching a fan-shaped stand designed to hold pens. It was fiddly work and she'd just got the soldering iron to the right temperature. She would once have put down her tools straight away. Tonight, she could barely stomach the sight of him.

He watched and waited while, with a steady hand, she finished her soldering.

'It's a fine piece of work.' He stood over her, hands in his pockets, an appreciative smile on his face.

'It's not finished. I've made this little ornament to put onto the lid.'

She pointed to a tiny replica of the torch of learning, which she'd copied from the bookshop sign. She wiped her hands on her long apron, still not looking at him. The acrid smell of hot solder filled the air and her father pushed open the French window. He took out a cigar, lit it and stood with his back to her. Blowing smoke into the damp garden, he said in an even tone, 'I should tell you Nora confessed to me about your visit to Paul's school. She was wrong to disobey me, and very wrong to involve you.'

He spoke into the dusk and she was glad he couldn't see the moment of surprise on her face. Didn't he know Nora would have told her about his attack on her? Kate had thought he'd be too ashamed to mention his discovery of their visit. But he obviously felt secure.

She waited for his rage to be directed at her, the way it had with Nora. Instead, when he turned around, his face was sad.

'I'm sorry you had to see me so... agitated before. I don't want you to think badly of your old dad, Katy.' His wide-eyed look of remorse might have instantly gained him most women's forgiveness, more so when he was youthful, when it might even have seemed charming.

'No, I'm the one should be saying sorry, Dad. I feel like I've come in with me two big feet and started messing up your life. Stirring up the past with all my questions...'

He chuckled. 'You could put it that way. You're headstrong and full of curiosity... but I can understand that.'

He walked to the centre of the room, still smoking his cigar.

'It's just hard, when there are so many blanks in your life, you just want to fill them up with... something.' She sighed, as pathetically as she could manage, and he gave her a look of sympathy.

'Tragedies will often do that to a person's mind, Kate – there's so much I can't remember about the war, yet I know it happened. I have the wounds to prove it!'

She began clearing away her tools. 'Do you mind if I ask you one more question that's been bothering me? I promise it'll be the last!'

He inhaled so that the cigar tip glowed. 'Not at all. Here, let me help.' He began gathering up her tools. 'What is it you want to know?'

'Were you there, the night Mum died?'

He paused, his pale, freckled hand hovering over the hammer she'd been using to shape the lid of the inkpot, and then he picked it up.

'What on earth makes you think that?'

'Because a memory came back to me – of seeing you there.'

'No, Kate, that's just your imagination. You were upstairs in the garret, fast asleep, when your mother fell!'

'I wasn't asleep. Someone was there and I've just got a feeling it was you. I don't know why. Was it you?' she persisted, feeling as if she was inching out onto a precarious ledge. 'All I want to know is what happened to her. Why did Mum have to die? If you know, just tell me, Dad!'

'She fell down the stairs in that hellhole we lived in. She died because we were too poor to own a decent house! And if she'd let me have what was rightfully mine as her husband, I'd have made a go of the business when I was a young man and made us rich! But no, she held on to the last of that cursed gypsy gold of hers. She was keeping it for you. That's what she always said. For you.'

His voice had grown quieter, hushed to a whisper, and he was looking through her. 'I told Bessie it'd do neither of us any good, sitting there doing nothing. I do believe it was cursed.'

Her heartbeat quickened and blood thudded in her ears. 'Did you need it for the business, or to pay off Mr Smith? Is that why you took the earrings after she'd died?'

He snapped his attention back into the room, his eyes sharp as tinplate. Without warning, he swung the hammer in an arc, the head brushing her hair as he brought it down, shattering the torch of learning ornament with the force of its impact.

'You will shut your mouth now!' He swung the hammer a second time, knocking the inkwell clean off its stand. 'And you'll say no more of earrings or Mr Smith! And if you do, you'll see that I only miss if I want to!'

He flung the hammer at her, and she was forced to duck for fear it would take an eye out. He began walking slowly towards her. She backed away to the end of the bench, till she felt the sharp edge of a metal-forming stake pressing into her back. He put his face close to hers.

'Are you trying to ruin my life, Katy? Trying to punish me, is that what it is? First you stir up Nora about Paul, now you're accusing me of having something to do with your mother's death! I know what you're up to, but even if it was true, you've got no proof. You're not clever enough. You've got the intellect of a tinker. Look at you!' he sneered. 'All the things you could have chosen to do with the means I've provided and you descend to the lowest level, back to the filth I pulled your mother from!'

He was inching closer and the spike of the forming stake was piercing her skin.

'Be very, very careful what you accuse me of, Katy.'

'No, Dad, I wasn't accusing you! You've got it all wrong.' She adopted Nora's musical tone. 'I was only asking if you knew any more than you've let on, because it's been worrying me all these years… in case it was my fault!' This had enough of the ring of truth about it and she could see it immediately have its effect.

'Your fault?' He took a step back.

Kate swallowed hard and nodded. 'When I was little, sometimes I used to wake up thirsty in the night. I'd moan and moan till Mum went downstairs and got me some water. I couldn't remember anything about that night, so I just thought that's what must have happened. Years and years I've blamed meself, if I hadn't moaned so much... if I'd just stayed asleep, she'd never have slipped on the garret stairs, she'd still be alive...'

He stretched out his neck and shoulders, which had been taut with fury. He relaxed like an unstrung bow. 'I've always wondered myself why she'd left you alone up there... perhaps it happened the way you said, but you can't blame yourself, Katy.' He nodded, taking a deep breath now. 'But that other thing – that you thought you saw – me, or someone else, taking her earrings, no.' He fixed her with steel-sharp eyes. 'That never happened. Do you understand?'

'I understand, Dad. It was just imagination – a story I made up.'

'Like one of those fairy tales your mother was always filling your head with?'

'Just like them,' she agreed. She slowly collected up hammers and pincers, and he helped, hanging them with care back on their hooks till all was in order.

'Well, Katy. I'm glad we've cleared the air. I'm sorry I lost my temper, and I'd prefer if you didn't say anything about this to Nora.'

When he was gone she grabbed the forming stake to keep herself from falling to the floor in a heap. Her legs felt as weak as her poor brother Paul's. The door of the studio opened again and she jumped.

'I've been meaning to tell you. I spoke with Mrs North

at her sister's charity concert the other evening and she tells me Mrs Cliffe gives elocution lessons at the bookshop. I suggested you'd like to join her classes. With Nora's help you've begun to dress like a daughter I can be proud of. I'm sure you'll agree it's time to get rid of that Bermondsey accent of yours. It spoils any good impression you might make. Goodnight, Katy.'

Her remaining strength ebbed away and she slumped to the floor, leaning her back against the bench, remembering Nora's words: where will I go? how will I live?

The same place and the same way I have since I was six, she answered.

She could have gone to Martin there and then; he would have taken her in with no worries about propriety. But then his mother would have given him hell. No, she would stay where she was, let her father think she was cowed and dutiful and stupid. The next morning a small but heavy parcel was delivered to her by hand. She signed for it, puzzled, and took it to her workshop. When she opened it, she gasped. It contained several square, solid silver plates, the sort she could use for raising into bowls or making cigarette cases. There was a card.

My dear daughter, Katy, I hope you can excuse my behaviour of last night. I said things in temper which I regret. Believe that I am proud of you. Please accept this token and forgive me?

That evening Kate found out that her father had left for a sales trip in Manchester, and the following day, she went to

Bermondsey. When she arrived at East Lane, she found her Aunt Sarah was still at work. She walked the short distance along the river to Southwell's jam factory and waited till the afternoon shift was over and a mass of women poured through the gates. She soon spotted Aunt Sarah. Wearing heavy clogs to protect her feet from floors covered in scalding jam, they gave her, and the other jam girls, a distinctive, shuffling walk. Seeing her grey hair tied in a bun and her large, stooped frame encased in a jam-splashed apron, Kate felt pity for her. The jam factories weren't for the fragile or the elderly. It was a punishing routine – stirring cauldrons of boiling jam, tipping the contents into heavy stone jars, hauling them onto a cart for transporting to the warehouse. But Aunt Sarah couldn't give up working; if she did, she'd starve. Her head was down, intent on getting home to her tea and then her feet up. She walked right past Kate, who called out to her.

'Kate! I didn't recognize you in your finery.' Aunt Sarah looked her up and down.

Not feeling much warmth in her aunt's greeting, Kate knew at least she could always appeal to her appetite. 'I thought I'd take you for pie and mash.'

'What, dressed like that?'

Kate wore a navy jersey jacket and low-belted white dress. It was simple, but expensive.

'Why not?'

'You don't look like a Bermondsey girl any more,' Aunt Sarah said and insisted she didn't want to eat her dinner being stared at. They went back to East Lane, where her aunt put out some cold mutton and pickles.

'How do you like living with Archie?' her aunt asked as she made room at the cluttered kitchen table.

Kate was silent a moment too long.

'Seen the other side of him now?'

The cold mutton was tough and she waited till she could swallow it, then pushed the plate away. 'I ain't got much of an appetite, Aunt Sarah. You may as well save this for tomorrow.'

'You don't look well, Kate. He's dressing you nice enough, but I should think that's cold comfort after the way you built him up. I warned you! He's disappointed you, ain't he?'

She wasn't sure if her aunt's lifelong loyalty to her brother had been completely broken or merely stretched. What if she couldn't trust her?

'More than disappointed, Aunt Sarah. He's turned on me.'

'Turned?'

'He threw a hammer at me.'

Aunt Sarah's small eyes narrowed and she gave a knowing nod. She wasn't shocked. 'What did you do to upset him?'

'I asked him about the night Mum died, and he went mad. Said I'd get worse if I didn't keep me mouth shut. But that just made me believe it more…'

'Believe what?'

'That he killed my mum.'

Aunt Sarah put a hand to her mouth. Kate had never seen her display such a range of emotion. It was like watching a sluggish Thames as the churning tide turned. Eddies of confusion, whirls of disbelief surfaced, disappeared, then resurfaced on her broad flat face, till she shook her head. 'No! You're wrong. Sylvie saw your mum at the bottom of them garret stairs and her neck was broke. Why would you say such a wicked thing about Archie?' Her aunt was breathless, sweat shining on her forehead.

'Because I saw him that night.'

'Saw him kill her?'

'No.'

'Well then.'

Kate explained exactly what she *had* seen and doubt clouded Sarah's small dark eyes. Doubt and fear.

'I know Archie was angry with Bessie because she had some of her gold left and she wouldn't let him have it. He needed money to start up this business. Mind you, she'd given him most of what she had already, and I suppose all the promises he made hadn't come true. They was living up in that garret and she was thinking of the future. But you can't cross our Archie. He won't be told "no".' Aunt Sarah rubbed her hand across the pitted wood of the table. 'I will tell you something, though, Kate, he moved heaven and earth to get that girl to marry him. Then once they was married, he ended up treating her like shit. It's my opinion he was more interested in her gypsy gold than anything else.'

She wondered now if that's all her father had seen in Nora as well. Poor Nora. She'd been worried Chibby felt trapped into marriage by her pregnancy, but now Kate suspected it was the other way around.

'Aunt Sylvie's always been Dad's biggest champion. Can you trust she's telling the truth about what happened to my mum?'

'Trust *her*? Well, I suppose not. At the time I did think it was a bit strange she was the one found your Mum. She had no time for her, never went inside her house, not for nothing, not even a cup of sugar! I never dreamed she was lying about it, though.'

'Do you think he could have done it?'

'If he was in a rage with Bessie he might've lashed out and hurt her – by accident. You never really knew him, love. But there was times when he'd give me a right-hander.'

'You?' Kate was genuinely shocked. 'But why did you

pretend he was something special all these years, then? Why lie to me?'

Her aunt thought for a moment. 'I wasn't lying. You can be special and still be a bastard, Kate. Ain't you learned that yet?'

She felt more than crushed, she felt pulverized to a fine powder that might dissipate on the wind of one more damning revelation about her father. Aunt Sarah put a rare comforting arm around her. 'I'm sorry you've had to find all this out about your dad. Truth be told, I used to like telling all them stories about Archie much better than I ever liked the feller himself.'

'I'm going to see Aunt Sylvie.' Kate rose and retrieved her hat and handbag. Aunt Sarah followed her.

'Not without me, you ain't!'

Aunt Sylvie's look of surprise was almost comical and it was probably only that surprise which got them through the front door. The kitchen was exactly the same. Laundry hanging on an overhead dolly, and a pudding boiling away on the range filling the air with thick, fatty steam. The same, yet different. Kate looked around at the scene of so many torments and realized how ordinary it was. And Aunt Sylvie, the torturer of her youth, how worn out and plain and insignificant she looked. There was nothing remotely scary about this woman. Kate was almost regretful that she didn't even want revenge. All she wanted was the truth.

'What do you pair want?' Sylvie stood with arms crossed over her faded pinafore. 'I ain't got all day, they'll all be home soon and expecting their tea.' She shot an accusing look at Kate, as if blaming her for no longer being there to cook it.

Aunt Sarah spoke first. 'Don't ask us to sit down, we wouldn't want to catch nothing.'

'All right, you can go and piss off out of it!' Aunt Sylvie uncrossed her arms. She looked ready to swing a fist.

'Don't start, you two.' Kate stood between them. 'Aunt Sylvie, I just need a few minutes. I've come from me dad's.'

'Oh, I know where you're living. His new favourite now! Looked after you all them years, I did – for nothing!' She clicked her fingers in disgust. 'Always promising he'd give me something for your keep and I never got a penny from him. But he don't want to know me, not now I've served me purpose.'

This was something new. Sylvie criticizing Archie? He had obviously told Kate the truth when he'd vowed to cut off both his sisters.

'What's he sent you here for – to do his dirty work?'

'Can we sit down?' She saw Aunt Sarah grimace and shot her a warning look. 'Dad doesn't know I'm here. And I don't agree with the way he's treated you both.'

Aunt Sylvie tucked in her chin, stared at her, and said, 'All right then, say what you've come to say.'

Kate took a deep breath. Trying to avoid accusing Aunt Sylvie of covering up a murder wasn't going to be easy. 'You know I've been living with him – in Belgravia.'

'Money.' Aunt Sylvie nodded. 'Belgravia – that's money for you.'

'I think he's in debt.'

'Well that ain't nothing new, he's always owed someone something. But Archie can get himself out of anything, plenty of old bunny, he could talk the leaves off the trees, couldn't he, Sarah?'

Aunt Sarah nodded.

'I think he's had all Nora's inheritance for his business and for his house in Belgravia.'

'Nora, that French tart?'

Kate swallowed her retort. 'They're married now.'

'Not before time. They had a boy, didn't they?'

'What boy?' Aunt Sarah asked. 'I don't know nothing about no boy!'

'That's because Archie was writing to *me* – not you!'

'He doesn't talk about Paul. He didn't even tell me I had a brother.' Kate tried to mollify Sarah, for she'd get no information if these two started arguing. She suggested a cup of tea and got up, reverting to her servant status without a thought.

The two sisters sat in strained silence while she made it, but once the tea was in their hands she felt her aunts were less likely to come to blows, and so she pressed on. 'I've come to ask about the night my mum died. Aunt Sylvie, are you certain it was an accident?'

Silence hung thick as steam in the kitchen. She could hear the water around the pudding basin bubbling and spitting in the pan. It needed topping up, but Kate didn't dare speak.

Finally, Sylvie put down her cup and let out a long breath. 'Whatever I tell you, you'll never prove nothing against him. *But* – she shook her head slowly – it wasn't no accident.'

Kate leaned forward, putting a hand over Aunt Sarah's to stop her interrupting.

'I remember it like it was yesterday. He come here in the middle of the night, in a terrible state. Blood all over his hands and his shirt. He says, "I've killed her, Sylvie. She's finally driven me to it, you've got to help me." And he tells me he'd got himself in trouble with Mr Smith, owed him a lot. He asked Bessie for the rest of her jewellery and she said there wasn't none left, he'd had it all. But he knew different. He turned the place upside down. "Sylvie," he says, "Mr Smith's threatening to cut me throat and chuck me in the Thames and she wouldn't help me!" Well, he hit her and she's cracked her head on the range and that was that. Dead.' Aunt Sylvie sat back, looking exhausted. She closed her eyes and Kate saw a single tear escape. As it trickled down her cheek, she opened her eyes and went on, 'Don't look at me like that, Sarah, what could I do? Bessie was dead. And his life was over if I said a word to anyone. So, I left him in here, sitting just where you're sitting now, Sarah. And then I went next door and found Bessie, laying on the floor with her head smashed in and her neck broke. I pulled her over to the stairs, cleaned all the blood up around the range. Then I went up the garret stairs to check on you.' For the first time in her account she looked at Kate. 'You was asleep and I picked you up and took you home.'

'I don't remember that,' Kate said in a hoarse voice that sounded very far away. 'I only remember Dad bringing me to your house, after Mum's funeral, and then leaving me there.'

'It's just as well you didn't remember – when I got you back home, he wouldn't even look at you. *Guilt.* Guilt, not grief. That's why he never wanted to see you. He'd robbed you of your mother, hadn't he? He went out that night, back up to Liverpool, so he could pretend he was away when it happened.'

'Why did you protect him?' Kate asked, dry-mouthed.

'He played on me soft heart.'

Aunt Sarah gave a snort of disbelief.

'Oh, you can laugh, Sarah. I wasn't always a hard woman. But I learned. He says to me, "Would you deprive that orphan child of her father, just because I've robbed her of her mother?"' She paused. 'And I looked at her, shivering she was and her arms stretched out to her daddy and I knew what I had to do. Well, the arrangement was that she'd live with me, just till his business was on its feet, and then he'd come back for her and see me right. And did he? Did he begawd.' She sat back, finished at last. 'So, is that what you wanted to know, Kate? Is it better, now you know the truth? Or should I have kept me mouth shut, like I have all these years?'

She didn't feel any better. But she did feel stronger.

'I'll go to the police.'

'You've got no proof.' Aunt Sylvie went to the range and inspected the saucepan. 'Me puddin's burned dry. Stan won't be happy when he comes home, meat pudding's his favourite.'

'*You* could tell the police the truth.'

'But I won't.'

Kate made a silver bowl. She hammered it so finely the indentations were barely visible. She soldered elegant, swan-necked handles on either side, burnished it till it was without blemish, and then she took it to Martin.

'Oh, Kate. This is beautiful! But where did you get the silver?'

'From my father.'

'Actually, I was hoping you'd reconsider the idea of putting your work into a gallery.'

'Can you sell it for me?' she asked.

Martin shot her a puzzled look. 'But you told me Chibby doesn't approve of "his women" going into trade,' he said tartly.

'I don't give a tinker's curse what he approves of. If you can get it sold, it would help me out. I need to get hold of some cash – quickly.'

Martin picked up the bowl. He ran his fingers around its curved body and along the elegant handles. 'So well balanced! I'll buy it. How much?'

She was taken aback. 'That don't seem right.'

'Why not?'

'Because if I gave it to you, I'd want it to be a gift.'

He looked at her, love warming those cool grey eyes. 'It's my gift to you.'

'I can't let you do that, but you're so kind to offer, Martin. I don't think I deserve you.' And she flung her arms around him and held him tightly. He laughed, delighted, because normally he found her not demonstrative enough. It's the Goss in me, she'd explained to him once, the only feelings we can't hide are when we're angry! And now the very thought of her father's blood running through her veins made her shudder.

The other trip that she needed to make while her father was absent wasn't so easy to arrange without Nora's knowledge. She told her she was going out with Martin for the day, but instead took the train to the small Sussex station near Paul's school. She didn't bother to knock on the front door. They would certainly have turned her away on this unscheduled visit. Instead she made her way to the back of the house, where, on open day, she'd noticed a metal fire escape. Now she climbed it to the second floor. On the way up, she heard sounds of lessons going on and discordant jangling from the music class, so hated by Paul. She came to a tall sash window and began to ease it open, but froze as it stuck and juddered noisily in its warped frame. It was open about a foot, but she couldn't risk raising it any higher. She squeezed through, putting one leg over the sill, then ducking her head and dragging the other leg after her. She was in a long corridor smelling of wood polish and urine. Walking softly forward, she checked each door. Paul had told her the dormitories were named after trees and his was called Thorn.

The reason she knew he would not be in class today was that he'd told her so. He'd slipped her a note towards the end of open day, begging her to get him out of the school. He knew he was being treated differently to the other children, he wrote. Tied into his chair all day, left in his dormitory without even a book – sometimes they even forgot to feed him. He pretended to his mother that the swimming and the pottery and the trips out were for older boys, but that wasn't true. He was left out because his fees weren't paid. He didn't want to upset his parents, but he needed to come home now. Could she help him?

Thorn announced itself with a picture of a twisted tree. She stopped and turned the doorknob. There looked to be a dozen iron-framed, thin-mattressed beds, each with a small chest at the foot. Paul was sitting in his wheelchair in front of the end window. He looked up as she entered and let out a cry of surprise. She put a finger to her lips, and hurrying to him, she hastily undid the unnecessarily tight straps. He rubbed at chafe marks on his wrists and neck.

'They say it improves my posture, but if I complain, nurse Jim only ties them tighter. Have you come to take me away?' He looked up with such trusting eyes that she hated to admit she had not.

'Not today.'

The eyes brimmed with tears and he bit his lip. 'Don't worry. I'm all right,' he tried to reassure her.

'I'm sorry, Paul. I can't take you home today – but until I can I've come to make things better for you here.'

He grasped both her hands. 'Thank you!' The teeth-grating sound of the percussion section drifted up from below and Paul smiled at her. 'At least if I'm up here I can escape the music class!'

'Paul, why didn't you tell your mother about the way they've been treating you?'

'I don't like it when she's sad and it would have made her sad,' he said solemnly.

She opened her bag and gave him some chocolate and a bag of biscuits.

'Oh, I'm not allowed – they say these aren't good for me!'

'Starving ain't good for you either! Where can we hide them?'

Paul giggled and pointed to a nearby chest. 'That's mine. Put them under the other things. They never go through it.'

'At least if they forget to come for you at teatime, you can nibble on these,' she said, stuffing them under his few possessions. 'I can't stay long. I just wanted to let you know things *will* get better.' She kissed him. 'And now, I'm going to see Mr Woolf!'

'You don't look much like Red Riding Hood!' he giggled.

She promised to come back soon and was rewarded by his open, eager smile. She wondered at how resilient he was, how such a small thing as a visit and a packet of biscuits could so cheer him. But then, perhaps in her darkest childhood days, she would have been the same. Any show of interest, or kindness, was enough to last a very long time.

She closed the door quietly and went to the main staircase. At the bottom she followed the directions Paul had given her, praying that she wouldn't encounter any curious teachers on the way.

She gave a brief knock on the principal's door and walked in. She opened her bag and drew out her purse. 'How much does my father owe you?' she asked.

The sale of the bowl, along with a cigarette case and a small vanity box which she'd made, had paid all the outstanding school fees. She added more cigarette cases and some pill boxes to her collection and was astonished at the prices her creations could fetch. They were only metal boxes, after all – though smaller and more refined than the tins she'd made at Boutle's, and, of course, of a far more precious metal. For her own amusement she tried out some jewellery – a pendant and a deep bangle with a repoussé geometric design. She was only satisfied when all the silver plates her father had given her were transformed into cash that would make Paul's life easier. When Mr Woolf no longer telephoned to chase payment, perhaps her father might wonder why, but she doubted he'd care enough to investigate. She had very quickly worked out why Archie Goss had given her a handful of silver when he was so deeply in debt. He wanted her close and he wanted her silent.

19

Elocution Lessons

'Aer naer brehan caer.'

There was a burst of laughter from the small group of students gathered in the reading room of the Bermondsey Bookshop. Kate turned and gave them a look of wide-eyed innocence.

'How now, brown cow,' Mrs Cliffe repeated.

'Hair nail brine car.'

'HOW! We are dealing with the vowel "O" here, my dear. Our concern is purely bOvine, nothing at all to do with hair, nails, salt water – nor motors, for that matter!' Mrs Cliffe was becoming exasperated, but her students were having more fun than they'd had in a long time.

Kate had decided it was best to go along with her father's request for the time being, but thought she might as well enjoy herself in the process.

'Once more, listen to my vowel sounds. How now, brown cow.'

'High nigh brine cai!'

'Better.' Mrs Cliffe sighed and, defeated, moved on to the next unfortunate.

At the end of class, Kate was about to rush downstairs to see Ethel and present her with the inkstand when Mrs Cliffe called her back.

'Kate, may I have a word with you?'

She sauntered over, feeling slightly sorry for dear Mrs Cliffe, who didn't deserve such treatment.

'You are a little minx.' Mrs Cliffe smiled good-naturedly. 'And I am perfectly happy to entertain you for a few weeks, but I know you're only here because of your father.'

'He asked you to make me sound respectable – but I don't really want to change the way I speak.'

'My dear, you already have. You've been living with Nora and Chibby for months and you have picked up their speech patterns quite naturally. You're a very good mimic. In fact, you don't need my classes at all. You could speak the Queen's English perfectly if you chose to.'

She had always liked Mrs Cliffe. She was no fool and Kate wondered why, then, she hadn't already seen through Archie Goss.

'Why are you going into business with my father?' she asked, without having meant to broach the subject.

'What an odd question! I should tell you that's a private matter. But I believe you're a good friend to Nora. And so am I.'

'Does that mean you're only doing it for Nora?'

Mrs Cliffe considered for a moment. 'Not *only*. I do believe it's a sound investment. But I suspect Chibby's business has swallowed up a good portion of his wife's fortune, so yes, it's mostly to help Nora.'

'It won't help Nora,' Kate said bluntly, and Mrs Cliffe's benevolent expression disappeared.

'What do you know about Chibby's business?' she asked.

'Not much. But I know a lot about Archie Goss.'

She saw Mrs Cliffe glance towards the staircase. Now the elocution class was over the reading room was open for members' general use, and someone had entered. It was Johnny.

Mrs Cliffe lowered her voice. 'This is not the place or time. Could you come to my house, tomorrow?' she asked and Kate nodded.

Johnny, who had seated himself in an armchair by a reading lamp and was flicking through a periodical, looked up and said goodnight to Mrs Cliffe as she left.

She felt awkward with Johnny now, ever since she'd told Martin she could love him. But why shouldn't she have? After all, Johnny had moved on himself.

'Don't tell me you're taking elocution lessons?' he asked, putting down the periodical.

She pulled a face. 'My father's idea.'

'Oh, your *fah*ther!' he mocked.

'Shut yer gob.'

'Ha! There she is.' He laughed. 'Come and sit down, tell me what you've been up to,' he said easily. 'And by the way, you don't need them.'

'What?'

'Elocution lessons.'

'I know. I'm doing it to keep him happy.'

'Oh? Not to keep you happy?'

She sat down next to him. 'No.'

'You're not happy at your dad's?' He seemed surprised.

'I'm not.'

'But I thought it's what you always wanted.'

'It was, but it turns out he's not the dad I always wanted.'

Johnny blew out a long breath. 'Oh, I'm sorry, Kate. But no parent's perfect. Do you think you might get used to his ways?'

'It's not that simple, Johnny. It's not his ways so much. I could put up with it if he was a drunkard, say.' She saw him wince. 'Sorry, I didn't mean—'

'I know.' He waved away her apology. 'I didn't put up with Mum, Kate. I just loved her.'

He was still impressive, and as she sat beside him, longing to tell him the truth about her father, she found herself in turns missing Johnny and feeling guilty about Martin.

'If he was just a bad dad, I'd still love him, but I've found out he's—'

'A bad man?' he finished her sentence.

She nodded.

'Can I help?'

'I don't think so. I've got to be going, Johnny. Is Ethel still downstairs?'

'No. She wasn't feeling well. Had to go home. Why?'

'I made this for her.' She pulled the cloth-wrapped parcel from her bag and uncovered the inkstand.

His look of surprise was enough praise. 'All those years at Boutle's weren't wasted after all! You've got a talent, Kate. Ethel will love it.'

'I hope so. Goodnight, Johnny,' she said, with a lingering sadness that she wasn't allowed to love two men at the same time.

★

The following day, Kate was shown into Mrs Cliffe's drawing room and the woman greeted her warmly. It was a cluttered room, every surface invaded by ornamental objects, little statues or lamps, and every wall covered in paintings of various styles and sizes. The objects were tasteful, expensive, evidence of Mrs Cliffe's generous nature, original pieces, many made by Martin's friends or Martin himself. Even the seat covers were hand embroidered in a modern, abstract design.

Mrs Cliffe offered her coffee from a silver pot on a silver stand and noticed Kate looking at the sugar bowl.

'I was entranced by your beautiful work. Simple, elegant, functional.'

'*You* bought it?'

'I'm proud to be your first patron.' Mrs Cliffe beamed.

Kate's delight was obvious and Mrs Cliffe said, 'I'm glad you approve of my putting your bowl to good use.'

'That's what it's for! I prefer to make things people can use – doesn't matter if it's a silver bowl or a tin box, so long as it looks good.'

'Things that you "believe to be useful and know to be beautiful"?'

'Yes! I like William Morris.'

'Oh, really? Now, Ethel told me on your first day you declared you'd come to clean, not read. She found it very amusing... but I'm pleased to see you broke your pledge at some point.'

Kate laughed. 'I suppose I did.'

'But now to more unpleasant matters. What can you tell me about Chibby Grainger that I don't already know?' Mrs Cliffe asked with a look of faint distaste.

'Tell me first what you do know.'

'I'm aware that, for all his charm and business acumen,

he isn't the ideal husband or father.' She paused. 'Of course, you know that I befriended Nora when she came to England and her own family shunned her. Her mother had been a dear friend of mine; I couldn't see Nora alone with a child – and no husband.' She looked to see Kate's reaction.

'Nora told me about that.'

'When I met your father, I was won over. He'd been fighting at the front and these things happen in wartime. I gave him the benefit of the doubt and, when he did the right thing, I believed Nora had found a husband who would love and protect her. But the marriage hasn't proved a happy one. I don't know if Nora's told you what happened to the child...'

'I've met my brother.'

'Really! Nora must trust you. I believe Martin and I are the only other people who know she's been visiting him over the years. Poor little soul.'

'I've found out more about the place he's in, more than Nora knows. He's not being treated as well as she thinks. And I've found out more about my father's first marriage.'

'Your mother died in a tragic accident, I was told.'

Kate shook her head. 'I don't believe that any more.'

Over the next couple of hours, while the sun moved round the room, blessing each object on her shelves and walls, Mrs Cliffe became enlightened about Archie Goss and when she finally understood, she said, 'If even half of what you've told me is true, I could never give my money to Chibby now. As you say, it would be the opposite of helping Nora. If he has robbed and murdered one wife, what's to say he won't do the same to another?' She shivered. 'I'll arrange for my solicitor to cancel our arrangement, and I'll move heaven and earth to see Nora safely out of that marriage.'

She looked at Kate with sympathy. 'But what about you?

You've been very brave to come here. You surely can't feel safe in your father's house? What will you do?'

Nora looked stricken. She crossed her arms, hugging herself against the truth.

'If Paul was being mistreated, why didn't he just tell me?'

'Because he was trying to protect you.'

Nora shook her head in denial. 'He's my son. I should have known. And how on earth did you pay the fees? Your allowance isn't enough. Besides, Chibby told me he'd settled the account after Mr Woolf's telephone call. I just don't understand.' She fiddled with a long string of beads, tugging till they broke and spilled onto the rug. Neither of the women moved to pick them up.

'My father gave me a present – some silver plates – and I made things. Martin helped me sell them. I used the money to pay Paul's fees.'

'I'll repay you – every penny.' Nora flushed. 'I'll get my cheque book.' She rose and hurried to a small bureau by the window.

'Nora, stop. We both know there's nothing in your bank account. He's had the lot, hasn't he?'

Nora stopped and turned, licking dry lips, unable to deny it. Kate pitied her – she understood only too well what the woman now had to face. The final death of her dream of a man who could take everything in hand, could manage and solve all problems, could talk of his own dream and make her believe in it, who, flawed though he was, loved her with all his heart.

'You've got to be honest now, Nora. And I'll be honest

with you.' Kate picked up her bag. She dug around till she found it. 'Here, look at this. Do you recognize it?'

'My earring! I thought I'd lost it – where did you find that? And what does it have to do with Paul's fees or my empty bank account?'

'Remember when we were trying on earrings, for the bookshop dance?'

'Oh, yes. But not this one. It's not a pair. I've kept it all these years... for sentimental reasons.' She took the earring, looking at it with a small smile of remembrance. 'Chibby's first gift to me. He found it quite by accident – just the one, in a ruined house that had been destroyed by shelling. He helped me put it on, like this – she raised the earring to her ear, and he called me his gypsy princess.'

The earring spun in her fingers and Kate felt a chill at the cruelty of his lie. She wanted to snatch the earring from Nora's hand. But she had done nothing wrong; Nora was no more to blame in all this than either Bessie or herself.

'Nora, are you sure that's your earring?'

'Yes, yes! What are you talking about, Kate, there's not another like it!'

'Yes, there is.'

And Kate took from her bag Nora's own tissue-wrapped earring. 'Actually, this one is yours, the earring Dad gave you.' She waited while Nora compared the two in shocked silence.

'They're the same! Where did you get the other one?'

'It was my mum's. Longbonnet – my Great-Aunt Rosina – gave it to me, said it was part of my inheritance. But I never knew what had happened to the other one. Not until that day we were looking for earrings in your jewellery box.'

Nora sat down, all the light in her eyes extinguished, and Kate carried on, feeling merciless. But it had to be done, like digging out a jagged splinter from an infected wound. She pressed on. 'My mum was wearing these the night she died. My Great-Aunt Rosina found one earring in the street – it had blood on it. The other one was nowhere to be found.' Kate let this sink in before continuing. 'Nora, everything he told you was a lie. There was no ruined house and you weren't the only gypsy princess he'd ever lied to. You know my mum was from a Romany family—'

Nora put her hands over her ears. 'No more, Kate. No more.' She looked so fragile, her face pale as porcelain, her thin hands pressing her temples as if she might crush her own skull like an egg.

'I'm sorry. I want you to know it all.'

When Kate had finished, she feared that she'd destroyed Nora. But it was her own tears that fell now. Nora had gradually straightened as the story unfolded of a man who'd bled one woman dry and moved on to another, who'd abandoned one child and then another, who had killed one wife, and then...

'If you stay, he'll do the same to you,' Kate finished. 'You need to run.'

'And so do you,' Nora whispered, glancing towards the door.

'Katy! Come here.' Her father stood in the doorway. Had he been listening? She hadn't heard the door opening. He could have been standing outside for a while. She got up, her legs like water, and managed to walk across the room. He encased her in a tight bear hug.

'And Nora! I've missed my two beautiful girls.' He wasn't

a jovial man as a rule. His humour was often dry and biting. Usually at someone else's expense.

'Did the trip go well?' Nora asked, and Kate didn't think her father could miss the tear-ruined eye make-up.

'Very. And I've just been to see Mrs Cliffe with the news that we now have several guaranteed contracts with top French manufacturers for the next three years!' He looked from one to the other, and Kate couldn't work out if his good humour was merely a screen. He rubbed his hands together. 'We need to celebrate, Nora. Champagne, I think.'

When they were seated in the panelled dining room, with the lamps lit and the crystal glasses glinting and the golden liquid bubbling, Kate's nausea became almost unbearable. He had been to see Mrs Cliffe.

She still had the old tin box. The one which had contained all her worldly possessions when she'd left Aunt Sylvie's. And that night, when the house was completely silent, she got it out again. In it she packed her mother's jewellery, the *Grimm's Fairy Tales* and some spare clothes. She wanted to take as many of her tools as she could carry. She felt no qualms that Archie had paid for them. It seemed like natural justice to recoup some of what he'd stolen from her.

She crept down to her studio and, as silently as she could, put hammers, forming pads and stakes, a fretsaw, a gas torch and her soldering iron into a leather toolbag. As she was about to exit the studio, she noticed a movement in the garden. Going closer to the French window she saw a ghostly figure, clothed in white, pacing the path. It was Nora.

Kate hurried to unlock the window and pulled her inside.

Although she wore a long dressing gown and was wrapped in a shawl, Nora was shivering.

'What are you doing?' Kate asked, looking out into the garden, just to be sure her father hadn't followed Nora downstairs.

'I couldn't sleep next to him, Kate. I can't bear to hear his breath or feel his body. It's not for what he's done to me, it's the harm he's done my darling boy! I loathe him.'

Kate was glad to see that anger had pumped ice into her veins again. She looked like the woman Kate had first known: impassive, cold, but no longer brittle – she'd frozen stronger than steel.

'Do you think Mrs Cliffe has told him anything yet? She told me she'd have to see her solicitor first!'

Nora shook her head. 'No, I don't think he knows. He seemed in such a good mood.'

'Well, you need to carry on as if you know nothing – just until Mrs Cliffe can arrange things for you. But, Nora, when she pulls out of the business, he'll know it was my fault. I need to be ready to go.'

'She doesn't have to tell him *why* she's pulling out. Surely it's safer for you if she doesn't.'

'He'll guess – who else could ruin his character? The silver was to silence me. I wouldn't be surprised if the only reason I'm living here is so he could find out what I remembered. Besides, I want him to know it was me who did it. It might be the only justice I ever get for Mum.'

She picked up the leather toolbag. 'Start getting your things in order. Mrs Cliffe won't hang about.'

'You're not leaving tonight?' Nora grasped both her hands and Kate hated the thought of leaving her here to play out her lonely charade of a marriage.

'I was afraid I might have to. But I'll wait until Mrs Cliffe's solicitor's letter has gone to Dad's office.'

'And what shall I say to him – once he's realized you've left?'

'Tell him I'm an ungrateful, spiteful girl and I don't deserve all he's done for me.'

Nora made a gesture of impatience.

'You don't have to mean it!' Kate hugged the woman, who was still shivering. 'But you're good at hiding your feelings, Nora. Just do what comes naturally.'

The following morning, she went to explain to Martin. His delight at her surprise visit soon turned to consternation as she told him what she'd learned about her father.

'How long have you and Aunt Violet been plotting this and not telling me?' Martin flicked a cigarette butt into his fireplace. He was as near to angry as he ever got.

'It was only yesterday. I've come straight here! Why are you angry with me?'

He took her hand. 'It's not you. It's at your monster of a father. To think you could be in danger from him once Aunt Violet's ditched him! I never trusted him, never liked him, after the way he'd treated Nora and Paul, but I never suspected the depths of... Listen, Kate, you're coming here, to live with me – today!' His normally languid manner was energized. He seemed invigorated by her crisis.

'No, I've got to wait for your aunt. And then I'll go back home.'

'To Belgravia?'

'No! *Home*, where I belong – Bermondsey.'

'Ridiculous. You don't belong there any more either.'

But he knew nothing about being rooted to a place. His childhood had been spent at a boarding school and his holidays mostly with Aunt Violet. Since the war, he'd moved about London, living near galleries where he made his living, or setting up camp wherever the latest artists' colony was flourishing – everywhere from Camden to Cornwall.

'Bermondsey's where I grew up – the river, the warehouses, the factories. I know it's just an ugly jumble of slums to you, but to me it's home.'

'How can you say that? You had a horrible childhood there – and your *home* was a nightmare. Is it because John Bacon's still there?'

'What?'

'Is he the draw?'

'Don't be an idiot, Martin. It's just that in Bermondsey I know I can find somewhere to live and somewhere to work – and until last year it was all I'd ever known. It's nothing to do with Johnny.'

She laughed at him, but he didn't look convinced. She was puzzled that he was still jealous of Johnny. 'It's you I love.' She went to him, putting her arms around his waist and looking up into his clear grey eyes.

'Do you?' he asked urgently. 'Then why not make a new life with me? I'm going to see Mother tomorrow – shall I tell her I'm going to marry you? She'll have to know sooner or later and I want to take you with me.'

Kate groaned. 'It's just not the right time, Martin. I'm not ready.' He let go of her, sulking, but she pulled him back. 'One day – when I've finished me elocution lessons and can speak proper!'

He laughed and spun her around till they tumbled together onto the chaise longue and he kissed her in a way that made her forget the crimes of her father and the tragedy of her mother, and she allowed herself, for a brief time, to be nineteen and in love with a prince charming who was everything Archie Goss was not.

She had, however, explained to Martin that he was to provide the carriage that would return her to Bermondsey. When Mrs Cliffe had done her part, his aunt would let Martin know and then he was to collect Kate in the Baby Austin. The following day she expected him to arrive soon after her father had left for the office. But after waiting all morning she began to worry that some legal problem had held things up. She sat in her workshop, pretending to sketch designs, jumping at every knock and dreading the charade she'd have to go through with her father that evening if nothing happened today. She was almost surprised when the maid came to inform her that Mr North was in the drawing room.

'It's done. Time to go!' Martin looked flushed and excited.

'I'm all ready.' She hurried to the door and was met by Nora coming in.

'I heard a knock...' She noticed Martin and, looking at Kate, understood what was happening. 'Mrs Cliffe's sent the letter to Chibby? You're leaving now?'

Kate nodded and was about to reassure her when Nora placed two hands on Kate's shoulders. 'Don't worry about me, Kate. Don't write, don't telephone and don't come back.'

Nora fixed Martin with a steady gaze and he blushed, and Kate saw he might still be a little in love with her. 'Martin will be our go-between. Good luck, Kate.' She put her cool cheek to Kate's and whispered, 'Thank you for making me brave.'

Kate gave her a final hug and collected the tin box and her toolbag. When the Baby Austin was on the road, she looked back at the stuccoed house, with its fancy railings and imposing windows, and, turning the corner, felt the dream of her new life fade away.

'Why are you crying?' he asked, taking his eyes off the road. 'Are you having second thoughts?'

She flicked the tears away. 'No. I'm crying for Nora. I don't like leaving her with him.'

Martin set his jaw. 'If he lays a finger on her, I'll kill him.'

How he would achieve such a thing she couldn't imagine. He'd be no match against Archie's muscular frame. But she believed he would try.

'But I don't think he'll turn on Nora, not yet. Once he's lost your aunt's backing he'll need whatever's left of Nora's fortune. And I told her she must give it to him if he asks for it.'

'You did what!' Again, Martin took his eyes off the road, staring at her as if she'd gone mad.

'If my mum had given up her little bundle of gold, she'd be alive today, but she wanted to keep it for me.' Kate thought of the jewellery sitting in the tin box behind her. 'I know which I'd rather have, Martin.'

'Good gawd, you sound like Queen Mary! Where you been staying, Buckingham Palace? We'll have to curtsy to her now, Conny.' Marge laughed and made room for Kate at the soldering bench.

'She can't help it if she talks posh.' Conny moved up too and Kate slipped into her old workplace as if she'd never been away.

Miss Dane jumped to her defence. 'Leave the poor girl alone, it's nice to have a bit of culture about the place. She'll probably end up in the office!' she said, coming to check that Kate had all her tools. 'I know you've been making your own bits and pieces, Kate, but you'll be out of practice. I'll put you on the easy stuff.'

Kate smiled at the woman. 'Don't worry about me, I'll be able to keep up.'

Miss Dane smiled too, patting her on the shoulder. 'We're not talking about your piddly pewter bowls. You've got to put your back into a two-gallon paint tin!'

Kate knew the objects were larger, but the process was similar and she didn't argue. Miss Dane had been kind to give Kate her old job back without any argument and for now, she needed to find a way of fitting in again. It wasn't until she'd been working for a couple of hours that she realized the supervisor was right. The ranks of coke ovens roared into life, sending the temperature soaring, and the harsh thunder from tin-stamping machines drowned out thought and speech. She'd forgotten what it was like to breathe choking solder fumes and soot, and before long the treacly thick air scorched her lungs as she took deeper and deeper breaths, searching for oxygen. Soon she was bathed in sweat and her back and hands were screaming for relief.

How could she have gone so soft in such a short time? But it wasn't her body that was letting her down; it was her mind. Her imagination, now so full of the beautiful life she was to have lived, the beautiful things she was to have made. It had turned her into a fragile fugitive, thrown down from heaven into the pit of hell. She was so lost in her own painful musings that she hadn't noticed Conny staring at her.

'The hooter's gone, ain't you coming for your dinner?'

'Dinner?' Her brain felt so assaulted by noise and heat she wasn't sure she'd pronounced the word correctly, nor even what it meant.

'Did I work through lunch?'

'*Lunch?* What have they done to you?' Conny shook her head. 'It's *dinner* time – half past twelve!'

'Oh, you mean *dinner?*' And seeing Conny's worried frown, she decided to lie rather than explain that she'd got used to eating 'lunch' instead of dinner and 'dinner' instead of tea. 'I was only joking!' she lied.

She walked with Conny to the dining rooms in the Methodist Central Hall and there Kate discovered that Conny's troubles were even worse than her own.

'Me stepbrother started again. I got too cocky, didn't I? But he hid the bleedin' soldering iron, come home blind drunk one night and there was nothing I could do. I'm up the duff.'

'Oh, Conny, I'm sorry. What are you going to do?'

'Don't know. Marge says there's someone that'll get rid of it, but I'm not sure...' Conny stroked her stomach.

'Have you told him?'

'Just laughed, said it was my fault for undressing in front of him. Well how can I help that when there's me and them two dirty gits sharing a bedroom? I pulled the curtain!'

Kate thought of her pretty violet bedroom back in Belgravia. If she'd stayed at Aunt Sylvie's this might have been her.

'I'll help you, Conny.'

'Oh, Kate. You don't have to tell me what happened at your dad's. But you're back here... so you ain't got no fortune coming, have you?'

'No, but I can make things now and sell them. I'm earning

good money for it too. And I'll get my old job back at the bookshop. You can come and live with me.'

'Where?'

It had been the safest place she could think of. He didn't dare come after her there – not back to the place her mother had died. It hadn't been hard for Aunt Sarah to get her the old place again. No one wanted to pay such an extortionate rent for a single attic room, and she said it had lain empty for most of the time Kate had been away. The only other tenant had been a hawker who'd lived there for three weeks and done a moonlight flit.

She hadn't meant to ask Conny to live with her, nor to go back to cleaning the bookshop, but Conny's need was great and at least she'd be able to help Kate with the rent.

'Are you sure?' Conny asked. 'We might not get on.'

'Do you snore?' Kate asked with a frown, and it was good to see Conny laugh.

'No. But you know you might be taking on one more than you bargained for, if I can't face getting rid of it…'

'Baby or no baby, you can't live with your stepbrother any more.'

'You've always been good to me. I don't know why. Everyone used to think I was so stupid. But you never did, Kate.'

'Don't cry, Conny.' Kate got up. 'Let's get back to the hellhole!'

At the end of the day she went to Miss Dane. 'I've got an idea to make things better for everyone in this place.'

'Oh, here we go.' Miss Dane put down the piecework sheet

she was filling in. 'Not been back five minutes and you're putting the world to rights.' But her scorn was only skin deep and Kate stood her ground, waiting until the supervisor was forced to ask, 'All right, what is it that the bosses with all their education haven't already thought of?'

'I realized today we might as well all be working inside one big chimney! No wonder everyone's losing time with the fume fever. I think we should replace all the coke ovens with gas stoves and gas torches.'

Miss Dane laughed. 'It might be better for our health, but it won't do the profits much good. Too expensive!'

'Not in the long run. I've been working with a small gas stove and a torch and you can get the temperature just right every time! Them coke ovens are either too hot or too cold, we lose hours firing 'em up and getting them to the right heat. The soldering work is much better quality using gas, it's all even. Besides all that, we won't be losing time with people off sick. I tell you they'd make back their investment in six months.'

'Learned everything about business from your dad while you've been gone, haven't you?' Miss Dane gave her a quizzical look. She hadn't asked what had gone wrong, but Kate knew that she and the other girls were curious.

'No. I worked it out all by myself. Will you just put the idea to the bosses?'

Miss Dane took off her glasses and rubbed her eyes wearily; they were red-rimmed from the soot that hung in the air.

'And gas ovens won't irritate you like the coke does, you'll be all bright eyed!' Kate added.

'You haven't lost your cheek! All right, I'll have a go.'

★

Kate threw open the garret window and stuck her head out. A mist had rolled up from the river, enveloping the warehouses and the turret on the school. The air felt damp as river ooze and bitter with soot. She breathed in deeply. She was back where she'd started, poorer by a dream, richer in knowledge. Now, she had to decide how she would live. She'd learned the folly of pinning her hopes on someone else to give her a better life, but she'd also learned her own power. At least her father had given her that; his Judas silver had woken a new dream, one that was within her own gift. She could make beautiful things – and she could sell them. She would hold on to that as she rebuilt her life. Perhaps it would be in East Lane and perhaps somewhere else. But she would remake it and it would have nothing to do with him.

However, she'd discovered that some things had improved in East Lane. She felt less persecuted. Once her aunts learned what she'd done, she found, for the first time in her life, that they approved of her. Aunt Sylvie, knowing that none of his profits would ever come to her, now took a vengeful pleasure in the ruination of her brother's business plans. Stan, with a new suit and a car, had become far too important to worry about harassing Kate. Mr Smith had entrusted him with running all of his debt collectors and tally men.

Then there was Conny. The young girl had moved in with few possessions. She used one of the ancient built-in timber bunks as her bed and Kate added more clothes hooks onto the beams. She thought she would miss the peace and quiet she'd always found in the garret, but their evenings became companionable. Kate arranged one corner of the garret as a workbench, with her tools hung on the rafters. She set about making small tin objects, which she thought Martin could persuade the gallery to sell. She made all sorts of decorated tins for face powder, pins or cigarettes. She included repoussé designs of dragonflies, butterflies and geometric shapes. Conny spent her evenings sewing clothes for her baby. Which, as soon as she moved in, she decided she would keep.

During her first week back in Bermondsey Kate went to the bookshop. She was pleased to find Ethel there, in animated conversation with a contributor to *The Bermondsey Book*. She had been ill, but today her fizzing energy seemed undimmed and when she saw Kate her bright smile was full of sympathy.

The contributor returned to his proofs and Ethel came to greet her with both hands outstretched. 'Welcome back, Kate. I hear you've returned to Bermondsey!' She lowered her voice. 'Mrs Cliffe told me. If there's anything I can do…'

'You could give me my old job back.'

'Oh, I'm sorry, I had to employ another cleaner! She's not so much fun as you were, Kate, but I don't feel I can send her packing.'

'No, course not. It was just an idea. But before I forget – I've got something for you. It's a bit late.' She got out the inkstand and presented it to Ethel. 'Happy fourth anniversary!'

Ethel let out a cry of delight. 'But, Kate, it's beautiful!' She examined the inkstand. 'And you made it specially for the anniversary?'

Kate nodded, grateful for Ethel's genuine delight, pointing out the Bermondsey Bookshop's symbol, the torch of learning.

'I made quite a few things while I was at Dad's. Even a silver bowl.'

Ethel nodded. 'I saw it, at Mrs Cliffe's. It's gorgeous.'

But the inkstand had given Ethel an idea and now she insisted on setting aside a table in the shop and another in the reading room dedicated to selling Kate's objects.

'I could make some fretwork bookmarks and copper bookends!'

'Perhaps a simpler version of my inkstand?'

Kate felt a pulse of excitement. Already she could see the objects that might appeal to the bookshop crowd. 'I'll sketch some designs tonight and see if you think they'll sell.'

Ethel smiled and beckoned her to a bookshelf. 'Mrs Cliffe also told me you've actually been making secret use of our bookshelves!' She pulled out a large-format book. 'She says you're particularly fond of William Morris. But you won't have seen this one yet; it's a new book about his designs.'

'But I'm not a member and I can't afford it yet,' Kate said, eyeing the book with longing.

'I'll make you out a ticket and you can pay in instalments when your first object has sold.'

Kate held out both hands. Once she'd come to clean and not read, and now everything had been turned on its head, including this.

20

Bleedin' Likely

'Chibby took it very badly.'

'Well, that's good! What happened?'

'He turned up at Aunt Violet's in a rage. Demanded to know her reasons for dropping out and the game old girl stood up to him! Told him that she'd heard things about his character that made it impossible to have anything to do with his business. Of course, he played the innocent, asked what the accusations were, and she let him have it. Aunt Violet's a dear, but she can be fierce as an Amazon in support of a just cause!'

'What did she say to him?'

'That she'd ignored for too long that he was a man who could abandon his child and beat his wife. But now something so heinous had come to light she'd been forced to act. She might have left it there, but he started screaming at her, demanding she tell him what it was. She told him she'd been informed, on good authority, that he'd robbed his first wife and been involved in her death.'

Kate hugged herself. 'She didn't pull any punches! But then I did tell her not to hold back. She was very brave.'

'I'm appalled at both of you! It could have been handled without putting either of you in danger. As it was, poor Aunt Violet had a water pitcher thrown at her head. It missed, but she ended up very, very wet and she tells me her mauve silk dress will never be the same!'

Kate burst into laughter, which she quickly stifled when she saw Martin's expression turn deadly serious.

'I'm making fun of the dear old thing, but really it's not at all funny. She could have been seriously hurt. Fortunately, she wasn't alone.'

'Who was with her?'

'Me! I turned up just as the pitcher hit the wall.'

'Did he say anything to you?'

'I'm not sure he even registered who I was, he was in such a mad rage.'

'And that was yesterday? Have you heard anything from Nora?'

'No, have you?'

'No.'

'Aunt Violet told me she'd make arrangements to get her out of Chibby's house. Let's hope it's soon.'

Kate had no fear for herself, but Nora was still wrapped in gossamer, trapped at the heart of her father's web, and she had a feeling she wouldn't be let go as easily as Kate.

Their conversation was cut short as they arrived at Martin's mother's house, an imposing four-storey in Kensington protected by its own set of wrought-iron gates. Martin pulled up the brake and put his hand over hers. 'Ready to enter the lioness's den?'

Kate blew out a long breath and smiled at him. 'If you'd lived with Aunt Sylvie most of your life you'd think your mother was a cuddly kitten. Come on, let's not keep the old gel waiting.'

As he pushed open the gates, he said, 'Now, you won't overdo the cockney Doolittle act, will you?'

Kate giggled. 'Don't you want me to have any fun tonight?'

He put an arm around her. He looked very elegant, in his black dinner suit and patent shoes, but she decided she definitely preferred him in a paint-spattered artist's smock.

His mother proved herself a terror. She'd obviously set out to intimidate Kate and dissuade her from marrying her only son. Her greeting was as steely as her hair, which looked like a polished helmet. Her clever eyes fixed Kate with a sharp attention and never left her all evening. Olivia, Martin's younger sister, and her husband had been invited along to oil the wheels. Fortunately, Olivia was as open and friendly as Martin, who'd made sure that Kate was seated between his sister and himself. The purpose of the evening was obvious to all. Kate was on show and she felt an almost reckless eagerness to see how quickly Mrs North could be brought to the point of forbidding her son's marriage to Kate. If Martin hadn't already had his allowance cut off for the lesser crime of actually courting her, she would have felt far more responsibility to pretend to be something she wasn't, but now, she was determined that they could take her or leave her.

She'd worn the black dress Nora had bought her for the bookshop dance. It was an outfit which made her feel as if she could take on the world – and Martin's mother – with ease. She noticed, as they were shown in, Olivia's look of approval and her sidelong glance at Mrs North, who gave her a stony smile in return.

When they were seated at the dinner table and the soup had been served, Mrs North started on her offensive.

'It's very nice to have this opportunity to get to know Martin's "Eliza" a little better.' Her smile was lethal. 'I hear you've been benefiting from my sister's elocution lessons!'

Martin's face froze in horror. Perhaps Mrs North thought she would strike Kate dumb, or that she wouldn't understand the reference. Instead she gave a sweet smile back.

'Yes! Isn't it a wonderful play? I loved the lecture G. B. S. gave at the bookshop, he was so entertaining. Ethel introduced us afterwards and I had a lovely chat with him about all the things he'd got wrong with Eliza's accent! And when I told him that she should have said "not *bleedin'* likely" rather than "not *bloody* likely", he took out his notebook and made a note of it!'

Kate gave Mrs North a wide-eyed smile and saw Olivia dip her head, stifling a laugh in her napkin. Mrs North fixed Kate with a look that would have frozen the soup. She felt Martin grasp her hand beneath the table and squeezed encouragingly. 'Actually, Kate was a real hit with the old chap,' he said, 'and Ethel appointed her voice coach when the bookshop drama group staged *Pygmalion*.'

She loved that Martin was so innocently proud of her, but Mrs North knew when she was being mocked. She attempted to out-stare Kate and, failing miserably, asked for the soup to be taken away instead. Towards the end of the meal, Martin tugged on his collar, loosened his tie and coughed several times. 'Mother, I've invited Kate tonight because I have an announcement.' He gave a forced smile. 'We are engaged to be married, and I would like your blessing.'

Olivia clapped and said, 'Oh, Martin, that's marvellous.' Her husband looked frightened and glanced at Mrs North, who flushed deeply. She turned to Kate. 'I'm sure you are a very lovely young woman, Kate, and I can see why my son is smitten, but he has not been kind in promising you marriage, nor in bringing you here. He knows my views on marriage between the classes, and now he's forced me to embarrass you.'

She turned her eyes on Martin, who gripped Kate's hand again, even more tightly. 'And as for you, if you insist on dragging the family down by marrying someone brought up in degradation and squalor, then you'll get not a penny from me. It will all go to your sister!'

Martin's brother-in-law stopped looking frightened and began nodding in agreement, until his wife spoilt the moment by exclaiming, 'But that's so cruel!'

Martin stood up, pulling Kate with him. 'Mother, I'm not interested in your money. Olivia's welcome to it. I came here for your blessing. That's all. Come along, Kate. I apologize for my mother's rudeness. Shall we sling our 'ooks?'

They ran hand in hand from the house, giggling, he drunk on his rebellion, she exhilarated by his sacrifice. And Martin was far from devastated to have lost his fortune. He seemed to have found a new sense of freedom and the next day was insistently determined to get her to agree to marrying without more delay.

'Why do you always want to wait? We've no one to please but ourselves now. My work is selling well. We won't starve. You can give up tin bashing and take up whitesmithing. It'll be marvellous! We'll be happy.' He kissed her but she stopped him, wondering if every prospective bride felt so hesitant.

'Martin, we can't go out and get married just like that. We'll have to make plans...'

'All right, here's a plan. A special licence, a register office, a reception in my gallery, a honeymoon in Cornwall.' He grinned and started singing, '"*It won't be a stylish marriage, I can't afford a carriage...*"' And Kate thumped him and then kissed him.

But her hesitation puzzled her as much as it did Martin. It wasn't because she doubted her love for him. It wasn't even that sometimes she thought he loved her more for what she symbolized than for what she was. She knew her very unsuitability sealed his rebel status, his bohemian image of himself. It wasn't because of Johnny, who had found happiness with the blonde from the bookshop. No. It was because of Nora and what she suspected Martin still felt for her.

Nora was free. Kate learned from Martin that Mrs Cliffe had made good her promise. Chibby had left for Europe to drum up other backers for his business and while he was gone, Mrs Cliffe had spirited Nora away too. Or rather, Martin had. Mrs Cliffe had rented a cottage from a friend in Sussex and had secreted Nora there. It seemed the ideal place – within Paul's reach, but out of Chibby's. It was natural for Mrs Cliffe to call on her 'chauffeur' to drive Nora down to Sussex – not in his mother's car, as that 'privilege' had been removed, but in his own. And for some reason the thought of the two of them motoring through the countryside in the red Baby Austin made Kate feel jealous. She was embarrassed by the feeling. After all, it wasn't anything like one of her jaunts with Martin; there was nothing carefree or joyful in poor Nora's situation. She was leaving her marriage with nothing, going into hiding in fear for her safety, with no clear idea of how she'd provide for her son, nor how she would live. The last thing on her mind would be a romance with Martin. And, of course, it would be the last thing on his mind too. Why would he throw his inheritance and his mother's good opinion away if he didn't love Kate more than anyone else in the world?

It was a Saturday evening. Kate knelt by the garret window, which she'd opened to let out the solder fumes. She was making a small tin bath for Conny's baby. She'd shaped each end into smooth curves with a leather-covered hammer and for the last two hours had been soldering the seams. Conny was on late shift and Kate hoped to surprise her with the finished article when she arrived home. She hadn't been able to bring her gas stove with her from Belgravia, but she'd found an alternative. Beside her was a small primus stove, with a cradle specially designed for heating soldering irons over the flame. She put the cooled soldering iron she'd been using onto the cradle and removed the hot one. Putting the iron's glowing tip to the seam, she applied the solder, which flowed magically upwards in silver teardrops, attracted by the hot tip. She'd almost finished the final seam when she heard a noise on the stairs.

'Conny, is that you? Let yourself in – I'm in the middle of something!' she called, disappointed that her friend had arrived home before she'd finished the bath. Oh well, she'd have to attach the handles later. She laid the still-hot soldering iron onto a tile and eased herself up. Throwing a blanket over the bath, she turned towards the door, ready for the grand unveiling. But the surprise was Kate's. She took in a sharp breath and held it as her father walked slowly into the smoky room. His large-framed, black-suited figure made the space, and her, feel small.

She stood, frozen by the shock. He was meant to be on the continent! He closed the door, took off his black homburg and laid it carefully on a chair before going to close the window.

'Katy, I was disappointed that you never came to say goodbye to "yer old man",' he said, grinning at his deliberate broad Bermondsey and not looking in the least disappointed.

She walked towards him, intending to show him out. 'All right, if you want I'll say it now. Goodbye, Dad.' But as she drew closer, he held up a hand to stop her.

'I don't understand why you didn't. It was rude, Katy, not to tell me to my face you were going. You were always entirely free to come or go as you pleased. Sit down.' He said it in such a way that she found herself about to obey. He seemed to own the room, and she gave an involuntary shudder, remembering that he had once lived here too. Her new memory of him vied with her old, causing her anger to boil up. She wouldn't be intimidated by him.

'No, Dad. I don't want to sit down. Why are you here?'

'I've come to see my ungrateful daughter!'

'That's not the reason. You're here because you're scared.'

He laughed and stared at her with disdain. 'Scared? Of you? Hardly. Actually, I've come to talk sense into you. Whatever you've been telling Mrs Cliffe, it's ruining my business. You'll have to go and retract it all. And don't deny it was you slandering me. You're the only one who witnessed...' He hesitated. '...that period of my life.'

Kate realized that, with a stupidity born of arrogance, he

still completely trusted that his abandoned sister Sylvie had kept her silence.

'I won't retract nothing. I've told Mrs Cliffe everything I've remembered. And that's what's scared you. What I remember.'

His eyes narrowed to sleepy slits and he was very still, almost relaxed, with his hands loose at his sides, his feet planted wide apart.

'So, tell me, what is it that you remember?'

'It was seeing Mum's earring in Nora's jewellery box that did it. It all came back. I remembered how you come home that night, you woke me up with all your shouting at her, and I remember how she cried out when you hit her, and I remember how I saw you rip the earrings out of her ears...' She was quiet for a second and could almost see the calculations going on behind those half-closed eyes. He was wondering how much of this she'd revealed to his wife.

'And that's what I told Nora. Just so she'd know what a wicked, vicious monster you really are!' She felt no fear at all, just a soaring exhilaration that she'd faced him with the truth. 'And I ain't taking back one bleedin' word of it!'

His stillness transformed in a fluid instant, so that she saw only the blur of movement as he sprang forward, snatched up the forming hammer from her bench, and whirled like a dervish in a low circle, swinging the hammer till it connected with Kate's temple. A moment's terror was all she felt as the murky light in the room was swallowed by the darkness.

She came to, she didn't know how long after, her throat dry as sandpaper, and found she couldn't breathe. Painful light burst in through the slits of her eyelids. She forced them wide open and found herself looking into the cold eyes of her father, understanding now why her heaving chest could suck in no air. His thumbs were squeezing her windpipe closed. She clawed at his hands, trying to scream, but producing only a choking rattle. From far away she heard him speaking and struggled to understand. She caught one word – repeated again and again – Nora.

'What did you tell Nora? Why has Nora left me? Where is Nora? Tell me!'

Her eyes felt as if they might pop out of her head and she knew, in one calm corner of her mind, that if she didn't dislodge his hold right now, she would certainly die. The force of his attack must have thrust them back into the room, for she'd felt her head crack against the tin bath's rim. But the jolt had also released his grip a fraction, and now, taking a drowning gasp of air, she flailed her arms and stretched her fingers taut till she felt the primus flame burn them. She recoiled, and as she did so, her fingers closed around the familiar worn handle of her soldering iron. She gripped it like a drowning woman would a piece of flotsam and, summoning all her strength, she swung it upwards, smashing it into his skull. He grunted, loosened his grip and staggered back against the door.

Move! But her body wouldn't respond. *Run!* She struggled to her knees, gulping for air. *Now!* But there was no way out. His unconscious figure blocked the doorway entirely. She had no strength to pull him out of the way. There was only one place she could go.

Everything seemed much darker now. She peered through a tunnel of red mist, her vision narrowed to what was directly in front of her. She felt a dull throbbing in her right temple and a searing pain across the back of her neck, but it was her throat that hurt the most – it burned as if a fiery noose had bitten through her skin. She crawled to the end wall of her garret, not stopping to look behind her. The unbroken darkness when she reached the far wall was almost a relief as she felt for her tin box. Behind it was the low hinged door that she'd used in her escape from Aunt Sylvie's on her first day at Boutle's. She shoved the box aside and wriggled through the hatch, pulling the tin box after her before closing the small door.

With pounding heart and her head bursting with pain, she staggered to her feet and stumbled forward through next door's attic. The connecting garrets were, from here on, open for the entire length of several houses. The bird droppings were deeper beneath her feet than before, and the spiders' webs, like thick curtains, clutched and caught her as she swam through them. And this time, her escape was slow, shot with pain and terror as she imagined hearing her father's footsteps behind her. She dared not stop, but blundered on till she reached a brick wall. Pressing herself against its solid, crusted surface, she felt her heart thumping. She was in the last house of East Lane, where mad old Longbonnet lived.

She wanted only to sink down now, to sleep. But a cracked, quavery voice seemed to echo through time and around the garret. 'This way!' it said, and she remembered the smugglers' escape route ended here, with stairs down to the yard and the river beyond. She reached up to a wooden pulley, and holding tight to the frayed fragment of rope, she followed it, almost blind now, to a narrow door in the back wall. Why couldn't she see? She wiped a hand across her eyes, and it came away wet, sticky. Her fingers felt her temple and probed the back of her skull. Her whole head was wet, as if she'd dunked her hair in the river. Perhaps she was drowning after all. There was a dormer in here, but no light seemed to reach her. She held her hand inches from her face. Dark, sticky ooze coated it. River mud. She edged on till she found the narrow door in the back wall. Only a few steps now, then down to the yard below and she would be free! But the door wouldn't open, it was stuck fast, and now she really did need to sleep. Sleep in the garret, her haven. Though this was a different house, wasn't it? She was confused. But it would do – to sleep in, even to die in, as her mother had done. It suddenly seemed unimportant to be free, and she let herself sink down and down, imagining she could hear the dark river lapping over her head.

21

Two of a Kind

Johnny stood in Kate's garret, listening to Conny.

'I come home from work and the door was open and I thought that was strange. But then I see the bath.' Her lip trembled. 'She must have made it for me baby. And I thought to meself, I bet she's hiding up the back of the garret, waiting to see how surprised I was with it. But then I saw this.' She pointed to a puddle of blood. 'I didn't know what to do, and you was the first person I thought of. The way she always talked about you... I thought she'd come straight to you if she was ever in trouble.' Here Conny broke down. 'Something bad's happened to her, Johnny. I got a terrible feeling.'

He put an arm around her. 'Don't cry, Conny. She's probably just...' He searched for an explanation which would convince him. '...just had an accident with one of her tools and she's gone to the doctor to get herself seen to.'

But in his heart, he felt otherwise. Conny was right – if Kate had hurt herself, he was sure she would have come straight to him. However far they'd drifted apart, he knew that much.

He looked around the attic and spotted something under Kate's bunk. He knelt down and reached under and his hand closed over a metal object. He had the odd sensation that it was burning hot and almost dropped it. As he stood up, inspecting the soldering iron, he felt something else – a sense of menace. He put the iron down, almost gratefully, on Kate's makeshift bench. Conny joined him. She looked at the soldering iron with a frown. 'Why would it have been under her bunk?'

'I don't know. It must have rolled there when she hurt herself.'

His unease was deepening. He couldn't stand here any longer, puzzling over the possibilities with Conny. He needed to find Kate – and quickly.

He tried to keep his voice even. 'I think it's worth having a search round the lane...'

'Just in case,' Conny said, and he nodded.

They hurried downstairs, and on the way Johnny checked with Mrs Wilson.

'I been out all day, Rasher, but the kids have been here.' She invited him into her kitchen, where her husband and small brood were seated around the table.

'Have any of you seen Kate today?' she asked. They looked up from their plates, shaking their heads. 'Only the front door was on the latch when I come in... I'm wondering if she left it open?'

'No, that was me...' the eldest Wilson child admitted. 'I left it on the latch when we went to play marbles in the kerb.'

It wasn't unusual to leave doors unlocked in East Lane –

there was so little for strangers to steal and neighbours wouldn't dare.

'How long did you stay out playing?' Johnny asked.

'Not sure, it was just getting dark.'

'And you didn't see Kate coming out at all?'

'Sorry.' The little boy shook his head and Mr Wilson got up.

'I'll help you look for her,' he said, passing his plate to the children, who fell upon his unfinished potatoes.

Johnny sent Conny to the top of the lane, to Aunt Sarah's, while Mr Wilson went off to check the opposite side of the street and the surrounding warehouses. Without much hope, he knocked on Sylvie's door. Stan answered.

'Why would she come 'ere?' Stan asked, picking his teeth. The family were obviously eating tea.

'She might be hurt, and your mum's the nearest family...'

Stan was suddenly alert. 'Hurt? Who by?'

'It could have been an accident. She was doing metalwork, a tool might have slipped. What makes you think someone did it?'

Stan shrugged. 'Dunno.'

Johnny leaned into the doorway and grabbed Stan's shirt. 'What do you know?'

'Nothing! I just heard something about her old man...'

'What about him?'

Johnny let him go, and Stan looked back into the passage and lowered his voice. 'I heard his business is in right trouble and it's all Kate's fault. Seems she's been opening her trap about him and he's lost his investors.'

'How do you know all this?'

'Let's just say I heard it at work. Anyway, Archie's not the sort you want to cross.'

'What's that you're saying about my brother? Get in here!'
Aunt Sylvie stood behind Stan and dragged him by the collar
as if he were a little boy.

'Rasher, you can sod off. Don't come around here asking
questions about my family business.'

'He wasn't!' Stan ducked out of his mother's grasp.

'It looks like Kate's been hurt,' Johnny explained. 'There's
blood in the garret and she's gone missing. I just thought she
might have come here.'

Now Sylvie's face hardened. 'Are you trying to say my
brother's hurt her?'

Johnny's heart was racing and he'd had enough. They were
all obsessed with Kate's father. 'Why the bloody hell would I
think that?' He looked from one to the other and a cold chill
seized him. 'But you two obviously do.'

Stan was sloping off back to his tea, but Sylvie turned and,
yanking him back, ordered, 'Get out there and help Rasher
look for her.'

Just then Aunt Sarah came hurrying along the lane with
Conny. 'Have you found her?' she asked Johnny, who noticed
a glance pass between her and Sylvie.

'No,' he replied. 'Perhaps you could check if she went to
the late clinic at the doctor's, Sarah?'

'She'll take till tomorrow morning on her legs,' Sylvie said.
'I'll get me coat and be there and back in no time.'

Stan went off to help Mr Wilson look around the
warehouses and wharves. Johnny went to the last house in
the lane with Conny in tow.

'Did you know that mad old Longbonnet turned out to
be Kate's great-aunt?' Conny asked as they hurried along the
dank street, their breaths trailing white vapour.

'I did. But I can't think why she'd go to her and not me.'

Conny gave him a questioning look. 'Only reason I can think of is because you're her ex?'

'Well, she's moved on,' Johnny said as they arrived at the end house.

And Conny sighed, 'Blokes are so stupid.'

Longbonnet came to the door in her coat. 'I was just going out with me supper delicacies, can it wait?'

'It's Kate,' Johnny said. 'She's missing.'

Longbonnet's kitchen was dark, except for a pool of light cast by the gas lamp on her table. The old woman's baskets were packed and covered in white cloths. But she took off her coat. 'Sit down there, and tell me exactly what you seen in that garret.'

As they were speaking, her ridged brown fingernails drummed a slow tattoo on the table. They told her about the upturned chair and the pool of blood and the soldering iron under the bed.

She plucked at her lip for a moment. 'And the door was left ajar?'

Johnny nodded. This was a waste of time Kate wasn't here. 'I just thought there was a chance she'd be here... but we'd better get going.' He stood up.

'Hold yer horses, I'm thinking!' The cracked voice had in that moment a surprising power. He sat down again, on the edge of the chair. 'She wouldn't have gone out and left her door ajar. But I remember there was a time, years ago – when she first started work – Janey locked her in, and Kate found a way out.'

Johnny nodded – he had heard the story from Kate before and always marvelled at her determination not to be imprisoned by anyone. 'But why would she not just come out the front door?' he asked, puzzled.

'Because she couldn't.' Longbonnet looked up at the ceiling. 'She's in my garret!' Longbonnet said it with such certainty that Johnny leaped for the stairs. But Longbonnet got there first and mounted them two at a time with surprising swiftness. She fumbled by the door for a candle and led the way into her garret. The small flame did little to illuminate the long, dark space and they stumbled about, searching with their hands rather than their eyes.

It was Longbonnet who reached her first, slumped by the door in the back wall. 'I've got her!' she called to the others, then put her face close to Kate's. She kept it there for what seemed like an agonizingly long time.

'Is she breathing?' Johnny whispered, a catch in his voice.

'There's breath, but it's weak. We need to get her warm, she's like ice.'

He put his arms under Kate and lifted her gently. Her head was against his cheek, and he felt her blood, wet and sticky. Longbonnet held the candle high for Johnny as he negotiated the ladder-like stairs to her bedroom. They laid Kate on Longbonnet's bed.

'Oh, look at her poor head!' Conny wailed. 'What could have happened? There's so much blood!'

Johnny looked up, his face ashen. 'She could have just fallen and hit her head.' But even as he said it, he remembered how Kate's mum had died in just such a tragedy in the very same place.

Conny was shaking her head. 'I've got a bad feeling about that soldering iron, Rasher. She taught me how to use it – to keep me stepbrother out of me bed. Much good it did me. Much good it did her, by the looks of it, the poor darlin'.'

Conny was overtaken by sobs and Longbonnet sent her

to the kitchen for water. 'Get some of me clean basket cloths while you're at it!' she shouted after her.

Johnny had never felt so helpless. He looked to Longbonnet. 'Has someone attacked her, do you think?'

'We can't know for sure till she can tell us. But if it's anyone, it'll be Archie Goss's handiwork. He did it to her poor mother, so why not to her? I wouldn't put it past him.'

'You think her dad did this?' Johnny leaped up. 'I'll murder the bastard!'

'No! I'm not saying he *did*, I'm saying we need to wait and see. Don't go off half-cocked. She needs you. Go to the phone box at Dockhead and ring for an ambulance. Well, get a move on!'

He didn't argue. She was right – there was nothing they could know for certain until Kate woke. If she ever did... But as he dashed along Bermondsey Wall to the phone box, he found himself reciting aloud the litany *I'll murder him! I'll murder him!* to the black night and the empty streets until by the time he got to the glowing phone box it had become his faith. He trotted back to East Lane, his chest still heaving, and when he saw Martin leaning against the red Austin outside Kate's, he embraced his rival. After telling him what had happened and what they suspected, Johnny repeated the murderous litany and Martin became his first convert.

'I need to see my darling girl,' Martin said as they entered Longbonnet's. He looked out of place here. But his eyes locked onto Johnny's, and in that instant they were not rivals but allies. After all, they both loved her. Longbonnet showed Martin upstairs and when he came down from seeing Kate, his eyes were red. He made no effort to disguise that he'd been crying and Johnny envied him. They heard the urgent clanging of the ambulance's bell as it turned into East Lane. Johnny opened the door, letting in the dank night air.

The ambulance's arrival had created a stir in East Lane and neighbours stood at their doors, talking to each other, speculating about who the unfortunate was and what had befallen them. It wouldn't be long before the story of yet another Goss woman's tragedy made its way into every house. But for now, they stood at a respectful distance, keeping their voices low.

Johnny was about to jump up into the ambulance when he hesitated, standing aside.

'You should be the one to go, Martin.'

Martin stepped in and then offered Johnny a hand. 'Come on. We'll both go.'

In the green-walled hospital corridor, the two men stood awkwardly side by side. Kate had been whisked away to a ward and now the doctor wanted to know who was next of kin. Martin stepped forward. 'I'm Kate's fiancé.'

Johnny felt a jolt. He hadn't realized it had gone this far and yet part of him didn't mind. It was her life he cared about, her life and her happiness, even if it was with another man.

'She seems to have suffered a head trauma. Here—' the doctor pointed to his temple—'and here.' He pointed to the back of his head. 'Possibly sustained in a fall?'

Johnny stepped forward. 'It's possible. She was making a tin bath – soldering.' The doctor showed surprise. 'She's a tinsmith, but she was working at home and we thought she might have had an accident with a tool?'

The doctor gave a dismissive gesture. 'Not unless she

deliberately hit her head with one. But presumably there would have been an oven, heat, solder? She could have been overcome by fumes.'

Johnny shrugged. 'Maybe. She'd been soldering for a few hours, in an attic, but there was a small window open…'

The doctor tutted. 'Still, very dangerous. The fumes are noxious.'

Johnny didn't want to say that Kate's lungs had suffered much worse in her working life. But neither could he disagree. 'And you are?' the doctor asked.

'Just a friend.'

'Will you let us know when I can see her?' Martin asked.

'Yes. You can wait here.' The doctor indicated some chairs ranged against the corridor wall.

'Do you think it was the fumes?' Martin asked when they were alone. His face was gaunt, pale and tight as one of his blank canvases, and Johnny's heart went out to him.

'It might have been. She knew the risks, but it's like her to push herself. The bath was for Conny's baby – she wanted to finish it before Conny got home, I expect.'

Martin nodded. 'I hope to God it was the fumes…'

'Me too.'

She was in a bed at the far end of the ward. They'd been warned by the sister to expect no response. The blood had been cleaned from her dark curls, which now spread in tendrils over the hospital pillowcase. Strange to see her face so pale. Her cheeks, normally pink from running or working or rage, were now white as the starched linen. She looked as if she had on one of her beloved bandanas, but this one was white instead of her customary red, and it hid her wounds.

Johnny held back, letting Martin go to her first. He took hold of Kate's hand and let out a low sob.

'My darling, I'm so sorry I wasn't there when you needed me. Can you hear me, dearest girl?'

Johnny stood rigid behind him, choking back his own grief and regret. He should have fought harder to keep her.

'Would you like to speak to her?' Martin asked, turning to Johnny. 'Another familiar voice... it might help.'

But what part of his heart could he bare in front of Martin? He moved closer and leaned over her, wanting to brush a stray curl from her cheek, but not daring.

'Kate, it's Johnny. I'm here too, it's both of us, me and Martin.'

And as he spoke, she stirred. Her lips parted and both men leaned in closer.

'Dad,' she said, her voice lower than a whisper.

It was an unlikely war council. Back in Longbonnet's kitchen, Johnny, Martin and Kate's aunts gathered. Conny had been sent back to her garret to rest. The news they had brought from the hospital sent the three warring women into an unlikely embrace. But their relief soon exploded into anger.

'I knew it was him!' Longbonnet said, pointing a finger at Aunt Sylvie.

Johnny needed to know how the old woman could have been so sure that Kate's attacker was Archie. 'What did you mean when you said he did it to Kate's mother? What did he do?'

Sylvie and Sarah exchanged a look, almost like children caught in an act of mischief.

'I can answer that,' Martin said, and he explained Kate's

recovered memory and what she'd done about it. There was silence in the little room as Johnny tried to take in the import of what he'd just heard.

It was Sylvie who spoke first. 'I'll give her that. Kate's the only one I ever knew who stood up to my brother. She won't be beat by nothing and no one.'

And Johnny muttered, 'Well, you should know.' At which the room again erupted into accusations and blame until Johnny, who had naturally taken the lead, hushed them. 'We can't do much to help Kate, but we can try to make sure Archie pays.'

'He's got to be held accountable, obviously, but he needs to be stopped, now!' Martin added. 'We need to act quickly. We should go straight to the police.'

'What can the coppers do?' Johnny replied. 'No one saw Archie go in or out of Kate's garret – it's only her word against his.' He rubbed a hand across his tired eyes, hoping Martin hadn't seen the tears that threatened.

'But we need to get him locked away! It was Kate tonight, but he'll be looking for Nora now.'

Johnny couldn't help agree with him in that. 'He's a bloody raving madman, he could do anything... It's a pity we didn't know what he was really like earlier.' Johnny shot an accusing look at the aunts. 'I'd never have let her go and live with him if I'd known what he was capable of.'

Longbonnet shook her head in frustration, so that her long earrings jingled. 'We can all blame ourselves till we're blue in the face. Fact is, Kate wouldn't be standing here talking, she'd be up and doing!'

'You're right. Martin, you know where Nora is and you've got the motor. Why don't you go to Sussex, make sure she's all right – and you'd better stay with her till I find Archie,' Johnny said, taking charge.

Martin agreed and, putting on his cap and driving gloves, shook Johnny's hand. He held on to it for a second and said, 'Take care of her for me.'

Johnny gripped his hand and, looking into Martin's eyes, promised, 'I will.'

When Martin had gone, Kate's aunts went home too and Johnny was left alone with Longbonnet. Snatching up his coat, he made for the door – he was bursting with an almost painful energy. He needed to be doing something.

But Longbonnet held him back. 'Take someone with you. Don't be fooled. Archie's got a posh voice and a posh suit these days but he's as strong as a docker.' She eyed Johnny's slim figure doubtfully.

'Well, what do you think I do all day – I *am* a bloody docker!'

'Yes, but you ain't no killer. Take Stan.'

'Take him? You must be joking! He's never been a friend to Kate. I'll find me own muscle.'

The upstairs sash window squeaked and stuck. Ginger Bosher gave it a shove then poked his head out. He didn't look pleased. 'Rasher, is that you?'

'I need a favour!' He tried to keep his voice low.

'At this time of night? We're all abed!'

'It's important, it's my Kate...'

Something about his voice must have convinced Ginger, and within seconds he appeared in his pyjamas at the front door. 'Fran's got the right 'ump with you! You woke the kids up.'

Ginger padded on bare feet into his kitchen and lit the gas mantle. As it flared and hissed, Johnny paced up and down, explaining what had happened and the nature of the favour he'd come to ask. Ginger made him sit down.

'You've got to go about this systematically, Rasher. You know what happens when you get yourself all stirred up and just rush in. You sit and have a think about all the places he could be, while I get dressed and smooth it over with Fran.'

As Ginger's heavy footsteps receded up the stairs, Johnny took a deep breath. His friend was right. Ginger could always manage to calm him down. There wasn't much Ginger didn't know about dealing with hotheads; his brother, Ted, had been a Bolshie who'd got himself put away for trying to bomb the Woolwich Arsenal during the war. Perhaps that's why Ginger had taken Johnny under his wing.

By the time Ginger came downstairs again, Johnny had a list of all Archie's possible locations. He'd got most of the addresses from Martin before he'd left. 'We should start with his office, it's the nearest, just over the water in Lower Thames Street. He might have bolted there first – to get cleaned up.'

Ginger nodded grimly and jammed a flat cap over his wiry red hair. Tying a white choker around his neck, he said, 'Come on, Rasher, let's go and sort this bastard out.' His tone was as matter-of-fact as if they were about to tackle a shipload of bananas instead of a killer. They walked briskly along Tooley Street before crossing a fog-shrouded Tower Bridge. The usual daytime and early-evening crush of traffic was absent now, with only a few smudgy headlights from the late-night buses crossing the bridge. Gas lamps flared along the north embankment, illuminating the inky water below, and they walked in silence, heads down, intent on getting over the bridge and out of the cold wind.

Once on the other side, Ginger asked, 'If he's there, what do you want to do?'

'I want to frighten him into admitting what he did to Kate, and maybe even what he did to her mum.'

'How far are you thinking of going?'

Typical Ginger, to ask if he had planned a cut-off point. 'As far as I need to – you can just stand there and look tough. Shouldn't have much trouble doing that.'

Ginger grinned. 'I can look the part. And I'll soon give him a pasting if I think he's lying to us – but I ain't toppin' no one.'

'Ginger! You've got kids. I wouldn't get you into that sort of trouble. I'll be honest, I want to murder him. But that's something I can do all on me own.'

'You silly sod, you don't even *think* that! Hear me?'

Johnny nodded and stopped. The whiff from Billingsgate fish market told him they were near. It wasn't easy to find but eventually they came to a narrow alleyway, leading to a tall house with a bow window jutting over the river. They had come to the office of Archie's fur business. It was in darkness, along with most other buildings in the street.

'Don't look like there's anyone in,' Ginger observed.

Johnny tried the door and, looking both ways along the street, he shoulder-barged it, bouncing back into Ginger's arms.

'Get out me way, you young streak o' piss.' Ginger grinned and hustled him aside, aiming his booted foot at the door. With one kick, the ancient lock gave way and the two hurried in. The main office, overlooking the Thames, was obviously empty and a search of the accounting and sales rooms also proved fruitless. But in a small downstairs cloakroom Johnny found something. He called to Ginger, who peered into a sink, stained with faint streaks of blood. 'Is that what I think it is?'

'We've missed him, damn it!' Johnny thumped the cloak-room door.

'All right, well, where would he go next? Home?'

Johnny blew out a long breath. He really didn't know. The mind of Archie Goss, a man who would kill his wife and batter his daughter, was closed to him. 'Let's have a better look round here. Maybe he's changed his clothes. If we could find a bit of bloody clothing, that might be evidence.'

But the streaks in the sink were the only signs Archie had left of his guilt, and even they could be explained away by something as innocent as a nosebleed.

They decided to go to Belgravia next and took the underground from Mark Lane station. After rousing the maid from her bed, they were told that Archie was abroad on a business trip and had been gone for some days. Johnny pushed past her.

'He ain't here! I told you.' She pulled her dressing gown close around her. 'Are you from that loan shark feller?'

Johnny turned back. 'What's his name?' The maid took a step back and Johnny smiled at her. 'We're not here to hurt you, miss. We just need to speak to Mr Grainger.'

'You and half the world,' she said, but seemed to soften at Johnny's smile.

'This loan shark...'

'I don't know his name. But he's got the same colour hair as him.' She pointed at Ginger. 'Spots all over his face, crooked brown teeth. Right charmer.'

'Thanks, love. Can we have a look round, then?' Johnny smiled again.

'Suit yourself. I'm going downstairs for a cuppa. When you're finished, you can come and have one too if you like – but don't bring him.' She nodded towards Ginger and Johnny winked at her.

There was no sign of Archie at the Belgravia house, and Johnny didn't stop for tea. They continued their search at Archie's club, slipping the doorman ten bob only to find that Archie wasn't there, and finally, they returned to the fur warehouses near his office. But with the city waking and the dawn rising pink over the Thames, they found themselves trudging back over Tower Bridge, defeated.

At Dockhead, Johnny shook his friend's hand and watched as Ginger turned his square, muscular frame in the direction of home, walking away with that distinctive rolling gait of his. Now Johnny turned in the opposite direction and headed for East Lane.

The search, the certainty that he would have his hands around Archie's throat by this morning, had saved him from thinking about what faced him at the hospital. But now he felt sick with apprehension. He went home to shave and change and then to Longbonnet's. After years of viewing her as the madwoman at the end of the street, he found she had suddenly become a sane ally. But when she answered his knock, her anxious, hopeful expression told him she'd heard nothing. Neither had Sylvie and Sarah. Archie might turn up later at one of his sisters', perhaps sniffing around for news of Kate, but Johnny couldn't waste any more time hanging around in East Lane.

He went out to the sound of Dockhead church bells ringing for early Mass. The main road was quiet and he jumped aboard a tram, just eager to be nearer Kate. The tram's jolting, clanging progress up Tooley Street did nothing to calm his anxious stomach. But as he stared up at the sooty railway viaduct leading to London Bridge station, his murderous litany of the previous night transformed into a supplication and he prayed silently: *let her live and I'll let him live, let her live and I'll let him live.*

It was Sunday, and far too early, of course, for visiting. He should have known the workings of the wards by now – his mother had spent enough time in Guy's Hospital as her health had drained away with the drink. He stood outside at a tea stall and with other early risers and down-and-outs drank thick brown tea from thick white mugs. Hearing the everyday talk of men worried about finding a bed for the night somehow steadied his nerves. He found a phone box and dialled the number Martin had given him.

'Mrs Cliffe? I'm sorry to ring so early, this is John Bacon – from the bookshop.'

The woman's clear, cultured voice repeated his name. Why should she have noticed him? 'I'm a friend of Kate.'

'Oh, yes, John! Our budding novelist.' And then, realizing that the phone call had nothing to do with the bookshop, she asked, 'Is there something wrong? Is it Martin?'

'No, but he did say you might be able to help me. Kate's been attacked and we think it was her father.'

'Chibby? Dear God, I was afraid of something like this – but I hoped he wasn't so vile as to target his own child... I blame myself. I should have protected her as well as Nora.'

Johnny tried to reassure her and then asked, 'I've looked everywhere, but I can't find him. Have you got any idea where he might be?'

He could hear Mrs Cliffe breathing and thinking; his money was going to run out soon and he was about to insert another penny in the slot. 'I really need your help, if there's anything you can do...'

'Yes. I think I *can* help you. I'll go to see Chibby's solicitor first thing tomorrow. If anyone knows where to find him, it'll be Mr Mordant. They're joined at the hip – two of a kind, I'm afraid.'

After the telephone call he felt suddenly cast adrift and walked towards the river. Drawn by the bells of Southwark Cathedral he almost went in, but instead descended the steps to the river, choosing the abiding Thames as a surer source of comfort. When he could finally get in to see Kate, he was taken by surprise. He'd expected she would be groggy, that the doctors might have news of a lengthy recovery. Surely if she'd roused herself enough to speak the name of her attacker, she should be conscious today. But his whispered greeting could not wake her at all. When the staff nurse came on her round, she told him Kate hadn't responded or spoken since that one word of yesterday – Dad.

It was a sleep so sound that he was reminded of 'Briar Rose' – a tale from her beloved *Grimm's*. Johnny shuddered. He wasn't normally a man who prayed and yet he found himself, for the third time, creating a prayer, or perhaps it was a spell: *if I kiss her she'll wake up.* He leaned forward and put his lips to her cheek. 'Kate, it's me, Johnny.' He waited, searching her pale, beautiful face for a sign, but it was impassive as stone. So unlike his Kate, with her ever-changing, intelligent eyes, her mocking smile, her sudden kind expression. She slept on as he sat there, and eventually, he stood up and said goodbye. If he could not be the one to wake her, he would bring her the one who could.

22

A Faithful Knight and True

Johnny had left it until mid-morning before phoning Mrs Cliffe. But now the telephone box at Dockhead was busy. He smoked a cigarette and dived into the box almost before the man had vacated it. Mrs Cliffe answered his call at the first ring and he could tell, just from her voice, that she had disappointing news.

'I'm sorry, John, but it seems Chibby couldn't have attacked Kate. He wasn't even in the country! I went to see Mr Mordant and he insists that Chibby has been in France ever since I backed out – no doubt trying to hoodwink other poor fools into giving him money.' Mrs Cliffe's tone was uncharacteristically bitter.

'So, you don't believe it was Archie who attacked Kate?'

'As a matter of fact, John, I do. But there's not an ounce of proof; it will be her word against his. I'm afraid Chibby's outfoxed us. Mordant *said* he'll be travelling back from the continent today, but who knows what the truth is.'

'But surely the police could check if he's actually bought a ferry ticket?'

Johnny heard a deep sigh down the telephone. 'Chibby might have sailed out and back overnight.'

'Or even sent someone else?'

'Exactly. He is a very devious man.'

'Well, I can't do any good here. I think Martin should come back from Sussex.'

'But what about Nora?'

'I'll swap places with him. Kate needs Martin.'

'She's no better, then?'

'No.'

'It's still very soon, John. She *will* recover, I'm sure of it.'

Johnny took no comfort in Mrs Cliffe's words. He turned his back on the man outside the telephone box who was waiting for him to finish his call. 'I know she will,' he said, 'I just think she'll recover better if Martin's with her. And I can guard Nora just as well as Martin can.'

There was a second's silence. 'Very well, John. I'll telephone Martin to expect you tomorrow.'

The following day Johnny packed a small bag, told Ginger he'd be away for a few days and then made his way to London Bridge station. He smoked a cigarette, staring at the departure board, thinking of Kate, only a stone's throw away in Guy's Hospital. He hadn't planned on visiting her – what would be the point? It wasn't him she needed. But the temptation proved too great and he decided he must see Kate one last time before leaving. He stowed his bag at left luggage and, dodging buses and taxis crowding around the station, he made his way to St Thomas's Street. As he was crossing the hospital courtyard, he noticed someone standing under the entrance portico. He was the sort of man you took notice of. Tall, and obviously well-muscled beneath his dark, elegant clothes. Johnny turned towards the staircase leading up to the ward and stopped with his foot on the first step.

It was him! Johnny hadn't seen Archie Goss since he was a boy, but now he was sure he'd just glimpsed the man he'd searched half London for. He dashed back to the portico, now crowded with nurses in a flutter of blue-and-scarlet capes, coming off duty. Johnny parted them, apologizing, then wove through a stream of visitors. He searched every face for the tall, dark-suited man. But he'd gone.

Damn. No! He couldn't lose him now. He sped back to the staircase, leaping up stone steps till he reached the landing and Kate's ward. He barged through double doors, shouldering aside visitors filing in quietly, and, ignoring the disapproving look of the ward sister, he rushed to the end bed.

A man was bending over Kate, whispering into her ear. It was Archie Goss. Johnny launched himself at him. 'Get away from her, you bastard!' His hands gripped Archie's throat and Johnny wrestled him to the ground, his fists flying fast as pistons, smashing into Archie's shocked face until it was smeared with blood.

The ward sister shouted for a porter to come quickly as visitors got to their feet, some standing protectively at their loved ones' beds, others calling for Johnny to stop. The two men tumbled along the ward, scattering chairs and visitors as they went until Johnny felt hands grabbing him. A porter and a burly visitor together pulled him off Archie, who staggered to his feet, brushing down his suit trousers and straightening his waistcoat.

'This is disgraceful behaviour!' The ward sister stood tall and imposing in her dark blue bustled uniform. Her face red with anger, she turned on Johnny. 'What do you think you're doing?'

'I'm protecting her from that man!' Deep breaths raked his chest.

The sister gave him a look that might have cowed the nurses beneath her, but couldn't stop him from struggling with the porter. The sister turned to Archie. 'Would you like me to call the police?'

Archie wiped his bloody nose with a handkerchief and fixed Johnny with an almost amused look. Arrogant, assured eyes assessed him – but at least Johnny had the satisfaction of knowing there'd be purple rings around them before too long.

'No need for the police, Sister,' Archie said calmly, 'but I'd appreciate some time alone with my daughter.' He gave the sister a smile, which revealed a bleeding split gum.

'Keep your hands off her, Goss!' Johnny shouted, and the sister nodded to the porter.

'You'll have to leave, now, sir.'

As the porter hustled him away, Johnny said, 'I *want* you to call the police, Sister! This man's put Kate in here. I won't leave till you get a copper!'

Archie put a hand on the sister's arm. 'This young man is clearly very upset. I'm quite happy to leave – for now. Provided he does too.'

The sister saw the eyes of the ward switch from the scene going on around Kate's bed to the other end of the ward, from which the matron was fast approaching. She looked furious. 'Sister! I can hear the noise all the way over in the next ward!'

'Very well,' the sister said to them quietly. 'Go, both of you. Now!'

The porter escorted them out of the hospital, watching them walk across the courtyard and out of the gates. Johnny groaned inwardly at his impetuous stupidity. His temper could have cost Kate dear. Now he'd tipped Archie off to their suspicions, the man would be doubly careful, perhaps doubly vengeful. But at least Kate was out of his reach – for now.

Once outside the gates Johnny turned to Archie. Shoving his face close to the other man's, he warned, 'You keep away from her, do you hear me?'

Archie flinched, though he didn't retreat. 'Ah! I remember you now, you're Rasher Bacon! Your mother was that disgusting, drunken slut who couldn't be bothered to wipe the snot from your nose when you were a ragged-arsed kid. She was anybody's for the price of a gin.'

Archie's cold eyes were mocking. He wanted Johnny to swing again; here in the anonymous street it would be easier for him to strike back.

'Listen to me, you vicious bastard. I know you hurt Kate. And I know why. And I'm going to the police about it. Why don't you come down Tower Bridge nick with me right now and accuse me of assault?' Johnny grinned, knowing Archie couldn't risk that much scrutiny.

For answer, Archie reached inside his jacket and pulled out a ticket stub. 'Accuse me of whatever you like. I came here as soon as I arrived back home from the continent. Why wouldn't I want to be at the bedside of my daughter? And I don't see how I could have been involved in her accident when I was out of the country!' He smiled confidently, but the muscles of his jaw were working hard. And Johnny knew that Archie Goss was rattled.

*

Kate had known he was there. He had kissed her. His name she couldn't remember, but she remembered his kisses. She'd wanted to wake up then, wanted to say his name. But she wasn't in a place where things could be named. Words were part of another life, the one beyond this fog, this continual searching for something lost. That feeling was at least familiar, something she could understand. It had always been with her: the seeking, the questioning. But as her mind roamed in this place without signposts, the past and the present and the future merged into one accusing presence, admonishing her over and over for asking all those questions. She felt regret. Why had she insisted on asking about him? She called him Dad, though he had another name. Why had she demanded answers? Even when whatsername, her aunt, had warned her it would cause only grief. She'd been right all along. The only certainty Kate had in this liminal place was that the longed-for man – Dad – had returned, not to love her, but to kill her, as he'd killed the other one. The woman who'd held her tight and read stories of monsters and promised that they were only fairy tales. She couldn't remember her name either. But she was someone, like herself, who'd been harmed by Archie Goss. And then, with a sharp pang of remembrance, she knew who that woman had been – her mum.

Now she felt water trickling down her cheeks and tried to blink. The light hurt and a shadow passed across it. She was grateful. The shadow took the pain away. She blinked again and saw that the shadow was shaped like a man. Forcing her lids open, she concentrated very hard. He was saying something, low, like a hiss, words she couldn't understand

and others she could. 'Katy... d'you hear me? I swear if you tell... I'll make sure you sleep forever... hear me?'

She opened her mouth to scream and then the shadow that was Dad was yanked away. There were shouts and clatters and thuds that hurt her ears – she could see it all. The one whose kisses she remembered had come back. His name was Johnny. She opened her eyes. She was awake, but he was too busy bashing the living daylights out of Dad to realize it, and, try as she might, she had no words to call him. It seemed easier simply to close her eyes and to drift back into the calm twilight world where there were no names, no words and no questions at all.

Johnny hadn't taken his train. He wouldn't leave Kate unprotected now – not even for a day. Martin must come and relieve him straight away. He rang the number of the cottage in Sussex and after several rings Nora answered. Her voice sounded strained and Johnny wondered how she'd react to her bodyguard being removed. But when he told her about Archie's appearance at the hospital, she made the suggestion first.

'But of course you mustn't leave her! Martin was very good to come, but I've told him all along it isn't right. His place is with Kate!'

He heard the sound of her hand muffling the receiver and then Martin came on the line. 'John? What's happened, what's he done to her?'

After Johnny had explained, Martin said, 'My God, he'll stop at nothing. But I'm not happy about leaving Nora alone. It was different when I knew you'd be coming to look after her.' There was a pause on the line. 'I feel terribly torn.'

And Johnny heard Nora's exhausted voice, faint in the room. 'For God's sake, Martin, go! Your fiancée needs you.'

And Johnny was glad it wasn't he who'd had to point out the obvious.

His plan was to stand guard outside the hospital gates for as long as was necessary. And it was there that Martin found him later that evening, as a fine rain smudged the sky above the hospital. It had been falling for most of the day and the streets around London Bridge were slick.

'I wasn't sure you'd be able to get here today.'

'You were quite right to call me back, John,' Martin said, shaking his hand. 'Thank you for keeping watch over her.'

'I couldn't take the risk of leaving – he might have come back. I've looked into his eyes, Martin, and he'll do anything to protect himself.' Johnny shuddered at the memory. 'Anyway, I'm sorry you had to leave Nora, but I don't think Goss will come looking for her right now. He'll want to keep his head down for the next few days. He certainly got the wind up when I mentioned involving the police.'

'I've left Nora in good hands. Aunt Violet's friend, the one she's renting the cottage from, is a retired army officer. Still fit as a fiddle, and he's kept his service pistol. He's agreed to go over and keep an eye on Nora while I'm away.'

'Just as well,' Johnny said, and shivered. He had stood sentinel by the ornate gates, checking everyone who went in or came out. Oblivious to the rain showers, he was now wet through.

'You poor chap, you're soaked! You'll catch your death. Get yourself home. Unless... do you want to come in and see Kate with me now?'

'Oh, I can't do that. Sister won't let me back in!' Johnny

said. 'You just go and try to get her to wake up. I'm going to the police.'

'But I thought you said it was useless. There's no proof.'

'No. But if the police are poking around, asking questions, it might make Archie think twice about going anywhere near Kate – or Nora.'

'All right, then. But change into some dry clothes first!'

Johnny nodded and walked away, hands digging deep into his pockets, longing to be the one going in to see Kate.

He took Martin's advice and went home, changing into dry clothes, before paying a visit to Tower Bridge police station, where the desk sergeant painstakingly took all the details and then seized, depressingly, on the most obvious explanation.

'So, you're saying your young lady was working in a garret full of flux fumes, fainted and hit her head on a tin bath?'

'No! I think she was attacked by her father, who's a violent, vindictive man!'

The sergeant carefully copied down Archie's address, but when he heard that the sole witness was the alleged victim herself, who had regained consciousness only to ask for her father, he pointed out, not unreasonably, that this didn't count as an accusation.

Johnny left feeling less than hopeful. He walked out of the police station, intending to go to the bookshop. Kate's friends there had asked for updates on her progress, and besides, he couldn't face sitting alone in his tiny house, with all its memories of Kate and the happy days before he'd ruined everything between them. He headed for Tower Bridge Road and had reached the railway viaduct when he heard his name being called. Softly at first, then louder. He turned to see Stan stepping out of a shadowed recess.

'You been to the old bill about Uncle Archie?'

'What's it got to do with you?' Johnny carried on walking, ignoring Stan, who hurried to keep up.

'Don't be nasty, I've come to do you a favour.'

Johnny slowed his pace and glanced at Stan. He had a new boil on his neck and he reeked of the same sweet cologne as Mr Smith. No doubt Stan thought it would improve his chances with the girls. Nothing would do that. Johnny stopped. 'What's the catch?'

Stan grinned. 'I've always been fond of Noss Goss, ain't I?'

They stood beneath the arches as trains rumbled overhead, three and four at a time, making it hard to hear each other. Stan beckoned and Johnny followed him around the corner into Tanner Street. The stink of brewing vinegar from Sarson's factory mixed with Stan's cologne immediately forced bile into Johnny's mouth. He'd eaten nothing all day and his anxiety was making him nauseous enough as it was.

'Look, I seen you standing outside Guy's all day – Mummy's little soldier boy guarding your girl. But what I'm saying is, I've been keeping an eye on Archie for my boss anyway, so I could do the same job for you... if you like.' And Stan rubbed his fingers and thumb together.

'Why would I trust you?'

Stan gave an uncomfortable shrug of the shoulders. 'Me mum told me to help you out.'

Johnny laughed. 'Who's Mummy's little soldier boy now? What's changed her tune, anyway?'

'It ain't that she's got much love for Noss Goss, it's just she hates Uncle Archie's guts now.'

'So, should I go back to the nick and tell them Sylvie wants to report her brother for murder?'

'She ain't that stupid. He'd have her next. But you and that posh git Kate's picked up with – you're amateurs. All I'm saying is, leave it to the professionals.'

'Oh, for God's sake, Stan. Grow up. You wouldn't last five minutes against Archie Goss.'

Stan was leaning against the high brick wall that stretched the length of Sarson's. The street was deserted and, without warning, he pulled open his jacket to reveal a handgun.

'I can look after meself. All I'm saying is, my boss is interested in Uncle Archie, so I might as well kill two birds with one stone.' He pushed off from the wall. 'Suit yourself.'

'All right. But just *watch* him – and let me know if he goes anywhere near Kate.'

'My pleasure,' Stan said, pocketing the notes Johnny handed him and patting the gun in his jacket pocket.

'And Stan. For Chrissake don't shoot him.'

'Oh, no. I won't do that,' Stan answered, with a brown-toothed grin.

Of course, it was Tuesday night. As soon as he entered the bookshop, Johnny realized with a jolt that elocution lessons were going on in the reading room upstairs. He could hear Mrs Cliffe's well-modulated tones, followed by her pupils repeating the exercises. It was one of the things he'd always found so comforting in the bookshop, its civilized routines. In his home there had been no set times for anything, so these dependable rituals touched a deep need in him. But now the sounds of improved locution drifting down to the shop brought sudden tears to his eyes. He'd mocked her. Told her she didn't need them. He'd pretended not to be interested, flicking through that stupid periodical, acting as if he had a life without her, as if he were serious about poor Pamela, who'd finished with him when she finally realized where his heart truly lay. His chest heaved in a shuddering sigh. He was exhausted.

The place always looked cosy, but tonight it felt like the home he'd always longed for, with its bright walls, its warm-coloured shelves of books, its fresh flowers and painted friezes. And there was Ethel, looking tired from her own bout of ill health but her eyes undimmed, greeting him with the warmth and brightness of a tropical bird amidst the grey and dun bricks of Bermondsey. She held out her arms and he fell into them.

Ethel handed the shop over to Lucy and led Johnny into the back room, where she made him tea and gave him the cake that the bookshop never seemed to be without. She sat him down, gently coaxing out the details of Kate's progress and the depth of his own regret at losing her.

'It's obvious you still love Kate, and fond as I am of Martin, I believe you should tell her so.'

Johnny drained down the last of his tea. 'But she loves Martin now, and why would she want me when I ruin everything with this...' He contemplated the crumbs of his cake. '...this bloody *rage* of mine? I'm scared I've made things so much worse.'

'But you haven't. You did exactly the right thing by going to the police. Chibby will be questioned, Kate has Martin with her and though you've been excluded from the hospital, you can carry on keeping watch over her – a faithful knight and true!' He smiled at the image and left feeling better for her comradeship and her cake.

Kate struggled to open her eyes. It seemed such hard work

she wished she could give up. But it was important not to. For the moment she couldn't understand why it was so important, but she thought it was to do with the one who'd kissed her. Each eyelash had its own weight, each needle of light piercing her lids its sting. An hour or a day seemed to pass before she could open her eyes, and when she did, her first sensation was surprise.

'Oh, it's you! I thought the other one was here...'

'Of course it's me, my darling.' And Martin put soft lips to her own.

She felt embarrassed to ask his name, but she had expected it to be the other one – yes, Johnny.

'Is this a hospital?' she croaked, smelling the disconcerting mixture of ethanol and stale bodies and feeling the stiffness of her bed linen.

'Yes, you're in Guy's. I'll get you some water.' He lifted her and helped her drink, and then a nurse came to shoo him away. There was too much she couldn't remember, but as he left, certain things came back in such a nauseating rush that she wished for forgetfulness again.

The doctor stood beside her bed. Mr North could stay, he said, for a short while. Of course, his name was North, Martin North. How could she have forgotten? Martin. Dear, devoted, annoying Martin, who'd refused to let her go. Unlike Johnny, who had done – too easily. She was half listening, half furiously trying to keep awake when she heard the doctor addressing her in a clear, slow voice.

'And can you tell us now, Miss Goss, how you sustained your injuries?'

Martin squeezed her hand and nodded his encouragement. He looked ill himself and the lines of his face were tight with worry. She wanted to make it easier for him, for herself. Archie was her dad's name. She knew him now, better than she ever had in her whole life. She knew what he'd done.

'I'm sorry, Doctor, but I can't remember,' she said, seeing a flicker of disbelief cross Martin's face.

'Well, not to worry. You've had a severe head injury. It's common to lose some memory temporarily. It'll come back. Meanwhile, you're to *rest*,' the doctor emphasized, giving Martin a warning look. 'Five minutes, no more!'

When they were alone, Martin leaned close. 'Is it true that you don't remember? When you came around before, you mentioned your dad, and your great-aunt Rosina is convinced Chibby attacked you... Have we got it all wrong?'

She leaned back again, wincing as pain throbbing in her temple reminded her of where the hammer had hit. She put a hand to the place where it hurt.

'I'm sorry, Kate, I'm tiring you out.' He got up, but she put a hand over his.

'I just want to let sleeping dogs lie, Martin. He got away with doing it to Mum and he'll see me underground and get away with that too. Just let me forget him...'

She felt her eyelids drooping and as much as she wanted to keep them open, they closed, letting her sink back into the world of forgetting, where his second kiss was entirely lost on her.

Johnny was waiting outside. Martin's broad smile told the news before he'd spoken the words. 'She's awake!'

Johnny's bursting relief could only express itself in one way and he found himself embracing his former rival, who laughed and patted Johnny on the back in return.

'She was a bit confused, thought I was you at one stage!' Martin said, giving Johnny an unexpected pang of jealousy, which he was determined not to let spoil this moment.

When Martin told him about Kate's decision, he was incredulous. 'What do you mean, she wants to let it go? She can't!'

'It's what she wants,' Martin said firmly. 'You go home and sleep, John. There only needs to be one of us here tonight.'

But Johnny couldn't rest. Every part of him was trembling now, partly from the tension that had been released once he knew Kate was all right, partly from the cold he'd caught standing in the rain, but mostly with a fierce desire to end Archie's ability to ever hurt Kate again. Even now he was pacing up and down in front of the hospital gates.

'Just calm down and listen. We've got to respect Kate's wishes, and if she prefers to pretend she can't remember a thing, then that's what we have to allow!'

'Didn't you manage to get any details from her? I can't believe you've just accepted it!'

Martin put an arm around Johnny, leading him to the nearby late-night tea stall. 'Come on, you need something inside you.'

'I've had enough tea for one night,' Johnny replied, shrugging Martin off, and then, remembering that Kate loved the man, added, 'Sorry, thanks for the offer to stand guard. I'll be more use tomorrow if I get some kip. Besides, I've got someone else keeping an eye out for Goss.' And he explained who the unlikely helper was, still unsure he hadn't signed a pact with the devil.

Finally, Johnny dragged himself home, stumbled up to his small, cell-like room and fell into bed. He shivered with cold and then burned, throwing off the blanket, before falling into a fevered sleep. He dreamt of hellfires and woke to a lurid light, the red lantern from the nearby pub reflecting off his window. Tears wet his cheeks as he remembered Archie's cruel words about his mother, selling herself for a gin. He hadn't been able to save her, nor Kate. He groaned, hating the worthless tears and half knowing they weren't just caused by guilt. He'd made himself ill, weak, useless. Stubbornly standing out in the rain, going back tonight, even when he knew Martin was there to look after her. God, she really was better off with North.

When he woke the sheet felt damp against his body and he couldn't lift his head. He could tell, from the light coming through his small window, that it wasn't early morning. He looked at his alarm clock. He'd slept well into the afternoon! So much for him being the faithful knight, keeping watch at the gates. The noise that had woken him, a loud knocking, resumed. He rolled his whole body over and fell out of the bed. It seemed the easiest way to get up.

'All right, I'm coming!' he croaked, and throwing on his shirt and trousers, he staggered downstairs.

'Gawd, you look rough, you been on a bender?'

'Why are you here, Stan?'

'Cos that posh git sent me to see if you was all right. You was meant to turn up this morning. I offered to stay meself, but he don't seem to trust me for some reason. What you been telling him, Rasher?' And Stan wagged a nicotine-stained finger at him.

'Well... thanks, you've delivered the message.'

'Don't you want to know what I found out?' Stan put

a foot in the door and Johnny felt too weak to argue. Stan followed him into the scullery, watching as Johnny began to shave with an unsteady hand.

'Need some help, mate?' Stan asked. 'You might slit your throat like that!'

Johnny shot him a look, which shut him up. He lathered the brush again.

'Archie's had a visit from the old bill this morning!'

Johnny paused with the cut-throat razor halfway down his soapy cheek. 'Stay long?'

Stan shook his head. 'Goss went running to see his solicitor afterwards, though. I followed him.' Stan seemed to want praise.

'Stay long?'

'Is that all you can ask? Seems the old bill checked his ferry ticket, even rung the French fur business he was meant to have gone to… Alibi's solid as a rock. Him and Mordant had a bit of a drink, celebrating.'

'Are you making this up?' Johnny wouldn't put it past him, if he thought he could get another bung out of it.

'See what I mean? Amateurs!' Stan said with a superior smirk. 'I got Mordant's secretary wrapped around my little finger. Do anything for me, she will.' He sniffed and Johnny wondered how much he had to pay her.

'So, he'll get away with it.' He finished shaving and threw the towel across the room, spattering Stan's suit with soapy water.

Stan hopped back. 'Oi, mind the new whistle! Anyway…' He turned to leave. 'Don't you worry about Goss.' He nodded slowly and the overpowering whiff of Mr Smith's favourite cologne caught in Johnny's throat.

*

A week had passed before she was able to formulate a question about Johnny. And then Martin told her why he'd been barred from the ward and how he stood at the hospital gates every hour Martin couldn't be here with her. Her memories began to return and on the day she was able to get up and walk unaided, she went to the window. There he was. Hands shoved in his pockets, alert, restless. Just like himself, except he looked thinner, paler. Occasionally he shot a look up at her ward. *Oh, Johnny... if only you could have been different.* And it was then that she realized how foolishly certain she'd been that he was to blame for everything going wrong between them. It had been so easy to blame his uncontrolled rage and his jealousy for breaking them up. But what about her? When he was ready to come back, to be different, she'd chosen another man over him – she'd chosen to go to her father and leave Johnny behind. The fault had been hers.

Now she moved to the middle of the window, so she could see him properly. Across the courtyard beyond the gates, he must have sensed something, for he stopped pacing, and then, searching the windows, he found her. Their eyes met and he raised a hand.

23

Nemesis

Two weeks passed before Kate was deemed fit to leave hospital, with the proviso she agree to a period of convalescence. Longbonnet offered to look after her, but Martin insisted that she needed clean air and quiet. He would take her to the Sussex cottage and to Nora. On the night before Kate was due to be discharged, she asked a young nurse going off duty if she would take a note down to the front gate.

Kate made her slow way to the chapel, cursing every time she had to stop for a rest. The chapel was always open – small candles burning night and day, evidence of prayers for loved ones; brave signs of hope. Tonight, it was empty. She sat in a pew near the back and waited. She heard him come in, and when he sat next to her, she turned to look at him. His eyes were liquid bright in the candlelight, his face gaunt and pale. He dropped his gaze.

'Thank you, for coming back to us,' he said in a voice not weak, but gentle. 'I don't know what I'd have done if—'

She put a hand over his. 'Martin told me you've been on guard out there every day since I came in. I should be the one thanking you, Johnny.'

He shrugged. 'I couldn't have been anywhere else.'

'But you've not been working – how've you been managing?'

'That's nothing. I couldn't have eaten if I tried.'

'Well, you can start eating now, can't you?'

He smiled and nodded, compliant. 'Now you're better I can.' It was hard to tell just how he'd changed, but she knew he had. Perhaps because they were in a chapel, it felt to her an almost sacred change. She searched for the word to describe it and found one from her Catholic schooldays: chastened.

'Martin's taking you to Sussex tomorrow?'

She nodded. 'I wanted to go to Longbonnet's.'

'Better to be somewhere Archie doesn't know about. Though now he seems to have got off scot-free, I shouldn't think he'd have any reason to come after you...'

Here was another surprise – he wasn't telling her off for not fighting for justice.

'Come and visit me?'

'Of course. But you should get back to your bed. It'll be a long drive tomorrow.' He stood and helped her up. 'Goodbye, Kate. God bless.' He kissed her on the cheek and left her standing in the chapel, astonished. He didn't believe in God. His blessing was even more precious for that and tears pricked her eyes as the door of the chapel closed behind him. Before she left, she went to the shelf of flickering candles and, on impulse, lit one for Johnny.

*

The sun came out for their drive down to Sussex. As they passed through the Weald of Kent and on to Sevenoaks, she remembered the days of motoring in Martin's red Baby Austin, when he would take her on a mystery tour to a village pub or a picnic by the river at Yalding or Eynsford. When he'd painted the *Bermondsey Triptych*, she'd felt her life opening out. She might be poor, but suddenly he'd shown her that she could be anybody she wanted to be, and now, with a rush of gratitude, she put her hand on his knee. He took his eyes off the road to look at her.

'Are you all right?'

'Of course I'm all right! I'm out of hospital and I'm going to be anyone I want to be!' He gave her a puzzled look and then smiled. 'Ah, the lure of the open road!'

He put his foot on the accelerator and they sped on towards Tunbridge Wells, with every tree and bush clamouring to burst its wintery straitjacket. She laughed. It might have been the open road, but she suspected it was the leaving of her father, and any idea of vengeance, behind that had made her feel so free.

They reached the cottage in the early afternoon. The sun had stayed out as hedgerows funnelled them in only one possible direction. They turned down a winding lane, overarched by old trees, whose fresh green buds hung so low they bounced against the windscreen. She felt a sense of anticipation, and as they turned another bend, the trees opened out and the cottage came into view. It was bigger than she'd expected – a two-storey, rusty brick building, with a thatched roof and a long, low annexe tacked on at one end. Leaded light windows flanked a small front door, outside which stood Nora. Her arms were folded beneath a pale woollen shawl she had draped over her shoulders for, though bright, the day held a remembrance of winter. She looked as if she had been there for some time, waiting for them. And yet when she saw them her face lit up with surprised delight.

She hurried across age-smoothed paving stones to the front gate, flung it open and stood by the car. 'You're here – Kate, Martin!'

Martin helped Kate out and Nora held her at arm's length, studying her. 'Oh, my dear Kate. I'm so sorry I couldn't have been with you. You've been through so much.'

Kate pulled her close, and Nora, in spite of all her natural reserve, didn't seem to want to let go. While Martin went to park the car in a disused barn next to the cottage, Nora led Kate into a cosy sitting room, fussing and making her sit in the most comfortable chair. She stood, holding Kate's coat and hat, and then seemed to remember.

'Mrs Wills "who does" has made us a cake! I'll fetch some tea.'

As she returned carrying a tray, Martin put his head round the door. 'Where shall I put Kate's things?'

'In the annexe, Martin dearest.' She turned to Kate. 'I thought it would be easier for you – there's a little bathroom next to the bedroom, so no stairs to bother about.'

'That's kind of you, Nora. But I'm not an invalid.'

Nora gave a wry smile. 'In fact, you are.'

Kate gave in, leaned back in her chair and allowed herself to relax into the comfortable warmth the place exuded. She studied Nora over her teacup.

'I'm sorry he had to leave you here alone.'

'Oh, Martin?' Nora seemed surprised and a rare flush warmed her cheeks. 'I wasn't alone. Major Crawford – the owner – stayed in the annexe. He loved it, I think – pistol to the ready in case Chibby...' She paused and rubbed her flawless forehead. 'Even his name fills me with loathing. Kate, I'm so sorry. I should never have let you come into that house, knowing what I did about him. How he'd treated me. I was so hopeful that finding his daughter would somehow change him.' She fiddled with the fringe of her shawl, the strain of the past month evident. 'How am I going to explain it all to Paul?'

'Paul is a clever little boy – he understands more than you think.'

'I suppose you're right, Kate. And besides, he'll have us... won't he?'

'Yes, he will.' And Kate understood that, with Nora's usual reserve, she was being invited to be part of a new family. She felt Nora was about to say something else when Martin returned and the atmosphere became immediately more jolly. He had that knack of making the everyday into something special and party-like, but after an hour she found herself retreating. She sat, listening to the pleasant notes of Nora's musical voice as she talked to Martin about his latest work and their mutual friends. Sights and sounds blurred and she must have dozed, for the next thing she knew, Martin was shaking her gently. 'Kate! Let me help you to your room. You're exhausted.'

She didn't refuse. In the small, whitewashed bedroom, he drew the curtains and kissed her goodnight, whispering how happy he was to have her there, safe and sound. It took all her remaining energy to get undressed and to sink gratefully into the deep feather mattress, pulling the fluffy bedspread up to her chin. In the annexe all was quiet, and as she felt sleep claim her, Kate's mind wandered to Johnny and his stubborn, lonely vigil and she wondered what he would be doing now.

★

During the night she was woken by what sounded like a scratching on the window pane. The night was darker than anything she'd experienced in Bermondsey, where the gas lamps burned along the lane or light from pubs spilled onto pavements. The blackness was thick, like an ebony woollen blanket surrounding her. She tried to ignore the sound and willed herself back into sleep, but it persisted. Perhaps the window latch was loose. She eased herself out of bed and felt her way to the window. She pulled aside the curtain and jumped back, with a cry of alarm. A face was staring at her through the window. A pale face beneath a black homburg hat. She screamed. The man pressed his face against the window pane. Then she screamed again, louder this time, but not out of fear – her scream was one of pure rage. The man was her father.

As she screamed, Archie's face, which she could have sworn had a look of terror on it, disappeared. It was as if he'd been yanked away by some unseen hand. She stumbled back towards the door, which burst open as she reached it.

'What is it?' Martin was at her side, his arms around her. 'Kate? Are you all right?'

She was trembling violently and stuttered out, 'N-no, I'm n-not! Dad's just paid me a visit.' She pointed to the window.

'Dear God, he must have followed us here...' Martin pushed open the window and looked out. 'Major Crawford left me his pistol. Stay here.'

'Not bleedin' likely!' Kate grabbed his arm and they made their way down the dark passage to the main house.

'Martin?' she whispered, hearing a creak from the floorboards upstairs. 'Did Nora wake up too?'

'No!' Martin grabbed the pistol from a drawer in the hall stand and leaped up the stairs. Kate stood, desperately wanting to follow but barely able to stand, let alone negotiate the uneven stairs. She began climbing them, tripping in the darkness, shivering in her nightdress from shock and rage, her heart thumping so loud she could hear nothing of what was going on upstairs. And then a crack split the night. She had never heard one before, but she felt sure it was the sound of a gunshot.

She discovered that the quickest way up was to crawl, one painful stair at a time. She called for Martin and Nora, but there was no answer. Dreading what Martin might have done and imagining the worst, she gripped the top banister and hauled herself up onto the landing. Crying with the effort, she staggered to Nora's bedroom. With her hand flat on the door, she paused. There was no sound coming from inside. She pushed the door ajar. Martin stood in the middle of the room with his arms around Nora, who had her back to Kate.

'Is he here?' Kate breathed. 'Did you shoot my dad?'

Martin stared at her. 'Kate?' he said, almost as if he'd forgotten that she was there. 'No, Chibby's not here.'

Nora left Martin's arms and ran to Kate. 'Did Chibby hurt you? You're shaking.'

'Only cos I want to kill him.' So much, she thought, for leaving vengeance behind.

'But did he threaten you?'

'No. He seemed more scared than I was!'

'Scared? Chibby? You must have been mistaken.'

'I'm going to look outside. You two stay in this room and lock the door.'

'Don't be foolish, Martin,' Nora said. 'Chibby could easily overpower you. I don't think he's come for Kate, it's me he's angry with.' And before they could stop her, Nora dashed from the room.

Martin roared at her to stop, but she was quick-footed and determined and as Martin raced out, Kate heard Nora unlocking the front door. There was nothing she could do except force open the window and lean out. She saw Nora running towards the lane and then stopping at the woods' edge.

'Chibby, it's me you want!' she cried out to the trees. 'Kate had nothing to do with my leaving. It was all me. Let her alone and I'll come back to you.'

She couldn't mean it. But if her plan was to draw him out, it failed. Nothing stirred in the wood, save the night breeze tossing the tree branches in a crazy dance that made shadows look like stalking creatures. Martin was close behind Nora and he clasped her tight to him. As he held the pistol high in front of him, even at this distance, Kate could see that his whole arm shook.

They watched for a while, waiting, Kate at the window, Martin and Nora below. But the silence of the night was broken again only by the call of a solitary owl.

With no possibility of sleep that night, they agreed to stay together in the sitting room, with the connecting door to the annexe locked. Martin found the remains of a bottle of brandy, which they polished off as they sat waiting for the dawn.

'So, if it wasn't you who fired the shot, who was it?' Kate asked as Martin handed her a glass of the brandy.

'It must have been your father.'

'But who was he shooting at – if not Nora or me?'

'I don't know. But whatever he wanted in coming here, I think he's gone now. If not, he would certainly have come when you called to him,' Martin said to Nora. 'I can imagine how it rankled with him that you dared to walk out. But, Nora, he's controlled you for long enough.' Martin gripped Nora's hand, and Kate was reminded of all the years he'd known her. He'd been trying to protect Nora for far longer than he had Kate.

'But I still can't understand it. Chibby's never been one to give up so easily.' Nora looked at Kate, who didn't say anything, but felt a deep unease. She believed her father was still out there, somewhere. And surely Nora knew that too.

In the morning, Martin telephoned the police to report an intruder and they were visited by a constable, who poked around the abandoned barn and ventured into the woods a short distance. He wasn't gone long. Nora asked him into the sitting room. He looked no older than Kate and he was visibly shaking.

'I think I've found your intruder, Mr North.'

'Really? I thought he'd be long gone.'

'I'm afraid he is... in a way.' The young constable adjusted his tight blue collar. 'I'm not sure if the ladies need to hear this.'

'I do,' Kate said, staring at him till he blushed. 'He's my dad.'

'And I do too – I'm his wife,' Nora added.

She saw the policeman's Adam's apple rise and fall. He blew out a long breath. 'If he is Mr Grainger, then you should sit down, miss, madam. It appears he's suffered... an accident.'

They did as they were told and the constable went on. 'I found the gentleman lying in the woods with a gunshot wound to the head. I can't be sure, but it appears he took his own life. The gun was still in his hand.'

★

For the rest of that day and most of the next, the area around the cottage swarmed with blue-uniformed policemen, clustering around the woods like flies, seeking out any clues to what had happened the previous night. A detective came too and asked them to go over in detail their various relationships to Mr Grainger. When they probed Kate about her own 'accident', she lied – what good could it do her now if her dad were dead anyway? She told him the report of an attack on her had been a mistake – a result of her mental confusion. It was left to her to identify the body. Nora said she couldn't do it. So Martin drove Kate to Tunbridge Wells and waited outside the morgue.

He was still recognizably her dad, though they'd covered half his head with a sheet.

'It's him.' She gave a brief nod to the policeman, who left her alone with the body.

Tears pricked her eyes and she allowed them to fall freely. Not understanding why she should be weeping, she rubbed away a tear, angry at her stupid weakness. What had she lost? The dream version of him had already long vanished. Perhaps she was just mourning the reality: a man who'd destroyed everything that got too close to him and had ended up with nothing. She took a deep breath, and walking from the room without looking back, she stepped into the weak sunshine, where Martin waited, leaning against the Baby Austin.

He opened the car door for her and once they were on the road, he asked, 'What do you want to do now?'

'What do you mean?'

'You're free of him.'

'Yes, I am – and so is Nora,' she said, turning her face

to the houses lining the road, watching them thin out, to be replaced by hedgerows, fields and woods.

The coroner's verdict, when it eventually came, was suicide. Archibald Grainger had taken his own life as a consequence of his business failing and his wife leaving him. Nobody disputed it, not even Martin. But whatever had happened that night, Kate was certain Archie hadn't gone to his death willingly. She had seen his face through that window, and what she hadn't told the others was that he'd opened his mouth in a silent plea to be let in. It was yet another question mark surrounding her father and one she'd probably never know the truth of.

Archie's funeral wasn't held in Belgravia, but in Bermondsey, which Kate felt was a fitting punishment. He'd reviled the place in life, even killed to escape it, and now it had reclaimed him in death. Kate had travelled up from Sussex with Nora on the train to London Bridge, leaving Martin to drive back to London. Her aunts had surprised her by insisting on arranging the service at Dockhead church. Aunt Sylvie had even ordered Stan and Janey to attend. Afterwards they were invited to her aunt's for tea and sandwiches. It was the strangest of family gatherings. Strained beyond any attempt at civility, Sylvie and Sarah had been brought together, briefly, by their shared sense of betrayal, but new hostilities had broken out over the funeral and now, as Sarah handed round sandwiches, she whispered to Kate that she would probably put another Goss into her grave today if her sister didn't stop going on about Janey and how well she was doing in her new office job.

Nora looked serenely on, but Kate knew that, like the

swan she so often resembled, underneath that calm she was ferociously paddling. Her unruffled veneer slipped only once, when she noticed Stan, seemingly for the first time. She leaned close to Kate. 'I believe I've seen that man at the house.'

'My cousin Stan? Yes, I saw him there once too – he was strong-arming Dad to pay back Mr Smith.'

'And who is Mr Smith?'

Kate clutched her own hand protectively, remembering that agony of crushed fingers. 'Oh, Mr Smith is someone you *always* pay back – one way or another.'

Stan must have sensed he was the subject of their conversation, for he started towards them.

'Oh no, he's coming over – don't look at him, Nora. Talk about something else!'

But it was too late. Her cousin stood in front of her, a glass of whisky in his hand. He stared at Nora and eventually gave her one of his vile grins. Kate turned to face him, pulling him to one side, blocking his view of Nora, as if his gaze alone could sully her, like a patch of Thames oil ruining a swan's down.

'She don't look much like a grieving wife, does she?' he said.

'Piss off and leave her alone, Stan.'

He giggled. 'She should be thanking me, she should.' Kate could smell that he'd had more than one whisky. 'And so should you,' he whispered, putting two fingers to his head and splashing her dress with whisky as he did so.

She hoped Nora hadn't seen the gesture and as he fixed her with a fuzzy gaze, she turned back to Nora, explaining, 'He could never hold his drink!'

She hustled him out to the scullery. 'Oooh, where ya taking me, Noss? All them years you wouldn't look at me!'

Aunt Sylvie cast a disapproving look in their direction and

Janey smirked. She heard her mutter 'slut' as they passed.

Grim-faced, she shoved Stan through the scullery and into the backyard. When he tried to paw her, she slapped him hard. 'You idiot! You don't go around making up stupid stories about shooting someone, just to make yourself look big!' She didn't like Stan, but neither would she see him hanged.

His fuzzy gaze hardened. 'Who says it's a story? And don't you talk to me like I'm a kid. I done a man's job out in that wood!'

'You?'

He smirked. 'My boss got fed up waiting for your dad to pay him back. I'm Mr Smith's right-hand man, me,' he boasted. 'He says I'm like the son he never had. Mr Smith wants something done – I do it.'

She was cold to her bones. 'Even murder?'

'Murder runs in the family. Didn't you bash Archie's head in with an iron? Don't tell me you wanted him to get up and walk away...'

A week later Kate stood on East Lane Stairs and scattered Archie's ashes into the swift-flowing Thames. It was a blustery day and the wash of the tide caught and crashed against the river wall, splashing up to where she stood. As the pale ash was torn apart on the wind, then caught in the eddying current, she pondered Stan's accusation. The remains of Archie Goss were finally claimed by the river and, borne rapidly downstream, they disappeared from her sight. No. She was not another murdering Goss. She'd never wanted to kill him. She'd loved him – just not enough to let him kill her.

24

The Whitesmith

1925–1926

The house in Belgravia seemed to be inhabited by ghosts. White sheets covered tables, chairs, clocks and bookshelves. Nora had arranged the sale of the house, with all its contents, shortly after the funeral. But she'd wanted Kate to have the rest of her whitesmithing tools and the metals she'd left behind. Nora had arranged for a packing crate and now Kate was fitting in all the heavy equipment and materials, stuffing newspaper around them.

'Why don't you come and stay with me in Sussex?' Nora asked as Kate finalized the packing. 'You've said yourself you can't go back to your garret. Martin can motor down to see us... It would be perfect.'

But the pretty cottage beyond the tunnel of trees no longer seemed a welcoming prospect. Surely the woodland would be as haunted as this house was by the ghost of her father. Nora had chosen to return to Sussex until the money from the house sale came through. Beyond that, she said, her only plan was to bring Paul home.

'I'm not sure I can live there, Nora. I'd be seeing his face through every window. But can I come with you when you fetch Paul?'

'Of course! I wouldn't think of going without you, Kate. Apart from anything else, he'd never forgive me!'

After arranging with Nora to travel down to Sussex early next morning, she went straight to the Bermondsey Bookshop. Ethel had sent flowers and cards, asking Martin daily for updates on Kate's progress, and Kate didn't want to leave without saying thank you. The woman had been in ill health herself and often absent from the shop, Martin told her, so her concern for Kate had been even more touching. Nothing had changed, except that there seemed to be even more people than usual browsing the shelves. Kate walked to the back of the shop. No, nothing had changed; there was Ethel filling a couple of small vases with snowdrops. And when she noticed Kate approaching, she gasped, 'Oh, my poor, dear girl, what has the brute done to you!', embracing Kate and then holding her at arm's length, her expression of concern telling Kate truthfully the toll her injuries had taken on her appearance. Everyone else had obviously lied when they said she was looking so much better. But Kate knew how thin she was, how wasted her muscles, how all her quick movements had slowed to a frustrating crawl.

'Well, today I definitely haven't run, so I suppose I can't read neither, can I?'

Ethel laughed. 'Ah, he never managed to crush your spirit!' And then she dropped her voice. 'Not as he did our poor Nora.'

'She turned out stronger than I could have imagined, Ethel. She stayed with him for the chance of getting her child back, and that's just what we're going to do tomorrow!'

Ethel went to the back kitchen to make tea and, once they were seated at the long table together, Kate asked Ethel about her own illness, which had left her paler and thinner. The woman brushed the question off, obviously more eager to talk about Kate's future. 'Might I suggest you carry on with your smithing?' She put a hand over Kate's. 'I want you to know that whatever happens in the future, you will always have a gallery at the Bermondsey Bookshop.' She looked at Kate with such sweet intensity it almost felt as if she were making a solemn vow. Then the bright smile returned. 'In fact, you need to start making more things for us; I sold the last of your pieces a week ago.'

'Really, which one was that?'

'The pewter Welsh love spoon.'

Kate smiled. She'd been proud of the intricate interlacing knotwork of the spoon handle, topped with two linked hearts.

'I hope it went to a good home. Do you know who bought it?'

Ethel's bright gaze dimmed slightly. 'Yes,' she said softly. 'It was John Bacon.'

Kate left the bookshop with a sense of sadness. It had felt as if Ethel were saying farewell, even though Kate had promised she would return. However, she suspected that Johnny would not. He'd told Ethel that he was going away, but he hadn't said where and he hadn't said for how long. She walked back to East Lane, intending to see Longbonnet, but with a lingering hope that perhaps Johnny hadn't yet left.

They sat in Longbonnet's backyard, in a square of early-evening sunshine. It had been a foggy day and patches lingered above the river, but now a rose-gold brightness made an oasis of the yard, where foggy dewdrops shone like jewels on furry-leaved herbs.

Her great-aunt Rosina puffed on the clay pipe. 'So, what you going to do now, darlin'?'

Kate shrugged. 'Everyone seems to be asking me that.'

It had been Martin's first question after Archie's death. Nora had asked her, then Conny and Miss Dane had asked her: What was she going to do? Was she coming back to East Lane? To Boutle's? Even her aunts had been interested enough to ask. Only one person hadn't asked her.

'Do you know where he's gone?'

Longbonnet leaned forward to pick a sprig of rosemary. She chewed on it, shaking her head. 'No. But he didn't look well. He come to me before he left, said he was going away for a bit, needed a rest.'

The news was like a blow to the stomach. 'Not well? Was it his lungs?' She'd never forgive herself if he'd caught pneumonia because of all those damp nights standing guard over her.

Longbonnet gave her a long look and said, 'It's my opinion there's not much wrong with that boy's lungs – it's his heart needs mending.'

'What do you mean?'

'Wake up, gel... he'll never get over you.' She picked another sprig of rosemary and handed it to Kate. The sweet, sharp aroma clung to her fingers.

That Johnny should have left without a word to her felt like a betrayal, and yet he had no obligation to tell her anything. Kate dropped her gaze and picked off the blue-green spines.

'He didn't *have* to lose me, it was just he always seemed to do the wrong thing at the wrong time. It never worked.'

'Wasn't the wrong thing when he searched half London for that murdering Goss, then stood outside Guy's making sure he didn't come near you, was it?'

Kate breathed a deep sigh. 'I'm not saying I wasn't just as much to blame. When Dad came along… I put him first.'

'Your father was a cold bastard,' Longbonnet said, returning to her pipe, and Kate shifted uncomfortably on the old wooden bench. 'He had ice in his veins, your father, and believe me, you don't want to go that way too.'

'I'm not cold-hearted! I'm just promised to someone else. And Johnny's made his own choices – he took up with another girl pretty quickly, now he's chosen to go away without telling me. I wanted to stay friends.'

Longbonnet rose with an audible crack of her joints and Kate realized she had no idea how old her great-aunt was. 'When you decide what you're going to do, you let me know. Don't forget old Longbonnet,' she said, kissing Kate, who was enveloped in the smell of rosemary and pipe tobacco. 'And don't forget that boy.'

Nora hadn't yet told Paul about his father's death. She'd arranged for a special visit, but hadn't explained to Mr Woolf the reason. Paul was in the common room, alone, and when they walked in, he greeted them with his dazzling smile.

'Mummy!' He used all his strength to shove the heavy wooden chair into action, but Nora already had her arms around him before he had moved a few inches.

'They didn't tell me you were coming until this morning.

And they never said Kate was coming too!' He put his arms out for Kate, who hugged him, so that they formed a tangled trio.

'We wanted to surprise you,' Kate said. 'We knew you'd make yourself sick with excitement and then you wouldn't fancy these.' She got out a bag of his favourite toffees.

'Thanks, Kate! They've been letting me have your parcels since your last visit,' he said, dipping in and giving her a toffee along with a conspiratorial look. He knew it had been she who'd made his life better, though how the fees had been paid he had no idea.

'Well, you look as if you've put on some weight and you seem stronger!' Nora said, holding his hand and sitting near him.

'The food's been better,' the little boy said vaguely, and Kate took his other hand.

'It's all right, Paul. Your mother knows why you weren't happy here. But she's got something to tell you.' And she gave Nora an encouraging nod.

After the news about his father had been broken, Paul cried. Kate wanted to tell him to save his tears, angry that the little boy's love had been so despised. And in the same instant, she remembered her own tears at the morgue. Deserved or undeserved, love didn't seem to discriminate, and she kept silent as Nora dried Paul's eyes and told him she had other, better news.

His smile burst from a tear-stained face. 'Today?' He looked from one to the other. 'I can come home today?' This time, when he gripped the hard rubber wheels, he found the strength to propel himself forward rapidly. 'Come on, Kate. Help me pack!' And she found herself hurrying to keep up with him.

Mr Woolf had wanted to delay things. It was a hasty decision, Mrs Grainger's mind was confused by grief, surely she could see Paul was flourishing under his care?

But Nora was implacable. 'You see, Mr Woolf, I have always thought that *I* am the one who can best care for my son. My husband and I were always at odds over the *care* Paul received here. And to a mother's eyes and a mother's heart, what you have offered has been no care at all. I *will* be taking my son home today.'

Nora swept out of his office with a regal assurance and Kate followed admiringly in her wake. Later, they walked out of the school, Kate pushing Paul in the clumsy chair, and as they left, her brother kept looking over his shoulder, just to be sure that the walls of his benevolent-seeming prison were truly receding forever.

Kate was concentrating hard. She had burnished the pewter loving cup till it shone like silver. She'd added a copper rim and handles, which she'd chased with a Celtic knot design of two intertwined swans. Now she was engraving the inside of the bowl with a message. It was for the wedding. She stood up to stretch, and breathed in the salt-tinged breeze that drifted through the open window. She never tired of the view. Today, a cornflower sky rested above an aquamarine sea, white-ruffled surf fringing creamy sand in the cove below. Her workshop was on a cliff top. It was sheltered by a crescent hedge of wind-sculpted thorns and separated from the cliff edge by a slope of emerald turf. She could not be further from her garret in East Lane and sometimes she felt the dizzying need to remind herself that this was her life now.

MARY GIBSON

And yet there were some things that were much the same as in East Lane. The small-paned window she could lean out of to see sky resting above water, and that same sense of a haven that she'd had in her garret. But now the vividness of the colours and the beauty for as far as the eye could see made this seem like a dream version of her life.

It had taken a long time to fit out her workshop exactly as she'd wanted it. She worked at a wooden bench that was beginning to acquire the smooth, worn feel of constant use. It wrapped around her so that, from her tall stool, she could easily reach spikes, vices, forming pads. Beneath it she stored her metals: tin, pewter, copper and a small amount of silver. From the ceiling, coils of wire and objects she'd made hung from low beams. Her bench was nothing like those at Boutle's. She had a gas canister to fuel a clean oven and blow torch, so the days of soot and ash were over. In front of her, a row of tools hung neatly on a wooden rack – there were chasing and engraving tools, hammers of several sizes, some leather-wrapped. She picked up a hammer now, very like the one her father had used against her. She rarely thought of that day, but sometimes the heft of a soldering iron in her hand would bring it all back. And at those times she would put down her tool and look through the window, reminding herself that this was now who she was: Kate the whitesmith, not Kate the tin basher.

Martin had brought her to this place to continue her convalescence. There was no question of going back to the garret with its memory of Archie's attack, nor of staying for long in Sussex, scene of his suicide. And suicide it still was in everyone's eyes. She'd told no one about Stan's confession. If she had done he would simply have denied it, and besides, whatever Mr Smith's reasons might have been, justice of a sort had been meted out.

Martin knew of this place on the north Cornwall coast because he'd once lived here, spending two years in a community of artists, who'd bought up some houses and cottages dotted along the cliffs above the small harbour. The place would be perfect, he'd explained. She could rest and benefit from the sea air, and he would have the much-needed peace and beautiful light to help him return to painting. After Archie's attack on Kate, he'd found working almost impossible, and she'd been as worried about him as he was about her for a while. He was anchorless without his work and so she'd agreed to come here. She'd imagined they would stay the month or so necessary for her recovery, then return to London for their wedding. But things hadn't gone according to plan.

She blamed the tin mine. It had caught her eye as they first drove along the cliff road to the village. Its tall, narrow engine house and sky-piercing chimney perched on the very edge of the cliff, a stark and dramatic connection to every part of her life since she'd escaped Janey and walked into Boutle's on that first day.

'Is the cottage far from here?' she asked, her eye on the mine.

'No,' he said, squinting at the road ahead. 'The cottage isn't far now. Why?'

She laughed. '*Why?* We'll be living near a tin mine!'

'Oh! *Tin!* Yes, of course. I suppose it's like taking a sculptor to live in Carrara!'

'If you say so. But I'd like to go and see it.'

'Carrara?'

'No! Idiot. The tin mine.'

And they had done, not long after settling in to the cottage. And as she'd walked around the mine she'd felt something settle in her. As if she'd been here before, as if it might once have been home. She liked to think that her roaming ancestors might have passed this way in the distant past. So, the tin mine, oddly enough, became the symbol that held her steady, and helped her heal, and instead of a month, they had stayed more than a year.

It had been more than a year. A year in which everything had changed. A year in which he'd grown stronger, fitter, browner, and one in which – the doctors assured him – the cure of freezing high mountain air had worked its magic. His lungs were clear. He'd never expected to return from Leysin, the Swiss sanatorium which Bermondsey Borough Council paid for locals to attend – if, of course, the medical officer thought the case was serious enough. Others were given a green wooden hut with louvre windows and ordered to sleep in their backyards – well away from spouses and children.

But here he was, back in England, with a new idea of his future and a new book written. He'd called it *A Really Common Reader – Adventures in a Bermondsey Bookshop*, and he had dedicated it to the memory of Ethel Gutman, his dear friend and mentor. It seemed fitting. Without her encouragement and enthusiasm, without her belief in him, he would never have dared believe in himself. She had died last spring, shortly after he'd left Bermondsey, and when he'd heard the news, he'd been so ill he thought he might be joining her very soon. But she'd given strict instructions that the Bermondsey Bookshop was not to die with her, and she had left him a bequest – to fund his literary career, she'd stipulated – her faith in him strong to the end. He thought perhaps he'd only decided to live because of that faith.

He hadn't intended to seek Kate out, not at first, but when the chance came to speak at the St Agnes Miners and Mechanics Institute, it felt as if fate had made it easier for him. He had a legitimate reason for being here. He'd come to give a talk about the new book. But the event wasn't until tomorrow and he would have time on his hands. He'd settled into his St Agnes bed and breakfast yesterday and had asked around at the local pub last night. He was pretty sure it must be Kate. They'd called her the whitesmith, and described a cottage near the coastal path above a small cove. He set out along the cliff path early. It was a mild morning, with a clear sky, and the path was dotted with small yellow and magenta flowers. He took off his jacket and hung it over his shoulder, feeling a rising sense of anticipation, yet still with no clear idea of what he would find, nor what he would say to her. He knew she was here with Martin, but he felt strong enough now to face her happiness.

At the top of a steep stretch of path, he stopped for breath. This must be the place. A whitewashed cottage with a wooden lean-to workshop, its windows facing the sea. The path took him around the side of the house. And then, from inside, he heard a sound: a baby crying. He stopped. A baby? This he hadn't expected. In that moment he realized he'd been lying to himself. She had a family, a husband, a craft, a beautiful place to call home. Why on earth had he come? He turned around and walked away.

*

Kate had finished engraving the loving cup with her simple message. She was glad that she could give a gift made with her own hands. Now she sat on a little bench outside the whitewashed cottage and closed her eyes, enjoying the spring sunshine, waiting for Martin. She heard a noise on the path and looked up. A man was walking away from her. He was in his shirtsleeve, his coat flung over one shoulder, his walk easy, his eyes on the path. The sight of the tall, slim figure made her heart leap. She stood and called out, 'Johnny!' She began walking, and then running, to catch him up. It was only on her second call, 'Johnny, stop! Is it you?', that he halted and turned around.

He looked so different from their last meeting. His face was tanned, relaxed; his body had lost its worrying thinness. 'It *is* you! But why were you walking away?'

She was bewildered and delighted, her heart thumping; she took his hand, to stop him from retreating another step. He responded with an awkward handshake.

'Johnny!' She wrapped her arms around him. 'Where've you been? Why didn't you write?' Tears were in her eyes as she let go and looked at him.

'I'm sorry. I was ill and to be honest, I thought my time was up. I thought it was best to leave you to make a life for yourself without worrying about me. And Kate, you have!'

He put his hands on her shoulders and gave her the same old smile, full of charm and amusement.

'But you weren't going to stop and even say hello?'

He put his head to one side. 'I knew you'd be married, I suppose, but I wasn't counting on the baby. You've got all your future here... why would you want the past coming back to haunt you? I'm just glad to see you've made a good life for yourself, Kate. I'll be going now.'

Kate grabbed his hand and pulled him towards the house. 'You're not going *nowhere*, Johnny Bacon. You come with me!' She dragged him back to the cottage and he ducked as they entered through the low door. She led him through the small, sunlit sitting room into the kitchen, where a baby sat in a high chair. A woman feeding the child rusks in milk looked up at Kate and said, 'Madam here's leading me a dog's life this morning, spitting it out all over the place!' And then she saw Johnny. 'Blimey, hello, stranger!'

Johnny gave her an awkward smile and Kate decided it was time to put him out of his misery. 'You remember my friend Conny from Boutle's? This is her baby, Kathy.'

Conny smiled adoringly at the little girl. 'I named her after Kate – and she's just as awkward, ain't you?' She pinched Kathy's cheek and was rewarded with a rusky smile.

'Oh, I see my mistake,' Johnny said, blushing as Kate went to pick up her namesake.

'Conny and Kathy both live with me now,' Kate explained.

'I'm her *apprentice*!' Conny informed him with exaggerated pride. 'Though I ain't half as good as our Kate. Never will be.'

'You're getting better!' Kate said, handing the baby back to her mother. 'Put the kettle on, Conny, while I show Johnny the workshop.'

A door in the kitchen led to the wooden lean-to Kate used as her workshop. Johnny bent to avoid the tin lanterns, jugs and mugs Kate had hung from the rafters, ready for sale.

'This is my bench.' She smoothed her hand across it and was pleased to see he was impressed. 'And here's my latest piece…' She handed him the loving cup.

'It's beautiful, Kate. Such fine detail on these handles! I'm so pleased you never gave it up.'

She took the cup and showed him the interior. 'See, I've engraved it. It's a wedding present for Martin.'

He looked bewildered. 'You two aren't married yet?'

She bit her lip and shook her head. 'Read it!' she ordered, and enjoyed seeing him understand.

'"With my love and blessing, to Martin and Nora on your wedding"! It's Martin and Nora that are getting married! Not you? He's not marrying you? Why not? The idiot – though of course Nora is marvellous...' He was spluttering and smiling.

'Not me. No, Johnny. Once Nora was free, I knew. For Martin, it had always been Nora. I let him go, Johnny.'

'He broke your heart!' And she saw his eyes flash with a protective fire that reminded her of the old Johnny.

'No. My heart wasn't broken.'

'So, he's not living here, with you?'

She shook her head. 'Actually he's in a cottage up the lane. But he should be here soon. Let's go and meet him.'

Outside the back door of the workshop was a garden, planted in the lee of the thorn brakes, and at the end was a gate, leading to a lane. As they began walking along the sun-splashed lane, she felt Johnny's eyes on her. He eventually asked in disbelief, 'I don't understand. You're still friends?'

'Yes, Johnny. We're still friends. I love him... but it's a different sort of love to— Ah, here they are.'

Martin came first, with Nora walking beside him and then Paul. His gait was ungainly as he swung one twisted leg around the other; he was slow, but he was smiling broadly.

'He can walk?' Johnny asked in wonder.

She raised her hand in a wave. 'Yes, he always could. He just needed the right care – proper exercise, good food to build up his muscles. It didn't take us long to get him on his feet.'

It was Paul who spotted them first and he waved excitedly back, then tugged at Nora's sleeve. A slow smile spread across Nora's face and Kate saw relief mixed with her happiness. It seemed her friend had been hoping for this moment for a very long time.

Conny brought out some kitchen chairs and a blanket for the baby to crawl on and they sat in the early spring sunshine, Johnny telling how he'd undergone the pioneering treatment for tuberculosis in Switzerland. 'I had to spend hours and hours lying in bed on a freezing mountainside. They used to park us in the snow and leave us all day. They say if it doesn't kill you it cures you!' He was silent for a moment. 'And when I heard about Ethel, that's when I decided I needed to live if I was going to write this book...'

He'd brought a copy with him and he handed it to Kate. She opened it, reading the dedication aloud. 'She would have been so proud of you, Johnny,' she said softly.

'We're all proud of you, dear chap,' Martin said. 'And we're all glad you decided to live...'

And Kate noticed the same look of relief as she'd seen on Nora's face. Obviously neither of them had believed her when she'd promised her heart wasn't broken. She'd been telling the truth, but what she'd never admitted, even to herself, was that her heart had been incomplete.

After they'd drunk too much tea and eaten too much cake

and Paul had made the baby laugh till she was sick, Conny went to put Kathy down for a nap. Martin and Nora took Paul back to their own cottage, and when they were alone, Kate said, 'Let me show you my cove.'

She led the way to a fork in the coast path, where some stairs had been cut into the cliff. They zigzagged down to a sandy cove and once there, Kate took off her shoes.

'Yours too!' she ordered and Johnny obeyed.

They walked through the yielding, fine sand, the only sound the calling of two gulls swooping above them and the regular crash of the surf. As they walked, Johnny asked her about her future. 'So, when those two marry, will you move back to London? It's beautiful here, but won't it be a bit isolated if you're on your own?'

'I've got Conny and the baby, but no, we won't be on our own. Martin and Nora are buying a house in the village; they're going to make their home here. Paul's thriving and Martin has produced so much since we came. It's good for us all.'

Johnny nodded. 'I can see that. You've never looked so happy – nor so beautiful.'

They reached the sea edge and Johnny took her hand. He traced the long white scar along her arm and said, 'We're a long way from home, Kate.'

'Not so far, Johnny,' she said, bending to pick up a bright object that had washed up on the tide. Handing him the old silver coin, she kissed him and he enfolded her in his arms. As they turned to face the horizon, it felt almost as if they were back on the riverbank, looking out at the Thames. But here, they couldn't see the farther shore, just an endless possibility of sky and sea.

Acknowledgements

Bringing a book to publication is very much a team effort and I have been very fortunate to benefit from the advice and help of many publishing professionals: my brilliant agent, Anne Williams, my talented editor, Rosie de Courcy, my eagle-eyed copy-editor Liz Hatherell and all the dedicated team at Head of Zeus. A big thank you to all of them.

I am also very grateful to Julie Orchin, for sharing with me her vivid descriptions of life in Bermondsey during the first half of the twentieth century. I would like to acknowledge G. R. Clift and his evocative memoir *My Life in Industry 1900 – 1954*, about his time at T. F. Boutle & Company.

Many thanks for their continued support to my writing pals at Bexley Scribblers and to my wonderful family. Finally, to Josie Bartholomew, special thanks for making it all possible.

Author's Note

The Bermondsey Bookshop was founded by Ethel Gutman in February 1921. It's stated aim was: 'To bring books and the love of books into Bermondsey.' With evening opening hours, a sixpenny 'instalment plan' for buying books, and free lectures and classes – everything was designed to make the shop attractive and accessible to local working people. In this aim it succeeded, but in the process, it also drew students and literati from all over London, with the Sunday-night lectures attracting celebrity speakers such as John Galsworthy and Walter de la Mare.

In 1923 the bookshop began publishing its own literary quarterly, *The Bermondsey Book*, which quickly became international, gaining critical acclaim and launching the careers of well-known writers such as H. E. Bates as well as local Bermondsey writers. The publication welcomed 'new voices' from any class of society. Contributions from hitherto unpublished working-class writers sat alongside pieces by H. G. Wells, Virginia Woolf and Thornton Wilder.

After Ethel Gutman's untimely death in 1925, the bookshop continued to be run in the spirit she had intended, by her husband Sidney Gutman, until its closure in 1930. The

Bermondsey Bookshop made a lasting impact on many Bermondsey people, some of whom still remembered it with fondness fifty years later.

About the Author

Mary Gibson was born and brought up in Bermondsey, where both her grandmother and mother were factory girls. She is the author of the bestselling *Custard Tarts and Broken Hearts*, which was selected for World Book Night in 2015, and five other novels, *Jam and Roses*, *Gunner Girls and Fighter Boys*, *Bourbon Creams and Tattered Dreams*, *Hattie's Home* and *A Sister's Struggle*. She lives in Kent.